Only One Woman

Christina Jones
Jane Risdon

Published by Accent Press Ltd 2018
Octavo House
West Bute Street
CardiffCF10 5LJ

www.accentpress.co.uk

ISBN 9781783757312
eISBN 9781783757329

Printed in Great Britain by Clays Ltd, St Ives plc

Foreword

When Jane asked me if I'd like to write a foreword for Only One Woman I was thrilled and excited to be invited to share some of my memories of the 1960s and how the song, Only One Woman, came into being.

When I moved to London in 1968 with my cousin Trevor Gordon and our band, we never expected what was going to happen to us. We played a club in London called the Revolution Club and it just happened that the Bee Gees ex-manager was in the audience. He knew my cousin from when Trevor lived in Australia and actually played and recorded with the Bee Gees; this was back in the early 60s. He gave Trevor Barry Gibbs' telephone number.

We eventually went over to Barry Gibbs' house and sat around playing acoustic guitars and singing Stevie Wonder songs and Beatle songs. It just so happened that Robert Stigwood - the Bee Gees' manager - was at Barry's house at the same time and wanted Barry to take my cousin and me into the studio to record a song that he asked Barry to write for us.

Before we knew it we were in the studio that same week with Barry, Maurice and Robin, with only a vague idea of a tune that Barry had written for us to record.

So we sang and recorded a 'la la la la' melody to begin, with Barry playing acoustic guitar. Trevor changed the melody a little and took a straightforward kind of 3/4 country tune to an R&B soulful melody. Eventually Barry wrote the words and came up with the song "Only One Woman."

When "Only One Woman" became a number three hit in 1968, in the UK, everything changed for Trevor and me. Suddenly we were recognised on the streets and it was strange.

I will be forever grateful to the Gibb Brothers for giving me and Trevor a career. Since those days my whole life has just been music thanks to my cousin and his encouragement, and also to the Gibb brothers for giving me such faith in my own talent. The rest is music history.

For me, Jane and Christina's book – "Only One Woman" - reflects very honestly those times and the feel of those times. I can picture myself back in London when reading some of the pages. The 1960s, for me, was probably the most wonderful time in the music business with such bands as The Beatles, The Stones, The Kinks, The Who, and The Bee Gees and more: the list is endless.

This book will take you back to that time; read on readers.

Graham Bonnet,
Studio City, Los Angeles, California
2018.

Renza's Diary
May 24th 1968 – late

What a flipping nightmare of an evening. I really thought I'd never get home in one piece. Everything that could go wrong, went wrong. Someone up there hates me I'm sure.

If only Selina hadn't lost her handbag at the Top Rank, I'd have caught the last bus back from Reading and I would've been home on time. Instead I'd gone back with the others to look for it – thankfully it had been handed in at the cloakroom and nothing was missing. Luckily I had just enough money for the train, which I'd had to run for. Selina's dad took the others home in his brand new car as arranged, and there wasn't room for me as well. I reckon he could've taken me but Yvette refused to let me sit on her lap in the front, in case I ripped her Mary Quant stockings. Sometimes I really want to do her a mischief.

They've got to do something about our local station, it's just too creepy for words. Steam from the train almost suffocated me as I crossed the bridge to the exit on the opposite platform; all very 'Brief Encounter' I remember thinking, in an effort to stop my mind wandering off into 'Hitchcock-land.' Talk about cough myself silly, and my eyes stung something rotten as I tried to find my way in the pitch black. The two over-head lamps didn't help much, they should do something about those flipping lights, I could've broken my neck, or even worse, tripped over in my new pink kitten heels and broken one of them.

I slowly took the steps down to the lane beside the station, glancing around me all the while – I admit it, I was a little freaked out. It's always deserted, and you can never be too careful. Not long ago a dangerous prisoner escaped from the nearby asylum and hid in the waiting room for days before being recaptured. Hardly anyone uses the station since the cut-backs by that old idiot, Beeching, and the trains are a bit hit and miss since they messed with the timetable, so the convict was able to wait for his twisted ankle to mend without much danger of discovery. For all I knew, another Jack the Ripper could've been lurking in there waiting for me to pass, that'd just been my flaming luck.

I was in so much trouble. Forty minutes later than agreed. She'd never believe me about the bag, but no other excuse came to mind as I walked down the lane. I was going to be so dead.

Oh God!

I had such a fright. Something or someone, made a noise behind me, so I stopped and listened, but I really felt like running. Some sort of night creature, silly girl, I decided as I walked on. But there it was again. Was someone behind me?

I turned and peered into the pitch dark – I'm still shaking as I write this. I told myself it sounded like a hedgehog – had to be. Don't panic, no-one comes down here at night I reminded myself. Oh cripes, that lane, I hate it. Anyone could jump out to get you, seriously, I've often wondered, who'd hear you yell? No-one, that's who. There aren't any lights or houses down there.

I must remember – next time the girls ask me to the Top Rank – to leave early and get the bus on time. Next time, who am I kidding?

I'm going nuts – I hope no-one ever reads this, I'd die, but I started singing quietly to myself – I do that sometimes when I'm feeling a bit nervous – well seriously spooked actually. I turned on to the main road relieved no-one had grabbed me, and headed for our house. That's when I heard him...

***

'What time do you think this is?'

Well, I nearly died of fright. I actually jumped. I couldn't work out where the voice was coming from. It seemed to echo all around me in the dimly lit street. Someone had followed me, that's what I kept thinking. I hurried past the bus stop when I heard him again. What to do? Should I run? If I screamed, bringing Mum and half the village outside, Mrs Digby would just love that and if I got murdered, well, it didn't bear thinking about. All this went through my brain at a rate of knots as I tried to work out where the voice was coming from. Would I make it to the gate? Bloody Selina and her stupid bag. I was going to die all because of her stupid bag.

'You're out very late.'

I froze. I was partly relieved it wasn't Mum or Mrs Digby's voice. It was definitely a man's. Who the hell was it? I was considering running but I didn't want to break another heel, not after the last time. The cobbler said he couldn't repair it if it snapped again. Besides, the bloke didn't sound like a cold blooded murderer, well, not really. I mean, what sort of killer asks you what time do you call this, before bumping you off?

'Well?'

The voice sounded even nearer and something made me look up towards the row of shops not far from our house. A window was open in the flat above the hairdresser's, Shirley's, and I could just make out a head and shoulders poking through. Someone with long dark hair; definitely a bloke.

Thank God, at least I hadn't been followed by a crazed axe murderer after-all.

'Mind your own business. What's it got to do with you when I come home?' I stopped walking and stood looking up at him. I couldn't make out his features in the dark, and being short-sighted, even full daylight wouldn't have made that much difference anyway.

'You're lucky you don't have school tomorrow, coming back this late.'

Flaming nerve! He sounded like my Dad. Who the hell was he, I wondered. Too young to be one of Mum's spies surely.

'Drop dead!' I turned and flounced off towards our gate, trying hard not to go over on my ankle on the uneven pavement. I had a bad case of the shakes thanks to him.

'I'll be watching you. Make sure you get your beauty sleep,' he shouted just as I closed the gate, anxiously glancing at the house in case Mum or Mrs Digby next door had heard someone shouting at me in the street.

I'd never be allowed to forget it if Mum thought Mrs Digby had heard me making a spectacle of myself in public. Even getting murdered would've been my fault, causing her embarrassment in front of the whole village. Perish the thought – a public spectacle, no matter it wasn't instigated by me. Fingers crossed most people were in bed by now anyway.

Just as I got to the front door, it was yanked open by Mum and she stood aside in the hall to let me pass. Dread flooded over me. She'd heard me shouting. I was dead!

She was about to start on me when thankfully one of the kids woke up, having a nightmare or something, yelling and thrashing about in the room they all shared. With a withering look at me, she stomped upstairs to see whoever it was.

I heard something about 'chocks away,' followed by a huge thud. Then Mum yelling, 'you can't go to the loo in there! It's the wardrobe! Get out of there!' followed by a lot of shuffling about.

That would be my ten-year-old brother Simon doing a parachute jump from the top bunk and then mistaking the wardrobe for the loo – it often happened after he'd been messing about with his Air-fix.

Blessing him and his night-games – for once – I used the commotion to sneak into my room and get ready for bed. Hopefully Mum wouldn't come into my room, and if she did I would pretend to be asleep. I'd get away with it – but she would certainly start on me in the morning.

I sighed heavily and prepared myself for not being allowed to go anywhere ever again in this lifetime.

Renza's Diary
May 25th 1968

I left to do my paper-round at 5am, the house silent as I wheeled my bike through the front gate. I glanced up at the flats over the shops to see if there was any sign of life.

The bloke who'd shouted was intriguing me. I couldn't work out why he'd been so interested in what time I got home. The flat must have been rented out recently because I'm sure the last time Mum had spoken to Shirley, who owned the salon beneath, she said it was still empty and that can't have been that long ago. It would be nice to have new neighbours – but not ones who were going to get me into even more trouble with Mum.

The air was really fresh and the sun was beginning to warm the ground as I cycled to the next village to collect my papers. The fields were covered in mist which hovered about three feet off the ground, and with the sun shining through the trees as I passed the hedges all green and lush, it looked so pretty, but a bit eerie. I loved this time of morning, hardly anyone around, and so quiet, having the village to myself, except for the milkman on his electric float. I nearly always passed him just before I reached the village pub, The Chequers. He waved and his dog, Silver, who always ran alongside him, barked hello to me.

I got back home about 8am after stopping in for breakfast with Nan, as usual, after I finished my round. There didn't appear to be any signs of life at the flat I noticed, as I wheeled my bike through the front gate. Mum was in a flap because she had been called in to work apparently, and so it was all go whilst she got herself ready and I helped with breakfast and dressed my younger brothers and sisters. Thankfully, she was in such a rush she forgot to have a go at me. Not that she wouldn't later on. Now I had all day to worry about what she was going to do about me being a bit late home and making a

5

show of myself in the street to boot.

Before she left she reminded me to get the washing out of the boiler and put it through the mangle and hang it out, and I had to make sure that Simon went to the local butcher's to pick up sausages for lunch and the Sunday joint. My Saturday well and truly sorted then.

I had hoped to meet Yvette in town and go for an espresso in the new coffee bar which had opened on the high street. Not having a phone there was no way I could let her know I couldn't come, unless I could manage to get down to the phone box before lunch to warn her. Everyone seemed to be getting phones except us, it just wasn't fair.

Yvette had wanted to come to our house with Selina, and had got all funny when I said Mum wouldn't like it and we should meet in The Cadena.

Actually, you'd have thought they'd have realised they weren't welcome because they'd both turned up, unexpectedly, on a couple of occasions recently and Mum hadn't liked it one bit.

No one with manners visits without an invitation, she told me after they'd left. It was embarrassing, she was so rude to them both, and she went on something rotten at me for inviting them without her permission. It was her house, not mine, and she would be the one to invite guests. Nothing I said would convince her I'd had no idea they were coming. They hadn't told me. I'd no idea why they wanted to visit all of a sudden. As it was they spent most of the time in the back garden being too loud, giggling and showing off all the time. They didn't even bother reading the magazines they had with them: *Jackie* and *Fab 208*. Mum binned them as soon as they'd gone, in case I was corrupted by their nonsense.

I'd no idea why they were trying to show off to Mr Digby, it was a bit sad. And of course it gave Mrs Digby a good reason to moan at Mum about me and my 'cheap' friends in our mini-skirts, flaunting ourselves in front of her innocent Geoffrey.

6

Huh! If only she knew what I knew about her darling Geoffrey. I dearly wanted to tell her.

Donald Digby, Peg Digby and their mother, take the utmost pleasure in getting me into trouble. Not that I've ever done anything wrong, but they spy on me and report stuff to Mum, exaggerating everything, knowing I'll get hell. Mum always believes them for some reason.

Once, Mrs Digby caught Mum over the fence, telling her she'd seen Dad in a new three-piece-suit and that Mum had better watch out because 'men of a certain age' were usually having an affair when they got new clothes.

Mr Digby – Geoffrey, the innocent – is a real creep, he makes my flesh crawl. Always leering at me and making weird remarks on the sly. We've caught him several times in our garden, peering through the sitting-room window when he thinks we've gone out. The whole family's more than a bit odd.

After a lot of yelling and some bribery, I managed to get Simon to go shopping so I could cook lunch for when Mum got back at 1pm. I legged it to the phone box before he went, and caught Yvette in the middle of a row with her mum about wearing too much eyeliner and spending all her pocket money on silly magazines.

She went into a bit of a mood when I said I had to stay in to look after the kids again, and I wondered, as I hung up, if she would send me to Coventry again, like she did the time she got funny with me when two blokes on a Vespa stopped to chat us up outside school, and both of them took more notice of me, as if that was my fault.

I was hanging out the washing when someone started whistling and shouting what sounded like 'I love girls with long blonde hair.'

I looked around but couldn't see anyone walking up the path beside the houses, so I just got on with making sure I hung the shirts the right way, otherwise Attila the Hun would be on me like a ton of bricks.

'Hello beautiful.'

I heard a vaguely familiar voice off to my right, and glanced around but couldn't see anyone. Not that I thought it was meant for me, of course.

'Over here, blondie.' The male voice sounded quite nice really and I followed the sound, looking upwards to see a very sexy, topless, bronzed specimen with long blond hair, squatting on top of the wall leading up to the flats over the shops.

My heart skipped a beat and I tried hard not to smile, but I could barely keep the grin off my face. He *was* talking to *me*. How about that.

I looked quickly over at Mrs Digby's in case she was lurking ready to report back to Gestapo HQ that I was flirting with a half-naked god in the back garden. The coast seemed clear. I smiled and silently cursed myself for doing the housework in scruffy clothes.

I didn't have any make-up on and my hair was a mess – trouble is, I'm not supposed to wear make-up anyway. Trust me to meet a a gorgeous boy looking like this, putting the flipping washing out for goodness sakes.

Standing there with a pair of Mum's undies in one hand and her bra in the other, I felt a bit silly as he looked at me and I short-sightedly squinted back trying hard to see his features, hoping my face wasn't too red. Then I realised he wasn't alone, there was another boy standing behind him.

Before I could hide Mum's undies, the other bloke stepped forward and said, 'hello again.'

I realised then that it had been him speaking to me all along, not the blond God.

I felt disappointment for all of two seconds until the boy with the long black hair and the most amazing bronzed muscled chest grabbed my attention.

He was the one from last night.

My knees felt like jelly and I could feel the dreaded red hot flush travelling up my neck to my face. I'm never going to be cool and sophisticated. Never ever.

'Are you going to say anything?' he asked, as the blond boy next to him suddenly stood up, revealing his tight white jeans and bronzed, well-toned chest muscles; I thought I'd just died and gone to heaven. They were both unreal. Wait until I tell you about this Yvette, I thought, you'll be eaten up.

'Oh, yes, um, hello,' I stuttered like a moron, mentally kicking myself for not being a bit more confident.

'I'll leave you two to it then.' The blond God boy smiled at me, waved and went back up to the flats, leaving the two of us staring at each other in silence.

The air around me seemed to have a funny tingle in it and I got goose-bumps as I tried to release my gaze from his.

'Broken up for the summer yet?'

I could hear the kids killing each other inside and I remembered I had put the potatoes on to boil ready for when Mum came back on her lunch break.

' Um, no, no I haven't, not yet, but I'm leaving school soon anyway.'

Now why did I tell him that? Why did I say that? It was like telling him we were moving away. And we were. To Germany. To live with Dad, who has been out there for the last six months working for the Ministry of Defence on attachment to an Army Base in the Ruhr Valley. The back of beyond if you ask me, I'll die stuck out there

The noise from indoors grew even louder and I knew I'd have to sort the kids and the spuds out before Mum came home. I could've cried.

I turned away from him, hurriedly pegged out the rest of the washing, grabbed the basket and ran back towards the kitchen with his call of 'I love girls with long blonde hair,' ringing in my ears.

Renza's Diary
May 27ᵗʰ 1968 – Spring Bank Holiday

'You talk funny.' My three-year-old sister Lucy was staring hard at the man in the dirty white overalls bending over the once white sheets, covering the carpet around our hearth.

Mr Fowler, the chimney-sweep and our other next door neighbour, glanced up and gave her a toothless grin. His craggy, soot-lined face was kindly, but sadly marred by his hare-lip. He nodded at Lucy and carried on shoving his brushes up our chimney. I was filled with dread in case she started to copy the way he spoke. He was barely intelligible because he didn't have a roof to his mouth, and Mum had drilled me about watching Lucy and her talent for mimicry during his previous visits.

'What you doing?' she asked, shuffling closer and stepping on to the sheet. She glanced around, knowing she had been told not to go near him whilst he worked.

I kept an eye on her from the kitchen where I was making Mr Fowler a cup of tea and hoping he wouldn't make too much mess because I would need to clean it up before Mum got in from work.

'Chimney,' said Mr Fowler without looking round.

Soot fell in a great black cloud, covering him and the sheets. My sister squealed and ran behind the sofa.

'Lucy, leave Mr Fowler alone and go out to play with the others,' I shouted as I placed the cup of tea and Rich Tea biscuits on the soot covered coffee table.

The back door flew open and five-year-old Jasper raced into the room, nearly landing in the hearth. Mr Fowler jumped up, bumping his head on the mantelpiece, causing Lucy to scream from behind the sofa.

When would Jasper ever learn to walk inside the house? He was panting and red in the face. Both knees were covered in grass stains and his backside was hanging out of his shorts. He was for it. After staring at Mr Fowler hard, he shrugged and turned to me.

'Been playing football with the band,' he panted, pointing in the direction of the shops, 'scored millions of goals.'

'What band, played football where?' I asked as I grabbed his arm and moved him away from the clouds of soot falling from the chimney.

'You know. The band. Your boyfriend's band.' He giggled as he shouted it out because he knew it would embarrass me.

Mr Fowler looked up and winked at me.

'You know full well I don't have a boyfriend. I've no idea what you're on about, but if Mum finds you've been playing with those boys of Barker, you'll be for it.'

The boys of Barker were local seven-year-old delinquents, and, for some reason Jasper was strangely attracted to them, much to my parent's bewilderment.

Jasper could never keep their exploits secret and would come back with tales of what they'd been up to, causing Mum to nearly faint with fear that Jasper would get sucked into their crimes, bringing the full force of the Law up the garden path, in full view of the whole village. Perish the thought.

'Yes you do have a boyfriend, so. And you kiss all the time,' persisted Jasper, causing Lucy and Mr Fowler to watch me carefully as I began blushing to the roots of my blonde hair.

Lucy shot past me on her way to the garden, shouting at the top of her voice 'Renza kisses her boyfriend. Renza kisses her boyfriend.'

Oh my God! If Mrs Digby got wind of this I was totally, totally and absolutely dead.

I don't have a boyfriend, Mum won't allow it, and besides, as I hardly ever go out, how the heck I am supposed to get one I have no idea. The girls at school have boyfriends and go to

11

discos and Youth Club, but I'm rarely allowed. I've only managed to go to the Top Rank twice recently because Mum's friend, the Honourable Charlotte Shand, allowed her daughter to go regularly and since she's not been raped, sold into white slavery or forced into a life of immorality and drug-taking, Mum reluctantly agreed to let me go with my school friends – not wanting to lose face in front of the Honourable Charlotte.

However, missing the last bus and getting back late on Friday led to World War Three and all sorts of threats when she finally decided to have a go at me. I'm keeping a low profile, being a good girl looking after the kids – unpaid flipping nanny more like – and doing the chores like the resident char lady. Anything for a quiet life.

I'm going to be in so much trouble if they blab to Mum about me kissing boys and such rot. She'd happily believe it.

Hopping from one foot to the other Jasper stuck his tongue out at me. I wanted to strangle him. 'For goodness sakes go to the loo and stop hopping around like an idiot.' I snapped going into the kitchen.

My heart sank when I looked out the window and saw Lucy and the other kids talking to Mrs Fowler over the fence. Goodness knows what they were telling her, not that she'd gossip, but even so...

Her house was set back a bit from ours and there was only a wire fence separating us. The Fowlers' house was Victorian, whereas ours was newly built when we moved in just under eight years ago.

Mrs Fowler often gave the kids sweets and pop if they were outside when she was gardening. The Fowlers were Jehovah's Witnesses, although originally Mrs Fowler had been Jewish. She once told me she'd found Jehovah when she was having a stout at the 'Cow and Gate,' where she used to play the piano on Saturday nights. According to Mum the Fowlers had never been the same again.

Apparently Mrs Fowler, who has known Mum all her life,

told Mum all marital relations had ceased from then on.

They'd had the one daughter, so Mrs Fowler had fulfilled her marital obligations. Mum went ballistic when I repeated this conversation one day when we were all having tea with Grandad Rossi. It didn't go down too well for some reason.

'Got a message for you from your lover,' Jasper sniggered, watching Mr Fowler as he waited for my reaction. 'He wants to go out with you and give you millions of kisses,' he persisted. I debated chopping his head off instead of chopping the veg for dinner.

'Oh shut up you little squirt.' I was getting irritable, what with the soot and the cleaning I was going to have to do, not to mention all the cooking and looking after the brats. 'I can't wait to go back to school and get some peace.'

'I bet you can't wait to kiss and kiss and kiss.' Jasper danced around the kitchen.

I waved the knife at him, sorely tempted. 'I'm warning you!'

'If you want to go out with Scott, then tell me coz I've got to be a secret 'messager' and let him know.' Jasper started fiddling with the carrots I'd chopped.

I smacked his hand away and got a lot of pleasure from the sound of the slap.

'Stop being such a horrid little boy and go away.'

'OK then, I'm gonna tell Scott that you love him and want to marry him and kiss him all the time,' shouted Jasper as he crashed through the back door.

'Scott who?' I shouted after him, but he was gone.

Mr Fowler came through the kitchen with his brushes and sheets and a large box of soot, well, what wasn't covering all the furniture and carpets that is. He said something which sounded like 'Catch your Mother later,' but really, I never could understand him. Such a nice man and such a shame, I thought as I resigned myself to the mess waiting for me. I smiled, nodded, and closed the door behind him.

I began wondering about the band Jasper mentioned, who

they were and where they came from, and how they knew Jasper. Were they the boys living over Shirley's? Was that where Jasper kept disappearing to?

Through the kitchen window I could see them sitting on the wall again: the blond God and the sexy black haired one. Imagine if he was this Scott, Jasper was on about... nope, get a grip, he's far too gorgeous to be interested in me. But then he did shout at me twice...

Watching them both sunbathing on the wall, I wondered if they were famous, but they didn't look familiar. Never mind that, I can't wait to get back to class and tell Yvette and Selina about the boys living over 'Shirley's.' They'll be so eaten up and for once they'll envy me.

I put the transistor on whilst I got on with my chores, singing along with Brenton Wood to 'Give Me Some Kinda Sign.'

Trust my life to start getting exciting just as we're leaving England.

Renza's Diary
May 30th 1968

Everyone at school wanted to know about the band living over Shirley's. Word soon got around, and suddenly I was really, really popular for once. Well, being so 'cool' all of a sudden might be all right for some, but being the centre of attention isn't all it's cracked up to be. I'm not sure I like it. It's embarrassing. Everyone crowding round me all the time, asking questions – as if I know anything – wanting to come round to the house. Mum would just love even more girls strutting around the back garden, much to the delight of Mrs Digby – I don't think so.

Even Yvette's talking to me again after ignoring me because Mum wouldn't let her and Selina keep coming over... now I get what the attraction was. Not me – they didn't want to see me. By conning their way into the back garden, they thought they'd get near the band so they could flirt with them – well thanks for nothing – someone could've told me they were there. Trust me to be the last to know.

Jasper has spent the last few days ferrying messages to me from the dark haired boy, who it turns out is Scott, he's a guitarist and the band is called Narnia's Children. I've never heard of them but according to Jasper – the expert on all things band-related – they're from an island somewhere – he's forgotten where – and are in England to tour and make records. They don't look foreign to me.

Anyway, Scott keeps sending me messages asking me out and I keep ignoring them. Every time I walk past the flat he's sitting at the window shouting out things like, 'I love girls with long blonde hair,' and 'I think I love you,' and 'Your legs look great in that uniform,' and all sorts of nonsense, which is really getting me into trouble with Mum.

Mrs Digby has cottoned on and I saw her grab Mum as she went to the post box yesterday. I got it in the neck as soon as I got home from school. The usual stuff about showing myself up, not acting like a lady and – the best one – 'wait until I tell your father how you've been carrying on.'

Apparently I'd managed to ruin her and Lucy's birthdays earlier in the week because of the worry and the embarrassment my behaviour is causing.

It's driving me mad! I've done nothing. Nothing!

I can't help it if some boy sends me messages and calls out to me every time I set foot in the garden or go outside to the shops or to school. How is that my fault? Jasper says he told Scott to lay off like I asked, but either he is fibbing or Scott couldn't care less that I am in such trouble.

Hopefully next week will be better. It will be my last week at school, I'm leaving before the school term ends so I can help Mum prepare for the move. I can't help it if Scott sees me hanging washing out, but Mum will be at work, so at least if he does yell at me, she won't be around to hear it.

I caught a glimpse of him, Scott, coming down the stairs from his flat with another older-looking boy this morning as I waited for the bus to school. They went round the back to the car park and soon after they drove past me in a yellow Bedford van. I nearly dropped dead because, as they passed me, the van made a funny noise like a gun shot, they waved and tooted the horn. Everyone at the bus stop stared at me. I just wanted the ground to open up – but I still can't help thinking it's so cool. A boy in a band likes me. A strange tingle sparks the length of my body every time I think about him.

Of course Mum says he is one of the great unwashed and a long-haired layabout, and she's seen lots of girls going up the stairs to the flat carrying overnight cases, and according to her, they're up there for days.

For someone who says she's not interested in them, she certainly keeps an eye on everything they do.

'Stop encouraging them,' she keeps telling me. Encouraging them? She's telling *me* to stop encouraging *them*. As if. 'I'm warning you!'

I shook my head at the unfairness of it all and went and sat in front of the television. *Top of the Pops* was on and Pan's People were dancing to Elvis and 'US Male'. I love Elvis but I'm not keen on Priscilla. Their baby Lisa Marie looks very sweet though. There've been loads of photos of them in the papers since she was born in February.

Ok, it sounds daft, but I was getting all excited in case Narnia's Children was on next. I couldn't tear myself away – just in case – which really annoyed Mum as she needed the kids' shoes polishing. I kept telling her I'd do it after *Top of the Pops* ended, but she was losing her patience. I hoped she wouldn't turn the TV off before I got to see who was Number One this week.

I'm not sure how famous Scott's band is, but I'd be so thrilled if they were actually on TV. Imagine that. I sat there with my fingers crossed, but they weren't on. Stupid of me to think they would be really, but The Equals were still in the charts which was fab and cheered me up a bit.

I love their new song 'Baby, Come Back'. They'd played it at the Top Rank on Friday and it was amazing. We'd danced all evening and it was the best fun ever. Not counting going to the Empire Pool Wembley, that is, when I'd been allowed to go as a special treat. That was really far out – all those bands on a Sunday afternoon and all that screaming.

At least people hadn't screamed too much when The Equals were on stage at the Top Rank. I wondered if people screamed at Narnia's Children.

I'd seen the band earlier in the evening, coming down the stairs carrying guitars and duffle bags. For one horrid moment I'd thought they were moving out, but then I recalled what Jasper said about them going away for a couple of days to play gigs in lots of different places. He'd said that Scott had told him to tell me he would be back soon and would be thinking of me and that I had to be a good girl whilst he was gone.

The flipping nerve! If only he knew – chance would be a fine thing!

I'd been upstairs and the kids' bedroom window was open as I was fixing Simon's latest air-fix model to the ceiling with drawing pins when I glanced out of the window and saw them together for the first time.

I'd nearly fallen off the top bunk. Yvette was right, they're all gorgeous. I can't understand how I'd missed seeing them all when everyone else seemed to know they've been here since April.

I'd just put the last pin into the Lancaster Bomber, placed between the Halifax Bomber and the Spitfire, when I'd heard their voices, and from where I was I'd a great view as they filed down the stairs and out to their van. Jasper, who knows everything, said the van was called Bessie Bedford.

Talk about dreamy. They all wore tight brightly coloured hipsters and shirts, except Scott who had on really snazzy purple cords and a tight black short sleeved sweater, which only came to his mid-riff. He was so tanned and had such a cute behind. I wobbled straining to watch, and nearly ended up in the toy box.

I wondered what songs Narnia's Children played and if they'd been on Radio One.

I love Radio One, Tony Blackburn is my favourite DJ. I was so happy when it started last year. I mean, I still love Radio Luxembourg, and the pirate stations, Caroline and London, are really far out, but Radio One is on all day and when Mum is out I put the wireless on in the sitting room and dance and sing myself silly.

What if German TV doesn't have *Top of the Pops* and other English shows? What will I do? Lately I can't stop thinking about Germany and leaving Nan and England and, dare I think it, now – Scott.

I told Nan I didn't want to leave school or go to Germany. I explained I needed to do my A Levels so I could eventually take up the offer of a job as an apprentice journalist — made by a friend's father, Mr Hardy, who was an editor on *The Sunday Times* — with day release for college. My dream, if only Mum and Dad would agree. Nan said I could stay with her and I didn't need to leave school, I'd be company for her too. But Mum and Dad wouldn't hear of it.

Mum needed me in Germany to help with the kids and made it clear there wasn't a senior school near enough for me to go daily and so I'd need to board, and they wouldn't allow that, either. So my chance at *The Sunday Times*, staying with Nan and being able to study, and possibly go to college was growing dimmer by the day.

It's so unfair. I feel like running away. Mum and Dad just want me to be a skivvy in Germany. It doesn't matter that I've got hopes and dreams.

What did anyone want six kids for anyway? Don't get me wrong, I love them all. We get on fine, but they think I'm their 'other mum'. Because I'm older than they are, it falls upon me to keep an eye on them, take care of them and generally be responsible for them. Simon thinks he can blackmail me when it suits him — he's Mum and Dad's favourite who can do no wrong, and boy, does he play on it. Sophia is the entertainer in the family, always good for a laugh, messes around playing the clown, and everyone loves her for it — she's Mum's other favourite. The others follow her as if she were the Pied Piper. Jasper is a lovely kid, always smiling, always seeing the good in everyone — hence his relationship with the delinquents of the village. Anything for a laugh, accident prone — with hilarious consequences — and the one who gets a clout if Mum hears a rumpus, regardless of who's to blame, Jasper gets it. Crispin is a lovely soul, gentle, sweet natured and a bit of a practical joker, even at such a young age. Little Lucy, such a sweetheart, loves her dolls and her pillow, which she cuddles for comfort, follows me around everywhere, possibly because I looked after her when she was a baby. They're great kids, but would I want six kids? Nope. I feel as if I've had mine already.

I counted my paper-round earnings and the money I got for working in the dry cleaners on Saturdays and school holidays... There's no way I could save enough money to run away. My life is one big unhappy mess.

I told Mum I had a migraine just to get some peace and time to think. My room is the only place I'm ever alone. It's heaven. I turned Radio Luxembourg up really loud, still trying to work out how I could get out of going to Germany.

'Turn that damn racket off and put your light out,' Mum shouted up the stairs. 'Some migraine!'

She slammed the sitting room door and I turned the radio down, searching for my earphones so I could go on listening without her knowing.

I'd been allowed to pick the colours for my room last time we decorated and I chose purple walls and a purple lampshade which matched my eiderdown. I think it looks really far out. Dad said it made him feel sick. I'm going to miss my room. My sanctuary.

We'll be moving into two flats in Germany, or so Dad wrote to Mum last week. The Ministry of Defence is converting them so we can use them like a house. I might have to share with Sophia if there aren't enough bedrooms. That's not funny.

Scott will forget all about me, I thought, as I listened to The Box Tops playing 'Cry Like a Baby'.

Just what I felt like doing.

Renza's Diary
June 6th 1968

The local paper had photos and everything. A big write-up about Narnia's Children stopping on their way back from a series of gigs to help put out the big wild-fire on the heath near Blackstone airport.

Mum pointed it out to me in the paper and I couldn't believe it. They were heroes. The fire brigade had been struggling to contain the fire when the band drove past and, seeing how bad it was, drove back to help fight the fire. The reporter said they worked through the night until about 8am alongside the firemen, and took photos of them all covered in smoke. There was another photo of them, too, what the reporter called their 'publicity stills' – they'd used in a programme for gigs and TV shows in Jersey. It all seemed too unreal.

I hoped I'd be able to hide the paper away in my bedroom without Mum noticing, just so I could look at Scott's picture again and again.

I heard the band's van come back when I was helping Mum to pack.

I pretended not to notice and Mum didn't say anything either.

Since leaving school a few days ago I've been busy helping get the house ready for the estate agents to inspect and assess for renting out whilst we are away.

Things we're leaving behind have to go up in the roof and the agents have been told it's off-limits to the tenants. I hope so, all my ballet and theatre books have gone up there, books I treasure because they were given to me by Mum's actress friend, Sheila, who made me promise to keep them always. I hate leaving them.

I finished packing my lovely books and washed my hair in the hope that if I saw Scott, I'd look my best for a change. He must think I always look like I've been dragged through a hedge backwards because he never sees me with make-up, my hair done, wearing something half decent, unless it's my school uniform.

'Get down here this minute,' Mum shouted.

'I'm in the bathroom, I can't,' I shouted back, putting my hair up in a towel.

'I know you can hear me – so heed me,' she yelled angrily. 'Now!'

I almost fell down the stairs in the rush to find out what it was I'd done wrong this time.

She was standing by the window with a piece of paper in her hand and she was definitely not amused.

'What may I ask, is this, madam?' She waved the paper at me.

'What is it?' I didn't have a clue what it was. I reached for it, but she yanked her hand away.

'*I'm* asking *you*.' She raised the dreaded eyebrow. Not good.

'And I can't tell you until you tell me,' I mumbled, worried sick.

'I think you know only too well. And I would like to know what exactly is going on, young lady! So, you'd better tell me – now!'

My little sister Lucy stood watching me carefully as I tried hard to think what it might be.

'Using a small child to run your illicit errands is disgusting,' Mum hissed as she pointed to Lucy who had a big sneaky grin on her face. She knew I was in for it.

'Sorry, what errands? What do you mean?'

The dread was crawling over my skin as I wracked my brains.

'Well, you can tell him the answer is no, my lady.' Mum thrust the paper into her apron pocket and waited, arms folded.

'Mum, I haven't a clue what you're on about, please tell

22

me?' I was beginning to feel sick.

'Casanova and you!' she yelled at me, and Lucy jumped behind the sofa.

'What?' My throat went dry and I felt dizzy. 'Who are you on about? I don't know any Casanova.'

Unless you count the bloke who had stalked me for months ages ago, and he's not allowed anywhere near me since the police sorted him out.

'Don't play dumb with me, you insolent little bitch!'

'But I don't know what you're talking about. And if you don't tell me, how am I going to know?' I was so near to tears. I'm sick of this all the time.

'You and that lout next door! Think I don't know? Think I am stupid?'

'Donald Digby?' I shouted in horror, 'that idiot and me? Are you nuts?'

The moment I said it I realised my mistake.

Her hand flashed across my face so fast I stumbled back and knocked the coffee table sideways, making all her ornaments fall over with a loud crash. Lucy screamed and ran out of the room and up the stairs.

Not so funny now, Lucy, I thought, as I held my hand to my throbbing face and weeping eye, where her ring had caught.

'Watch your mouth.' She picked up the ornaments and examined each one carefully to see if I'd broken any. Apparently not, thankfully.

'How long has this been going on behind my back?' she asked, angrily brushing her hands through her newly permed hair.

I tried very hard not to cry in front of her. 'Mum, apart from going to Youth Club that one time when you made me go with him, I haven't seen Donald or spoken to him in ages.'

'Did I mention Donald Digby? Well, did I?' she snapped. 'Don't try to be funny.'

23

'Well, who then?' I sniffed, unable to stop the tears any longer. They streamed down my cheek from my eye, which felt as if it was swelling up to the size of a football.

'That creature next door, the one with the harem,' she snorted and took the paper from her pocket again. 'That long-haired hippy living in the flat – don't play dumb with me.'

'I don't know him, Mum, I've never spoken to him and I've never met him.'

'Really? You expect me to believe that when he's sending you obscene messages and getting little Lucy to bring them? Do you think I came down with the last shower?'

'It's true, honestly you can ask him.'

'Oh, don't you worry, my lady. I will. He is going to feel the edge of my tongue before long, disgusting creature. Here.'

She thrust the piece of paper at me at last and I slowly opened it:

'I want you to come out with me. I've been dreaming of you every night since I first saw you. You've got my messages so will you come out with me, please? We are away for the next week but when I get back I'll come round and take you out. Promise. Please give Lucy an answer today so I have something to look forward to. You are gorgeous. Love Scott. Xxx'

I swallowed. My heart skipped several beats with pleasure and I felt all warm and tingly. Then I saw her face. Oh, my goodness. I was in so much trouble. My heart thudded like crazy and I felt faint.

'I'm going to be sick,' I yelled, running for the stairs. 'Leave me alone.'

Amazingly, she did. Well, at least long enough for me to bathe my eye where she'd struck me.

Oh, Scott, I thought, you have no idea what you've done...

***

An hour later Mum stood over me as I replied to Scott's message, dictating what I wrote. When I came downstairs we'd had a blazing row, and eventually I think I'd convinced her I was telling the truth.

Even Jasper defended me for a change, telling her that he knew I hadn't spoken to or even met Scott because Scott was always moaning about me ignoring him. For once, I could've kissed Jasper.

'Tell him you will consent to go for a walk with him, only, and that he is to come into the chemist's when I'm on duty and tell me when he'll be round for you,' she instructed, as I wrote with shaking hands.

'Once he's been out with you and finds out what a boring, uninteresting, nothing person you are, that'll sort him out, and he won't want to see you again. He won't bother you again.' Then she added, just for good measure, 'Once will be enough and he'll stop pestering you.'

I had a horrible feeling she was right.

Jasper took the note round to the flat and I made tea. I called Simon and Crispin when it was ready and wondered if I dared ask to watch *Top of the Pops* later.

Cathy McGowan – I love everything about her and I always look forward to seeing what she's wearing and how she's done her hair and make-up. I miss *Ready Steady Go!* She was fab in that, but she's great on *Top of the Pops* – she's one of their best presenters, and so is Samantha Juste, I love her too. The News came on after *Top of the Pops* and I cried when I heard Robert Kennedy had been killed, just like his brother JFK. That poor family. In April Martin Luther King was assassinated too. I hope my Aunt Celia is safe living there because it seems to me America is a dangerous place to be, even though I love American groups.

Renza's Diary
June 14th 1968

He turned round as I came into the sitting-room and smiled the most sunny smile I've ever seen in my whole life. It caught my breath and I felt the familiar red blush creep right up my neck to my freshly washed hair.

'Hello,' he said.

'Hello,' I replied croakily, my throat restricted.

'Well, this is all very cosy.' Mother was sitting in her usual chair with a view of the garden path and the main road running alongside it.

Scott and I locked eyes and the world sped away from me so that there was only him and me. Somewhere in the distance I could hear Mum mumbling but it was in a tunnel, miles away from the two of us.

I saw his face properly for the very first time. I saw turquoise blue eyes, and a chiselled jawline in a determined but kind face. He was staring at me as if in shock. Unblinking and intense. He was so totally, totally gorgeous. Scott Walker and Peter Frampton all rolled into one.

He was about six feet tall close up, with broad shoulders and the slimmest tiniest hips in white cords. His shirt was pale blue with small paisley flowers on it – Dad would have something to say about the flowers, not to mention his long hair!

My head was spinning and I felt as if the floor was dropping away from under me.

I tried desperately to come back into the room but I was flying, light and feathery, my heart skipping about like a child on the way to a sweet shop.

'... So mind what I've told you, do you hear me?' Mother's voice was starting to penetrate my head. I forced my eyes away from Scott to look at her.

'Earth to Renza, do you hear me?' she snapped as she

stood up and came over to me, wagging her finger in my face.

'Yes Mum,' I mumbled but honestly, I hadn't a clue what she was waffling on about. I hadn't heard a word.

Scott continued to stare at me and I started to wonder if I was a disappointment. I had my new blue and white sleeveless polka-dot mini-dress on with the thin belt and the cut-away neckline, not plunging or anything like that, but it might have been a bit low... and I was wearing my pink kitten heels with matching clutch bag and a little make-up – sadly nothing like Cathy McGowan's – which so far had gone unnoticed by the bloodhound. My auntie Celia, who lives in America, sent me some perfume for my sixteenth birthday and I'd dabbed some behind my ears, on my wrists and a bit in the hollow of my neck, like they tell you to do in *Jackie*. My almost waist length hair was behaving for once. I'd nearly been sick about four times since I heard the front door go.

'What have you done to your eye?' Scott spoke at last and it was the first time I'd really heard his voice. Up until now he'd always been shouting to me. He had a warm voice, very well-spoken. Mother must be pleased about that at least.

'She walked into a door,' Mother said, glaring at me. Daring me to say different.

I just nodded.

'Nasty.' Scott peered closely at me. 'Poor you.'

'Right, you have my permission to go for a walk round the village,' Mother told Scott pin-pointing him with her brown eyes, one eyebrow raised. 'Nothing more.'

'Thanks Mrs Rossi,' he said gravely, fixing her with steely eyes.

'No funny business and no showing yourself up in public.' She jabbed me in the shoulder.

'She'll be perfectly safe with me and you've no need to worry about anything at all,' Scott said with a bit of an edge to his voice. He didn't appear to be frightened by my mother.

'Hmmm!' Mother's head jerked back sceptically. 'All right, you can take her away now.'

She opened the front door and Scott allowed me to step outside first. Got manners too, I thought, as I wobbled past him, grateful that for once I didn't have five kids trailing along with me.

Mother watched us all the way to the gate and I could feel her eyes on my back as we walked along past his flat in silence. We must have gone about two hundred yards before he spoke. I'd been wracking my brains for something to say, so when he spoke, I almost cried. I felt so tense and so on the brink of something momentous, I could hardly breathe.

'This is ace,' he said huskily, staring straight ahead.

'That's nice,' I said like a complete idiot, my voice shaking so badly I wondered if he noticed.

We turned to walk up Farm Close, Scott on the outside nearest the road. He put his hand in the small of my back as we crossed the road and I jumped as the bolt of lightning shot through me. I stole a glance at him and he was grinning.

Frantically I tried to think of something to say, something witty, sophisticated and intelligent, but I found myself incapable of coherent thought. My mind was devoid of anything except the awareness and presence of the boy walking close to me. My breathing was shallow and I just knew my voice would come out in a squeak. I cleared my throat as quietly as I could.

'Your mum is a bit much,' he said finally. 'I had the Spanish Inquisition while waiting for you.'

'What do you mean?' I had a good idea but I thought I'd better ask.

'Wanted to know what my father does for a living, what my mother does, how many brothers and sisters I have, if I am a Catholic − I take it you must be − where I went to school, how do I make any money, and when am I going to get a proper job? I even had to tell her my age − I'm 18 by the way – and I know how old you are.'

He laughed, a lovely throaty, sexy knee-weakening laugh.

'Sorry. I'm so sorry,' I muttered, feeling deeply ashamed at her behaviour. At least he wasn't too old for me, I thought, relieved.

'No problem. I gave her the low-down and no doubt she's suitably shocked.' He chuckled as we turned up towards Strawberry Way where the rows of small Victorian houses gave way to the grand houses of the local aristocracy, with their sweeping tree-lined driveways and beautifully tended grounds.

'Wow, my father would think he'd died and gone to heaven if he could handle these if they came on the market.' He whistled and stopped to take in the huge white gabled house where my school friend, Bernadette Dunlop, lived.

'What does your father do then?' I asked, feeling a bit like my mother: nosey.

'He owns an auctioneers and estate agency in Brighton.'

Mother couldn't find fault with that, I thought, she would approve of a business man.

'You said she'd be shocked, why?' I was beginning to relax a little now that we were having a proper conversation.

We continued to walk up Strawberry Way, Scott stopping now and again to admire the houses and the grounds, as a particular one caught his eye.

'Yeah, I thought I'd fill her in on my life-story to save her giving me the third degree later. She seemed satisfied.' He laughed again. He'd certainly got my mother summed up.

'Oh, I'm so sorry, she's a bit direct I'm afraid.' Understatement. I could imagine what she'd been like. So embarrassing. 'What did you tell her?'

'I live in Jersey with my mother and her second husband and their daughter. My dad has just remarried and has a young wife. He owns his own business and I haven't seen him in years. I have a brother who sometimes lives with my mother and sometimes with my father. My step-father has his own business in Jersey. That's it really.' He was watching me closely, those turquoise eyes boring into me. 'Oh, and my parents divorced when I was twelve, so obviously we're not Catholics.'

'Oh!' was all I could say. I wondered what Mum had made of it.

'I know lots about you.' He laughed. 'Your brother Jasper is a mine of information and very keen to tell me all about you and your family.'

He brushed his thick black hair from his eyes and turned towards me, slowing his pace.

'Oh.' I managed again.

His eyes had an almost hypnotic effect on me and I just stopped and gazed into them as he stepped towards me. The air around me was stifling; I couldn't breathe.

We stood looking into each other's eyes. My throat was dry and my chest was struggling to cope with the blood pumping through my veins, thudding in my ears like a drum solo by Keith Moon of The Who.

'So, here we are then,' he said gruffly, not taking his eyes from mine.

'Yes.' I think I said it out loud, but my mouth felt as it if had gone on holiday leaving my brain in a vacuum.

'So, what are we going to do?' he asked, licking his lips. His eyes had a twinkle in them as if he knew a really funny joke.

'About what?' Someone spoke and I realised it was me, my mouth and brain had reunited.

'About us of course.' He was so matter of fact. His smile was slow and sexy.

'Us?' I dragged myself back from the mist-filled place I was falling into as I registered what he'd said. Was there an 'us'? He seemed a bit sure of himself, I thought. Flipping nerve.

He grinned. 'We do need to sort this out.'

'Sort what out?' I was more than mystified and intrigued.

'Us, of course. You're going to Germany in August, so we

30

need to sort stuff out,' he said earnestly. 'All this...'

He put his hands on my shaking shoulders and drew me close to him so that I could feel his hot breath on my cheek. My knees were about to let me down so it was just as well he took me in his arms and almost lifted me off my feet, as his lovely soft lips brushed mine. Keith Moon played another deafening solo in my ears. I could feel the whole length of his body pressing against mine, almost willing me to pass through and into him.

His heart hammered against my chest and the smell of his aftershave filled my senses, his cheek was soft and his hair fell over my face, soft and feather-like. I really had died and was in heaven. Scott Walker and Peter Frampton began to fade from my memory as Scott what's-his-name took over.

I vaguely wondered what his surname was. I was being kissed by a total stranger I'd only met an hour ago. Mrs Digby would love this, I thought, as he pulled away from me and sighed.

I stood, eyes closed, hanging on to him in case I fell over. It seemed as if he was kissing me forever, but it was just the briefest touch of his lips on mine. I seriously believe I won't survive a proper full on kiss. Gordon Bennett! I felt like Doris Day in *That Touch of Mink*, when Cary Grant kissed her for the first time. Trouble is, she broke out in a rash every time he came near her.

We carried on up the road towards my house in silence. He put his left arm around my shoulders and took my left hand in his right. I was lost for words. It was all a bit much, but I still managed to keep an eye out in case anyone who knew Mum was around.

As we turned into the drive Mum's bedroom window shot open and she stuck her head out and hissed, 'what time do you call this?' It echoed in the silence of the late evening.

'Sorry Mrs Rossi, we forgot the time as we chatted.' Scott looked suitably repentant. 'I'm so sorry, but there are some

31

lovely houses around and I was telling Renza about my father being in the estate agency business, so we were just trying to guess the prices – got a bit carried away.' He gave her his most charming smile.

'Since when have you been incapable of walking unassisted?' She glared at me and I moved away from Scott's protective arm.

'Just keeping her safe,' Scott told her, grinning broadly.

'Say goodnight and get in here now.' Mother shut the window and the curtain closed.

I watched the window as I said lamely, ' Err, well, thank you for taking me out. It was lovely,' and I turned towards the front door. I felt so miserable. Mum said go out with him once and he wouldn't want to see me again. I waited for the brush off.

Before I reached the door he grabbed my arm, pulled me round and leaned towards me, kissed my forehead and squeezed my arm. Winking, he said, 'We'll do this again, seriously. I'll call round tomorrow, tell your mum.'

And he was gone.

I closed the door and leaned against the cool glass, completely blown away. I still didn't know his full name but it didn't matter.

Scott Whatshisname wanted to see me again.

Renza's Diary
16th June 1968

Of course Scott didn't show up yesterday. I knew he wouldn't and I knew Mum was right. I felt confused and disappointed and so unhappy. Goodness knows what I did wrong. What's wrong with me? I mean, I'd spent hardly three hours in his company and now all I could do was think about him, dream about him. And he wasn't interested. My heart was broken.

Luckily Mum didn't have time to shine the light in my face and give me a good grilling because Dad's cousin Gideon turned up out of the blue, and wanted to take me for a spin in his car. I tried my best to get out of it. Not that I didn't enjoy his company, I did, but I wanted to keep an eye on the stairs to the flat to see if Scott would appear.

By midday I had run out of excuses and with no sign of Scott decided, well, gave in, and reluctantly agreed to go and see an exhibition of Gideon's art in a leading London gallery.

Gideon was a talented artist, so clever, but sadly he suffered with his nerves, badly, since being bombed in his submarine during the Second World War. He had what the family called 'funny turns' and there was never any warning when he was going to have one.

He wasn't violent or anything like that, he just sort of went off to another place in his head for a while and sometimes he didn't come back for days and had to go into a special hospital.

He still lived with his widowed mother, Fenella, who tried hard to care for him, but she was getting quite old and you could see what a strain it was on her.

She's our favourite great aunt. You can hear her coming a mile away, with all the jangling charms on her bracelet. And whatever the weather, she had something fur on, either a big fur coat, or a stole, or a hat. She was like a model, tall, elegant and very beautiful, without a hair out of place. But she was only too happy to roll up her sleeves and bath one of the little ones if she got the chance.

Great Aunt Fenella had lived a wonderfully exciting life and had travelled all over the world, she had many stories to share. She'd even lived in Borneo. I loved it when she told us about her life there. Especially the story of her going up a river in the jungle in a small canoe, with natives taking her to join her husband, whom she hadn't seen in a while – he was an engineer inventor. She had on her best Bond Street outfit, complete with huge picture hat (this was in the 1920s), and suddenly a huge gust of wind took her hat off and she had to content herself watching it floating down the river, much to the amusement of her oarsmen.

I could always imagine it. The big white memsahib looking ridiculous.

Gideon and I were just getting in the car when I saw Scott walking towards us. I silently cursed Gideon and his flaming art, and then I cursed Scott for leaving it too late to visit me.

Taking a deep breath, I prepared myself for the brush off, my heart feeling like a lump of concrete as Scott said hello to Gideon and smiled at me.

Scott beckoned me to one side and I gave Gideon a huge smile, following Scott behind the car. I saw Mum twitching the curtains upstairs, her eyes boring into us.

'Just thought I'd pop round and let you know we are doing a gig in Luton and might not be back until late tomorrow. If we get back at a decent time, I'll come round then, OK?'

Those beautiful eyes held mine totally and utterly and I think I muttered, 'OK, then, see you tomorrow,' but I can't be sure.

He smiled at me again and patted my arm, and then he was gone.

Mother opened the bedroom window and shouted, 'what the hell are you playing at keeping Gideon waiting? Get in the car, now!'

Still in a bit of a dream, I got in the car. Gideon smiled at me and put the radio on. Flipping classical music. Oh boy, the trip into London was going to be so unreal. His car was ancient and it back-fired all the way up the London Road, it was so embarrassing, people stared at us and I felt a right twit.

Gideon wasn't the talkative type, thankfully, so I leaned back in the cracked leather seat and shut my eyes, re-living the last few minutes with Scott. He'd looked so sexy in his purple cords and tight black top which ended just under his ribs. He was so muscular and brown – just like a rock star. I wish I'd asked him more about his band the other evening, instead of acting like a dim-wit, all starry-eyed and gormless. I could kick myself. Closing my eyes, I felt his lips on mine, his arms around me for the millionth time. I just kept re-living every second of it, unable to believe what had happened. Actually I wasn't sure just what had happened. Was this like *falling in love*? I tried not to think about it and concentrated on this impromptu trip to London instead. One thing I was pleased about was that I'd dressed nicely for a change, thinking Scott and I might spend some time together. I'd decided to wear my black midi skirt and Mum's 1950s platform heels which tied across my ankles. I wore my white lace blouse with the high collar and a cameo broach at the throat, finished off with my black waistcoat – I thought I looked like a trendy cowgirl.

Going into London I didn't want to look like a country bumpkin. I hoped that Scott had liked what he saw. I just couldn't tell.

'Was that your boyfriend?' Gideon spoke at last, his eyes never leaving the road.

'Err, no, well, not really,' I stuttered, 'we've only just met – sort of.'

'Good looking chap, bit of a heartthrob I suppose.'

Gideon surprised me as it was generally thought that he was in such a world of his own he never saw or heard what the rest of us mere mortals did.

'He's in a group,' I said, sitting up and gazing out of the

windscreen as we came into the Cromwell Road in London.

'An artistic soul then, that's nice.' Gideon slowed down and turned off into a side street. 'I like that.'

We parked the car and I followed Gideon along the street full of hippies and really hip people wearing the latest fashions and hair styles – it was so exciting and I felt as if my eyes would pop. I made a mental note of what they were all wearing so I could find similar clothes next time I had some spare cash.

We went into a large white Georgian building, decorated richly with a chandelier hanging from the ceiling. The walls were lined with Gideon's paintings, most of which I recognised from the studio in his home.

'I wanted you to see them before the exhibition opens. I know you appreciate the creative side of people, Renza, so you're having your own private showing with me, before the opening next week. I hope you like what you see.' Gideon peered intensely at me with a look of hope in his dark grey eyes.

'They're amazing, wonderful, you're so talented. I hope you sell bucket loads and make millions just like Dali and Picasso.' I'm not a fan of Picasso or Dali; at least you can recognise what Gideon has painted.

Gideon went off to see someone about his exhibition and I found a seat and went back to thinking about Scott.

He seemed to be all I could think about since we had our date.

Date! Wishful thinking! Our walk.

Renza's Diary
16th June 1968 – early evening

Amazingly we headed to the Dorchester on Park Lane for dinner. Gideon said he'd told Mum he'd feed me, so we might be late back. We took a black cab because Gideon didn't want the hassle of finding a parking space and dealing with parking meters.

The Dorchester was amazing, glittering and very posh. Everyone was dressed in evening clothes or really way out fashions with the wildest hair-styles and jewellery. The women looked just like models and the men looked like film stars. My eyes almost popped. A man in a bow tie played music I didn't recognise, seated at a grand piano, whilst waiters flitted about like black penguins smiling and serving drinks and meals. I felt so sophisticated when we walked in, although I could see people watching us, no doubt wondering what a middle aged man was doing with such a young girl. I wasn't fussed. I know I can pass for older than sixteen. I felt like Lady Muck.

A few months ago I'd been out with Phillip Swartz whose family own the grocers and Post Office not far from Nan's. His mum was friends with mine and he apparently 'fancied me' and wanted to take me out, so between them they arranged for him to take me to a discotheque. I didn't have a choice and I felt really stupid going out with someone of twenty-five, but he was nice.

We had a good time, but he was shocked when I said I was only just sixteen, no one had told him. He thought I was twenty. I reckoned Mum thought she would marry me off to a rich bloke and get me off her hands. He said he loved taking me out and he really liked me, but I was just too young for him. I've never been so relieved in my life. I spent all night worrying in case he wanted to kiss me goodnight. He kissed my hand instead. He was rather dishy though, a bit like Dave Clark from The Dave Clark Five, but really, he was almost an old man!

Gideon ordered for us. I looked at the menu but it all seemed a bit posh and expensive to me and so when he said he would order I was really relieved. We had oysters in their shells and something called garlic bread which I'd never had before but I really liked it, even though it hummed a bit. Then we had pheasant and some sort of sauce with lots of vegetables and roast potatoes. The oysters and pheasant were 'out of season' according to Gideon, but apparently posh chefs can get them from overseas. Well, that's a relief then.

I'm not much of a meat eater, I'd rather have just had the vegetables, but at home if I say I don't want to eat any of it Mum says I'm trying to be different and being awkward, so I just ate what I was given. Besides, I wouldn't have upset Gideon for the world. I even drank the claret which was poured for me when we'd finished our citrus torte, and afterwards we were served the cheese board and coffee. I thought I was going to pop.

Gideon was interested in my writing career, or rather my fading hopes of one, and he said he'd try and get Mum and Dad to think again, but I told him it was far too late. He asked me about Scott and his band as well, but I was at a loss what to tell him really – what was there to tell?

So we talked art and music and films, and then we talked about the Vietnam war and the unrest in France and in Eastern Europe, and how being in Germany might not be too safe, what with the Soviet Union and Berlin Wall.

It was almost worth not seeing Scott to be here at this time in this fantastic city. I really was having the best time.

We took another taxi after dinner, and stopped off at Carnaby Street. I couldn't believe it. I was standing in the most trendy, fab and groovy place on the planet, and it was all so mind-blowingly exciting.

Everywhere I looked I could see Mods and Hippies and really cool looking people with the most far out clothes you could imagine. Girls were in minis with John Lennon caps and long over the knee boots; maxi and midi skirts were everywhere and in every colour and pattern you could think of. It was crowded with people shopping and tourists and people just like me.

'I want to go into Lady Jane, and have a look round!' I was almost squealing with excitement and anticipation. Not that I could afford anything, but just to go inside.

Gideon went into Lord John whilst waiting for me. I couldn't imagine it was his type of place, but he kindly stayed in there for the twenty minutes I spent in heaven with the most grooviest gear ever.

Eventually I felt sorry for Gideon and fetched him out. Then we wandered into Pop.

When we came out I spotted a really famous band, The Mojos, who I recognised from the television, coming out of the really trendy hairdressers called John Stephen.

I could hardly believe that I was standing feet from The Mojos, in the most famous street in the world. There was a huge photo of Long John Baldry in the window and it seemed he had his hair done there too.

Suddenly a crowd of screaming crying girls came charging towards us as they also spotted The Mojos. Gideon grabbed my arm and we ducked into a music shop. The group were surrounded and ended up signing autographs and having their photos taken by the fans.

It was just like being at the Empire Pool Wembley after the pop concert I was allowed to go to. Amazing.

The record shop was full of kids looking through the records, standing in the booths, listening to songs with headphones on, and there was just this loud muddle of music – all sorts of songs bleeding through the booths and into the shop. Some girls were dancing to the music, swaying from side to side, eyes closed.

There were posters all around the shop for different bands and events. There was a fab poster of The Who, advertising their Magic Bus Tour, and another one for the West End musical called *Hair*, with Oliver Tobias on it, which, so I heard at school, had lots of naked people running around on stage. I tried not to imagine the gorgeous actor, Oliver Tobias naked.

I was knocked out by the atmosphere and the variety of people, the music and fashion – it was all so unreal, so far removed from my life at home. I'd seen a famous band and lots of trendy people. Unreal.

We popped into a coffee bar across from the record shop and ordered two espressos; "people watching" Gideon called it. Imagine if Twiggy or David Bailey went past – I'd just die.

After a while Gideon said, 'We'd best get going or your mum will do her pieces if we're too late back.'

So we took another taxi back to the car and set off home.

'Gideon, I've had the best day ever, thanks so much for bringing me with you, it's been the most wonderful day.'

'My pleasure.'

He went to chat to Mum when we got home, and I went straight to bed so I could replay the fab day I'd had, over and over in my mind. But as I drifted off to sleep it was Scott who filled my mind. I couldn't stop thinking about Scott and tomorrow.

Renza's Diary
June 17th 1968 – early afternoon

Scott stood at the front door smiling broadly and looking out of this world. His hair was caught by the sun over his shoulder, glossy and falling over his eyes, which seemed even more turquoise than I recalled.

'Hello, want to go for a walk with me?' he asked, one hand resting on the door jamb.

'Oh, err, I'm not sure,' I stammered, glancing over my shoulder nervously. 'I'd have to ask Mum first.'

'Ask her then,' he said, reaching out to touch my hair. My knees nearly buckled.

'Please wait here, she doesn't like people coming inside uninvited,' I told him, feeling really stupid. He must think I'm such a little kid.

'No sweat,' he winked at me. 'We can go to that big park place down the other end of the village if you like.'

'It's a military college actually, one of my favourite places.'

'The place with the huge gates?'

'Yes that's it, it's gorgeous in there, I think you'd love it. Hang on a minute...'

I shut the door a little and went to find Mum.

When I'd found her and told her Scott was at the door and wanted to take me for a walk to the college she looked amazed.

'What the hell for? I thought he'd have lost interest by now, I don't understand him.'

She'd been making pastry and cakes for teatime and had flour all over her hands and apron, which thankfully meant she wouldn't want to be seen looking like that. Not that she would ask Scott in anyway.

'The college you say, well I suppose so. Make sure you get back here before teatime, and no going behind the bushes or anything like that.'

She didn't look too happy so I decided to get going fast before she changed her mind. But she hadn't said no – and I couldn't believe it. I ran back to the front door.

'Won't be long – got to brush my hair.'

In actual fact I belted up the stairs, had a panic about what I was wearing and decided to put my grey bell bottomed hipsters on and the pale blue skinny rib jumper with the polo neck. I cleaned my teeth and dabbed myself with the American perfume with the unpronounceable French name which my aunt Celia had given me. Thankfully I had clean hair.

I put a little mascara on – Mum would go nuts if I put too much on in case anyone saw me – and I grabbed my blue shoulder bag and hurtled down the stairs.

At first I thought Scott had given up waiting and had left. I opened the door wider, relieved to see him by the gate talking to the blond God, and the rest of his bandmates, who I'd only ever seen from a distance.

Gordon Bennett, they were a good looking bunch. I'd love to see Yvette's face if she went past now...

The blond God saw me and waved me over. I shouted 'bye' to Mum and closed the door before she could check me over. I made my way nervously towards the boys, disappointment washing over me. He never mentioned them coming with us.

'Hey babe.' The blond God smiled at me and I nodded back. The dreaded flush was already starting to spread across my throat.

'So, babe, how are you?' said the dark haired, dark eyed boy, with a sort of angelic face.

'Fine thanks,' I said lamely, feeling anything but a babe.

'Yeah, babe, how's it hanging?' The lean tanned one with Marc Bolan locks, smiled at me.

I'd no idea what he meant but smiled and nodded in response. The older-looking one who I'd seen in the van that day when they tooted, simply nodded at me. I nodded back.

'I'm Rich, the roadie.'

I had no idea what a roadie was but looked suitably impressed and muttered, 'Oh, far out.'

What a twit I am, I thought as soon as I opened my mouth. Some babe I was.

'Her name isn't babe – as you well know. She's Renza. Renza, let me introduce the rest of the band.' Scott laughed. 'This is Zak, lead vocals,' he said, pointing to the blond God. 'And this is Joss, our bass player,' he added, pointing to the boy with the black hair and angelic face.

'Hello,' I said, glancing at the house to see if Mother was hiding behind the curtain, spying. She was. I looked over at Mrs Digby's and saw her watching us out of the bedroom window. I wished the boys would go away before I got hauled back inside.

'And this is Mo, our drummer and my co-writer.' Scott put his hand on the Marc Bolan look-alike's shoulder.

'Hi there, Renza,' he said, smiling warmly. He winked at me. 'You've really done a number on Scott, Renza. From the first moment he saw you he's been determined to have you to himself.' He laughed as Scott punched him.

'It's called love at first sight, you know.' Mo added grinning at me.

I blushed in horror and Scott's face went red but he didn't look angry, he seemed very accepting of what his band-mate said. He winked at me, nodding and grinning broadly. Love at first sight, cripes, that's something else…. flipping heck. Me?

'All right you lot, clear off and let us get going.' Scott opened the gate and put his hand in the small of my back, guiding me on to the pavement. I breathed a sigh of relief; they weren't coming and we were leaving before Mum could change her mind.

'We'll see you later, don't forget. We're working tonight. I'll come and pick you up so don't go too far inside the college,' Rich told Scott.

Scott walked on the outside of the path and thankfully

waited until we were out of Mum's view before taking hold of my hand. It felt strong and cool and soft, though I had noticed before that the tips of his fingers were quite hard. I asked him about this and he told me it was from playing guitar with his fingers and not using a pick.

I desperately tried to think of something else to say, but just as I opened my mouth Scott said, 'you look gorgeous.'

I blushed right up to my roots and held my head down, letting my hair fall all over my face, saying nothing. Too shy to even say thank you. I hoped Scott wouldn't mention anything about the love thing – I'd die – but deep down I was thrilled. A gorgeous boy loved me. I felt all excited and terrified at once. There's no future in anything anyway, because I'll be gone before long and he will soon find someone else, but even so ...

Scott was watching me out of the corner of his eye, making me feel embarrassed. I wondered what he was thinking, but daren't ask.

'They all seem very nice,' I managed as we passed the recreation ground where the local cricket team were in action against some team or other. Dad would've normally been playing with them, if he hadn't been in Germany

'The band?' Scott squeezed my hand tightly, 'yeah, they're cool guys.'

'How long have you been in the band?' I asked, thinking it would be good to ask him lots of questions and then there wouldn't be awkward silences.

'Well, Zak and I have been in bands together since we were about 15, and this one has been together since about 1966 I guess.'

'Oh, that's nice. How long have you known the others?' I sneaked a look at him out of the corner of my eye, taking in his long slim legs and slender hips in tight black trousers. His broad shoulders were covered by a purple shirt – so far out!

'Well, the other two joined not long after, I'm not really

sure how long ago.'

'That's my nan's house over there,' I told him, pointing to the red-brick house with the huge front garden full of chrysanthemums and peonies.

'That's nice,' he said politely.

Oh, I am so lame.

'That's the farm where I used to collect eggs, feed the cows, and sometimes help with the haymaking and potato picking when I was little.' I pointed to the 16th century farm house and out buildings nestling back from the road.

'Before we moved into our house we used to stay with my nan when we were home on leave from the army – we lived mostly overseas, so did my cousins, and sometimes we'd all descend upon Nan at the same time. It was fun, but very crowded.'

'That's nice, you having a real family and everything,' he said at last. 'I never really had one. When my parents divorced neither of them wanted my brother and me once they remarried. We reminded them of their unhappy marriage I guess.'

'That's sad,' I said, feeling so sorry for him, he seemed as lonely as me. I wanted to give him a big hug. 'But big families aren't everything. I can't wait to get away from them all.'

'I think I can see why.' He laughed. 'Your mum is a bit full on and all those kids all the time... Not that I don't like them, I do, but they never leave you alone.'

'Tell me about it.' I sighed. He put his arm around me and it felt great.

We passed the Gypsy Cottage with the Romany caravan in the garden next to the huge pile of logs which they used to sell, along with pegs and lucky heather. I made Scott laugh when I told him about the time my nan bought some 'lucky' heather from Old Ma Lee who came to the house selling bundles of it. Nan gave her a few shillings for several bunches and it was only after Old Ma Lee had gone, she realised she'd just paid her for her own heather. Old Ma Lee had picked all Nan's heather and then had the nerve to sell it back to her!

We entered the village end of the college and I showed him where Yvette used to live, just inside the gates before her family purchased a house in town. 'I think I've seen your friend,' he said. 'She and another girl kept visiting you when we first moved into the flat. Got the idea they were trying to get off with us.'

He laughed again, a lovely throaty, warm laugh, which made my knees go weak.

'Yeah, Mum sent them packing. She hates people coming round.'

'I noticed, but she better get used to me coming round because I'm not stopping.'

Scott turned to me and grabbed my shoulders and bent his head to kiss me.

I closed my eyes and felt the soft lips touch mine and I was in heaven. I melted into him and never wanted it to end. He held me tightly and pressed himself against me, but I didn't mind like I did when Mum's friend Mrs Hudson-Smith's wet son, Harold, tried to kiss me. That was like being smacked in the mouth with a wet fish. I couldn't stand the idiot, but Mum wanted me to go to the school dance with him because she thought he was such a nice boy. He was a letch. I had the devil's own job getting rid of him. Gross!

Scott sighed in my ear and I came back to the real world, leaving Harold behind and feeling nothing but Scott's body so close to mine and feeling so right. I tried to breathe slowly and not to make a mess of the moment.

We walked along contentedly – at least I was feeling content – and as we passed the statue of Queen Victoria I told him the story of a friend of Mum's whose ex-boyfriend drove the statue all the way from London, after the war, telling her he'd been followed by a fat old lady all the way. The girl was jealous until she realised it was Victoria.

'I love all your stories,' Scott said, looking around admiringly at the grounds, the sweeping lush lawns dotted with the huge Wellingtonia trees, oaks, pines, and the acres and acres of all variety of trees in the woodlands surrounding the colleges.

There were all colours of rhododendrons throughout the grounds as far as the eye could see, and we took in the two huge lakes with their secret islands in the middle where the ducks and swans lived. Scott gazed at the huge white building, the Old College, with the famous pillars and steps leading up to the main entrance where the Adjutant, on his white charger, climbs following the Officer Cadet Passing Out Parades. Then he looked over at The New College, with its red brick and tower overlooking the polo pitch.

'Wow, this place is amazing, it's gorgeous here. I can see why you love it.' Scott waved his hand round as he surveyed the beauty of our surroundings.

I pointed to the cricket pavilion on our right, across the road from Queen Victoria and the first of the lakes. A match was being played by cadets and a visiting team – all in their whites. It was the perfect English summer scene.

'Your dad's played cricket here, so Jasper said.'

'Yes, gosh he's got a big mouth. What else has he told you?' I'm going to kill Jasper slowly, painfully, and with great pleasure. Such a big blabber.

'Don't blame him, I've picked his brains ever since I first met him. He and your little sister, Lucy, knocked on our door when we arrived here and asked if we wanted to come out and play!' He laughed his head off at the memory. 'Jasper comes every day to play football with us and hang out... And of course, act as my 'messager.' He's a nice kid. They all are.'

In very small doses, maybe, I thought.

'What's that down there by the water?' He pointed to the wooden boat house where the cadets kept their rowing boats.

'It's the boat house.'

Everything seemed to interest and delight him, it was infectious. Scott grabbed my hand and took off down the hill, dragging me towards the wooden building, laughing when I nearly ended up on the grass, my shoes sticking as we ran.

'I'm going to break my neck, what's the rush?'

'Can we go inside?' he asked trying the door. It was locked.

We walked round the back as a group of officer cadets came marching towards us in their check hacking jackets, slacks and flat caps – their 'walking out' gear. As soon as they passed, Scott pulled me to him and gave me the biggest bear-hug ever. Then he buried his face in my hair and gave me little light kisses all along my neck and face. It was unbearable. Then he found my mouth and I just went to another place for the longest, sweetest time.

After a while we sat on one of the benches facing the main lake and watched the swans and ducks. There was almost total silence – apart from the sound of the odd duck quacking and a few birds flying overhead, and the occasional thwack of a cricket ball on willow, the clapping of the spectators on the cricket pitch behind us across the road behind the trees. We might have been on another planet, all alone.

The water lapped gently at the edge of the lake and the fragrance of the newly mown grass and vegetation filled the warm air. Sunshine danced on the almost ripple free water in-between the water lilies, throwing soft reflections of the elegant, fluffy white swans, as they dipped now and again after fish, and the ducks went bottoms up when they spotted food.

I leaned against Scott, his arms circling me, as we watched the reflection of the Old College in the water just to the left of us, a perfect replica of the white building floating on the surface.

We chatted now and again and learned more about each other and each other's family and background, and it was gradually easier for me to relax and enjoy myself in his company. We discovered we liked the same music and bands, and we both had the same albums by little known (in England) American rock bands. We enjoyed similar movies and books – mostly – and we both loved the countryside. I'd never felt like this before and it was a little confusing. I was beginning to feel as if I'd known him all my life. He said he felt it too. I had to put all thoughts of August out of my mind.

The perfection of the afternoon soon came to an end. The yellow van appeared on the road near Queen Victoria and Rich ran over to us waving his arms.

'Been looking all over this place for you, I said don't go too far into the grounds and here you are, almost out the other end!' he panted, reaching us, a bit red in the face.

Scott stood up and looked down at me. 'Gotta go, Renza. We're playing in London tonight.' He helped me up and put his arms around me, holding me tight.

'Sorry love. You can get home all right, can't you?' Rich smiled at me, and started back to the van where I could see the band watching us.

'Oh, yes of course, thanks,' I said, not wanting Scott to go.

'I'll see you tomorrow, thanks for a lovely afternoon. Mind how you walk home.'

Scott kissed my forehead and then he was getting in the van, and with a honk of their horn he was gone, they were gone, and I was alone with the ducks and the swans and the hollow-sounding thwack of the cricket ball on the bat, on such a perfect summer afternoon.

Stella's Diary
18th June 1968

'Miss Deacon? Stella? How are you feeling, dear?' The nurse peered down at me. 'Can you breathe normally? At all?'

Flat on my back, staring at Oxford Radcliffe Infirmary's cream ceiling and trying to ignore all the lights dazzling me, all the tubes attached to me, not to mention the weight-belt fastened round my waist and squeezing the life out of me, breathing was about the only thing I *could* do. I nodded.

'Good,' the nurse said briskly. 'Nearly done now. They'll just check the X-rays, and make sure they don't need to repeat anything, and if it's all clear then you can go. You're not in pain?'

I shook my head. I'd had a pethidine injection prior to the investigation procedure. It was lovely. I was floating. Which was just as well as this particular test involved my kidneys being injected with dye and then a massive belt fastened round me and pumped up increasing the pressure to something akin to being sat on by a baby elephant – apparently so the doctors behind the screen could see exactly where the fluid went.

I'd been having various out-patient investigative tests on and off for almost two years. I'd had the agonising stomach pains for much longer, more or less since I'd started my periods. Once Dr Kingston, my doctor at home in Harbury Green, had decided they were neither growing pains, or each time I went to see her with yet more embarrassing non-stop periods, "simply part of becoming a woman", she'd sent me to the Radcliffe for tests into everything else.

This one was for the kidneys. I was 19 years old and felt about 90. Probably looked it, too.

There was a bit of a flurry and several white-coated figures loomed over me.

'Miss Deacon,' a voice boomed. 'Good news. Your kidneys, while showing slight inflammation, which isn't unusual under the circumstances, are in otherwise fine fettle and functioning normally. I know – um, ah, yes, Dr Kingston, your local doctor has been treating you for suspected pyelonephritis and nephritis – and I'm delighted to tell you that today's X-rays, combined with our previous tests, confirm that you have neither.'

I tried to smile. The pethidine made it difficult to move my lips. And anyway, if it wasn't the kidneys giving me the crippling pains and making me faint, then what the heck was it?

The nurse bustled round undoing drips and the belt and generally freeing me from my shackles.

'Sit up slowly,' the white-coated doctor boomed. 'And take it easy for the rest of the day. Don't eat anything until this evening and just take a few sips of water if you're thirsty. Your innards will take a bit of time to revert to normal after the weight belt. We'll send a letter to your local surgery with today's results and our findings generally. You clearly have a problem, Miss Deacon, and we feel we've exhausted all the tests we can do here. I think maybe the problem lies with your reproductive system. I'd like to refer you to my colleagues over at the Churchill.'

With the help of the nurse, I sat up. The room swam dizzily.

'I'll contact the Churchill's Gynaecological Department and ask them to make an appointment for you as soon as possible. In the meantime, please go back to your local surgery if you need further help. Good day, Miss Deacon.'

And followed by his white-coated coterie, he swept out.

The Churchill. Women's problems – everyone knew that's where you went with women's problems. Another hospital... More tests. Gingerly, I slid my feet to the floor.

My mum, all fly-away hair and big glasses and her nose, as always, in a book, was waiting for me outside in the Radcliffe's grounds, sitting in the sun by the fountain.

Still feeling very wobbly, I sat beside her and told her what had happened.

'That's a shame, Stell,' she squeezed my hand. 'I'd really hoped we'd get to the bottom of this today. Your dad and I hate seeing you in so much pain... never mind, love. The Churchill is a wonderful hospital, they'll get you sorted out. How do you feel?'

'Sore round the middle where the belt went. But they gave me pethidine, so not too bad – although I'm still a bit squiffy. And I'm cross that no one seems to know what's wrong with me. And I'm hungry – and I'm not allowed to eat. Apart from that, Mum, I'm hunky-dory.'

She laughed and hugged me. 'We'll take it nice and easy walking back to the station, then. Oh, Stella, I do hope they can make you better soon.'

'So do I,' I said, groaning as I stood up and the Banbury Road dipped and swayed. 'I'm so fed up with feeling ill.'

And I wasn't the only one, I thought as, arm-in-arm, Mum and I took a slow stroll through Oxford's sunbaked streets back to the railway station.

Mike, my boyfriend, was getting pretty tired of me cancelling dates or having to go home early because I felt ill. Mike, I thought, as Mum and I walked down Hythe Bridge Street with the heat bouncing from the pavements, was going to be pretty cheesed off that yet another hospital appointment hadn't discovered what was wrong with me – and more importantly, what was needed to make me better again.

Mike... sometimes I wished Mike was more understanding – but then, what 20 year old boy wanted a girlfriend who had out-of-the-blue chronic stomach pains, occasionally fainted when they got really bad and – when the pains were at their worst – looked like a haggard old crone and had to go to bed and stay there?

Mike was my first proper boyfriend. Of course I'd had dates with the local boys before, and been walked home from youth club, and got off with the boys at Oxford dances and clubs, and things like that, but they were all casual and short-lived, and studying for my 3 A levels, and being at an all-girls' grammar school, meant that – well – having a proper boyfriend had come pretty late in my teenage life.

Mike and I had met at a dance last Christmas at the end of 1967. I'd left school that summer, after the A levels, and was a few months into my job in the civil service, and he was doing a mechanical engineering apprenticeship.

My job, as a clerical officer in the nearby Atomic Energy Research Establishment, was a lot less grand than it sounded. I worked in the claims department with two other girls – Debbie and Sally, who I'd been at school with – one older lady, and a middle-aged man, checking, calculating and authorising subsistence payments to the employees who needed to travel or work away.

Even though – much to Mum and Dad's delight – I'd been offered a place at college in London to read English, I'd opted to go out to work after A levels because honestly, I'd had enough of studying. The college had said I might change my mind and they'd keep the offer open.

This seemed like the best option and Mum and Dad had agreed it had to be my decision, but they hoped I'd reconsider in the future. Mike hadn't.

When I'd told Mike about it, he'd said they needn't bother keeping my place open. Girls didn't need to be educated and certainly not get degrees, he'd said. Girls always wanted to get married and then they'd stay at home and look after the house and their husband and their children. Like his mum.

I'd hooted with laughter and said there was no way on earth I'd be tied to a house and a husband and kids – even if I did get married – which I doubted, and that I'd do whatever I wanted to do in my life and no one would stop me... then I'd realised this was possibly insulting to his mum, so I'd trailed off and changed the subject.

My mum, who was a teacher at our local infants' school,

and both my nans, who worked in our local shops, had never given up going out to work, and were all fiercely independent, free-thinking women. But when Mike was around, I felt it was probably better to keep my opinions on women's education and emancipation to myself.

Mike was tall and good-looking in an athletic sort of way, with very short brown hair and brown eyes, he played football for our local team, and he had a car. Lots of the Harbury Green girls fancied him and envied me. I knew that.

Now, I was pretty sure that Mike was getting fed up with me. It bothered me, of course, but being ill bothered me more. Sometimes I just wanted to shut myself away and cry.

'Nearly there,' Mum's voice cut through the memories, and she grabbed my hand as we crossed the road by the railway station. 'We should be in plenty of time for the quarter past two train. Shame it's a stopper... but we should still be home by three.'

I nodded. The train could take forever as long as it meant I could sit down for a while.

The stopping trains from Oxford chugged along slowly between half a dozen rural stations. The journey, in summer, always reminded me of Edward Thomas's poem, Adlestrop. The fast trains – directly from Birmingham to London – also stopped at our small market town before rushing onwards to Reading and Paddington because Harbury Green, tiny as it was, was a Great Western Railway junction with lines that led westwards to Bristol, Devon and Cornwall. You could get a train nearly anywhere from Harbury Green, and practically everyone in the village relied on the railway for work, play and holidays.

Queuing at Oxford station, we handed our tickets over for clipping, and I felt so wobbly Mum was almost holding me up. People stared at us. They probably thought I was drunk.

'Stella?' she looked at me. 'You're not going to faint, are you?'

'No... Sorry... I'm ok. Just a bit shaky. And I was thinking about Mike earlier – and being ill. He's not going to like it that I have to have more tests...'

'Don't be silly, Stell,' Mum guided me gently on to the platform. 'He'll want you to be well again, however long it takes. If he loves you, he'll understand.'

I didn't say anything. I wasn't even sure that Mike loved me anymore. He had at first, of course. And I'd been crazy about him.

But now...

Renza's Diary
June 22nd 1968

The past few days have been like a dream, like a movie, or one of those wonderful books Daphne du Maurier writes so well. Romantic. Unbelievable.

Mum must be developing a split personality or something – spooky. She's allowed me to go out for walks with Scott nearly every time he asks me, whenever he has been home, which hasn't been a lot because the band have been busy talking to some famous songwriters about recording some of their songs. And of course most nights they gig all over the country. But we have spent a few lovely afternoons and evenings together, on the odd occasion he hasn't been off somewhere glamorous and she hasn't stopped it. I keep waiting for the axe to fall.

A couple of evenings we have walked to the college, around the lake, and on the way back we've stopped at the phone box so he can ring his mother in Jersey. I've spoken to her a few times, and his little sister, who is about four and a bit of a handful by the sounds of it. His mum said I can go over and stay with them whenever I want.

Fat chance. Nice of her to ask though. I wonder if Jersey is a bit like the Isle of Wight where Yvette and I spent Cowes Week once, staying with my dad's aunt, Ivy, who owns an inn on the Medina River.

Yvette and I had to earn our keep and helped out cleaning the rooms and making beds and sometimes we even got to work in the bar. Dad and Mum didn't mind me going to Cowes because Great Aunt Ivy would be keeping us under control.

It was a really exciting time, the inn was near the river where the floating bridge came across, and so there were people walking past all the time. People on holiday and others attending The Cowes Week Regatta which was on just up the road, past the hovercraft hangars, and near the Royal Yacht Club. We could see it all.

There were so many rich people about, coming into the inn, or on the beaches. It was so exciting. We spent most afternoons walking up and down the sea front watching it all. Of course, we also watched the boys.

It was great being away from home – from Mum especially – and, dare I admit it, the kids. I was free and able to be myself instead of having to be a good daughter and the helpful big sister all the time; the very first time I'd been away from them all since Simon's birth. I remember really not wanting to go home.

Not long after we got back home, Yvette's middle brother Jacob was killed in a road accident, and she didn't speak to me for ages afterwards. We were meant to go and see Traffic at the Finsbury Park Astoria, but she couldn't come, so the rest of us from school went without her. It was miserable and so sad. But Traffic were amazing, and the other bands were great as well. Not long afterwards there was that terrible disaster in Wales – in Aberfan – when the coal tips collapsed on the village and the school – 1966 wasn't a great year really.

No, on second thoughts, perhaps I don't want Jersey to be like the Isle of Wight, too many weird memories. I can't see Mum and Dad ever letting me go all the way to Jersey anyway, it's near France apparently, far too far away. I haven't mentioned it.

Mum did ask me if Scott's parents were rich because to live in Jersey you have to be a millionaire. As if I would ask him! Now I knew why she had changed her opinion of him – she was on the hunt for a rich husband for me again. Well, I was never getting married, so she can plot all she likes. I want to be an independent woman, like Katherine Hepburn is in her movies and in real life too, so I've read. I want a career and to travel, not a kitchen sink and nappies.

Scott and the band are coming round this afternoon to paint the garage door and to do some gardening. Rich has been chatting to Mum a lot and getting quite friendly with her; she thinks he's sensible and mature, possibly because he is a bit older than the others. She has even made sandwiches and cakes to have with their tea later on. Mum has definitely gone a bit funny in the head. I feel like I'm treading on egg shells, waiting for the real Mum to suddenly reappear and then what?

I've been invited to one of their gigs in Wiltshire next week, on Salisbury Plain, and Scott is going to ask Mum if I can go. I feel sick with worry in case she says no and gets mad at me for letting him ask her. But I really want to go.

The band had my transistor on in the back garden as they dug the vegetable patch and Rich painted the garage door. So far Radio One's played all the songs I love and the band's been singing along to them. When Otis Redding's 'My Girl,' played Scott kept winking at me. I couldn't help smiling but then I remembered crying for days when Otis died last year, and I felt sad.

The younger kids have been hanging around, getting in the way. Jasper tried to fight Scott and the others whenever he could get near enough to head butt them, or generally annoy them. Lucy kept getting in the way of Rich and the paint pot, but thankfully the others were still at school and wouldn't be back for ages.

I've spent the afternoon trying to keep the peace. Mum's been upstairs packing stuff, but every now and again I caught her watching us all from the back bedroom. Keep watching all you want, Mum, I thought, because there's nothing to see.

Eventually, she came downstairs and into the garden with the tea and cakes. I still can't believe it – but I guess she still thinks they are all millionaires so she's going to suck up as much as possible.

'Mrs Rossi, these cakes are wonderful, just like my mum makes.' Rich was on his third piece of ginger cake. Mum absolutely radiated pleasure at his compliments. I knew he had her just where he wanted her, crafty devil.

'Did you know we're playing at Merryhill, on Salisbury Plain – you know – in Wiltshire – next week at the big army base there? It would be great if you and Renza could come,' Rich said as he popped another piece of vinegar fruit cake in his mouth.

Scott and I exchanged horrified glances.

Mum stared at Rich for a few seconds. 'That's nice of you to suggest it, but I'm afraid I couldn't, much as I'd like to, it's hard to get babysitters for all the kids.'

Get her! I nearly choked.

'In that case, how about Renza coming with us?' He smiled at her and then sighed, and put his head on one side. 'These are the best cakes ever, I think they might even beat my mum's you know.'

And he put yet another scone on his plate.

Before Mum could answer, Scott said, 'that would be great, we'd look after her and you know she'd be safe with us, Mrs Rossi.'

'Yeah, all those soldiers as well, Mrs R, safe as houses.' Mo said, grinning widely.

I held my breath unable to move, waiting. She glanced at me briefly and then turned to Rich. 'If you can guarantee her safety and her arrival home at a decent hour, I might be inclined to allow it. But of course, I need to ask her father first.'

'Of course she'll be home safe and sound about an hour or two after the gig, I promise.' Rich smiled at her. 'You have my word.'

Scott winked at me.

'We'll sort the details later, Mrs R.' Rich nodded at her.

'Well, as long as she doesn't get home after the milkman.' Mum smiled, but I knew she was deadly serious. But, astonishingly, I thought she'd just said yes.

***

Later on, when the kids had had their tea and all the washing up had been done and shoes polished, Scott came round for me. Mum said we could go for a walk as long as I was back before ten, because she had an early morning start at work.

We didn't want to go as far as the college this time, instead we headed in the opposite direction under the railway bridge past open fields and farm cottages, and out of sight of prying eyes much to my relief.

We walked hand in hand and chatted easily now my nerves had settled down and I'd discovered Scott was really nice, as well as being sex on legs. I wasn't in such a state every time he came near me. He still got me all of a quiver, but I could control it now, thankfully. It was worrying me. I really wondered what he made of me being such a pushover whenever he touched me. Maybe I ought to play a bit hard to get.

He started talking about the gig at Merryhill and I was so excited – I'd never been to a concert where my boyfriend was in the band! I guessed I could call him my boyfriend now. My boyfriend. Wow.

Scott laughed when I asked him what I should wear. I didn't want to let him down by looking like a country bumpkin. He said, 'nothing would be nice.' I blushed to my roots. One day, I promised myself, I will stop blushing.

Stella's Diary
22nd June 1968

'We're going to meet up with Sam and Patsy at the pub,' Mike said as I scrambled into his car outside our house. 'Then we can decide what to do after that. Ok?'

He leaned across and kissed me. Briefly. The evening sun dazzled through the Wolseley's windscreen. For once, I felt ok. No pains, and I'd managed to get my hair to go just right which was nothing short of a miracle because my hair drove me mad.

For ages now it had been fashionable to have a Cathy McGowan waterfall of sleek, straight hair – preferably blonde – and mine was brownish-red and naturally curly. Not nice curly like Marsha Hunt's – no, left to its own devices it looked like my nan's perm. So embarrassing.

Eventually, I'd decided that if I couldn't have the same hair as everyone else, then I'd go all out to be different. So, I'd chopped it very short, razored it into haphazard layers, dyed it coal-black, then backcombed it so that it was a huge mass of spikes with a long dead-straight fringe which, if it all went right, tangled with my false eyelashes.

Anyway, tonight it had behaved really well and even my false eyelashes had gone on first time. Mind you, I hadn't gone the whole hog: I hadn't done my eyebrows.

Last year, after A levels, I'd shaved my eyebrows off. It had been really trendy to be eyebrowless during 1967's Summer of Love. Free at last from the shackles of the sixth form, we'd become Flower Children, and spent our days and nights in Oxford's Fantasia Café high above Carfax, inhaling Gauloises fumes, drinking coffee and listening to 'All You Need is Love', or sprawled by the Isis in Christ Church Meadow re-enacting 'Itchycoo Park.'

My eyebrows had never grown back, so using eyelash glue, I'd stuck an arch of multi-coloured sequins where my eyebrows had been and dusted my eye-lids and cheeks with smaller sequins and glitter. My sparkly face and brows had become a bit of a trademark, but this year, since I'd been feeling so ill, I hadn't bothered with them much.

Not that Mike would mind – he'd never been a fan of my glittery make-up. I suspected he thought it was a bit hippy-ish.

Anyway, tonight I was wearing a new navy and white polka dot coat dress with white collar and cuffs. I'd made it myself, like I did with most of my clothes, and it had been quite tricky. I'd hoped Mike might say I looked nice.

He didn't. He didn't even ask if I felt ok. Maybe he didn't want to know the answer. He'd certainly gone very quiet earlier in the week when I'd told him about being referred to the Churchill.

As we drove towards the pub he just talked about work and football and his car – all the usual topics – and I sort of stopped listening to him and listened instead to The Herd singing 'I Don't Want Our Loving to Die' on the radio. How apt!

We reached the pub. Sam and Patsy were sitting at one of the trestle tables outside and smiled at us.

They were Mike's friends really. Not mine. Sam and Mike worked together and played football together. Sam and Patsy were engaged and had been since she was sixteen. Patsy had glossy red hair with flick-ups, like Lulu, and wore very grown-up clothes. She was a bit younger than me but looked and acted much older. I was never sure if I liked her or not. I thought probably not.

If we went out in a foursome it was usually with Sam and Patsy, rather than my best friend, Vix, and her boyfriend Jeff. Mainly because Vix didn't like Mike – and the feeling was mutual. It was all a bit wearying to be honest.

Sam and Mike disappeared into the pub and Patsy, half-way through her glass of Babycham, looked at me. 'Nice dress.'

'Thank you.'

She leaned across the table. 'What do you think about

Cornwall, then?'

'What?' I squinted into the still-hot evening sun. 'What about Cornwall?'

She laughed. 'Oh, don't say Mike hasn't told you! We're going on holiday – to Cornwall. All four of us.'

I was suddenly very cold despite the heat. 'What? When? No, honestly, Mike hasn't mentioned it to me – I mean...'

Patsy laughed again, flicking back her hair. 'What's he like, eh? We've booked the last week in August – because it's the boys' factory holiday week – in Polperro. You'll have to get the time off work and start saving.'

I sighed. 'Oh, gosh... I don't know... I mean... I've got to have some more hospital appointments and I don't know when they're going to be, and...'

Patsy frowned. 'I'd shut up about the hospital appointments if I were you. I think Mike's getting pretty fed up with hearing about them. He won't want you spoiling his one week's holiday by going on about how ill you are.'

'I don't keep going on about it!' I snapped. 'But if I have an appointment at the same time as the holiday – then I won't be going to Cornwall.'

Patsy smirked and twiddled the impaled cherry in her Babycham. 'I wouldn't tell Mike that if I were you. There's plenty of other girls who'd jump at the chance... you know what I mean?'

'Not really.' I glared at her.

'Oh, Stella!' she trilled with laughter. 'I'm only teasing. Don't look so cross. We all had a fab time when we went away together before, didn't we?'

I didn't reply. I didn't actually trust myself to answer.

Because the possibility of a hospital appointment clashing with the week away really wasn't my main problem about going on holiday.

In early May we'd all had a weekend away at a caravan site in Hampshire. The weather had been gorgeous and we were close to the sea and it was all very pretty. It was also the first time Mike and I had been away together and I'd known he'd expect me to sleep with him.

It was something I'd been managing to avoid for the whole five months we'd been together. But once we'd arrived at the caravan site and I'd realised that there were two double bedrooms it had been something I couldn't avoid any longer.

I'd sort of fudged the issue with my mum and dad, saying there was a crowd of us going. And it wasn't even about the morality of sex before marriage: this was the swinging sixties after all and nearly everyone I knew was on the pill and sleeping with their boyfriends.

No, it was just me being more than a bit scared, and dopey and hopelessly romantic. And I'd wanted the first time to be special and with the boy I was going to spend the rest of my life with. And I was pretty sure that wasn't Mike...

Anyway, it was awful. Truly awful. Mike seemed to enjoy it but I hated it. It was embarrassing and uncomfortable and all over so quickly. I couldn't for the life of me understand why everyone raved about it. I simply couldn't understand why anyone would want to have sex. Ever.

And as far as I was concerned it had been a one off. Using my illness, and much to his annoyance, I'd managed to avoid Mike's attempts to do it again ever since.

The thing was, despite all this, I didn't really want to finish with Mike. We did have fun together and we got on ok. It just wasn't how I'd imagined my first gown-up relationship was going to be.

As a pin money hobby, I'd been writing short stories for the teenage magazines since I was fourteen. They were all sweet and romantic, with mutual adoration, gentle hand-holding and moonlight-kisses, and every one of them had a happy-ever-after ending. That's what I'd expected to happen in real life, I think.

I read voraciously, too. From Dickens to Denise Robins and

back again. I always lost myself in whatever I was reading: I *was* that heroine... and I yearned for the adventures and love affairs they had – all the excitement, and daring, and head-over-heels giddiness and cascades of rainbows and twinkling stars and bluebirds.

Oh, in my heart of hearts I knew it was totally stupid. Stuff like that would never happen to someone like me. But it didn't stop me dreaming...

'Are we – er – staying in a caravan again?'

'No!' Patsy's eyes sparkled. 'We're renting a cottage. I got it out of The Exchange and Mart. Just the four of us. Playing house. It's going to be fab!'

I groaned. It was going to be anything but.

'I've booked it as Mr and Mrs Stewart and Mr and Mrs Metcalf,' Patsy continued, chuckling to herself. 'Because we have to collect the keys from the cottage's owner when we get there and it's married couples only. So, I've got you this... it's a present...'

She scrabbled in her handbag and pushed a small paper bag across the trestle table. I peered inside.

A wedding ring. Oh, God!

'Woolies' finest!' Patsy grinned. 'I've got one as well. Hopefully our fingers won't go green before the end of the week.'

'Who's turning green?' Mike came out of the pub then carrying a tray with two pints of beer, another Babycham, a pineapple juice for me, and four packets of crisps. 'Not morning sickness. A bit late, is it, Patsy?'

She shrieked with laughter and punched him playfully as the boys sat down. The drinks slopped into the tray.

Sam pulled a face. 'I bloody hope not. I'm not ready to be a daddy yet. I keep telling her to get on that pill.'

They giggled together.

'You're a one!' Patsy chuckled. 'Anyway, no – we were just talking about going to Cornwall – weren't we Stella?'

'Yes, we were...'

Sam sniggered. 'You'll have to get fixed-up as well, Stella, cos we're gonna have a whole week of sun, sea and sex.'

Patsy laughed. I didn't.

Mike looked at me quickly. 'Ah, yes – I was going to tell you about that – about going on holiday – it was just with you being at the hospital again and everything... Anyway, what do you think? Cool, isn't it?'

I sipped my pineapple juice. Slowly. 'I wish you'd asked me first, actually. But, yes, if I'm ok, and can get the week off and it doesn't clash with any of my hospital stuff, then I suppose it'll be fun...'

And then I uncrossed my fingers.

Renza's Diary
June 29th 1968 – Merryhill Base

The gig was amazing. It was packed – lots of kids and soldiers of course – full of screaming girls, so noisy. Scott's band was the star attraction, having come from overseas (well, Jersey), and, as Rich told me during the evening, they had proper management and an agent, plus as well as writing their own songs, they had songwriters working for them too. Serious stuff.

Narnia's Children, I soon discovered, were professionals, unlike the support act, The Fulcrum, a local amateur band looking for a record deal but so far hadn't got any interest. They had a big local following, but Scott's band had a national following and some fans came to all their gigs, wherever they played. It was great, learning all this. Rich said that Narnia's Children even had several record companies interested in them and there was talk of overseas tours, and they were recording soon with a famous company. They had lots going for them. Going to one of Scott's gigs for the first time was so thrilling – and I basked in the glory.

Mind you, it had got a bit scary when I went to the loo. Being an army base there were lots of women soldiers and I have to say some of them were real hard cases by the look of them. Anyway, I found my way through the heaving crowd to the ladies and waited in line for a cubicle to become free. Several mini-skirted girls were ahead of me, chatting and giggling and discussing which one of the band they fancied and which one they were going to get off with given half a chance.

There were a couple of female soldiers behind me, chatting and passing remarks about the girls in front. I didn't think anything of it. I'd been thinking about how sexy Scott was, the way he held his guitar so low and moved on stage.

The girls in front of me went into the cubicle and one of them shouted to me to hold the door because the lock was missing. I grabbed the door as best I could and tried to keep it shut. But all the time she chatted to her mates about how she fancied Scott and went into great detail about how she thought he was eyeing her up all night and how she was going to go backstage and make a play for him. Over my dead body, I thought, and was tempted to let go of the door and expose her.

'Are you going to be all day?' I wasn't going to hold it much longer and all the other cubicles were full so this one was going to be mine, if she ever came out. It sounded like Niagara Falls on the other side of the door.

'Go play with the traffic,' came the reply. Girls tittered behind me.

'Come on, you've been in there ages. What're you doing?' said the soldier behind me. 'Need any help?' Everyone laughed again.

The door flew open and a Phyllis Diller look-alike shoved past me, giving me the evil eye.

'No chance,' I muttered, thinking of her plans for Scott. Before I could move she turned and pushed me into the cubicle. 'It's all yours.'

I turned to the soldier behind and asked her if she would hold the door for me, at which she smiled sweetly and nodded. Her friend giggled. I was getting myself organised when the door flew open and the two soldiers stood grinning at me.

'Please shut the door,' I said, my hipsters almost at my knees. I held my hand out to push the door closed again, but the blonde soldier who had agreed to hold the door pushed the door open again.

'Don't be unfriendly,' she said, moving closer to me.

'What?' I moved as far away from her as I could in the tight space and nearly toppled into the loo. 'Please go away.' My hipsters fell around my ankles.

'You want to be nice to us, don't you?' Her tubby freckled faced friend was trying to get into the cubicle as well.

'What are you on about?' I started pulling my hipsters up. 'I want to leave, let me leave.'

I felt threatened. I couldn't understand what I had done to upset them. I didn't think I'd been unfriendly, why did they want me to be nice to them? I struggled to zip my hipsters up and tuck my skinny rib in.

Something about their faces and their stance made me frightened and I could feel my heart pounding and my face getting red. I tried to get past again, but they blocked my way and the blonde one made a grab for me. She got hold of my shoulders and pushed me against the wall, as her friend tried to get in far enough to shut the door, but thankfully the space was too small for the three of us.

'What do you want?' I yelled at them, struggling against the hands holding my shoulders. 'What have I done to upset you?'

My captor laughed and bent her head towards me. The penny suddenly dropped: bloody hell! She was going to kiss me. Oh my God! My mind went blank with shock. I turned my head away and my hair covered my face.

She grabbed my head and forced it round and her friend leaned over and pushed my hair out of the way. She grabbed my left boob and squeezed. I struggled and kicked and yelled at the top of my voice, 'Help! Help!'

The tubby girl looked over her shoulder and checked no one had come into the loo. Then she held my face in her hands whilst her friend tried again. I twisted and turned and wriggled about, I was in a panic. I couldn't for the life of me think why they were doing this to me. At first I thought they were going to beat me up, I'd heard about girls who did that to other girls, but kissing me!

That was really weird.

'Scott! Scott!' I yelled at the top of my voice, though how he could help me in the ladies loo, I had no idea.

'Shut up you stupid bitch.' The blonde girl twisted her face up and grabbed my hair, pulling it really hard. I yelled louder, the pain was terrible.

'Hey, what the hell is going on in there?' a female voice asked from the other side of the cubicle wall, and both girls stopped and stood quiet.

The blonde one put her hand over my mouth. I thrashed about with my legs, kicking her and biting her hand. She yelped and jumped back, her hand falling from my mouth.

'Help! Please help me,' I shouted and kicked out again so that the two girls had to back out of the cubicle to avoid a good shin kicking.

'What is going on in there?' the woman outside shouted again. 'I'll get someone to sort you out if you don't stop it and come out.'

'I'm being attacked, please get help,' I yelled as my assailants backed out of the cubicle and left me, panting hard and holding on to the wall for support.

I heard the door bang as they left and a middle-aged woman appeared in the door.

'Are you OK, love?' she asked kindly, holding her hand out to me. 'They've gone now. You can come out.'

I took her hand, emerging slowly, looking around to check they'd really gone.

'What on earth was going on?' the woman asked.

'I don't know,' I trembled, hardly able to get the words out. 'They forced their way in and grabbed me and tried to kiss me... I don't know why they'd do that. I was terrified.'

'Well, they're gone now so don't worry any more.' The woman smiled at me kindly. 'They won't try it again, they'll get into serious trouble if they're reported.'

I was still bursting to spend a penny (well more like half a crown by now) and the woman held the door whilst I relieved myself. What Mum would call the 'Relief of Mafeking' whenever she was that desperate to go.

'Hang on whilst I go to the loo and I'll come out with you and check they really have gone.'

'Thank you.' I held the door for her, my heart at last beginning to slow. 'You with anyone, love?' the woman asked, pulling the chain. The door opened and she came out moving towards the sinks.

'My boyfriend's in the band,' I said and stopped her trying to wash her hands before she tried the taps. 'Nothing works.'

'Ah, thanks.' She opened the door to the hall and the noise of the crowd and the support band nearly deafened us. She looked around and then beckoned me out. 'All clear love. You go and find some friends and stay with them.'

'Thank you so much,' I shouted as she walked away waving over her shoulder.

I looked around cautiously and made my way through the crowd looking for the stage door where Scott said I should wait when they came off stage. Smoke hung thickly in the air mixed with every kind of perfume making a heavy cloying atmosphere. I pushed past couples snogging and dancing, and others just standing watching the band. Their music was all right – but not as good as Narnia's Children.

I found the door and leaned against the wall, feeling sick and giddy. I was still frightened and kept checking the faces around me for the two soldiers.

My brain was sluggishly trying to process what had happened and I still couldn't believe it. Two girls were trying to kiss and grope me. How weird was that?

The stage door opened and several girls came out laughing and chatting, holding autograph books. I moved aside so they could pass and glanced inside before the door shut, searching for Scott. I wondered if I should go inside but I didn't like to.

Leaning back against the wall again I shut my eyes.

'Hi...'

I opened my eyes and there was Scott. He bent and kissed me on the forehead.

'Waiting long?'

'No, not long.' I was so relieved to see him I nearly burst into tears.

'You OK?' He peered into my eyes.

'I had a bit of a nasty time in the ladies,' I said as he frowned and put his arms round me.

'Tell me,' he said and held me tight.

I tried to explain what had happened and he looked furious. He glanced around. 'See them here at all?'

'No, the lady who helped me said they wouldn't dare come back because they would get into trouble, being soldiers and all that.'

'Right, well, they will be if I see them, I can tell you.' He kissed me again and smiled. 'Quite an experience. I'm sorry, I shouldn't have brought you and left you on your own, but there wasn't anyone you could be with tonight. Usually we have friends with us.'

'Don't worry, I'm all right now,' I said unconvincingly.

'We're leaving soon. Gonna party with The Fulcrum for a while. They live in Salisbury somewhere.' He brushed his lovely thick black hair from his face and smiled. 'Don't panic, we'll get you home on time, we don't plan staying long, but it's good to hang out with the competition.'

'Oh, OK, as long as I'm not late. Mum will kill me if I am.'

'We'll have you home before the milkman, as instructed! Let's go and party...'

As we left the hall, loads of girls ran towards us, screaming and yelling, trying to grab the boys. The band stood and signed autographs and smiled and chatted to the girls, and got covered in kisses for their trouble. I spotted the girl from the ladies who'd said she was going to pull Scott. She gave me a look of sheer hatred when she saw him put his arm round me and help me into the van. I smiled sweetly at her as she poked her tongue out at me.

'Where exactly are we going?' I asked Scott as the van travelled down rough country roads to the strains of Radio

Luxembourg playing 'Dedicated to the One I love,' by The Mamas and Papas, one of my favourites.

'Not sure where, but not too far. They wanted to hang out after the gig, so we're gonna do it for a while, don't fret, we'll be home in time.' He kissed my cheek. 'That right, Rich?'

'Yep, won't be hanging out too late,' Rich turned round, 'the boys gotta get their beauty sleep these days.' And he went back to driving us along the bumpy country road.

After about fifteen minutes we arrived at an old rundown house, the downstairs looked dark and dreary until I spotted the flicker of candles against the windows. I felt a bit unsettled about going in there.

'Do they live here?' I asked, jumping down from the transit.

'Let's hope so,' Rich said as he woke the others who had been snoozing throughout the short trip. 'Because this is where they said to come. Let's go and see what's what, shall we?'

Renza's Diary
June 29th 1968 – later

What a dump! The local band seemed to live in part of an old house which looked derelict from what I could see. There wasn't any furniture to speak of, just old packing cases for tables, piles of cushions and beanbags on the red thread-bare carpet. At least, I think it was red but it was hard to tell in the candle light coming from the Mateus Rose bottles dotted round the room.

The light flickered on Che Guevara and 'Ban the Bomb' posters, giving them a bit of a sinister look. Very anti-establishment here – Dad would go nuts.

Distorted shadows fell on couples lying around, mostly snogging or smoking, and a few were standing swaying to the music from the Philips cassette player in the corner. I was saving up for one I'd seen in Rumbelows. It was going to take another month to have enough and I hoped it wouldn't be gone before we moved. I should never have got the Cathy McGowan mini with the zipped front like Twiggy, it was far too expensive, it had left me without any money until the end of the month.

I hadn't had chance to wear it yet because I was trying to hide it from Mum until she was in a good mood – whenever that was going to be. I earned the money for my clothes, so I didn't see why I couldn't wear what I wanted. But no, she had to inspect me every time I left the house, lecturing about what I'm wearing: too short, too long, too much leg showing – moan, moan, moan.

The dress is gorgeous though: paisley pink, sleeveless and with a fab mandarin collar – very sexy – and with my long white lace-up boots I am going to blow Scott's mind when he sees me in it.

Scott had vanished into the gloom with the rest of the boys, and just as I was about to follow, someone lurched up to me and shoved a pile of home-taped cassettes into my hands. 'Here, doll. Put some music on, there's a love. Your choice but make it cool, right?' And lurched off again.

I was just about to say I wasn't the DJ and didn't know how the cassette player worked when I noticed a couple heaving and groaning on a pile of grubby cushions almost by my feet.

I tried to avert my eyes and not blush – but too late. They rolled over and nothing in the world could have prepared me for the shock of witnessing two bearded men coming up for air following a long, fierce, snogging session.

I only just stopped myself shrieking out loud and tried not to look at the couple, both with long blond locks and tight bell-bottoms, as they got down and dirty again on the pile of cushions. I'd just assumed it was a guy and a girl. Well, I would. I mean, blokes kissing blokes? And they were groping each other.

I felt myself going scarlet as I had made eye contact with them. My mouth gaped open, and total confusion almost paralysed my brain. They were nearly having sex in front of everyone, including me – a convent girl – for goodness sake!

They just grinned at me and then started groping each other again. I looked away confused and embarrassed, and tried to concentrate on the cassette tapes in my hand.

But I couldn't help myself. I couldn't take my eyes off them. I watched them from underneath my long fringe, fascinated yet repelled at the same time.

Had anyone else noticed it was two blokes? Of course, I had heard about people like them, I mean, we got Sex Education at school, and hadn't I been rescued from two girls trying to kiss me in the loos at Merry Hill for goodness sake. But actually seeing them, and watching them nearly 'doing it', well, that was something else. Part of me wanted to giggle. But I was cool, sophisticated, part of the 'in crowd'. Wouldn't do to make too much of it, otherwise I might look as if I didn't belong and I really did want to belong.

I was supposed to be picking tapes to play and that was hard enough. Working out which songs would be hip and which ones might not be was giving me a migraine. I gave up and put them with the pile on the floor, deciding to let someone else pick the music.

I glanced round the gloomy room looking for Scott, or at least something to focus on and take my mind off the couple who were getting a bit too much for me to handle on my own. I eventually spotted Scott chatting to The Fulcrum's drummer. Someone else had taken over the music and The Beatles, sang, 'Girl,' in the background, which made me want to laugh out loud. Not a hip thing to do. Wonder who chose that one? Someone else had seen the blokes, I bet.

I sat on the edge of a packing case and tried to catch Scott's eye but he was too engrossed as he and the drummer poured another glass of Watney's from the party tin.

Typical, he's having another beer and I haven't had a thing to drink yet.

When we'd arrived he'd told me not to drink or eat anything without showing him first. No explanation why, and that was ages ago. He'd gone off to the loo and hadn't made it back to me yet. Clearly too many distractions, not just the beer.

Everyone else seemed to be getting seriously mellow. Why the hell couldn't I at least have some food? It had been hours since I'd eaten and the sickly sweet smell in the room was making me feel a bit light-headed.

The Beatles' 'Lady Madonna' repeated on the cassette player as if the tape had got stuck. It was their latest hit, I loved it. I looked over and saw a girl in a flowing kaftan re-insert the tape and it played again.

She watched it for a moment and then started swaying to the music all on her own in the centre of the room, her arms raised over her head, which seemed to rotate. I'd get dizzy doing that. I waited, but she didn't fall over. Several blokes watched her closely.

Trying not to look at the two bearded beauties again, I stood up, smoothed my new purple Samantha Juste hipsters, and tucked my pink skinny rib into them. I wandered towards the wallpaper table and what was left of the food: a few soft looking sausage rolls and a couple of scotch eggs which had probably been sitting out for hours, I didn't fancy the look of them. A few packets of Smith's crisps and some peanuts was the alternative. I grabbed a packet and a handful of nuts and tucked in whilst I studiously avoided the lovers on the cushions.

'Hi babe, what's your name?' I turned to see a tall skinny bloke with long black hair and a pair of lime green bell-bottoms grinning at me, cigarette dangling from his rather thick lips. I peered hard at him and then realised he was one of The Fulcrum's guitarists, so it must be his party.

'Saw you at the gig tonight,' he added, flicking his ash away.

'Err, yeah,' I said looking for Scott. I was trapped between the table and the guitarist, who kept blowing sweet smelling smoke at me. I felt sick from it.

'How about you and me then, babe?' he moved up close to me and put an arm round my waist. He smelled of Old Spice. I can't stand Old Spice.

'I'm with my boyfriend,' I said lamely as I wriggled away from him.

'Don't look like it from here babe,' he said as he grabbed me again. 'Let's go over there and get to know each other.' He tried to pull me into the shadows.

'No, please.' I tried not to whine, it's not cool to whine. The magazines all say boys hate whiney girls. 'I really am with my boyfriend, he's over there.' I pointed to Scott still chatting to the drummer.

'Yeah, cool... come on babe, don't be like that.' He tugged my arm again and held me tightly.

'Please, leave me alone,' I whispered through gritted teeth, 'I don't want to go over there with you!'

Someone changed the tape and Amen Corner's 'Bend Me, Shape Me' got a lot more people on their feet, and I started to get a bit claustrophobic as they seemed to close in on me. My head was spinning.

'Hey, man, what gives?' I nearly fainted with relief as Scott came up to us and put his hand on the guitarist's shoulder. He grinned at me and winked.

'Scott! Hi man, nothing much.' My captor let go of my arm and took a long drag on his roll-up. 'Your chick?' He nodded towards me and blew smoke into my face. I started to cough and my eyes streamed.

Scott said, 'Yeah, she is,' and took my arm and guided me over to the drinks. He opened a Pepsi and handed the bottle to me. I gulped it down, handed the bottle back to Scott, and fished in my new Mary Quant shoulder bag for a hanky to dab my eyes. It came away all black from my mascara and eyeliner, and I had to fish around some more to find my mirror.

'Oh, now look at my eyes,' I sniffed. 'Is there a ladies where I can redo my face?' I looked like a panda with two black smudges where my perfectly applied Dusty Springfield look had been.

'You don't want to go in that loo, babe, trust me.' Scott held my Pepsi in one hand and stroked my hair with his other.

My legs went to jelly. I came over all unnecessary every time he touched me, and I felt myself getting all hot and bothered. Scott looked curiously at me for a few seconds and then laughed out loud.

'Look at you, getting in a tizzy.' He laughed and handed me my Pepsi. 'Drink that up and I'll hold your mirror so you can do your face. We can go over there by the candles. I'm sure you'll be able to see well enough to put your war paint on again.'

He held the mirror whilst I tried my best to repair my face. I felt his eyes upon me the whole time, watching me with an amused expression. My hands shook as I tried to re-

78

apply my eyeliner and mascara. Damn the plastic eyeliner liquid, it never goes on easily and dries so fast. I put some spit on the mascara cake and dabbed the brush over it, and applied several layers to my lashes.

'The stuff chicks mess with,' Scott watched me closely, 'you don't need any of that, Renza, you are way cool without it you know.'

I blushed – again.

'Oh God – what time is it?' I asked, as The Beach Boys started to sing, 'Darlin'.

'About midnight. We'll go soon, don't worry, you won't be late.' Scott put his arms round me and held me close, and we swayed in time to the music.

My legs did a good job holding me upright but my body felt in a state of collapse. So close, and held so tightly, it was heaven. Scott stroked my hair and I closed my eyes and wished that it would never end. It was too much.

I came back to reality with a jolt when someone bellowed close to my ear.

'Scott, man, great gig, hope you cats come and play with us again.' The bass player with the local band held his hand out and they shook hands. He peered at me, giving me the once over.

'No sweat,' said Scott, 'where're you playing next?' And he let go of me suddenly, so I had to struggle to support myself.

'Back at Merryhill. We have three nights here before we go to Germany,' the bass player said, tossing a peanut into the air and catching it in his mouth.

'Oh, yeah of course. Well, we're back here in about a month I think. We're off to Scotland tomorrow, Elgin and Wick, and some other places I can't think of,' Scott told him.

Oh, yeah? It was news to me.

More couples were dancing now, swaying next to us as Scott dropped his bombshell.

'Then we're off on some cruises in the Med for a few weeks. It's good money and our manager says it's great exposure.'

My mind went blank for a few seconds: a few weeks, in the Med? He'd never told me any of this... *a few weeks?*

Scott must have seen how stricken I was as he put his arm round me and squeezed me tightly. 'Sorry Renza, only found out earlier and was gonna tell you, but you know how it is,' his voice trailed off when he saw this didn't help.

I felt my whole world was coming to an end.

A girl in a tight fitting bolero top and hipster trousers came over to us and flung her arms round Scott, kissing him on the mouth, a bit too long and hard for my liking. Scott didn't seem in too much of a hurry to push her away, and she melted into him as if she was trying to come out the other side.

'Scott lover, how's it hanging?' She sounded just like Fenella Fielding, all breathy and wanton.

'Yeah Scott, just how *is* it hanging?' I snapped and flounced off to where I could see Rich sitting on his own, hugging a beer.

'Hi Renza, babe, what's up?' Rich held the glass up to me in greeting and took another drag on his ciggy.

'Who's that girl talking to Scott?' I asked plonking myself down next to him on the huge bean bag. We both nearly fell off as it settled itself with my extra weight.

'Hey, don't waste good beer babe.' Rich held his glass away from me as I wriggled to get comfy.

'Rich, who is she?' I asked again as I saw her drape herself all over Scott and nestle into his shoulder. The bitch! Scott didn't seem too bothered.

'She used to help Stephan – he's the band's manager I told you about earlier – in the office in Jersey and then she came to the mainland with her boyfriend. She's no one important, she sometimes hangs with the band when we're over.'

'Hmm!'

I watched her like a hawk. Scott looked over and waved.

The nerve!

Rich took a few gulps of beer and patted my leg. 'Don't fret about Scott, he's mad about you. She'll get the message after tonight.

I looked round the grubby room with its crates and boxes, and fake Greek Taverna decorations hanging from the walls, the fake fishing nets, glass baubles attached, and wine bottles with candles burning in them. And the couples seething in a mass on the floor, in the shadows, and on the cushions, doing goodness knows what, and I wanted to go home.

Actually, I wanted to get Scott to myself. Back home. In the village. Where things were normal.

'Magical Mystery Tour' came on and I suddenly thought about having to miss The Beatles at the Hammersmith Odeon, because I was 'Mrs Spoffington' in the school play, and couldn't get out of it. Instead of The Beatles giving me the thrill of my life I was stuck on stage singing 'Oh I do like to be beside the sodding sea-side,' to a hall full of boring parents. Not that mine bothered to go.

'Rich, mate, hi. Good gig. Stephan about tonight?' A huge man of about thirty came up to us and nodded at me. 'Want to sort some stuff out with him.'

He was wearing beads and a kaftan with an orange and green squiggly pattern on it, and had his ears pierced. His long black hair hung in tight curls around his shoulders. Mum would just love him.

'Oh Renza, this is Psychedelic Smith,' Rich said. 'Remember we told you about him, he's our fixer.' I remembered. Apparently he was helping Stephan get Narnia's Children a record deal. Everyone had to kiss up to him I was told. Well, thankfully, I didn't.

Psychedelic Smith dismissed me with a brief smile before turning back to Rich.

'Stephan's back in the smoke mate, got *Top of the Pops* with The White Knights, so he's gotta be there for that.' Rich drained his glass and put it on the floor next to him.

'Right, yeah, going up the charts fast. That's cool, I'll ring him later. I'm in town tomorrow and want to arrange some record company auditions for the guys. Got some label interest.'

'Do I need to re-organise anything for the boys?' Rich asked.

'Nope, I'll sort some dates out with Stephan, he'll let you know in good time. I've got some songs lined up for the guys to hear, so we'll sort some dates for visiting publishers in town too.'

I couldn't help wondering what Mum and Mrs Digby would say if Psychedelic Smith turned up in the village to visit the band. I giggled quietly.

Psychedelic Smith began to roll a ciggy and offered one to Rich.

Rich shook his head and got to his feet. 'Nah, mate, gotta drive back soon or her mum'll kill me if she's not home on time, won't she, babe?' Rich smiled at me and looked at his watch, then went off to round up the band.

Psychedelic Smith took a few more drags and offered me one. I shook my head. I could just see me floating in the front door with Mum waiting up to look me over and make sure I hadn't 'been up to anything'.

'No thanks.'

The Demis Russos look-alike shrugged and headed for the kitchen. Dad would have a blue fit if he knew I was 'fraternizing,' with blokes in dresses.

I knew the only reason I'd been allowed out so late with the band was because Mum quite liked Rich and he'd sweet-talked her into letting me go to the gig. God! If she could see me now, in this horrible house with everyone stoned, she'd have a migraine for a week worrying in case the village found out.

I looked at my watch. If we didn't leave soon I was going to be seriously late and that would mean all hell breaking loose.

Scott was nowhere to be seen now and Rich was chatting to 'The Bitch' by the food. I know it is horrid calling her that but she's got right up my nose, wall-papering herself all over Scott.

People were still wrestling on the floor which meant I had to watch where I looked: I didn't want to appear a Peeping Tom, though it was hard not to cast a sly glance now and again. I mean, seriously, some were actually 'at it' in full view. Anyone would look, wouldn't they?

Thinking about it, how do you 'do it' in public without all your bits and stuff being on show? I couldn't see anything, you know, rude or anything, but they were definitely 'doing it', I just couldn't fathom how.

'You look deep in thought,' Scott made me jump, 'what're you looking at?'

Before I could answer he followed my gaze to the nearest couple. He threw his head back and laughed loudly. I blushed as if I'd been caught out doing something naughty.

'Ah!' he said, 'I see.'

I felt really stupid. I could feel the heat rising up my neck to my face, thank goodness it was so gloomy.

'Bit of an education eh?' He grabbed my arm and led me through to what could only be called an apology for a kitchen. 'Can you wait here while I get the others? We should leave now. Don't move. I won't be long.'

And off he went again.

The room was horrid. The sink was all cracked with brown stains and the green larder door was hanging off. A few tins of baked beans and soup was all that I could see on the shelves. A dirty milk bottle was on the draining board with about a dozen tea cups and spoons, all in need of a good wash. Dirty dishes were piled next to them, some with food still on them. I screwed my face up in disgust. How could anyone live like this?

An old gingham curtain hung in tatters at the filthy window which had a crazy paving of cracks across the top. A pedal bin stood in the corner overflowing with baked bean tins and

Woodbine packets. The room stank of mould and rotting food.

I waited and tried not to think of what was surrounding me. Even my boots were sticking to the linoleum. What the hell was keeping Scott? 'Watcha.'

I looked round to see 'The Bitch' as I'll always think of her, standing in the doorway. She must've followed me in.

'Looking for Scott.'

'Well, as you can see he isn't here,' I said frostily.

She laughed and leaned against the door jamb. Looking me up and down, she rummaged in her pink PVC bag and took a thin black cigarette out.

'Light?' she asked as she placed it between her full, pale lips.

'Don't smoke,' I said, and then kicked myself. I shouldn't have let her know I wasn't that cool; too late.

She laughed. 'What, too good to do the dreaded weed, eh?' and she rummaged a bit more and came up with a box of Swan Vestas. 'You must do something, coz Scott wouldn't waste his time otherwise.'

She smirked and winked knowingly at me. I glared back.

She had long dark hair, cut like Cher's, and her eyes were deep blue, peering out from her panda black eye make-up. She had a spot of acne on her chin, and that made me feel great.

The room filled with a pungent odour as she lit up and exhaled, blowing the smoke upwards. She folded her arms and continued to appraise me with an amused look on her face. The Hollies' 'Jennifer Eccles' drifted into the room and she tapped her foot to the beat.

'You're the kid from where they live now,' she stated flatly. 'Not what I expected.'

I couldn't think what to say. She made me feel like a stupid school kid and all my newly assumed sophistication was fast evaporating under her scrutiny. I shifted from one foot to another and flicked my hair forward so that she couldn't see my face. I watched her from under my fringe. She had a smile on her face as she smoked and watched me back.

Scott appeared in the doorway. He winked at The Bitch. She smirked.

'Come on, Renza, we're off,' and he held his hand out.

'See you soon,' he said, and blew her a kiss. She pouted her full lips and blew one back with a loud smacking noise, raised her eyebrows as I passed, and whispered, 'I can have him anytime I want.'

I said nothing, but my heart was in my boots and I wanted to cry. I was in way out of my depth: the sneering girl, obviously enjoying my discomfort, whose relationship with Scott was too free and easy for my liking, Scott going away for weeks without even mentioning it, and this awful, gruesome house party... I just wanted to go home. Yet Mo said Scott loved me – I tried to hold the thought – but he'd never actually told me, not properly. Perhaps he's changed his mind now he's been out with me a few times, especially now he's seen this girl again. I wish I had the nerve to ask him. But Rich said she'd be history after tonight, so perhaps I'm just being silly.

And I'd forgotten how far out in the sticks we'd gone to party with the band. Sitting in Bessie Bedford we were encased in total darkness, with no street lamps or nearby houses to comfort me. The wind was howling across Salisbury Plain and there was more than a spot of rain in it.

Rich tried three times before the engine decided to kick into life.

Bessie back-fired several times before we set off down the overgrown lane to the road. Although it was summer, there was a chill in the air and Scott put his parka round my shoulders when I shivered.

'Won't take long, should be a clear run back,' he said as I strained to see my watch in the gloom. I snuggled into his shoulder and he squeezed me tight.

'I can't be later than one,' I said. 'Mum will kill me.'

'Stop yapping,' murmured Zak from behind the back seat

where he was settled in amongst the gear. 'Some of us need a kip.'

'You shut up,' came the reply from the other side of the gear where Joss was propped against the wheel arch.

The seat behind Scott and me was occupied by two girls I had never seen before. They were already in the van when we got in and apart from a muttered hello, hadn't said a word to anyone, though I think I heard them whispering to each other now and again.

Mo sat in the front with a girl on his lap and she looked fast asleep. I had never set eyes on her before either. Only Rich hadn't pulled. He drove in silence, chewing gum and smoking now and again. Thankfully he wound the window down when he did. My head throbbed. Everyone was tired. I had so many things to think about, to worry about, to talk to Scott about – but I couldn't do any of them right now. Not in front of everyone, and I was so, so tired.

I sleepily wondered what it would be like to be married to Scott – not that that was ever going to happen – and closed my eyes and drifted off to sleep.

Renza's Diary

June 30th 1968 – early hours of the morning

I must have dropped off for ages because all of a sudden I wasn't saying, 'I do' to Scott, he was telling me to wake up. I shook my head and tried to open my eyes fully, but they just wanted to close and take me back to my wedding.

'Renza, wake up, please, wake up.' Scott's voice penetrated eventually and I made myself come round.

'What?' I said dreamily, and then I had a horrible thought, had I been snoring? God, I'd just die if I'd done that in front of him. He would never go out with me again. I checked my chin to see if I had been drooling but everything seemed OK.

'Van's broken down,' Scott said and it took a while for his words to register.

Of course, once they did, I panicked, sitting upright and looking round frantically. 'Broken down? How? I mean when? I mean ….Oh God, she'll kill me and I won't be able to go out with you again. Well, if you ask me that is…'

'Shut up!' Zak groaned sleepily from the darkness.

'Rich, where's Rich?' I asked when I saw he wasn't in the driving seat.

'Gone with Mo to see if they can find a phone box or a garage for a breakdown lorry,' Scott said, checking his watch – he had one of those that glowed in the dark.

Not members of the AA then.

'When? How long ago? I mean, have they just gone or what?' I just stopped myself grabbing Scott's arm and shaking it, I was in such a state.

'Chill, will yer?' Zak snapped from behind us, and he threw an apple core at us.

'Shove it.' Scott threw it back.

'All of yer, shut the hell up!' Joss yelled. 'Nothin' we can do about it, so chill, chill.'

'Oh God! what happened? Why can't anything be done

about it? About what?' I was in deep trouble if the van didn't move soon. My life would be over, well, it wouldn't be worth living anyway. Dad would be told and go mental. Mum would kill me.

The girls in the back slept on oblivious to the drama. I wondered if they would be in deep shit if they didn't get home soon. The one who had been asleep on Mo's lap was sprawled across both front seats, slobbering every now and again, but dead to the world. Would her parents be doing their pieces if she was late?

'Think the fan-belt has gone or the gasket or something. I dunno.' Scott scratched his head frowning. 'Rich said he couldn't see in the dark.'

'Use my stockings,' I said helpfully. 'My dad says that if the fan-belt goes you can use stockings to sort it out.'

They all laughed. 'Really, it's true,' I said earnestly. I wore them under my hipsters.

'Don't let us stop you, babe, get them off then,' said Zak, suddenly wide awake.

Joss laughed and Scott grinned, 'Come on boys, give it up. Much as I'd love her to take them off, I'd rather she did it just for me, eh Renza?'

'No, no, I didn't mean... I mean – I meant, well I didn't mean...' I was mortified. What on earth was I thinking?

'Well if yer dad says you should take 'em off to fix the van, better do it.'

Zak laughed his head off and I felt the dreaded blush rush up my neck and face.

'Much as I'd enjoy it, babe, forget it.' Scott's dark hair brushed my cheek. 'Let's wait and see what Rich and Mo come up with,' and he hugged me tightly.

I was in a state of complete panic. He just didn't get it. Mum would go nuts if I didn't get home soon, she'd never let me out ever again. I wished we had a phone like some of my other friends, then we could ring and explain.

Oh God! Explain. She wasn't going to believe we broke down. She just wouldn't. I was in for the Third Degree, the lamp in the face, the bloody Gestapo interrogation. Oh God!

'Don't worry, Renza, I'll talk to your mum.' Scott stroked my hair and kissed me on the nose.

I tried to smile at him but my face felt like stone. I nodded. I didn't want to seem too scared of my mum. After all, I was a cool chick and wasn't fazed by such things. He didn't want a little kid worried sick about being late. He wanted a woman who stood up for herself and could handle anything. Well, anything except Hitler at home.

Well, he would soon find out. He would never see me again after she had finished with him.

The Bitch... now, she was the type of girl he wanted, all sexy voice and sophisticated. Not me, oh not me! not me! not me!

The radio was going all fuzzy and Scott leaned over the front seat and fiddled with the dial, but couldn't seem to get the station back. Instead he found a woman singing that bloody advert I can't stand which was always on Luxembourg on Fridays.

'Friday night is Marmi night,' or some such rubbish. She drove me nuts.

I leaned against Scott and shut my eyes and went through the scene waiting for me at home. I kept them shut to keep the fear from showing in them. Despite being scared stiff, I was still very tired.

I must have dropped off again, the next thing I was aware of was voices. Men's voices.

Struggling awake I wondered where I was for a few seconds. Then it hit me with that awful dread that comes over you sometimes when something terrible has happened, when you first wake, it doesn't register at first, and then suddenly it dawns on you and you remember, something unpleasant.

I remembered something unpleasant. Mum!

I looked around but couldn't see anyone. The van was empty. The girls had gone and so had Scott. I couldn't see out the windscreen, it seemed to be covered in something. I tried to see out of my window but it was steamed up. I clambered over the seat to the sliding door and tugged it open.

God, it was freezing and almost dawn by the looks of it. I could hear the birds.

We'd been here all night. Oh God! Oh God! Oh my God!!

Mum would go mental if I came home after the milk man. 'What would Mrs Digby have to say about it?' she'd yell. 'How am I going to hold my head up in this village with you behaving like a trollop?' I could just hear her. 'I'll never be able to step out that gate again!'

Only this time I will have given her good cause.

'You OK, babe?' Scott came towards me as I clambered down from Bessie, shivering in the dawn chill despite having his parka.

'What's happening?' I cried, 'why are we still here?' I looked around and saw two men in overalls with their heads under the bonnet, which I realised was blocking the view from the windscreen.

'Rich and Mo managed to get them to come out from a local garage,' Scott said rubbing his hands together.

'What's wrong with it?' I stamped my feet and pulled Scott's parka round me.

'No idea, haven't said yet.' He glanced over at the two men, frowning.

'Do you think they'll take long?' I watched them work. 'How long have they been here?'

'About an hour.' Scott grimaced at the look of horror on my face.

'An hour!' I nearly fainted, the blood rushed so fast into my head, my face felt on fire. I grabbed Scott's arm before I fell over. 'I am dead!'

'No you're not, I'll explain, don't worry. Chill.' Scott put his arm round me and pulled me close, kissing the top of my head.

Chill! I was on fire: my heart was thumping through my chest, my ears ringing. I really mustn't pass out, I mustn't!

'Cor, it's cold,' a voice from behind me made me jump and I looked round to see one of the girls from the back seat standing with Joss's jacket round her shoulders, which couldn't have really helped much considering she only had a black micro-mini on and a bare goose-bumped midriff, with a thin black skimpy top covering her huge bust. 'I'm freezing.'

She was quite petite, with a Mary Quant sort of face, and big brown eyes which seemed to take up most of it. She chewed gum noisily, her mouth open, which sort of ruined her otherwise cute look.

'Me too.' Her mate walked up and stood next to her puffing hard on a roll-up, screwing her face up in an attempt to avoid the smoke going in her eyes. She had a Twiggy haircut, which suited her elfin face. Her blonde hair framing huge blue eyes peeping out from black eye make-up. Like me, she had gone for the Dusty look around her eyes and a pale foundation which made her lips look white. The pan stick had been applied expertly but she had forgotten to do her neck and even in the half light of dawn, I could see the tide mark where her make-up ended and her true skin colour showed.

This girl had a crochet mini-dress, in mauve, with a little white top covering her shoulders, long white boots which came over her knees and a huge 'Help!' ring on her middle finger of her right hand. She was really hip...well if you ignored the tide-mark that is.

'What's your name then?' asked the would-be Mary Quant, her teeth chattering.

'It's...' but before I could say another word Bessie gave a huge splutter and belched smoke, shaking violently as Rich tried the ignition. Then she died again.

'Bloody bitch!' shouted Rich, climbing down from Bessie

and slamming the door.

The two men in overalls put their heads under the bonnet again and did whatever they do under there, as we all stood around, shivering and waiting. Hopefully.

Mo came over with his arm around the girl who'd been on his lap, she was tall and skinny with brown hair which hung a long way down her back. She wore a red PVC mini skirt with a belt of metal hoops and a cream skinny rib polo neck – just like the one I had seen in *Jackie*, last month. I often bought teen magazines on the quiet and hid them under the loose floorboard in my bedroom, so Mum wouldn't find them. The girl was very pretty in a Julie Christie sort of way. Mo kept kissing her and stroking her hair as she giggled like a loon.

'How's it going then?' he asked Scott, nodding at Bessie.

'Not sure, mate.' Scott looked fed-up and sounded it. 'Rich says they know what they're doing.' His warm breath floated towards me on the cold air.

'Hey Renza, you're gonna be for it.' Mo winked at me and laughed.

Scott hugged me close. 'Cut it out Mo, she's having a nervous breakdown without you adding to it.'

Bessie spluttered again as Rich turned her over. More smoke belched out the back and she shook and spluttered, but then she started to sound a lot smoother and the smoke stopped and she settled down. The two men went over to the window and spoke with Rich for a few moments and then called Scott over.

'You got the band cheque book, mate?' Rich asked, waving the invoice the men had given him.

'In the glove compartment, passenger side Rich,' Scott said and ushered us all back in the van.

Rich wrote the cheque and the two men waved goodbye and got back into their recovery lorry and drove off. I waited for Zak and Joss to get settled in the back with the gear and for the girls to climb into the back seat. They giggled and fidgeted and eventually sat down together. Mo and his girlfriend stood snogging in my way so I waited patiently for them to get in the front seat, so I could slide the middle door open and get out of the cold.

Meanwhile the sun began to rise high over the trees and the bird song got louder. Mist started to rise, hovering about three feet off the ground, which was eerie and made me think of ghouls and ghosts and Mum!

As I waited for Mo to finish his meal – because he certainly was making one of kissing his new girl – I noticed that messages had been written on Bessie's paintwork in lipsticks of many colours. I hadn't seen them before so I guessed they'd been done at the gig in Merryhill.

Big love hearts with arrows passing through them: 'I love you Mo' and 'I dig you Joss' or telephone numbers with, ' Call me Scott, I'm yours' and 'Zak I want you in the sack'.

But all I could think about was Mum going ballistic and giving me serious grief over this. 'Your father will go mad if he hears about this,' and 'What will Mrs Digby next door think when she hears you've been out all night with several men, in a van covered in obscene messages?'

As if I was responsible. Oh God, I could just hear her.

Mo and his girlfriend eventually got into the van. She climbed on his lap, then they were at it again, oblivious of everyone else. I felt like offering him a knife and fork, he was making such a feast of her.

Scott got in after me and leaned across the front seat where Mo was in danger of forgetting he was in company, and put the radio on. He swished through several station settings and stopped on a fuzzy station with foreign people chattering fiercely.

Rich groaned. 'No, for Christ's sake, not a bloody foreign station, Scott. I need to concentrate.'

Silently I thanked Rich.

Eventually he found a station playing 'Jennifer Juniper',

which was quite relaxing and I felt myself getting heavy-eyed again. But I forced myself to stay awake so I could try and think up excuses for being late. My mind wouldn't allow me to concentrate though. It flitted here and there, from Scott in his tight bell-bottoms and his cute rear, to The Bitch and her threat to 'have him' whenever she wanted. I re-ran the episode in the loo with those horrid girls until my heart thudded so hard I thought I'd pass out.

To distract myself I thought about the Philips cassette player I really needed to have and soon, but then I worried about Scott going to Scotland, then on a cruise for absolutely yonks; I would die not seeing him for ages. Then panic set in as I went over the scene which no doubt awaited me at home. Soon my eyes started to close.

***

I woke up as Rich parked the van behind the shops where their flat was. A blast of cold air hit my face as the doors opened and everyone climbed out. I began to shake and it wasn't from the cold. My life was about to end. Mum was sure to ban me from seeing Scott and the band ever again. I was going to die.

'Come on Renza, let's go and face the music.' Scott put his arm round me and kissed me tenderly on the mouth. He nestled his face in my hair and whispered, ' no one's ever gonna to split us, not even your mum.'

'Hang on mate, I'm coming with you.' Rich locked the van and came over to us. He winked at me and stubbed his roll-up out on the concrete flower pot by the staircase leading to the flats.

It was nearly 7 as I opened the gate. Rich and Scott came behind me, wouldn't do for me to be seen in public with a bloke's arms around me. Ma would freak!

I wobbled up to the door and was about to knock when it flew open and the Wicked Witch of the West stuck her angry face out. I didn't bother knocking my heels together in the hope that they would take me 'Home' because I was flippin' home – unfortunately.

'And what time do you call this my lady?' she hissed, keeping her voice down so as not to wake the neighbours. 'Even the bloody milkman got here before you.'

She peered over my shoulder at Scott and Rich who were standing about three feet away. 'You've got a bloody nerve,' she glared at them both. 'What the hell have you been up to, staying out all night?' she folded her arms and cocked her head to one side, waiting.

'We're very sorry Mrs Rossi. The van broke down on Salisbury Plain and it took ages to get to a phone and then get someone out to see to it.' Rich stepped forward with an apologetic smile.

'Likely bloody story,' came the retort.

'It's true, Mrs R,' Scott ventured, moving forward with a look of contrition on his face.

'Think I came down in the last shower?' Mum stepped outside and gave them the once over. 'You think I don't know what you've been up to?'

She looked up at the windows of next door trying to see if Mrs Digby had been listening. As far as I could see the curtains were still closed. Thank God.

'Come on, Mrs Rossi,' Scott pleaded. 'Nothing has happened. The van broke down.'

'Really,' Rich added, 'you must've heard it making a racket all week.'

'So why didn't you get it serviced before you dragged my daughter half way across the country then?' Mum snapped angrily.

'Because it settled down and anyway it costs a lot to get it serviced,' Rich explained, but the look on Mum's face said she was having none of it.

'Ha!' Mum turned on Rich. 'Get yourselves proper employment and perhaps you could afford a decent van.' She stepped further into the garden and glanced up at the next door's windows again.

'Well that's your opinion, Mrs Rossi, and of course you're entitled to it,' Scott snapped back with some force.

Mum gave him one of her raised eyebrow looks. I knew that this was a 'Red for danger' sign, which should not be ignored, Scott didn't.

'Yes it is, and I am, and I will remind you that she is MY daughter and I make the rules in this house and I do not approve of her running round showing herself up with the likes of you.'

The one eyebrow remained raised. Bloody hell.

'The likes of me?' Scott went white. 'And just what is the "likes" of me?'

'One of the great unwashed and unemployed,' hissed Mum in his face, making him step back, just missing her immaculate flower bed. 'I knew there'd be trouble, your parents being divorced, and your hair.'

'One of the unwashed?' Scott drew himself up to his full six feet and put his hands on his beautiful, slim hips. 'And what have my parents got to do with anything? And—'

'Come on,' Rich stepped between them,'let's not get into throwing insults. Look, Mrs Rossi, we're sorry and we assure you nothing at all happened to her. Everyone was with her all the time and we looked after her really well, didn't we?' He turned to me nodding.

I nodded back. 'Mum, there were at least seven others with me the whole time, three other girls and the band, nothing happened, really.' I gave her the wide eyed innocent look which hardly ever worked, but was worth a try.

The gate opened and the paper boy came up to us. 'Morning,' he said and handed Scott the paper.

'You're late,' snapped Mum and snatched the paper from Scott as if he was about to steal it.

'At least I beat the paper boy.' It came out before I could stop myself.

'You, get inside, I'll deal with you later.' Mum shoved me through the door. 'Wait until your father hears about this, he'll have plenty to say!'

I glimpsed Scott winking at me and went into the sitting room to wait for the end of the world.

Mum stood on the step. 'You, out of my house, now!' she yelled and shooed Scott and Rich towards the gate. 'Stay away from my daughter in future or there'll be serious trouble.' She walked to the gate and shut it after them.

Scott and Rich stood on the other side and I heard Scott say, 'I'm sorry but I will not. She is over sixteen and can make her own mind up. I'll see her again and I hope that you don't give her any grief over this, she's done nothing wrong and neither have we.'

'We're sorry she's late, Mrs Rossi,' Rich leaned on the gate. 'You're right to be upset and that's normal, but she's home safe and no one is any the wiser.' He glanced up at the neighbour's windows. 'Please, don't take it out on her.'

Mum walked back to the door as I stood at the window and waved to Scott.

'We'll come and do the garden for you and finish the garage doors when we get the time off again,' added Rich hopefully. As if that would gain him gold stars!

Mum said nothing and slammed the door. My stomach hit the floor.

Renza's Diary

June 30th 1968 – later the same morning

Screams filled the house and I ran downstairs as fast as I could, avoiding breaking my neck on the various toys left on them by the kids. I'd been dozing, glad that Mum had to get ready for work. She'd ordered me to bed earlier, promising she'd 'deal with me later'. A short reprieve.

I ran into the kitchen to find Lucy and Crispin white with terror and Mum flat on her back on the floor. Our once red and white kitchen was now mainly red. I stared, not able to take anything in. What was she doing on the floor?

Lucy tugged at my arm and I looked at her for the first time. She was covered in what looked like blood. Glancing at Crispin I saw he was too. Actually Mum was covered in blood and so were the kitchen walls and ceiling.

Mum was muttering something, but Lucy started to scream again and I couldn't hear her. I yelled at the top of my voice for Simon to get downstairs right away.

'Mum's had an accident! Don't argue! Just get here now!'

I bent down to Mum, ignoring the two stricken little ones, trying to work out what had happened. Footsteps thudded down the stairs and Simon appeared in the kitchen in his pyjamas. It was still early. He gawped at us all, turning white when he saw Mum.

'Run next door and call for the doctor,' I yelled at him as I made tourniquets for both of Mum's arms. The blood was pumping like mad. It had spurted on the ceiling and the walls were running with it. It smelled funny. 'Get Sophia to grab these two and sort them out! Take them out of here! Quick!' I held both of Mum's wrists tightly. He stood gaping at me. 'Don't hang about, go now!' I screamed at him, 'and mind all the glass on the floor.'

'Not in my pyjamas,' he moaned.

'She'll die if you don't get to the surgery now, bugger your pyjamas!' I wanted to thump him.

He jumped and ran out the door.

'Sophia, get here now!' I shouted as loudly as I could. The front door slammed. Trust Simon to forget to call her.

The two little ones just stared at Mum, wide eyed and stricken, but I couldn't worry about them. Mum was out cold and I was on the verge of panic. I hoped the doctor would be quick. I was covered in blood and my fingers slipped as I held the deep cuts in her wrists to try and stem the flow. It was not spurting as much as before, but it was still pumping with her pulse. I hoped Simon explained that Mum had cut her wrists.

I grabbed two tea towels and bound her wrists with them, still pressing hard on them both. I prayed the doctor would be available or at least someone from the surgery would come, one of the nurses perhaps. I told the kids to move away from the broken glass on the floor and yelled for Sophia again. Eventually I heard her coming down the stairs. Crispin started to cry for Sophia.

The doctor was let in by Sophia who'd nearly fainted when she saw the blood; she hates blood. He came in with his big black bag and knelt next to Mum and asked me what had happened and how long ago. I told him what I could – which wasn't much really – but Lucy said Mum had opened the broom cupboard and knocked a crystal vase off the shelf, she tried to save it from smashing on the floor, bashing it against the door as she reached out with both hands to grasp it; it had shattered between her arms and the shelf, cutting both her wrists.

He bandaged her wrists, gave her something from his bag and told me to help her on to the sofa. Luckily Sophia had the sense to grab some towels and place them on the sofa first. If we got blood on it, we'd be dead.

Mum seemed drowsy but otherwise all right. Doctor French said she should go up to bed when she could manage the stairs and not to worry, she hadn't lost as much blood as it seemed. Because it had spurted so forcefully, it had sprayed a greater distance, making it appear as if there was more of it than there actually was. Also, the colour of the cupboards made it look worse.

I'd got to her in time apparently. Saved her life. He said he'd removed shards of glass from her wrists and there didn't seem to be any left. He'd send the nurse round to stitch her up as soon as he got back to the surgery, which, lucky for Mum, was next to the chemists where she worked, at the end of the shops. If there hadn't been a doctor so close, he said, it would've been a different matter.

'Lucky for your mother she has such a sensible daughter,' he told me, patting my arm as he closed his bag. 'Your quick thinking definitely saved her life,' he added as I showed him to the door. 'Good job I've known you all for so long. We get so many pranks and false alarms these days...' He shook his head, lips pursed.

'Thank you, Doctor French, I'm sorry to have dragged you away from surgery this morning,' I said, my heart still doing the tango in my chest.

'Renza, no problem. I'll call at the chemist and tell Mr Blackmore that your mother won't be in this morning, and that she needs rest for the next few days. Keep her in bed and keep her quiet, and any sign of anything wrong, you send one of the kids round. Use the phone box to ring me at home, if necessary, and I'll come.' He got to the gate and smiled. 'You did well, are you sure you are all right?'

I nodded.

'Good, I'll pop in after surgery in the morning to check on her, but I am confident she'll be fine. The district nurse will be round to sew her up as soon as I get back.'

He waved and walked off, stopping at Mrs Digby's gate, waving to her as well. I guessed she was on sentry duty, having seen the doctor calling. I wondered how long before the whole village heard about it.

Mum will have had a heart attack, a miscarriage or a stroke by the time Mrs Digby has finished. Or worse still, she'll think I'm pregnant, and that will make her really happy – she'd love that bit of gossip.

Back inside I cleaned up the mess in the kitchen and Sophia made some coffee – since giving up tea and sugar in the war so her father could have her rations, Mum only drank coffee – and I managed to force Simon, after numerous threats, to take the little ones upstairs to bath and dress them.

Doctor French said they were both all right, just a bit shaken up, and he said they'd soon get over it. I thought Simon could take them down the Rec for a while to play football or something, take their minds off it all, especially Lucy who was always asking Mum if she was going to die, usually when Mum was dozing in the chair. Lucy would try and prise her eyes open, to make sure she was still alive.

Thinking about football, I noticed Jasper was missing. Where had he been when the drama kicked off? Sophia said he went out earlier, as soon as he was up, doing something naughty, but I thought he'd gone to ask the band to come out to play.

The nurse came about ten minutes after Mum had finished her coffee. Mum was starting to complain about all the jobs she needed doing and wasn't able to, now that she was forced to rest. Of course I knew what she was telling me. My last chance to see Scott before the band went to Scotland later in the day had just gone out the window.

Mum complained all the way upstairs to bed, but the nurse soon told her to stop and save her energy, she was sure I was 'a very capable girl' so could be trusted to do what she wanted. Mum just sniffed and then gave me a long list of jobs she wanted me to do straight away, no messing around.

After the nurse had gone she summoned me back

upstairs. Her eyes were closed and she looked really pale lying in bed. I felt sorry for her, her wrists must hurt and I expect she was upset at smashing one of her wedding presents.

'Don't think this lets you off the hook for getting in with the paper boy. It doesn't.'

I groaned inwardly; even now, like this, she was going to give it to me. I sighed. Waiting.

'Your father will hear about this behaviour, don't doubt it. Just because I'm incapacitated for now doesn't give you an excuse to run around with that lot behind my back.'

'I'm not,' I said, standing at the foot of her bed, miserable and fed-up. I was beginning to wish I'd let her bleed to death. I couldn't believe I'd actually saved the bitch's life. What was I thinking?

She didn't look at me, but she smiled. 'You did a bit of quick thinking this morning, just like when Jasper put the fork through his foot in the garden; you acted quickly then.'

'Yes,' I said and waited. She didn't say anything for a couple of minutes and I thought she was asleep so moved to leave. 'And when Jasper put the spade through the top of Sophia's head that time, you were a good girl then, getting help for her so fast.'

'Yes.' Where was this going, I wondered uneasily.

'Stop all this journalism and writing nonsense, you're going to be a nurse,' she said sounding really satisfied.

I nearly fell over. A nurse! What on earth was she on about? Me a nurse!

'Your father and I had considered teaching for you but with the move and the school situation being what it is, nursing will be fine. We can sort you out when we come home from Germany. By that time you'll be nineteen and ready for college, and the discipline from one of the teaching hospitals will do you good, you could live in. Sophia will be old enough to help me by then.'

I just stood with my mouth open. Speechless. I really wanted to put the pillow over her face and shut her up, once and for all.

Bloody nursing? Teaching, for God's sake?

What the hell was I doing this morning, helping her? I really should've let her bleed to bloody death.

'Now get downstairs and sort those kids out and then you can start on the ironing. It won't do itself.'

Shaking my head, giving her one long look, I trudged downstairs.

The back door slammed and Jasper arrived all muddy and red in the face.

'Where have you been?' I despaired looking at him. 'Don't go in the sitting room for goodness sakes, you're all muddy.'

'Been playing with your boyfriend and the group in the Rec,' he said kicking his shoes off, aiming at the corner of the kitchen. 'They're going to Scotland today and Scott said he'll come and say goodbye before they go. Wanted to know if Mum was on the war-path still.'

He ran himself a glass of cold water.

'Oh grief, go back and tell him not to come round, she'll go nuts.' I grabbed his shoes and thrust them back at him, pointing to the door. 'Now! Go!'

'Keep your hair on, Sis, I'm hungry and anyway they're down the Rec.' He took an apple from the bowl, rubbed it on his shirt and took a huge bite.

'Then get back down there and tell him Mum's had an accident and I can't see him even if she wasn't on the war path, which she is.'

I started pushing the iron over the tenth white shirt, back and legs aching. I hated ironing, so many shorts, trousers, and blouses. The sheets were the worst, so big and heavy and trying to get them wrinkle free was a nightmare. Dad's army uniform used to be torture – when he was in the army

-getting all the creases right and the cuffs. I was so glad he didn't have all that anymore.

'Is she dead?' Jasper screwed his face up as he asked me.

'Who? Mum?' I sprinkled water onto the handkerchief and placed it over the shirt collar. 'No, more's the pity,' I mumbled under my breath.

'Who tried to kill her?' He looked deadly serious.

'No one tried to kill her, she cut herself on a vase she dropped and I had to get the doctor because she was bleeding so badly.'

'Cor, how much blood was there? Can I see it?' He looked as if he really expected me to have saved it just to show him.

'Don't be silly. It's all cleaned up now anyway.'

'I bet it was just like Dracula killing everyone and getting blood everywhere and then he drinks it all up... I want to drink it all up — I'm a vampire.' He started hunching his back and prancing around the kitchen like Quasimodo, making Dracula noises. I couldn't believe it. Little monster.

'Go and tell Scott I can't see him and find out when he'll be back,' I snapped, getting a bit fed-up with collars and cuffs and button holes.

Scott hadn't been sure how long they'd be away this time. We hadn't really had chance to discuss it on the way home, and what with everything else going on this morning... I hoped he knew by now as I didn't want to spend ages wondering. I'd enough stress already.

'Give me some money then and I'll go.' Jasper held his hand out smiling.

'No!' I slammed the iron down and he jumped.

'Everyone pays Simon to do stuff, so why can't I get paid?' He looked sullenly at me.

He was right, Simon always managed to get his palm crossed with silver when asked to do anything. I usually had to keep begging him and then, just when my patience was about to snap, he would agree to do a chore provided he got paid... By which time, if it was shopping for a meal, I had to give in because I needed him to go before Mum got back from work, and I had to have food ready for when she walked in. Little swine knew it, too.

Jasper was normally happy to do chores and never asked for anything so I wondered why the sudden demand for money.

'What's the money for?' I asked him, putting the last shirt on a hanger.

'I'm going to buy some football boots, just like Georgie Best's got.' He looked dreamy as he said it. 'Mum said if I want them I have to save for them and I only get thruppence a week for pocket money, and Simon said I had to ask for money if you wanted me to do stuff for you, so how much?'

'I'll give you sixpence, but only this once because it's important, but don't ever ask me again, and you can tell Simon that I shall be telling Dad about his little racket, so he can forget getting any more out of me!' I raised my voice. 'I have to earn my money doing work AND pay for all my own stuff. I don't get pocket money, and I don't see why I should pay anyone to do things for Mum either.'

I closed the ironing board with a clatter and slammed the hot iron on the draining board with a bang.

Jasper looked sheepish and shuffled, 'Sorry Renza, I didn't mean to upset you.'

'I'm not cross at you, don't worry. Wait while I get my purse.' I smiled at him, and patted his blond head. He was harmless, and such a smiler I could never be cross with him for long.

Simon on the other hand...

Renza's Diary

June 30ᵗʰ 1968 – later the same day

Jasper handed me a note from Scott later that afternoon telling me he wasn't sure how long they'd be in Scotland, but he would see me when he got back and he hoped Mum would be all right. He'd got dates for the cruise, somewhere in the Mediterranean lasting for about ten days he thought. He wished I could go with him. He'd signed it *'All My Love xxxx'*

Fat chance, I thought as I read it for the millionth time. Four kisses must mean something, and 'All My Love' was good, I told myself. I would love to go on a cruise, somewhere romantic, with long sunny days, warm balmy nights.

'Make sure you put salt in the potatoes,' Mum shouted, breaking into my daydreams. 'I know you and your salt-free nonsense. I'm not eating anything I can't taste.'

I'd been up and down the stairs to her all day taking orders for this or that to be done, taking her coffee and reporting on what I had been up to since the last time I'd been summoned. My legs were killing me and I was totally fed-up with being at her beck and call all the time. I just wished she'd go to sleep and not wake up!

I'd already done the potatoes and made the rest of the dinner.

'All under control Mum,' I yelled back from the bottom of the stairs.

'No need to shout, I'm not deaf!' Loss of blood hadn't affected her voice.

I went down the garden to get some mint for the potatoes and saw Donald Digby sitting in a deck chair doing something with a transistor radio; it looked as if he was repairing it. He looked up as I bent to pick the mint near the fence.

'Heard your mum tried to kill herself this morning, Mum told me. Said your mum found out about your dad having an affair.'

'What?' I stood up horrified. 'Your mum said what?'

'Yeah she heard it in the village. Your dad's been gone a long time now and Mum heard he'd got some foreign bird and run off with her, and your mum cut her wrists when she found out.' He put the radio down and stood up, moving towards the fence.

'Well, you can tell your mum and the bush telegraph that my dad has not run off with anyone, he's working in Germany as you well know, and we are all going over soon. And as for cutting her wrists, Mum caught a crystal vase with her arms and it smashed.'

I wanted to smash his sniggering face in.

'Yeah, well you would say that wouldn't you, but Mum and Peg heard it from someone in the chemist who heard the doctor telling Mr Blackmore she wasn't going to be in to work, and that you'd saved her life.'

His face was all twisted and horrid and I really felt I wanted to do him a physical mischief.

Donald was up close now and he reached across the fence and grabbed my left hand and gave it a nasty twist backwards. I yelled out in pain and he grabbed my other hand and twisted that at the same time. I thought I'd faint.

'Ouch, stop it, what are you doing that for?' I cried, sure he'd broken my fingers and my wrist. My eyes were filling with tears and the more I tried to get away from his grip, the tighter he held me and twisted.

'Think you're all so posh and better than us, you stupid cow,' he hissed through clenched teeth. 'You're the village tart, Mum says, showing it all off for everyone to see.'

'Get lost, Donald, and let go of me or I'll get Mum to call the police.' I couldn't think what else to say. The pain was unbearable.

'Suicide is a crime, your mum will go to prison if it gets out what she tried to do,' he threatened, 'so you won't be telling anyone.'

'What's wrong with you? You're always trying to hurt me, you little shit.' I struggled, and eventually he let go of one wrist but as I tried to get my other one free, he grabbed it and started to give me a Chinese burn. I yelled at the top of my voice.

'Hey! You, leave my Donald alone, you little hussy.' Mrs Digby opened their sitting room window and stuck her head out. 'Not content with flaunting yourself all over that long-haired lot next door, you're interfering with my Donald as well.' She looked puce with rage.

'Interfering with your Donald – you must be joking!' I cried rubbing my wrists now that he'd let go.

Donald stood back from me looking suitably shocked at being interfered with; big wide-eyes appealing to his mummy. I could just imagine him saying something like, 'Mummy make her stop, I don't like it,' or some such rubbish!

I glared at him and he gave me a look of triumph as Mr Digby came round the side of their house. 'You, get away from my son, you little tramp.'

Tears filled my eyes and with a huge lump in my throat I just shook my head, and turned and ran back inside, the mint left on the path where it had fallen.

'What the hell is going on down there?' Attila the Hun shouted from upstairs as I closed the back door. 'You flirting with that drip next door now?'

I leaned against the kitchen door, tears streaming down my face.

Please, Scott, come and take me away from this place and these bloody people. Please.

Stella's Diary
July 1st 1968

'So, what are you going to do?' Vix, my best friend, stared at me. 'Are you going to tell Mike you can't go to Cornwall? Seriously, Stella – look at you. What if this happens while you're away?'

It was late afternoon and I was in bed. At home. My lovely, scruffy, untidy, animal-filled, happy home. My refuge.

I really loved my bedroom – all sunflower yellow walls and curtains and buttercream paintwork. Like sunshine. Actually, outside it was quite dark and raining gentle summer rain. The transistor radio on my bedside cabinet was playing softly. The Alan Price Set 'Please Don't Stop the Carnival'. I loved that song. It painted such vivid pictures. It was all very cosy.

I'd had a really bad attack at work and had fainted in the office. I'd been sent first to the on-site medical centre, and then driven home by one of the lady chauffeurs in one of the huge shiny limousines the Atomic used for visiting dignitaries. Doubled-up in pain on the back seat I'd totally failed to appreciate the sheer luxuriousness of my transport – but I did manage to say a big thank you to the lovely lady driver who had helped me indoors and then rushed off, presumably before I could be sick on her pristine navy uniform.

Our next-door-neighbour had run across to the school to tell my mum, Dr Kingston had been sent for, and visited, and prescribed Aspro, a hot water bottle and bed-rest until the spasms passed. My mum, having arrived home from school just in time to listen to Dr Kingston, then see her out of the front door, had poo-pooed the Aspro idea and had given me two Feminax tablets instead.

Luckily you didn't need a doctor's prescription for Feminax. You could buy them over the counter at the chemist and they contained morphine and I'd taken them for years when my periods were really bad. They not only killed the pain within minutes but had me flying high as a kite.

'Far better than Aspro,' Mum had said, straightening the eiderdown, making sure my hot water bottle wasn't too hot, and that I had a glass of Lucozade and a pile of books to hand. 'I'm not sure Dr Kingston knows what she's doing with you, Stell. I'll be glad when you get the appointment at the Churchill. Are you ok, love? Need anything else?'

'No, thanks Mum. I'll just rest. And if Vix comes round please tell her to come up. Even if I'm asleep.'

'Of course,' Mum smiled kindly at me. 'And don't worry, love. You'll soon be better.'

Now Vix, who was very pretty, tall and slim, with Cilla Black hair, and with her acid-green shift dress barely covering her bottom, was perched on the end of my bed, accompanied by one of our dogs and two of the cats. Vix and I had met on the first day at infants school and had been best friends ever since. We told each other everything and I trusted her with my life.

I shrugged. 'I'm playing it all by ear at the moment. I mean, Patsy has booked it all anyway, and I don't have to make up my mind for another few weeks. I've got some money saved but I'm not paying it until I know I can go. And if I get a hospital appointment, then – '

'Shut up!' Vix laughed. 'We both know that's not what I meant. Well, it was sort of – because one, I think you're mad to be going away with people you don't really like, and two, I reckon if you were ill on holiday Mike and the other two would just leave you to it, and three, how dare Patsy make arrangements for your holiday without even asking you, and four, Mike was even worse for conveniently forgetting to mention it – but, actually, I was really meaning the bed-sharing thing.'

'Oh, God – I'm not thinking about that. I can't think about it. Not now. Probably not ever.'

Vix sighed. 'Do you love Mike?'

'Yes, of course I do... well, you know – I think I do... Oh, I don't know... I like him loads, and I'd hate it if he wasn't around – but...'

'There shouldn't even be a but,' Vix said primly. 'If you love someone you just know – there's no ifs and buts. Like me and Jeff. We just *know*. We've always *known*. Anyway, you could do so much better than Mike. He's...'

'Boring, unreliable, selfish and self-obsessed,' I finished with a grin. 'I know. So you keep saying. He loves you too.'

'Well, he's not my choice – and I'm not going to interfere – but I still think he's a bit of a weasel and you could do so much better. Anyway, if you go off on this holiday, and if you're thinking of having sex again then you'll have to get yourself on the pill – can you imagine the disaster of being pregnant with Mike's baby?'

'Bloody hell!' I snorted with horrified laughter. 'That's never going to happen – not in a million years – I'm never having sex again! And I thought you were supposed to be cheering me up.'

Vix was on the pill. As soon as it became available the previous year, Vix had gone to Dr Kingston. Of course, being an old fuddy-duddy and "you're not a married woman" type doctor, Dr Kingston had refused to prescribe it, so we'd caught the train to Reading and gone to the Brook Advisory Centre.

Vix had said it was the mature and sensible thing to do. I'd simply sat in the waiting room, surrounded by girls – and some boys – all of whom looked years younger than me, and read the posters on the walls and hoped I'd never have to decide about contraception or sex or anything else in that line ever.

And after the fiasco in the caravan, nothing had so far changed my mind.

I snuggled further under the eiderdown. 'The thing is, I reckon, that if I met someone, and fell madly, crazily, deliriously in love at first sight – I mean, all trumpets and confetti and celestial choirs love at first sight – then I'd actually want to make love with them, and it would be sensational, and everything else in the relationship would just fall into place.'

Vix peered at me. 'And you're away with the fairies! How many Feminax have you taken? That sort of thing only happens in your stories – it never, ever happens in real life.'

'No...' I sighed drowsily, 'but wouldn't it be fabulous if it did...?'

Renza's Diary
July 2nd 1968

Narnia's Children's van was not in the car park behind the shops when I looked this morning and it was still not there at lunchtime. Jasper had been round to their flat twice to see if they had returned and had bumped into a girl letting herself in with a key. After asking her if she wanted to play football, and apparently being told where to shove the football, he got the message and came back to tell me.

'I dunno who she is, she was horrid to me, so I don't like her,' he told me when I cross-examined him for about the tenth time, trying to glean more information from him. Trouble is, he soon caught on and started to embellish the story each time he told it.

'She's a famous singer and she's married to Scott,' was his parting shot as he sped out of the garden where I was hanging washing. His instincts are good; he knew I was about to clout him.

I strained to see if the girl was on the balcony but there was no sign of her. I spent the whole morning worrying about who she was. Perhaps it was 'The Bitch,' perhaps she wasn't history after-all. Scott told me he had a girlfriend back in Jersey, Marion, whom he'd dumped soon after he set eyes on me, and he said she had taken it badly and made all sorts of threats, so I couldn't help wondering if she had come over to 'do me a mischief', which apparently she promised to do if she ever came across me. Mo told me on the quiet that Scott had been engaged to Marion. Oh cripes, I hope it wasn't her. Surely he'd have told me she was coming.

Mum was up and about and not in a good frame of mind. She wanted me to go with her to town and get some new shoes and some stockings to take to Germany. She wasn't sure what the choice might be like over there, or if there was even a shoe shop anywhere near where we'd be living, so to be safe she wanted to get some whilst she had the chance. Nan was going to keep an eye on the kids.

I was over the moon at the thought of shopping with her. It normally ended up in a row.

We went out for the bus at noon and joined quite a long queue, all of whom knew Mum, and greeted her as we walked up. I just got the evil eye. I guess it was my purple mini dress and long white lace-up boots, judging from the looks I got, and the various sniggers I heard. Mum had gone on and on about me wearing boots in the middle of summer, but according to Marjorie Proops's newspaper column, everyone was wearing them. Some girls had mums like mine and so the 'Problem Page' was full of girls asking for advice about parents, and rows over clothes. Mum only gave in because she was worried we'd miss the bus.

I stood to one side whilst Mum and some of her old school chums chatted about this and that, and now and again I caught one of them glaring at me disapprovingly. I pretended not to notice, besides my feet were getting very hot inside my boots and I really needed to scratch my heel. Pride would not allow me to have a go at it though. Besides, I daren't bend over in case I showed the tops of my stockings. It was bad enough trying to keep my suspenders from showing. I really wanted to see if they had some tights for sale in the shoe shop. I'd seen some in the paper; they are going to be the next big thing, doing away with having to wear stockings and suspenders they say, so I want to see if I can buy some if they are not too dear. I've not told Mum in case she thinks they are too tarty.

Old Ma Lee was chatting to Mum and throwing her hands up in the air every now and then as she told her some story or other. I hadn't been listening but I could see some of the other ladies in the queue giggling on the sly, so I moved a little closer to eavesdrop.

Old Ma Lee was one of the local Gypsies whose family had been in the village over a hundred years and Mum knew her really well, having been classmates with some of Ma's grandchildren at school. The old Gypsy was in her usual long black skirt, men's army boots with a black trilby hat on her head, grey shawl draped over her shoulders held in place with a huge red semi-precious stone given to her by her grandmother, so she'd told us once before. Ma had a huge wicker basket over her arm and a blue and white gingham table-cloth covering the contents of the basket.

She was smoking a clay pipe which she tapped on her hat every now and again, and which she had to relight several times. She offered Mum a couple of puffs much to the amusement of the other ladies. Suffice to say Mum was not impressed at all. Besides, Mum had white gloves on covering her wrists which were still bandaged and I think she was worried people would draw the wrong conclusions about her accident, so was keeping the evidence covered up.

Mum never went out without a hat of some sort. Today she was wearing a pink feather thing which was like a large Alice band — like Audrey Hepburn wore a lot — and it matched her pink two piece suit. She had navy stiletto shoes on and a matching navy handbag. Fully made up, without a hair out of place, she could've been going to London for afternoon tea.

'Dun up to the nines, missus,' observed Ma Lee, giving Mum the once over and nodding to herself, 'where's you orf to then?'

'Shoe shopping at Barratts,' Mum replied, fully aware of the stares she was getting as everyone tuned in to the conversation.

'So you ain't no ghost then after-all.' Ma Lee looked relieved.

'Ghost? What one earth are you on about Ma?' Mum was puzzled.

'When you died, Missus, so youse come back then, but yer say youse no ghost.' Ma took long puffs on the pipe and blew smoke at Mum.

I tried to hide my smirk but it was hard because several others were struggling not to grin as well. Old Ma Lee was a notorious believer in ghosts and spirits and ill winds. Her grandmother had second sight apparently and sometimes Ma Lee said she had it as well.

'I'm sorry Ma, but I've no idea what you are on about,' Mum said frostily, looking at her watch and then making a show of watching for the bus.

'When yer done yerselft in t'other day, Missus.' Ma sought agreement from the ladies in the queue, nodding towards them encouragingly.

I thought I was going to burst. Oh my goodness, this was too funny for words.

'When I done, erm did, myself in?' Mum asked in amazement. 'I never did myself in. What are you on about, Ma?' Mum had a quick look round, and shook her head at the others, in a sort of 'what on earth is the woman on about?' look.

No one moved a muscle. Seven pairs of eyes and ears were trained on Mum and Old Ma Lee by now. Waiting.

'Our Effy dunned herself in.' Old Ma Lee crept closer to Mum who was backed up to the bus shelter wall by now, with no escape.

The whole bus queue shifted closer so they could hear better. As usual the bus was late so Mum probably had no hope of salvation any time soon.

'She comes back all the time,' Ma informed us all wisely.

'Oh Ma, you are so funny, and you will have your little jokes,' Mum tried to turn the tables, 'you and your ghosts and ghoulies.'

'I ain't worried by no family ghosts and ghoulies missus, just a worried youse gorn and made yerselft into yon spirit, and then come back again as I can see with my own eyes.' Ma peered closely at Mum and several heads leaned closer to have a better look as well. 'Youse gorn and dieded, and comed back again then?' she asked, poking Mum in the chest with her clay pipe. 'Is that it?'

Mum tried to side-step her but a rubbish bin prevented her from moving, so she had to remain jammed up against the wooden shelter.

Old Ma Lee rummaged in her basket and pulled out some heather wrapped in newspaper, and shoved it at Mum who was forced to accept it. The paper was wet and soggy where Ma had watered the heather. I wondered whose garden she had pinched it from.

'For youse to get yerselft back from the dead a-permedly,' she told Mum, looking round at the others, 'coz she mighten be called back again and she needs protectionation from the other side,' Ma informed us all.

My stomach was hurting from suppressed giggling and my face ached as well. I daren't look at the others as I could feel their mirth in the air. It was all too funny. Such a blast. Trust Mum to get caught by Ma on one of her 'Spiritual' days. I'm going to miss all this when we're in Germany.

'Really Ma, you do come out with some corkers.' Mum tried to laugh it off as Ma blew more smoke in her face.

'Ain't no corker missus, 'tis the truth so help me.' Ma tapped her trilby three times and stamped her feet. I've seen her do this before. No idea why. 'Youse don't want being carried off into the darkness again, it ain't right and youse can't keep a-coming back neither.' She put her pipe into her skirt pocket and put her basket on the ground whilst she tapped her hat with both hands and turned round twice. 'Now youse don't go a killing yerselft again — tell Ma you won't.'

Major Piggott-Brown's wife stuck her head into her handbag, apparently searching for something at this point, and Miss Dashwood placed her hanky to her nose so she could giggle in secret. Several other ladies did their best not to openly laugh. As did I. Poor Mum, she was beside herself at the

117

thought that everyone now believed she had tried to do herself in. Of course no one believed she had died and come back from the dead. Well, no one except me and Ma Lee – I secretly agreed with her thinking – Mum could well be something from 'the other side'.

A steady stream of smoke started to appear from Ma's pocket and I wondered if I should let her know. I think she'd forgotten her lighted pipe. A couple of the ladies nudged each other when they noticed the smoke, but no one said anything. I stared at Ma hoping she would notice me looking and I could tell her she seemed to be on fire, but she was muttering to herself and trying to wave her hands over Mum's head, but she was far too short to reach and was tottering on her tiptoes in the attempt. The army boots not being conducive to going up on pointes, Ma made a very comical prima ballerina as she tried to carry out her exorcism.

I had to stop myself humming 'Fire,' by The Crazy World of Arthur Brown. The singer used to set himself on fire as part of their stage act. Yvette saw them at The Top Rank in June and she said something went wrong and his hair caught alight and suddenly the Fire Brigade was spraying extinguisher all over him – just too funny.

Mum kept trying to duck and dive, mindful I think of her recent perm and her new hat. Suddenly Ma reached into her pocket and grabbed her pipe, patting her skirt rapidly – realising she might be about to go up in flames – she must've felt the heat. She was hopping from one foot to the other as she tried to waft the pipe over Mum's head, tipping ash all over the place. Mum started to complain. I couldn't speak or look away. It was such a blast. Mum's wild eyes kept appealing to me but I was beyond helping her. I was on the verge of hysterics.

A bicycle bell sounded and we all looked round to see Miss Glossop on her 'sit up and beg', wearing her red fez and long black cloak which she wore in all weathers. Her bright red cupid-bow lips greeted everyone with a cheery smile, and an expansive wave of her hand as she passed by. Her little Scottie dog was sitting on the child's seat behind her, wearing a blue fez and a tartan coat. He yapped wildly as we all stared after them.

Her intervention gave Mum the chance she needed to escape from Old Ma Lee's ministrations, and she rushed to my side. Before anyone could say or do anything else, the bus arrived.

All the way to town I had to listen to Mum doing her pieces about Old Ma Lee and what she had been saying. Priceless. If I ever get to write a book Old Ma Lee's going to be in it and all the Gypsies will be too. They're such characters.

I hate shopping of any description and especially when I'm with someone else. Mum drives me nuts whenever we go together, which I try to avoid like a dose of acne. Barratts didn't have anything she fancied and didn't stock tights – or as the sniffy assistant told us, 'pantyhose' – so we ended up in every shoe shop in town. She must have tried on a hundred pairs of shoes in every colour and design known to man before she settled upon a pair of black patent leather court shoes. Nothing special as far as I could see and I swear she'd already tried similar shoes on in Clarks two hours ago. We both managed to buy half a dozen pairs of 'pantyhose' each along the way. So goodbye suspenders and stockings – praise the Lord and pass the gravy, as Nan would say.

On the way back to the bus stop we met up with one of Mum's friends – as you do – and stood for ages whilst they chatted and discussed all the goings on in the village, every now and again uttering sounds of shock and horror as some poor devil's business was chewed over. We were outside the cinema and I wandered off to look at the posters for the forthcoming films on release in England later in the year. Not that I would be around to see any of them. I wondered if the

Germans had a cinema near us or if they even had English language films.

Every now and again a car would go past, tooting the horn. This may well have been directed at Mother – she thought it was, I think – and sometimes boys would shout out – obviously to me. Mum would give me the evil eye as if it was my fault.

A couple of 'group' vans went past as well, covered in writing by fans and with the name of the group written on the sides. Quite exciting really.

Another lady joined Mum and her friend, whose name escaped me, and soon she was laughing or tut tutting, depending on who and what they were discussing. I recognised the newcomer as being the wife of a local celebrity who was a former Canadian Cowboy called Cheyanne Harry, who used to entertain the cinema queue by doing tricks with his lasso during the Second World War, capping it all off by whipping a cigarette out of his wife's mouth with the lasso. They lived in a caravan down the lane beside the ford and had travelled all over the place doing their act. Cheyanne Harry had been stationed in the area during the war, marrying a local girl, and staying here when the war ended.

I couldn't help wondering what Scott would make of all these weird people. Perhaps there were weird people living near him in Jersey. I wondered if I'd ever find out.

After dinner I looked out to see if the band had come back, but there wasn't any sign of the van in the car park at the back of the shops. I felt really fed-up wondering if they'd come back during the night or later tomorrow some time. I hoped they'd be back by the morning because they were all going on some cruises later in the week and I wouldn't see Scott for ages, and I didn't want to miss a single minute with him before then.

He'd said they were going to Lisbon, Tangier and Madeira, stopping off at all sorts of wonderful places on the way there and back, and that lots of rich and famous people would be on the cruise and it was a great chance for them to make some money and new fans. I guessed so. He'd be back before we went to Germany and that was all I cared about. I wished I could go with him but as I couldn't, I couldn't care less about the stupid cruise. I wondered if the girl in the flat was going with them. I hoped not. I wanted to know which one in the band she was 'with' – although as long as it wasn't Scott, I didn't care.

Renza's Diary
July 7ᵗʰ 1968

Narnia's Children headed off before it was light on their way to Southampton where they were to board the SS Northern Star for their cruise to Lisbon, Tangier, and Madeira. I heard Bessie backfiring as she passed the front of the house and I ran to catch a glimpse of them but to no avail. There wasn't enough light to see into the van so I went back to bed feeling Scott's loss already.

He'd spent the last evening with me walking around the College grounds – our usual 'date' – arms around me, telling me how much he would miss me and that he'd send me postcards from every port, and how miserable he was going to be, and that he just knew he wouldn't enjoy any of it.

All I worried about was some rich girl getting off with him so that he would soon forget me and when he got back he wouldn't want to know me. Scott reassured me, well, tried to, and told me that Stephan, the group's manager, and Rich were staying behind and would be in the flat and they'd keep an eye on me and help Mum if she needed anything doing.

I found out that the girl in the flat was 'with' Zak at the moment. I laughed at 'at the moment' and thought that just about summed him up from what I could tell. Another one who'd be history within a day or so. According to Scott, they never lasted. I never saw her or any of the others. Trust Mum to see it all.

I couldn't help wondering if I might soon be history too, after the cruise. Nothing seemed real, and far too good to last knowing my luck...I know, I'm being 'negative.' But I can't help having 'wobbles.'

The cruise was going to last ten days and as well as the ports Scott told me about, they would be stopping off at other places on the way out and on the way back. He said that they would be playing for the crew in what is called

'The Pig' – where the crew have a club with a bar and stage – as well as playing for the paying guests on the cruise. They had to play in the evenings for passengers and then in the early hours of the morning for the crew. The rest of the time they could do what they wanted.

All this sounded wonderful, all those exotic places I could only imagine. Just like Whicker's World with Alan Whicker on TV when he travels all over the world, showing us what life is like in far off places. It's not that I haven't travelled, I have, but when I was much younger. We even lived in Singapore, before the others were born, and Germany – once before – and although I can recall bits and pieces it's not like being older and really being able to appreciate it all.

I'm going to miss Scott when he's away, he's the only person I've ever really been close to and can talk to – who has ever said they cared for me. Scott said I belong to him now. I've never belonged to anyone before. I love that feeling. He makes me happy. He likes all the things I like: reading, movies, looking at the stars, history and, although he doesn't write stories, he writes songs and they're just like stories I think. We could talk forever once we get started.

I put the transistor on quietly and listened to The Walker Brothers, they are so gorgeous, singing 'I Will Wait for You,' such a melancholy song.

Scott says he's not alone any more, but he will be when I go in August. I don't want to leave him. I wish we could just be together, somewhere on our own. His family seems a bit messed up, that's why the band means so much to him I'm sure. I never imagined someone like Scott could ever be lonely, but now I know he has been just like me.

I have my brothers and sisters I suppose, but they're not really much company, and Mum and Dad are too wrapped up in their own lives to bother with me. I've always wished for something in my life to make up for my crushing loneliness. It helps to write it down here and get it off my chest, but now I have someone to talk to: Scott. I just know I shall read my diary over and over whilst he's away. Just to be close to him.

Tony Blackburn is playing The Zombies, 'Time of The Season', and all I can think of is Scott's arms around me yesterday, his gentle breath in my ear as he whispered the words of their song to me, before his earthquake of a kiss.

Time to get up soon and face the next ten days without the love of my life.

Stella's Diary
Saturday 12th July 1968

Still no word from the Churchill Hospital about my appointment, but I'd had a good day today. I'd been taking Feminax every time I'd had really bad pains and they worked! Mum had said I shouldn't overdo them as obviously I might become addicted – but honestly, until someone came up with something else to stop me being in agony, then I'd take the risk.

There was the problem of being spaced-out most of the time. However, I could get away with that at work, it was a very relaxed office – that was an understatement! I couldn't always get away with being away with the fairies when I was out with Mike though – he got a bit ratty when I fell asleep in the car!

Mike picked me up from home tonight – I wasn't quite ready so he had a few minutes to chat to Mum and Dad – well, they did most of the chatting, Mike doesn't say much. They do like him, though – they think he's "steady".

I'm not sure "steady" is a compliment, actually. My dad is anything but steady – being a bit of a drifter job-wise – and a bit of a joker, and big and gentle and well, just carefree – I think he's like Mr Micawber. And Mum is just a lovely fluffy smiley person who cooks a lot and takes in waifs and strays, and wants everyone in the word to be well-fed and happy.

Vix says our house is like living in The Darling Buds of May.

Anyway, when I came downstairs, Mike looked quite relieved and actually said I looked nice! I was wearing the polka-dot coat dress again so he obviously hadn't taken much notice of it last time. I'd sighed and said thanks and that he didn't look too bad either.

Which he didn't. He was wearing his faded Levis and a black jumper – and he looked – well – conservatively neat. And, yes, ok – steady.

Tonight we'd been to see a film in Ashworthy – our neighbouring town – as Harbury Green doesn't have a cinema. Just the two of us. No Sam and Patsy tonight! I'd leaned my head on his shoulder in the darkness and thought if I hated the film I could fall asleep and he wouldn't notice.

The film was my choice: Up The Junction. If I'd left it to Mike it would have been Zombie Creatures from the Black Lagoon or a Western or something full of blood and guts.

Anyway, there was no chance of me falling asleep! What a film! I loved it! Oh, if only I could write something like that... Ok, it wasn't cheerful or very romantic and it certainly didn't end happily – but it was so *real*!

In the car on the way home, with the radio on in the background – it was all smooth and smoochy stuff tonight: Louis Armstrong and Herb Alpert. I chattered about the film to Mike. How Adrienne Posta reminded me of Vix, and how Suzy Kendall – the rich girl who'd chosen to slum it in a working-class area just to see what it was like – had been lucky to be able to choose to change her lifestyle, knowing that she could always escape back if she wanted to. And how sad it was, that her boyfriend ended up in prison, and how awful it was for Adrienne Posta's character to get pregnant and be so scared.

Mike didn't say much, just shrugged a bit.

'But, if you had the chance,' I glanced across at him as we pulled up at a Belisha Beacon to let someone cross the road, 'wouldn't you like to do something like that? Change your life? Experience something different just for a little while? Have an adventure? Meet new people... do new things...?'

'No,' Mike shook his head. 'Why would you want to do something like that? We should be satisfied with what we've got. There's no point in wanting anything else, that's what my dad says. A good job and money in your pocket, a few beers on a Friday night and football on a Saturday. That'll do me.'

I sighed. 'But the film... it just showed how different another life could be – even if it wasn't wonderful all the time, it was still like an adventure – didn't you see that?'

'What I saw,' Mike grinned as we drove away from Ashworthy, 'was that Suzy Kendall has a cracking pair of legs.'

I sighed and slid down in my seat.

Renza's Diary
July 13th 1968

The last few days have been really miserable. Mum has been in a mood and is getting stressed about us all travelling to Germany on August 15th. We have to get the train to Gatwick and then fly from there. She keeps telling me that she will be relying on me to help with the kids and the luggage and everything. As if I needed to be told over and over.

Stephan and Rich have been round helping with the garden and finishing odd jobs for her, so she's happy with them. They're happy because she's feeding them, and I am sort of happy because they've been telling me the latest news about Narnia's Children, and yesterday they took me to London to meet Rich's family who live in one of those new high rise blocks in an area called Ongar. I can't say I liked the place, but his parents were really nice and they gave me their address and told me to write to them from Germany.

Mum shocked me by letting me go with them and she didn't even give me the evil eye on the quiet when they weren't looking. She said yes right away. Probably because Scott wasn't there, or because she liked Rich, or she thought Stephan would make me a wealthy husband. We went in Bessie and drove up past Fuller's Brewery and I had a good look round the city as we drove. It was exciting and I loved every minute of it. We sang along to the songs on Radio One, and I almost cried hearing The Walker Brothers sing 'First Love Never Dies.' We waved to all the girls who stopped to stare at Bessie with all the fan's scribbled messages covering a large portion of the van.

The postman came this morning as I was dressing Lucy, and Sophia came rushing in with a postcard for me, from Scott. She announced it to everyone and then read it out loud, shouting until Mum came out to the landing to hear what it said.

I wanted to cry. It was for me, not them.

'*Dear Renza and Family*', Scott wrote on 11th July, '*I'm having a wonderful time and I'm afraid I've got rather sunburned. We docked at Tangiers this morning and I picked up quite a few bargains. Lisbon was wonderful as you can see from this postcard – huge, really beautiful buildings. The food on board is too much – seriously too much. Seven course lunches and dinners and all you can eat all day with buffets and snack bars and loads to do on deck*'. His writing was really untidy. '*Anyway, see you all in 6 days time I hope, love Scott 'Narnia's Children'. Xx*'

The photo on the postcard was of three views of Lisbon – Lisbon by night, all huge important looking buildings and fountains lit by coloured lights.

Sophia shouted to Mum, 'there are two kisses on it, Mum,' before she let me have it to read.

Rich told me the boys were having a great time in Lisbon, going ashore during the day, getting drunk before their evening performance for passengers, and then later at night – when they were 'off duty' – in 'The Pig,' performing for the crew, they really let their hair down and got totally wasted. Not my idea of fun. The boys had all sent cards to Rich and Stephan and given them the 'real' story of what went on. There were lots of dancers and show-people performing on board and the band were able to mix with them as well as the passengers.

It all sounded wonderful and glamorous and I couldn't help wondering about Scott and the rich women on board. But then he had sent me a card. Only one so far, but he had remembered to do that. Or had he sent it to cover up for what he was really up to? My head ached with the worry of it all. Nan came to lunch today and I felt so sorry for her. She looked so unhappy and kept saying she would never see us all again and how lonely she would be when we had gone. She asked Mum about me staying behind with her again but Mum was having none of it.

All of a sudden Nan looked really old and seemed to have

shrunk. I thought she was finding it hard to hear and I told Mum I thought she was going deaf. Apparently Nan had complained of headaches and I had to repeat myself to her over and over. I think Mum put it down to Nan trying to find a reason for me or all of us to stay, but I wasn't so sure. I knew she was eighty something, but in the last month I swear she'd aged ten years.

Dad told her, before he went away, that she could come out to Germany whenever she wanted and that she must come for Christmas. Mum kept telling her as well. But Nan seemed convinced she won't be seeing us ever again. It was heart-breaking. I was really going to miss seeing her every morning after my paper-round, having my breakfast with her, and I'd especially miss our chats.

Of course she'll have my cousins visiting when they are in England on leave, and then there's my uncle and auntie who used to live with her, but she spends far more time with Mum and with us kids, and it was going to leave a huge hole in her life. I was worried for her.

Every Sunday morning she would walk down to collect me to go to Mass with her at the local Catholic Church across the road, and I wondered what she'll do when I'm gone. She would always have Sunday lunch with us, and when Dad was here we would go for a drive after lunch and later, on the way home, stop off at a nice country pub somewhere and have a drink in the garden. Nan would have her stout or 'something stronger', Mum would have a gin and tonic and Dad had his pint. We kids would have Pepsi and a packet of Smith's crisps and we all thought we were so grand – it was a treat, as much for her as for us.

Nan would often take me on one of Crocket's coach trips down to the south coast in the summer. We'd get the coach early on a Sunday morning and the men on the trip would load crates of beer into the boot and off we'd go. We'd stop at what seemed like every pub on the way down and back – the men leaving the women on the coach with the kids and bottles of pop and crisps. Mum would send us off with packets of sandwiches to eat on the beach – which was usually pebbly – and often in driving rain and wind. Nan loved it.

Once Jasper came as well. Though given his track record for accidents, I was always a bit worried about him going anywhere with me. Not long before Lucy was born we were out for a drive, without Nan, and he managed to fall out of the car after being told not to play with the door handle. He had insisted on sitting in the front of the car even though Mum was pregnant at the time and needed the room. Dad gave in and Jasper sat up front. We were all crammed into the back and as we went round a bend in a country lane, Jasper managed to open the car door and went flying out.

All hell let loose with Mum and the kids all screaming and Dad slamming the brakes on so hard we all fell forward. The last we saw of Jasper he was going head first into a ditch and the car was moving away from him as he crawled out and started yelling at the top of his voice, 'don't go, don't leave me.'

Dad got out and tanned his backside, even before checking he hadn't broken his neck or worse! The car was full of screaming, deafening, hysterical kids and Mum heaving her bump all over the place trying to get out of the car, screeching like a hyena. She was so mad with Jasper, I thought he'd be better off if he'd knocked himself senseless so he wouldn't feel her thumping hell out of him.

About a week later we were going shopping and were on the top deck of the bus when he decided to stick his head out of the smallest window on the bus. As the bus sped along the road he was hit in the face by the branches of trees, yelling at the top of his voice all the way as Mum and I frantically tried to get his head back in. For some reason he'd managed to stick his head out of the window but he couldn't, whatever we did, get it back inside. We had to ask the bus conductor to get the driver to stop the bus, find a phone box and call the fire-brigade. We had a long wait for them to arrive and remove the window – and Jasper.

Mum wouldn't go outside for a month because of the embarrassment and poor old Jasper was confined to the house where he managed to get his head stuck in a saucepan, resulting in another session with the fire brigade, and not long after that he stuck a garden fork through his foot whilst helping Dad dig to Australia in the back garden – well, remove the roots of a huge rhododendron which was in the way of the new patio. Poor Nan, even though she probably dreaded taking Jasper anywhere because of his exploits, I knew she'd miss his antics and us all, and would probably put up with almost anything if we'd stay behind.

The kids have always followed me around, especially Jasper and Lucy, always wanting to come with me to the shops or whatever. Anyway Scott and I soon found out they were being paid by Mum to spy on us because, for some warped reason, she thought there'd be something she needed to know. Fat chance! They'd hide behind the sofa hoping to see us kissing so they could earn sixpence, or they'd trail behind us when we went for walks, hiding behind bushes and walls, but their giggling often gave them away. Mum rewarded them with a gold star on the back of the larder door for any information collected and these counted towards more pocket money when added up, so the incentive to spy and make stuff up was overwhelming of course. And that meant more aggravation for me. Simon on the other hand wanted money from me so that he wouldn't tell Mum anything – not that there'd been anything to tell. How I wished there was!

It amazed me that Scott was happy to put up with it all. I can't imagine many boys having five kids trailing behind them every time they went on a date.

'I feel like the flaming Pied Piper,' he laughed, when he spotted them for the first time. 'We'll have to be extra clever or there'll be no room left on the back of the larder door.'

Renza's Diary
July 18th 1968

I heard the band come back during the night. Rich told me last evening when he saw me in the garden that he and Stephan were going to Southampton to pick them up and he said that Scott would most likely come round to see me once they had settled in and caught up with some sleep. I reckoned the last ten days at sea had been nothing but a continuous party.

I couldn't sleep once they'd woken me up with Bessie backfiring all the way up the road. I tried hard not to allow those horrid little thoughts creep into my head; had he found someone else, did he still love me? The next minute I was excited at seeing him again, bursting with happiness and I knew everything was going to be wonderful. They say you're the last person to know if you've gone mad, but sometimes I really think I'm losing it. He loves, me, he loves me not; how to go nuts without really trying. I've even resorted to avoiding the cracks in the pavement, and telling myself that if the next song on the radio is a certain song, it's a sign he loves me, or that he doesn't love me. This has got to stop. Today is going to be a happy day. Scott loves me.

A little later I switched on Radio Caroline and listened to music as I tried to doze. It was difficult lying down with the earphones in but I didn't want to wake anyone. I had to stop myself singing along with the songs and I hummed quietly to myself whilst jigging around, sort of dancing lying down. I was so happy and couldn't relax, thinking of Scott being home and seeing him again. Yes, it's going to be a happy day.

The other day Rich told me that the band was going to be recording soon and they were going to 'Tin Pan Alley' in London to look at some songs the publishers had, which the band might like. Psychedelic Smith had arranged it after-all. Rich said that I could go with them if I wanted. Oh boy, I really want to go with them, every second with Scott is precious to me as August looms over us.

Apparently Scott would sort it out and then he and Rich would ask Mum if I could go. Even though they write their own songs, Stephan wanted them to record some by famous writers as that would help them get good exposure.

The Herd came on singing 'I Don't Want Our Lovin' to Die', followed by Marmalade with 'Lovin' Things'. I felt really happy for the first time in ages as I did my horizontal dance; all silly unhappy thoughts banished.

Scott came round at lunchtime and gave me a camel leather shoulder bag which I have to say smelled really funny, but I didn't tell him. I was so thrilled he'd thought of me. It was so wonderful seeing him again, all lean and tanned and even more handsome than I remembered.

As soon as I answered the front door he grabbed me and kissed me so hard and so long I thought I would suffocate.

'I've missed you so much,' he said.

'I missed you too. It's been horrible without you.' I kept one eye on the sitting-room door as he kissed me, in case Hawkeye or one of her Mohicans appeared at the wrong moment and caught us.

I nearly had to give the bag back as Mum put her oar in. She said that if you took gifts from boys they always wanted something in return!

'Mrs Rossi, please let me give her the bag. It's a present, nothing else,' Scott had pleaded all wide eyed and innocent, and for some reason she'd shrugged and said it was all right.

Renza's Diary
July 20th 1968

Narnia's Children, Rich and Stephan were crammed in Bessie, with me sitting on Scott's knee for our trip to 'Tin Pan Alley'. Scott's arms held me tightly as we lurched along, Bessie was obviously getting too old for all the work she had to do.

We parked near Soho and went into Denmark Street and up some stairs at the side of a music shop into a little cramped room full of people who looked like musicians, all going through sheet music and chatting to the publishers about songs.

The person 'dealing' with Narnia's Children had set aside some sheet music and also some records which he called 'demonstration recordings' for them to listen to. Apparently singers recorded songs written by the songwriters to demonstrate to other singers what they sounded like, so they could decide if they wanted to record them or not. However, they said that whoever produced the record in the end would probably change things a lot anyway. It was all very exciting.

We even listened to a song recorded by The Bee Gees, called "Coalman", which Stephan wanted Narnia's Children to record, but no one was keen on it, even though The Bee Gees were apparently considering it for their own long playing record at some point.

Cilla Black was in there, choosing songs, and I thought she didn't look that special close up. There were a couple of others, who I knew were famous but I couldn't recall their names, and Scott frowned at me when I asked him who they were. So I shut up. It was still all so new and rather thrilling for me.

After a couple of hours the band had chosen some songs and we left with sheet music and recordings for them to keep of songs they were interested in. Apparently they were due back in London tomorrow to have talks with some famous songwriters and record producers, so I wouldn't be seeing Scott again until Sunday, if they weren't playing.

On the way back we stopped off on the London Road and went inside the Little Chef for Coca Cola and a hamburger. I'd never been inside before or had hamburger and fries. Stephan had a pink milkshake – it was very American.

The band was fascinated when I told them that this Little Chef was the very first ever to be opened in the whole of England. I'm full of these little gems according to Rich.

Scott stayed behind with me when the others went back to their flat and Mum said we could go for a short walk if we wanted. We wanted. We set off on our usual route around the village and mercifully this time none of the kids were stalking us.

The cruise had been great fun and everyone ate and drank too much and partied too hard, Scott said.

'You'd love it babe, there was so much to do on board and the shops and restaurants were amazing, so cool, so hip,' he said excitedly, eyes shining. 'And the people: so much money, so glamorous and sophisticated.'

We strolled round the recreation ground which was deserted for once.

'Tell me about the places you visited on shore.' I wanted to know everything. We held hands and every now and again Scott gave me a big hug and a kiss. It was wonderful to have him back.

'Well, the crew were great and we spent a lot of time with them, playing for them at night after we finished with the passengers,' he beamed. 'We played in The Pig, and all the showgirls and dancers were there and so were the other entertainers. We played with Jean Kent, remember her?'

'She's the one in *Crossroads* I think,' I said wondering what she was doing on the cruise. 'Was she a passenger then?'

'No, she was singing on the cruise, as an entertainer. Lots of people from TV and the radio do the cruises apparently, there's lots of money in it.'

'Sounds wonderful.' I loved *Crossroads*, it would be on TV just as I used to get in from school each afternoon.

'We went ashore a lot and went shopping in the markets and had a good look round the towns. Some of the ports were not too great though. All nice and pretty as the ship comes in, but when you go ashore and see the streets behind the facades, it is really horrid and dirty, and the poverty in some places was dreadful.' Scott screwed his face up as he recalled some of the places. 'Tangier was filthy and smelly, and the beggars – even little kids – were everywhere. Little kids coming up and trying to sell us their sisters and their mothers for you know what... You know,' he said, his eyes all wide expecting me to catch on – and I did.

'Grief!' was all I could manage as his words sank in.

'They thought we were a famous band, some called us The Rolling Stones, and followed us everywhere trying to sell us stuff. We had the devil's own job to get away from the hordes of begging kids and hawkers, we felt like the Pied Pipers of Hamlyn.'

'It sounds a bit frightening but so different.' I tried to imagine what it must have been like.

'It was a bit. We managed to barter our clothes for things, like your bag and bits and pieces. We kept being followed by Arabs who wanted to sell us hashish and stuff.'

'Hashish? What's that?'

'You know, drugs and stuff.' He looked around furtively as he said it.

I immediately felt guilty and looked around as well. It would be just my luck if Mrs Digby or another of Mum's spies was listening.

'Drugs!' I whispered, 'cripes'. I stopped and looked hard at him. 'And did you?'

'What?' He tried to look innocent. It didn't work.

'No, don't answer me, I don't want to know.' I was

worried and couldn't cope with the answer at the moment.

'OK,' he grinned. 'But honestly, we had such a laugh. Every morning we'd get woken up by our steward – we were treated like the officers on board – with a tray of beer and other alcoholic drinks and he would stand over us in a menacing way until we drank everything. At first we refused but he made it clear that wasn't an option.'

'How odd.' I was flummoxed.

'Yeah, he was cool though. His name was Vera.' Scott laughed out loud at the look on my face. 'Coz, he was – you know – and actually all the stewards are, you know, really camp, even more than Zak when he's on stage.'

'What? You mean...?'

'Yeah they are, don't look so prissy.'

'I'm not prissy, just surprised they're allowed to work there so openly.'

'They even wear their make-up and some dress in women's clothes when they're not on duty.'

We sat on the bench overlooking the fields next to the Rec. Someone was walking their dog in the distance. The cows had already gone for milking.

'When we went ashore Vera came up to us and said if we had any trouble, to let him know, and he opened his jacket and showed us a gun.' Scott nodded as I looked at him in disbelief. 'Seriously. They're hard nuts, those guys. They used to fight anyone who crossed them. You'd have laughed the night they had a big bust up in the restaurant where the Captain was entertaining the VIP passengers.'

He laughed at the memory and I waited for him to carry on.

'Do you want me to shut up?' he asked.

'No go on, it's fascinating.' I was interested and a little shocked, truthfully.

'Well, the Captain has a special table where he entertains the VIP guests each night, different people are invited and it's all silver service and posh. Anyway, this one evening we were all eating and chatting – we were on the table next to the Captain's table – when all of a sudden one of the stewards ran into the kitchen, and started yelling and shouting at the chef. All hell broke loose in there and we could hear lots of people shouting and pots and pans crashing, and crockery being broken, and all of a sudden the door burst open and the steward came flying out chased by the chef who was brandishing a huge meat cleaver, which he was trying to embed in the waiter's head. Behind them came the whole of the kitchen staff carrying pots and pans and knives.' He was talking fast, excited at the memory.

I sat open-mouthed and waited for him to carry on. The sun had started to go down and I thought we ought to make our way back in case Mum was getting annoyed.

'It was hilarious, the passengers all yelled and women screamed and the Captain started shouting for security who came and started arresting everyone, and they took them off to the Brig – that's a jail – they have one on board apparently, and they keep guns on board, too, so they told me after.'

'Wow, that's like something out of a film...' I said trying to imagine it all.

'It was unreal. And to top it off, after everyone had settled down, Joss went up to the Captain and told him he was a groovy guy and patted him on his bald head – he was such a short-arse and bald as a coot.'

Scott laughed and I giggled at Joss's cheek.

'There must have been some lovely girls, in the shows and travelling as passengers I suppose,' I said hoping it didn't sound as if I really wanted to know.

'We met lots. Some of the girls in the shows were stunning. Quite a few of the passengers were old, rich and on the look-out for a new husband mind you, and plenty of the younger women passengers were on the look-out for a rich husband as well. Bit of a cattle market to tell the truth. We had a lot of girls hanging around and got lots of phone numbers and messages from them.

On the last night everyone autographed the menus and we got lots of cheeky things written on ours.'

I practically seethed with jealousy, but decided not to push that one for fear of what I might discover, so I suggested we walk back home. We stood up and started heading back.

'I want you to come down to Brighton to meet my father and his new wife,' Scott blurted out suddenly, stopping and grabbing me in his arms.

'Why?' I mumbled against his chest, the smell of him so familiar now.

'Just want you to, haven't seen him in years, not since the wedding.' He kissed my cheek.

'Ok but you better ask Mum then. How are we getting there? We'd have to come back the same day.' Ever practical I always had to have a good plan to set before Mum.

'We'll get the train down and can be back the same day. So, how about next Saturday?'

Renza's Diary
July 26th 1968

The train arrived at the station in Brighton in the late morning sunshine and Scott and I walked to the carpark where his dad said he would meet us. I think Scott was just as nervous as me. He and his dad were a bit like strangers he told me, but he did get on with his new step-mother who was only seven years older than himself.

Mum gave in and agreed to let me go without a murmur. I think she has decided to let me see Scott because they will be gone in a few days and that will be that. She's told me several times not to attach myself to him too much because I would be, 'out of sight, out of mind' in no time.

We hadn't seen much of each other since last Friday because the band had been gigging all over the place and, anyway, Mum had got me spring cleaning and helping sort out the last minute things needed doing before we left for three years. I'd also tried to spend as much time with Nan as I could because she was worrying me.

Scott's dad wore a trilby hat and a smart sports jacket and trousers and highly polished brown shoes. He even wore driving gloves for goodness sake. Scott had warned me he was a bit of an old fart, very proper and correct and he wasn't wrong. He shook my hand formally and we got into the silver Rover – the seats still smelled of new leather, though he said he'd had the car years. It was spotless.

We drove in silence at about fifteen miles per hour, in the centre of the road and I felt really uncomfortable. Scott kept glancing anxiously at me and I tried to smile but my face felt frozen. His dad cleared his throat several times as if he were going to speak and then didn't say anything. It was dreadful.

After a while we arrived at a large detached house in a road not far from where Scott grew up, and he chatted about school and his mates and how he'd lost touch with them. He hoped to meet up with one of them, a bloke in a band, later on if there was time. Scott had gone to an all-boys grammar school and had been in the choir at church which surprised me. Apparently choir practice was a bit unruly, paper aeroplanes and darts flying around and he said they did the same during weddings. Very angelic.

His dad hardly spoke except to agree with him about something or other. A young dark-haired woman – Philippa, the step-mother – came to meet us in the sitting room, which was nice enough I guess, and made us a cup of tea and we had cake. We made small talk but I wasn't really paying attention as I felt so uncomfortable and ill at ease, and I let Scott chat to them as he had not seen them for ages.

His step-mother seemed quite bossy for someone so young and Scott's dad seemed to do everything she told him to do. She worked as some sort of posh secretary or something. I could imagine her running the place. Soon I was getting grilled about my family, what my dad did and what Mum did and what sort of school I went to, and what were my plans for my future and stuff like that.

I realised what Scott must feel like when Mum gives him the third degree. Barry McGuire's 'Eve of Destruction' kept playing in my head for some reason. Every now and again Scott would catch my eye and wink. I smiled brightly back at him, my head throbbing from the strain of it all.

After lunch – salad made by Philippa from stuff she'd grown herself with warm bread, also made by her fair hands – we got into the car and took a drive to somewhere along the sea front, where we stopped outside a guest house.

We were visiting relatives – aunts and uncles who owned the guest house and Scott's ancient grandfather, called Pop. I also met Scott's cousins, Skaggs and Jools who were very nice and friendly and about our age.

We had afternoon tea with them and my head was reeling from all their questions and information being given to me about individuals present, not present, or who had passed away. I knew I'd never remember any of it and Scott whispered he hadn't a clue who half of them were either.

Finally we said goodbye and headed back to his dad's house and the friend of Scott's was waiting for us, Cliff, bass player in some band Scott used to play with before he went to Jersey with his mum and joined bands there. Cliff and his girlfriend, whose name I never caught and neither did Scott, had a Robin Reliant – a red one – and when it was finally time to leave for the railway station, we all piled into it, Scott and me in the back with all Cliff's band gear and them in the front. He'd offered to take us and Scott's dad seemed relieved. So was I. Another trip down the centre of the road at fifteen miles an hour with a line of cars hooting behind us was something I gladly passed up. Even if it did mean squeezing into the back of the tiny three wheeler.

Scott said it was great seeing Cliff again and catching up on things. I was happy for him but it had bored me to death sitting with his family and then later with Cliff and his girlfriend listening to all their chatter about people and places and events which meant nothing to me. I'd drunk enough tea to start my own reservoir. I kept having to go and spend a penny and it was so embarrassing. All that tea!

On the way back from the station we stopped at the phone box and Scott rang his mum and told her what we'd been doing. He put her on the phone to me briefly but I could hardly hear her as his half-sister was airing her lungs in the background again. His mum wished me luck in Germany and hoped I could spend Christmas with them all in Jersey when Scott and the band were going to be over playing at a club called Lords.

I said I'd ask Mum, but I didn't hold out much hope. Scott said he would pay my airfare but Mum would never allow that. Imagine what he would expect in return for an airfare! The leather bag was bad enough!

Stella's Diary
July 31st 1968

It was nearly 3 o'clock in the afternoon. It was stiflingly hot despite a fan whirling above me, and the air was thick with the cloying scent of mixed antiseptics. Lying on the uncomfortable bed, I had been watching the clock on the wall in the Churchill Hospital's outpatients cubicle for the last hour. Under my hospital gown I was naked. I had several wedges of cotton wool anchored by sticking plasters fastened to several of my veins. I'd had blood tests and X-rays and two very uncomfortable and embarrassing examinations.

'Just stay there and have a little rest,' one of the trio of doctors had said cheerfully. 'We won't be long.'

While a nurse busied around just out of my eye-line, clattering metal things into other metal things and humming quietly to herself, I watched the hands on the clock move slowly round.

I hoped and prayed that today they'd have found out what was wrong with me, could give me some medicine or tablets or something to make me better and let me get on with my life.

Mike had said more or less the same thing when I told him I had this appointment. He also kept on about the holiday to Cornwall – less than four weeks away now – because he'd paid my share of the cost to Patsy and thought I really should be paying him back. I'd got fed up with saying that if I was ill, or had a hospital appointment then I couldn't and wouldn't go. And that I wouldn't be paying him for a holiday I didn't have. And honestly didn't want... but I hadn't been brave enough to say that. Yet. Anyway, if today's results were good I might feel completely different in three weeks' time. Maybe...

'Miss Deacon!' The youngest of the three doctors I'd seen earlier, swept in, followed by a nurse. He'd clearly drawn the short straw. 'Sorry to have kept you. Can you sit up? Good... Right, now, the news isn't very good I'm afraid...

um – do you have someone with you?'

Oh God! I stopped struggling to sit up and stared at him. 'My mum's in the waiting room – but... is it really bad?'

'Fetch Miss Deacon's mother, please nurse.' The doctor said, still smiling. Then he looked at me. 'It's complicated, Miss Deacon. It might be better to have someone else here – two pairs of ears and all that.'

I was going to die!

I knew it!

I burst into tears.

'Oh, lovie,' the clattering nurse dashed across and handed me a bundle of tissues. 'It's not that bad... come on... I know you've been through the mill, my love... come on – don't cry...'

Her kindness made me sob even more. By the time my frantic-faced mum came into the cubicle, I was awash.

'Oh, Stella!' Mum hugged me. 'Oh, good Lord – what have they done to you?'

'I'm going to die!' I howled. 'I'm going to die!'

'No, you're not.' The young doctor, looking slightly disturbed at my sobbing, said quickly. 'Of course you're not.' He looked at the notes on his clipboard. 'My dear Miss Deacon, while the results of these tests are possibly what you don't want to hear, I have at no time hinted that your condition is terminal.'

'There,' Mum smoothed my hair away from my face and handed me more tissues. I hadn't worn much eye make-up – and obviously no false eyelashes or sequins – but I still knew my mascara would have run. 'Come on, Stell – dry your eyes and let the doctor tell you what's happening.'

Between my sniffs and gulps – yes, I was pretty ashamed at falling apart so spectacularly, but honestly, I was petrified – the doctor said it all in an unemotional voice.

Again, today's tests had been inconclusive. It would appear – as far as they could tell – that I had some form of ongoing septic inflammation around the pelvic area caused, possibly, by one or more undiagnosed and untreated abscesses, and probably cysts, which could be ovarian but also may be adhering to my fallopian tubes and uterus. Mum squeezed my hand very, very tightly.

'It really does mean,' the doctor said, 'that I have to refer you upwards to Mr Glendenning's clinic. You need further exploratory treatment. Mr Glendenning is our top man here in all matters of this nature – one of the top Gynae Consultants in the country – you'll be in excellent hands. In an older patient I would have no hesitation in recommending an immediate and total hysterectomy, but as you're only 19...'

Mum and I looked at one another. Hysterectomy? An operation? Major surgery?

'Er...' I gulped, 'I hope I won't need that...'

The doctor nodded. 'So do I. And in the meantime, I do appreciate that you are in considerable pain, Miss Deacon, and I hope that we can sort this out very quickly for you. I'll pass all this on to Mr Glendenning's team, and also your local practitioner. You do understand all this?'

I nodded.

'Good. And do you have any questions?'

I shook my head. I had dozens but I didn't think he'd be able to give me the answers.

'Good,' the doctor shook Mum's hand. 'I hope we'll have all this sorted out for Stella very quickly, Mrs Deacon. I'll make the appointment with Mr Glendenning's clinic a priority. You should have a date through within eight weeks. In the meantime, please contact your local doctor if you need any further help.'

And he rushed out.

The nurse almost bundled Mum out of the way. 'I'll help you get dressed Stella – just take it easy, lovie – don't dislodge the cotton wool pads, there's a good girl, otherwise you'll bleed all over my nice clean floor.'

And for the first time that day, I almost laughed.

Renza's Diary
July 31st 1968

Scott and I had been out for a long walk after tea and he had to call his mum.

He asked me to wait outside the phone box which was a bit odd, but then I thought they must have something private to discuss. After about twenty minutes, during which time I'd been tooted at by two group vans passing by, which was a laugh, Scott banged on the window of the phone box. As if it was my fault... I had my purple and green psychedelic silk dress on and my long white lace up boots thankfully, so I knew I didn't look like a witch for a change. There are so many groups around these days. I hope he is not turning into my mum.

When he came out he said he wanted to pop up to his flat for a minute and chat to Rich and if I wanted I could go up with him. I wasn't too sure, because of what Mum would say. I'd have to creep up there without being seen by Mrs Digby for a start. But I'd never been up there and was curious.

'You can come and listen to some recordings we made if you want, see if you dig them or not,' he said as we crept along the path behind the shops heading for the stairs, both keeping an eye on my house and next door.

The flat was a bit of a mess, but clean, and the whole band was there with Rich. Stephan had gone to visit the White Knights, who he used to roadie for, before becoming their manager as well. They were selling their van to Narnia's Children, since Bessie was on her last legs. Then he was going to find the band a new place to live in Bedfordshire. Apparently the band needed a cheaper place to live and he thought Leighton Buzzard would suit them better and was near to the Knights as well. They needed to move within a week or so. More upheaval... more moving away.

Scott and Rich went into one of the bedrooms for a chat and I had a cup of tea with the band and listened to the songs they'd recorded on a very small reel to reel recording tape. The songs were good, I thought. Some had even been written by Zak and Scott.

They told me that one of them was written for me called, 'You Didn't Have To Go Away.'

That was news to me. Scott had written it on his own. Another one written for me, so they said, was called 'Because Of You Girl.' I was so overwhelmed by it all. I glowed inside and couldn't stop smiling. Scott promised me I could have tapes copied which is cool because Dad has a tape player with him in Germany.

After a while, Scott and Rich came back. I said goodnight to the band and Scott and I left the flat and made our way down the stairs. At the bottom he turned to me, took me in his arms and said, very seriously, 'Rich says, will you marry me?'

'What? Marry Rich? Why?' I was really taken aback and confused.

'Err? No, not Rich – me. Will you marry me?' He looked deeply into my eyes.

He was so earnest I almost laughed.

'Well? Will you marry me?'

'I can't, don't be silly, I'm only sixteen. My parents would kill me.' I still wasn't sure if he meant it – he looked serious enough – or if he was really messing with my head for kicks.

'Well, I don't mean now of course, I mean later on, maybe in a year or two.'

Scott kissed me again and I tried to focus my thoughts and take in what he was saying. My heart was doing a jitterbug in my chest and good old Keith Moon was on the drums in my ears again. I stood looking at him in the light from the overhead lamp, eyes shining, hair flopping over his forehead, his lovely mouth half smiling as he waited for me to answer him. I thought about his gorgeous body, long slim legs and those sexy hips and I knew, just knew, I was going to say yes.

Bugger Mum and Dad.

Renza's Diary
August 1st 1968

Talk about floating on air. I know I was behaving strangely, but I couldn't help it. I was going to get married to the most gorgeous, wonderful boy in the world, and I kept breaking into song without warning, and for some reason Gilbert and Sullivan's, 'Three Little Maids from School,' was great to sing at the top of my lungs.

Mum caught me singing heartily, dancing round the washing as I pegged it out, and banged on the kitchen window. 'What the hell are you doing? Half the bloody village can hear you. Put a cork in it!'

The Rottweiler next door stuck her head out of the bedroom window and made a big show of sighing and tut-tutting and when I blew her a kiss and waved, she nearly fell out. Even Donald sneaked a look from behind the sitting-room nets. I blew him a kiss too. I reckon I made his day.

Even doing the vacuuming wasn't such a chore. I danced back and forth with it, singing over the noise which made the kids giggle and Lucy hide behind the sofa.

I didn't care. Scott and I were getting married.

Soon they were all going to be history.

Renza's Diary
August 3rd 1968

I thought Mum would stop me going for a walk with Scott this afternoon when he called round, but she didn't say a word. Not like this morning.

'What the hell's wrong with you, all this bloody singing and dancing?' she asked when I skipped round the kitchen putting crockery from breakfast away, singing my head off. 'Are you drinking?'

'What? No of course not, how could I be drinking?'

'Well, something's going on, I'm not stupid. What's with the non-stop Victor Silvester and bloody Maria Callas all of a sudden?'

'Nothing, nothing's going on. I just feel like singing, I'm happy I guess.'

'Well that's a bloody first then!' She peered at me hard and shrugged. 'If it's that apology for a male specimen you're getting loved up about, forget it. As soon as you've gone he'll be on to the next one.'

'Nothing to do with Scott and he's not a specimen or an apology for anything, That's horrid.'

'You mark my words my lady, you are just another ship in the night. I know his sort.' She prodded my shoulder hard. 'You'd better not be up to no good either, or your father will tan his hide within an inch of his life, and you'll have me to answer to. Understood?'

'For crying out loud, now I can't sing or do anything. This is so unfair.' I ran out of the kitchen and upstairs to the bathroom, locking the door, tears burning my eyes and hatred searing my heart.

'Don't get too comfortable up there, I want to do my face before my appointment.' Mum yelled after me. I'd forgotten she had to have her wrists checked by the nurse this morning. I'd really like to do her face, I thought, as I blew my nose.

Scott came round after lunch and we went for our usual walk around the Rec. We couldn't stray far as the band was gigging later.

'Don't talk until we get to the Rec, she's got radar for ears.' I whispered as we closed our gate. Peg was behind us with her excuse for a dog – her Toy Poodle or whatever it's called. She supposedly 'walks' it every day though how the poor thing gets any exercise I don't know. She carries it everywhere.

He pulled me to him as soon as we got into the Rec out of sight of prying eyes.

'You've been crying.'

'I'm all right.' But I wasn't. Tears welled as soon as I spoke.

'Don't cry, I hate it when you cry.' He hugged me close and stroked my hair. 'What happened? Has your mum been on at you again?'

'She's just so – you know – horrid. She can't be nice for one second. Always saying nasty stuff and getting at me for no reason. I can't stand it.' I sniffed and fished in my pocket for my hanky.

Scott took it and wiped my eyes and nose and kissed my cheek. 'Don't let her get to you, she's just a miserable old woman who hates everyone and everything.'

'She says you'll forget me as soon as I've gone. I'll be another ship in the night.' More tears fell and Scott wiped them away again.

'What's with the ships?' He laughed. 'Flipping heck.'

'It's not funny. I was happy then she started on about me singing, and you and me...'

'I heard you singing, it was lovely. You should sing more often. I loved it.' His turquoise eyes twinkled as he looked into my red rimmed, swollen eyes. I hoped my nose wouldn't drip.

'I like it when you're happy and you're not a flipping ship passing me in any night, so stop being silly. Come on, give me a lovely smile.' He tipped my chin towards his face and bravely kissed my nose. I tried not to sniff.

'Nearly, try harder,' he laughed as I tried to smile.

After a few more kisses on my nose, I couldn't help myself – he always made me smile. And my nose miraculously dried up.

'There, that wasn't too hard was it?'

We walked for a while longer, chatting about the future and getting married. It was all a dream really. I couldn't believe it. When I was with him everything seemed possible.

'You should do one of those postal courses, you know, for journalism.' It came out of the blue. 'I've seen them advertised in the papers, The London School of Journalism, and you can do it even if you live overseas. I'll try and get the details for you if you want. You mustn't give up on your dreams Renza, even when we get married, you should follow your own dreams.'

'I've never heard of it, I bet it costs an arm and a leg. I can't afford anything like that and Mum and Dad wouldn't pay for it either, but thanks for thinking of me.'

'When the band makes some money, I can pay for it. Don't worry about them. I want you to be happy and if doing something like that makes you happy, I'd pay anything,' he said and kissed me long and hard.

In that moment I believed him.

Renza's Diary
August 15th 1968 – 8am

Scott and I said goodbye before the taxi arrived to take Mum, the kids and me to the station, a short walk normally but with so much luggage we had no choice but to book one.

Nan had been round yesterday with my aunt and uncle to say goodbye and it broke my heart to see her face and her tears. She looked such a lonely figure as she walked back home with them. We watched and waved her out of sight. My aunt and uncle would look after her, but....poor old Nan.

Since they didn't have a gig, I'd managed to say goodbye to the band and Rich, spending the rest of the evening with Scott yesterday, after Nan had gone. We were both so choked up we could hardly speak as we had our last 'date,' walking in the College for the last time.

When we did speak it was about keeping in touch, not forgetting about getting married and when, if ever, we should tell our parents, and when we could see each other again. I couldn't bear it. Tears were near the surface the whole time and I kept thinking three years is a lifetime and what if I never got to come back and visit before then?

Scott told me the band had a possible tour of Germany on the cards at some point, but he didn't know when or where they might go. He was going to Jersey in October and would be staying there for Christmas as they'd been booked at The Tropicana, and then they were off to France for New Year playing in Paris and Toulouse, before coming back to Leighton Buzzard where they were meant to move during the next week or so.

I felt a wave of panic. What if I never got a forwarding address?

Scott laughed and said that he would never let me go and would always find me wherever I was. We were meant to be together forever, and we would be.

He hummed softly in my ear as we held each other round the side of the house waiting for the taxi, The Marbles' latest song, 'Only One Woman,' now forever, 'our' song.

'Don't ever forget the words; they mean what I mean.' His voice broke as he whispered to me.

I sobbed silently into his shoulder. 'I won't.'

'Don't forget to send me a photo for under my pillow.'

He squeezed me tight and I clung to him unable to speak. I nodded. I'd soaked the front of his black shirt, but I didn't care. I knew I looked a mess.

After a while I managed to whisper, 'Don't forget to write to me. You've got the address of the base where Dad is, and when you get the photos from Madeira printed, promise you'll send me one. I'll sleep with it near my heart every night and as soon as the moon is up, don't forget, we both look at it the same time and think of each other like we agreed.'

'I promise. I promise everything. Don't forget I love you and you are the only woman for me – I want only one woman – he sang quietly for the last time; and I've got the picture of the woman I love etched on my heart forever. I love you, Renza.'

I loved the way lyrics of songs meant so much to him and how he sang them to me. He had one for every occasion. So romantic. I'll never be able to hear The Marbles without reliving this moment.

'I love you, too, and I'll find a telephone somewhere so I can ring you when you're in Jersey, and I'll write with the days and times I'm able to ring you, once I know.'

'I hope your nan will be all right. I know I've never met her, but do you want me to call in on her and see if she is all right, while we are still in the village, I mean?'

'Oh, that's so sweet, but my uncle and his wife are close to her and will keep an eye on her, and she has a good friend she goes out and about with sometimes – Mrs. Dubarry – so I think people are going to keep her company while she gets used to us not being here, and Dad wants her over for Christmas anyway.'

How wonderful of him to offer, I thought.

He kissed me again, his voice choked up, on the verge of tears. 'Make sure you write to me tomorrow, even if you're tired out. Don't go messing around with those German blokes either, or I'll be over there to sort them out.'

'I won't – and you make sure all those girls keep their distance and you aren't tempted,' I whispered, trying to smile and make a joke of it.

'Renza! The taxi is here. Come and sort these bags out,' Mum called through the open front door as Crispin shot round the corner to find me.

'Renza is kissing! Renza is kissing!' he started to shout as I put my hand over his mouth and he tried to bite me.

Scott let go of me and Crispin head-butted him somewhere he shouldn't have, and poor Scott doubled up in agony as Crispin shot off before I could break his neck.

Our special last moments together had been ruined and we didn't get a chance for any further conversation or a proper goodbye kiss. It was all go with bags, giant pandas, and rounding up kids and scrambling into the taxi.

Scott shouted goodbye to Mum and the kids and looked longingly at me and I bit my lip as I watched him fade into the distance, waving and waving us out of sight.

Renza's Diary

August 15th 1968 – 10pm

Dad was waiting for us as our plane landed at Dusseldorf airport. He had a mini-van with a driver on loan from the base. We were all too tired to speak much as our plane had been delayed, so by the time he collected us, the kids were whining and Mum was in one of her 'Don't you dare say a word,' moods. Wonderful.

We'd been given two flats to live in, one above the other. It was all very German and bleak. The outside walls were grey concrete and there was a huge cellar which smelled funny and looked a bit creepy. I was given a room of my own upstairs, thank goodness, which I was going to be allowed to turn into a bed-sitting room. My parent's room was downstairs and the kids had rooms next to mine.

The view from my front bedroom window looked out on to a sort of green with trees at the front, and behind the trees was a row of those horrid grey concrete flats the Germans are so fond of. Dad said these were married quarters for the army families.

The rear bedroom window opened out on to a sort of balcony which overlooked a short stretch of grass and bushes – hardly a garden – and behind was a row of houses belonging to German villagers. All pretty depressing, though Dad says there is a Sports Platz – playing field – up the road a way and from there the views of the river Ruhr are fabulous. I don't care if it is the most beautiful place on earth, it meant nothing to me. I won't be walking there with Scott.

How I missed Scott. I thought my heart would break.

Stella's Diary
August 15th 1968

'A week tomorrow and we'll be going away,' Patsy said, smirking. 'I've almost finished my packing – just got a few more bits to buy. Are you excited?'

'Not really,' I didn't look at her. 'If any of you had bothered to ask me *before* you booked it, then I'd have said I wasn't going. And honestly, right now I'd be scared to go. I mean, it's hundreds of miles away and if I was ill...'

'You sound like my nan,' Patsy spat. 'Like an old woman! You can't expect Mike to go on his own, it isn't fair!'

'He won't be on his own. He'll have you and Sam, and he's paid for me so you're not out of pocket and—'

'I don't know why he puts up with you!' Patsy glared at me. 'You're always moaning about being ill. I don't even know what he sees in you. You might be a bit of a brainbox with your A levels and your story writing, but you're no fun. Anyway, if you don't want to go with him, I know someone who will.'

We were sitting outside the pub again. Mike and Sam were inside playing darts. My pains had been on and off – and I'd had an appointment through the post for Mr Glendenning's clinic – in September.

'Really?' I raised my bald and un-sequinned eyebrows. 'That's what you said before. I didn't believe you then and I don't believe you now.'

Patsy gave a little smug shoulder-shimmy. 'Well, then, that's all you know, Miss Clever-Clogs.'

I leaned across the trestle table. 'Go on, then. Spill. You know you're dying to. But let me tell you one thing, I *know* Mike has quite a few girls who fancy him, but he's going out with me – and he won't be taking any of them in my place. So, if you know so much, tell me her name. No, see you can't, can you? She doesn't exist! You're making it all up and—'

'Bernice Perkins.'

I sat, stupefied. Silent. It was a hot evening but I was suddenly icy cold. I just stared at Patsy.

Patsy stared back.

I swallowed. 'And who is she when she's at home?'

'No one. No one...' Patsy spluttered, going very red. 'I just made her up to annoy you.'

But alarm bells were ringing. I wasn't stupid.

'No, you didn't.' I said. My voice sounded like it was someone else speaking. 'You know her. That name just tripped off your tongue.'

'I just wanted to make you cross,' Patsy insisted. 'Because you're not coming to Cornwall... forget it, I was just being stupid.'

'Rubbish!' I started to shake. I wasn't sure if I was angry or scared or both. 'Who the hell is Bernice Perkins?'

Patsy looked as if she was going to burst into tears.

I shrugged. 'Ok, I'll go inside and ask Mike who she is, shall I? I mean, if he's taking her to Cornwall in my place, I guess he'll know who she is.'

I stood up, pushing myself away from the trestle table so violently that Patsy's Babycham spilled.

'Don't! Stella! Don't!'

I looked down at Patsy. I was freezing cold and felt faint – nothing to do with the pains – everything to do with the fact that this Bernice Perkins was real. I knew she was real. And so did Patsy.

'Ok – before I ask Mike – you tell me who she is.'

Patsy chewed her lips, avoided my eyes, and tried mopping up the Babycham with her hankie.

'Patsy!!!!'

'She's a hairdresser. At Lynette's Salon. In Ashworthy.'

I clung to the edge of the trestle table. And exhaled. My heart was thundering in my ears. 'And Mike... Mike – um – knows her...'

'Yes.'

I leaned down. 'How well does he know her, Patsy?'

'Oh... they're just – um – friends... she's – um – nothing. I mean – oh, Stella – forget it. For God's sake don't tell Mike – he'll... oh, shit.'

'I won!' Mike said happily as he emerged from the pub. 'Best of three! Drinks are on Sam so he's at the bar now – and being a bad loser...' He stopped and looked first at me, then at Patsy. 'What the hell is wrong with you two? Had a row?'

'Congratulations on winning the darts match,' I smiled glitteringly at him. 'And who's Bernice Perkins?'

'Jesus fucking Christ!' Mike glared at Patsy. 'You told her? You stupid big-mouthed cow!'

'Thanks,' I said, blinking back tears and swallowing the bile that was gathering in my throat. 'Well done, Mike. Now there's no need to go through the third degree. No doubt Bernice is as small-minded and boring as you are – so you're well-matched and I hope you'll be very happy together. Goodbye.'

I turned away and started to run down the lane that led to the main road and home.

'Stella!' Mike's voice followed me. 'Stella! Please! For God's sake – don't go! Come back – listen – she's nothing – it meant nothing! Stella!'

'Go to hell!' I howled. 'Go to bloody hell!'

***

'Stell?' Dad looked up from his paper as I hurtled through the back door and into the kitchen. He moved one of the cats to one side and stood up. 'God, Stell, are you ill? What's happened? What's the matter?'

'Nothing...' I muttered. 'I'm fine, Dad. Just fine. I'm going upstairs.'

'You're crying, are you in pain? Have we got the pills you need? Your mum's out – Townswomen's Guild – it's the miniature garden in a saucer contest tonight and she's done Versailles. Oh, Stell, love. Come here...'

He folded me against him. He smelled of home, of safety

159

and happiness. I burst into tears against his old, worn jumper. Two of the dogs tried to join in.

'There, lovie, there...' Dad held me like he had when I was little and had woken with a bad dream. 'You cry it out. Do you feel really ill? I can get a hot water bottle.'

I cried some more and snuffled incoherently into his chest.

It was over. Me and Mike. My first – my only – proper relationship. Finished.

I told him. I stumbled over some of the words but he got the gist.

'Right,' he said, gently disentangling himself. 'Now, you sit down here... there... and I'll make you a cup of coffee with milk, and we'll have a splash or two of rum in it, and then we'll talk about it again. Ok?'

Obediently, I sat at the kitchen table. The cats twined round me, the dogs sat at my feet. The kitchen, cluttered, scruffy and in need of decorating, was like the most fabulous place in the world. A haven. Gradually, gradually, the tears subsided.

The pains in my stomach were now replaced with a massive ache in my heart. It really did hurt – right under the ribs. My heart was broken... well, badly bruised anyway – but not quite as much as my pride.

Mike had found someone else. Someone better than me. And everyone knew about it – everyone except me. Oh, the humiliation...

I knew I'd never trust another boy as long as I lived.

Stella's Diary
August 22nd 1968

The mid-morning bus from Harbury Green to Ashworthy seemed to be taking ages, dawdling through the villages, stopping what seemed like every 30 seconds or so to pick up or drop off half a dozen women with children and/or shopping.

I'd taken the day off work today – not because I was ill this time, the pains had been dealt with by the trusty Feminax the minute they reared their head – but an official day's holiday, because there was something I had to do. I'd dressed very carefully in a rainbow print floaty mini-dress and my long white boots. I'd even done the sequins.

I hadn't seen or heard from Mike since the break-up – and I'd had a week of very mixed emotions: suddenly crying for no reason and then being swamped by a feeling of relief that it was over – because I'd always known it would have to be over at some point – then crying again because it had been so lovely to start with and I'd miss him being around and feeling lonely and sad. Then getting really angry and hurt because he'd been two-timing me – and then the tears started all over again...

Mum and Dad had been great, and Vix had managed to hide her delight that Mike, the weasel, was out of my life, and say all the right things and be lovely to me.

I didn't expect to hear from Mike again. Neither of us was on the phone at home, and he lived and worked on the other side of Harbury Green so we could always manage to avoid one another. And it wasn't as if we'd left records or books or anything at each other's houses. No, it was over. A clean break. I'd had a boyfriend and now it was over and I was single again. It would all be ok. That's what I kept telling myself.

It didn't always work.

However, I did convince myself that all I needed now was for the forthcoming appointment at the Churchill to say that there was a miracle cure for my messed-up innards, and without the pains and the worry, I'd be footloose and fancy-free and able to start a whole new stage of my life.

Well, that's how it would go if I was writing a story – I had a feeling it probably wasn't going to be that easy in real life.

The bus eventually pulled into Ashworthy's market square, and I stood on the cobbles, taking deep breaths of the hot, summery air and looking at everyone bustling around in their bright summer clothes. But I wasn't here to sight-see or enjoy the view – no, I was on a mission.

I headed away from the town centre, past the cinema where Mike and I had watched Up the Junction so recently, and into one of the side streets. Lynette's Hairdressing Salon was right at the end, taking up two shops fronts and gaily painted in pink and white.

I took a deep breath. I'd told no one what I was doing or where I was going – I knew Mum and Vix would have tried to stop me – but for me, it was the right thing to do.

I pushed open the door. It pinged with a little bell and, as I stood at the desk, a middle-aged lady, all big auburn curls and pink nylon coverall, bustled towards me.

The salon was hot and sweet-scented and very busy, with at least half a dozen hairdressers, all young, all dressed in mini-length pink nylon, either washing or curling or cutting hair, or checking how their clients were doing under the hood dryers.

'Good morning,' the middle-aged lady, whose name badge pronounced she was indeed Lynette, beamed at me. 'And how may I help you? Do you have an appointment?'

And yes, she did look slightly askance at my shock of coal-black, layered, back-combed, spiky hair.

'No,' I smiled at her. 'But I'd like to make one if that's possible.'

'Yes, yes of course. Have you been to us before?'

'No, but you come highly recommended by a friend of mine.'

Lynette beamed even more as she reached for the huge

desk diary. 'Wonderful – we do appreciate word of mouth recommendations. Now – what were you thinking of having done – and when would you like to come in? And do you have a particular stylist in mind?'

'Well, my hair's such a mess, I want a complete change. And yes, I do have someone in mind.' I crossed my fingers. 'Actually, my friend's hair was so fab that I hoped I could have the same hairdresser for mine?' I gave a little laugh and shook my head. 'I mean, look at it – it's going to take some work... I wonder if she'd have time to advise me now and then I'll make the appointment?'

'Yes, yes, of course. A good idea.' Lynette continued to look ecstatic at new business. 'Do you know her name?'

'Betty... um... Beryl... no! Bernice! That's it... Bernice...'

'Oh, yes – Bernice is very good. Very good indeed. I'm sure she'll be able to help you – I'll see if she can give you a few minutes to discuss the appointment.'

And Lynette wobbled off towards the back of the salon.

I could feel my heart thundering and my palms were sweating.

And then – there she was.

Bernice.

Undulating towards me in her micro-mini pink nylon overall. She was pretty. In a plump and blurred sort of way. And her hair was very blonde and piled high on top of her head with artfully-arranged tendrils snaking down either side of her face. Her eyeshadow was blue and her lipstick sugar-pink. She was probably my age but looked older. Like Patsy. I was sure they'd get on like a house on fire.

For a moment as Bernice approached the desk, smiling a rather vacuous but sweet smile, I wondered if she'd know who I was. I was pretty sure if she knew about me then she'd know about my wacky hairstyle and the sequins. I'd given her the chance...

But she was either a very good actress or she had no idea at all about who I was. She wasn't showing any signs of recognition. Mike had clearly not bothered to describe me to her. I obviously wasn't that important.

'Hello,' she smiled at me. The sugar-pink lipstick was also on her teeth. Her accent was pure Berkshire. 'Lynette says you'd like me to do your hair...' She stared at it. 'It's a bit weird... did you do it yourself?'

'I did. It shows, doesn't it?' I managed a little laugh. 'But now I'd like it done properly. A complete change. Maybe go blonde or have a perm or something.' I crossed my fingers even more tightly. I was actually quite amazed to find that I didn't hate her. 'I'll leave it you.'

Bernice giggled. 'Well, I do like a challenge. I don't think going blonde would be a good idea on top of all that black dye – maybe we'd have to strip it out over several appointments... a perm might be quite nice though... now, when would you like to come in?'

'As soon as possible, please.'

Bernice hauled the big desk diary towards her and flicked through to the pages with her name on them.

I swallowed and leaned forward. 'How about one day next week?'

'Oh – I'm so sorry...' she smiled hugely at me. 'I can't do next week at all. I'm going on holiday.'

Walk away now, I told myself. Walk away now.

I didn't.

I smiled. 'Oh, you lucky thing. I've heard Polperro is fab at this time of year.'

The sugar-pink mouth gaped.

I sighed. 'I'm sorry, but I honestly don't want you or anyone else to do my hair. I love my hair. I just came in to give you this – you'll need it far more than I do...'

And delving into my bag I dropped the Woolworth's wedding ring on to the diary page.

Frowning, she looked down at it and then up at me.

'Oh...' the penny dropped. 'You're...'

'Yes, I am. Goodbye, Bernice. Enjoy playing at being Mrs Metcalfe – and good luck. You'll probably need it.'

Before she could say anything else, I pinged my way out of the door. And then I ran away from Lynette's Salon and towards the bus stop without looking back.

Renza's Diary
August 29th *1968*

Scott's first letter was written on the 16th, telling me how much he missed me, how much he loved me, and that he'd gone to the local pub with Mo to drown his sorrows, and how the band had had a big fight when Joss couldn't get into the flat one night and smashed the door down in his temper.

He said that he was worried about the Russian invasion of Czechoslovakia and spoke of the riots in Paris by students or something, and he promised undying love, making me more miserable and hating this God-forsaken place even more. He sent me his new address as they were moving the following weekend to Leighton Buzzard.

I wrote back the same day, pouring my heart out to him, how thoroughly miserable I was and how I was missing him so much I couldn't eat or sleep properly. I felt totally bereft. I told him we were on a 'full alert' because of the Russians and things were pretty scary, but not to worry, we had nuclear missiles if we were attacked. I'm sure that comforted him as much as me.

I told Scott I haven't seen many young Germans living locally, everyone seems so old, dressed mostly in black, and miserable looking. Mum says the youth have left for the cities and work opportunities. I wrote that I knew he'd be happy to know there weren't any boys here to tempt me. There're mostly young army families here, with their little kids, and a few Ministry of Defence families like ours, but no-one around my age.

I told Scott the flats we have are on top of each other – on one side of a little green with other quarters opposite. A few steps lead up to the green from the street where other army families live in proper houses. In the war the village had been flooded by the RAF bombers known as The Dam Busters, with their bouncing bombs. I remember seeing the film. It must have been terrifying. Every building in the village has water marks where the river had risen up the walls. I told Scott I found it a depressingly grey place, lacking in any sort of life and he should look up the local dams in Britannica.

Most families go to the Mess for Sunday lunch and they usually show a movie in the afternoons. They showed two on Sunday. I've seen *The Sound of Music* – not my thing at all, and *Guess Who's Coming to Dinner* with Sidney Poitier. I love him. It's something to look forward to I suppose, as long as they don't show old fogey films.

Going down the steep cobbled streets is horrid, and Mum makes me walk behind her as she's embarrassed at the way the old women lean out of the windows shouting and laughing at my fashions. I'm only wearing what everyone in England wears: minis, midis, maxi dresses and hipster trousers. Nothing radical. The locals are openly hostile to the families, and I told Scott that's because I'm creating a spectacle of myself with my fashions according to Mum. He'd laugh at that I'm sure. It had to be my fault.

It's a good job we can go into Dortmund to shop at the NAAFI a couple of times a week, because I remember little German from the last time we lived here, and Mum's never been good with languages, so shopping locally is not on. I can imagine Scott laughing when he reads about the German drivers who take us to NAAFI. They keep asking us to buy them coffee, cigarettes, and booze. Apparently it is still rationed in Germany. They drive like lunatics, just like those in Naples he told me about, hands waving all the time and turning round in the driver's seat to chat, not that we understand half of what they say.

The Mess is open all day every day and every evening too. There's always something on entertainment-wise and it seems a lot of men spend most of their time there when not working. Narnia's Children would love the bar, I told Scott, all the drinks are really cheap. The building is where Goering used to give big

Nazi speeches during the war. It's creepy.

I've been given special membership so I can accompany Dad to events if Mum can't – when Mum is in a huff more like – and so I can go into the Mess bar as apparently they'll turn a blind eye to my age on Tombola and Quiz nights. Big deal. Mum and Dad let me go with them recently and one of the army wives babysat the kids. I'll be turning into Darby and flipping Joan if I'm not careful. I don't know if I can stand three years of this.

We've got TV here, but it is all in German of course. They seem obsessed with programmes about the war and concentration camps and stuff like that but I haven't bothered with it much. Dad likes to watch it. I think it gives him an excuse to be on his own in the sitting-room, because Mum won't go in there when it's on.

Renza's Diary
September 2nd 1968

Scott's written several times so far. I love getting his letters and hearing all about Narnia's Children and what they're up to. He sent me his photo in his last letter, taken in Madeira. He looked so sexy and handsome, I couldn't stop looking at it. It's under my pillow in a plastic sleeve and I kiss it goodnight before I go to sleep.

He also remembered to send me the tape recordings of the songs he'd written for me which I first heard in their flat. It makes me cry hearing them.

I sent him a copy of the photo I had taken for my ID card here. He said I looked gorgeous in it. The letters and photos serve only to enhance my misery and despair. I'll wither away like the old people in the village long before I get to go home to England and Scott again. He will have found someone young, beautiful and trendy long before then. I'm doomed.

I must bore him to death with my letters telling him about the kids, the NAAFI and what's going on in the Mess. I have *such* an exciting life in comparison to his...

Stella's Diary
September 12th 1968

'We're going out!' Vix bounced into our kitchen after a cursory knock on the back door. 'And grab your brolly, Stella, it's tipping down out there.'

The dogs rushed to greet her. The cats, curled in front of the coke boiler, didn't bother. Mum and I had just finished tea. Dad wasn't home from work yet.

'Blimey, you're drowned!' I pushed my plate away. 'And going out? Are we? Have I forgotten something?'

Vix shook off the raindrops and grinned. 'No. Spur of the moment. Jeff's doing overtime and I've got a bit of a treat in store for you. You do feel ok, don't you?'

'I'm ok. But I'm not sure about going out.'

'Go on, Stell,' Mum said. 'I'll clear the table and wash up. You run along. It'll do you good to get out for the evening. You've been nowhere since you and Mike... well, you know...'

Yes, I knew.

'Ok. Give me time to get ready and —'

'You don't need to get ready. You'll be fine as you are.' Vix eyed-up my boring work outfit of neat black skirt and cream blouse. 'We're not going far, and we're not out to impress anyone, so no need for make-up or hair or anything like that either. And don't ask me where — it's a surprise. Just find your boots and your mac and your umbrella and we'll be off.'

An evening out would be nice for a change, I thought, as I rummaged through the corner cupboard in the kitchen where we kept coats and shoes and lots of other miscellaneous stuff. Dad always called it the avalanche cupboard. It was aptly named, I thought, as I fought my way through a mass of coats until I found my PVC mac.

Vix and I had bought or macs at the same time — hers was electric blue and mine was scarlet — and they just skimmed the tops of our thighs. We had matching long white PVC boots, too. The rest of us, in between, got wet.

Mum shook her head, chuckling. 'You both look very sweet and fashionable, but neither of you look exactly waterproof. You need a good gabardine and a sou'wester apiece.'

'Mrs Deacon!' Vix pulled a face. 'Really! You'd make us a laughing stock! Come on, Stella – let's go.'

Ten minutes later, having splish-splashed our way along Harbury Green's darkening, deserted and wind-swept roads, with rain dripping from the edges of our umbrellas, trickling down our macs and leaking into our boots, we reached our destination: Vix's Nanny Ivy's house.

For as long as we could remember, Vix and I had shared our grandparents, so Nanny Ivy's house was as familiar to me as my own. I loved it: it was crammed full of fat furniture and every surface was covered with nick-nacks and ornaments, all mementos from Nanny Ivy's many seaside coach trips.

Nanny Ivy shook her head. 'Lovely to see you both, but what a night to pick for visiting, our Vix. More like Christmas than early September. Come along in the pair of you! You look like drowned rats! Here's some towels, no Vix, love – don't put those macs there – let 'em drip in the sink – I'll get the kettle on and make us a nice cuppa. You go through to the living room. I've lit the fire.'

So there we were. Me, Vix and Nanny Ivy, sitting round her little table in front of the fire, drinking tea from big white cups, listening to the rain pitter-pattering against the windows and Vix's Grampy Wilf snoring softly in his big armchair.

It was lovely and cosy of course, but a bit disappointing and surely not what Vix had meant as a treat in store?

Nanny Ivy beamed at me. 'Now, Stella, Vix says what with your tummy troubles and you and young Mike not courting any longer, you want to know what the future holds, is that right?'

And then the penny dropped! With an almighty clang!

I grinned at Vix. 'You! You might have told me!'

'And then you wouldn't be here,' Vix chuckled. 'I know you don't believe in Nanny Ivy's fortune telling, but I do and I thought if she could give you some good news about the future it'd stop you worrying.'

Nothing was going to stop me worrying, least of all Nanny Ivy's sooth-saying, but I thought it would be rude to say so. 'But what if the future looks bad?' I asked. 'I mean, I might not believe in any of it, but...'

'I never give bad news,' Nanny Ivy interrupted. 'I'll always warn against something and suggest another path to take if the portents aren't good – there's always a choice to be made. And no! Leave that cup, Stella! I'll do your tea leaves as well.'

I obediently returned my cup to its saucer. 'As well as...?'

'The tarots, my love. The tarots.'

Oh, the tarots – of course!

Vix and I had played with Nanny Ivy's many sets of tarot cards for as long as I could remember. We'd played Snap and Happy Families and built card houses, and I'd loved the ancient mystical illustrations and the jewel-colours – but as for their alleged fortune-telling properties, I'd always been a total disbeliever.

Mind you, Nanny Ivy had lots of regular clients in Harbury Green who called for readings – including my own nans – and they all swore by her and her turn of the cards.

'Shall we get started?' Vix switched off the standard lamp, so the only illumination in the room came from the dancing, flickering fire. 'I've never been allowed to sit in on a reading before and I can't wait to find out what's going to happen.'

I glared at Vix across the table and shook my head, as Nanny Ivy handed me the pack of cards. Vix grinned back at me. She knew she'd won.

'Hold them tight for a moment, Stella.' Nanny Ivy said. 'That's right. Good girl. Now cut them... and again... lovely... now I'll have them back – thank you.'

Nanny Ivy took the cards I'd handled, deftly shuffled the

pack, and started dealing out the ornate cups, wands, coins, hearts and pentangles before turning them face up.

Vix leaned forward. 'Oooh look, Stella – the tower – oh no it isn't – it's the lovers!'

'Hush,' Nanny Ivy frowned, but kindly. 'These are turning up for Stella, not you.'

I watched as Nanny Ivy's heavily-veined hands flicked at the cards. The Lovers... the Hanged Man... and Death... Oh my God.

Vix gave a little scream.

Nanny Ivy sighed heavily. 'For heaven's sake, girls! Shush!'

'But it's death!' Vix said, sounding rather too ghoulishly excited for my liking.

'Shut up,' I groaned.

Nanny Ivy sat back. 'Right. Stella. These cards are fascinating – because they all link to your health and your future.'

'And death,' I sighed. 'So please don't tell me anymore. I honestly don't want to know.'

'Yes you do,' Nanny Ivy insisted. 'The Death card doesn't mean the end of life – far from it! Death just indicates the end of what's happening to you now. It signifies change, transformation and healing... so it's a really good card for you.'

I said nothing but I wasn't convinced. Not even a little teeny weeny bit convinced. I still thought it was all mumbo-jumbo.

'Look, Stella,' Nanny Ivy continued to tap the cards. 'The Hanged Man here means that you will soon be given a chance to let go of your past life and experience something new. That could be a new job or...'

'A new boyfriend!' Vix chirped happily. 'See, Stella – it's all really cool.'

Nanny Ivy frowned again at the interruption. 'Well, yes, maybe. However, the Hanged Man turned together with Death, means that all the current bad times will be taken away. In a

173

nutshell, the cards are telling you that you will get better, you will feel well again and your health won't be a problem anymore.'

'Really?' I frowned. 'Are you sure? You're not just being kind?'

'No, my love,' Nanny Ivy smiled gently. 'The cards are always truthful – and so am I.'

'But,' Vix said, 'you've left out the Lovers card, Nan. As well as Stella getting better it must mean she'll have a new boyfriend. And hopefully a much better one than Mike.'

Nanny Ivy shook her head. 'Don't be reading too much into the Lovers, young Vix. None of these cards should be taken at face value, you should know that by now. No, the Lovers usually mean a person being a bit torn. They can mean that your heart wants to do one thing but your head advises another. It could mean a new boyfriend for Stella, of course, or a new job, or a new way of life – but whichever of those it is, Stella will have to choose between her head and her heart. And it won't be an easy decision.'

Still nonsense. I giggled. 'Thank you. That was fun... I may not believe in it, but it all sounds ok.'

'Ah, but we haven't finished yet – the tarots have given us the story so far – but there could be more.' Nanny Ivy said briskly. 'Give us your tea cup Stella, there's a love.'

I watched, fascinated, as Nanny Ivy swirled the dregs of my tea, upturned the cup into the saucer so quickly it was like a magician's sleight of hand, and then peered into the remaining leaves.

'Well I never!' Nanny Ivy's eyes shone. 'There's a turn-up!'

'*What*?' Vix and I said at the same time.

'Well,' Nanny Ivy sat back in her chair. 'You're a lucky girl, Stella. The cards have said you'll soon be cured of your illness and have the chance of adventures – and now the tea leaves have predicted that you will have a new love in your life – and very soon.'

Wow! I really tried not to laugh.

'Cool....' Vix breathed. 'See, Stella – I told you it was all going to be ok. When is he going to be here, Nan? Is it someone we already know? Who is it? Is it -?'

'Hold your horses,' Nanny Ivy chuckled. 'That's the funny thing – the tea-leaves have never been so strong in their message. They say that Stella's new love is going to be a tall, dark handsome stranger from over the seas...'

My shriek of derisive laughter drowned out the drumming of the rain, the crackling of the fire, Grampy Wilf's snoring, and Vix's whoops of excitement.

Dear Lord in heaven! I really should have seen that one coming! The tall dark stranger line! What a load of complete twaddle!

Renza's Diary
September 14th 1968

Something terrible has happened. Dad rushed home from work at lunchtime with a telegram from Mum's brother. Nan has had a stroke or something and is in a coma in hospital and it seems she won't live.

Mum took the news really badly. We all did. Apparently Nan had been on a coach trip to Derry and Thom's in London, where she'd had afternoon tea on the roof garden with a friend. On the way home she'd complained of a headache. She wanted to nap, she told her friend, but when the coach stopped her friend couldn't rouse her and she was rushed to hospital, but there seemed to be no hope.

Dad's booked Mum and me on the first plane from Dusseldorf – he thought she would need me with her – and he's taken time off to look after the kids, who are all in school except Crispin and Lucy, so the kids won't be too much trouble for him to cope with.

We arrived in England early evening and my uncle met us at London airport with the news that Nan had died whilst we were in the air. She'd had a brain haemorrhage apparently and never regained consciousness. It was something of a blessing – poor Nan would've died of shame had she woken up in hospital without a change of undies. Nan was terrified of hospitals.

Through my tears and grief, I chuckled at this thought, a bit of her Irish coming out in me. Sorry Nan.

I kept thinking of poor Nan, telling us she would never see us again and wondering how she knew. She died almost a month to the day we'd said goodbye to her.

Renza's Diary
September 20th 1968

Nan's funeral was so sad. It rained the whole time but there were so many people there, even people who had known her since she first came to the village back in the twenties. It was clear that she was much loved and respected by many, from all walks of life too.

Mum and her siblings have spent the last few days going through her things, sorting out her affairs, and I've tried to help as much as possible. It's just awful.

But, every cloud and all that – tonight I'm seeing Scott. Narnia's Children have two nights booked for the opening of the local Country Club, performing with Grapefruit, an amazing group I love. I adore their songs, especially 'Elevator' and 'Dear Delilah'. It's so exciting.

I couldn't believe Mum said I could go when I'd asked her. She didn't argue or moan, she just said yes. I felt bad asking her, considering what had happened, but it's going to be a chance to be with Scott and I honestly don't care what they all think.

This is part of their tour and they've been playing in Reading and other local places, and it's just luck – or fate – that they're going to be in the next village at the same time. Scott wrote telling me his dates and their schedule in his last letter, so as soon as we got back to England I phoned him at the Leighton Buzzard house and let him know I could come to the gig.

He was amazed to hear my voice and it was magic for me too.

There's someone from Capitol Records, Apple – the Beatles' new company – and also from President Records, coming to see them play tonight and the band's really nervous. It's a really important gig for them. The record company executives had asked the band to perform some of their own compositions, because they were interested in their song-writing, just as much as their image and performance.

Good job things with Joss have been sorted out and all the bad feeling since the big fight's forgotten. I'm really nervous for them, too.

Scott said that Brian Auger and The Trinity, featuring one of my favourite girl singers, Jools Driscoll, were going to be there as well, though he wasn't sure if they were going to play. I love their song, 'Wheels on Fire'.

'Wow, you look beautiful!' Scott grabbed me the minute he saw me, and he took my breath away with a long soft lingering kiss which sent shudders of delight throughout my body, and good old Keith was back, drumming with a vengeance, only this time he had company.

If we ever made love I seriously believed I wouldn't survive.

'You don't look bad yourself.' I stood back and took deep breaths. His hair had grown longer and was shining under the lights of the dressing room. He was bronzed still and his turquoise eyes twinkled as I remembered. His lips were pink from our kiss and I felt the urge to kiss them again. And again and again.

'Where are the others?' I asked looking round the cramped dressing room with all their clothes strewn about, Coke bottles and crisps packets scattered over every available surface. I could smell aftershave and that 'male' odour rooms take on when a number of men are shut up together for some time. Not nice.

'Chatting up some girls they met earlier, waiting outside for us,' he smiled and ran his thumb over my lips. I nearly fell backwards at the jolt of electricity that shot through me.

'I've missed you so much, I haven't been able to concentrate – been drinking far too much trying to put you out of my mind' he said huskily as he took me in his arms and pressed himself against me, his lips finding mine again.

Reluctantly, I managed to prise my mouth from his. 'You'll never believe how much I've missed you. I can't believe you're here, now, it's like a dream.'

'Come here and show me how much,' Scott mumbled into my neck as I closed my eyes.

The gig was over far too soon. They were amazing, I couldn't take my eyes off him, the way he moved, held his guitar and his voice. Sheer magic. The band sounded a lot tighter than last time and they played all of their own material. If I were a record company representative, I'd sign them. When the gig ended, the band went off to meet the various record company people who'd turned up. After spending about an hour with them Scott reappeared.

'Sorry about that, you know how it is.'

'Actually I don't, not really, but I know it's important to you all.' I watched his face flushed with excitement. Perhaps one day I'd be au fait with it all.

'How did it go?'

'Ace, it was ace. There were five labels out there tonight and all of them stayed to chat with us.' He couldn't stop grinning.

'What does it mean?' I started grinning too, his was infectious.

'It means that Stephan and Psychedelic Smith have a lot of negotiating to do we hope. Stephan thinks there'll be a bidding war.'

'Wow.' I couldn't think what else to say as he grabbed me close. I'd no idea what he meant, but I didn't care.

'The others will be back in a minute, come here and let me say goodbye to you properly.'

Renza's Diary
September 21st 1968

Before we returned to Germany Nan's belongings were divided up between Mum and her sisters. It was so sad seeing her possessions being bundled up. She had drawers full of Christmas and birthday gifts still wrapped in the paper in which they'd been given to her; she'd not worn or used any of them – keeping them for best she used to say, or a rainy day. I cried when I thought about her saving things for a time which never came. I cried thinking of leaving her behind in that horrid grave yard, alone and in the rain, and I cried for Scott.

Our last moments together had been bitter-sweet. It hurt so much part of me almost longed to get it over with. The tension was too much to endure. But leaving him behind was an altogether different kind of agony.

Stella's Diary
September 26th 1968

Today is my 20th birthday. I'm no longer a teenager. There wasn't an awful lot to celebrate to be honest. No boyfriend, a job that bored me, and of course, being ill.

I seriously don't think I'll be around to see my 21st. Does that sound over-dramatic? Maybe – but honestly, I feel so rotten. Again. So much for Nanny Ivy's daft predictions of a cure! Mum, Dad, my grandparents and all my friends have sent cards today, Vix will be round tonight, and I've had some lovely presents, and been spoiled as usual, but I feel truly awful.

I've been off work all this week, in bed. The weather has turned really autumnal – usually my favourite season with the colours of the leaves and the frosts and mists and the cosy dark evenings – but it's just dismally rained nearly every day. I've been reading Gone With The Wind, for the umpteenth time, and promised myself that one day, if I ever get better, I'm going to be just like Scarlett O'Hara and to hell with convention! The idea of crying 'fiddle-de-dee' and flouncing and stamping my foot in Harbury Green made me giggle despite the pains.

Because yes, the pains were back with a vengeance. And there was to be no more Feminax. Dr Kingston had made a home visit and practically shouted with horror when I told her how many Feminax I was taking. She tore Mum off a strip, too.

'Honestly, Mrs Deacon, I'd have expected better from you. You're an educated and intelligent woman – surely you must have realised that the amount of opium derivative contained in these tablets is a sure path to addiction? The instructions for use on the packet are there for a very good reason! You surely can't have imagined that dosing Stella up with them like damn Smarties was a good thing?'

And Mum, always so gentle and quietly-spoken, had taken a deep breath, pushed her glasses more firmly on her nose, and glared at Dr Kingston. 'Yes, of course I was aware of the risks – but they worked. They stopped the pain. She, Stella, is my child and she was in agony. I'd do it again if I had to. And, if you'd done your job and managed to prescribe something other than an Aspro and a hot water bottle and tell her it was 'women's troubles' and tried to get to the bottom of what exactly is wrong with Stella sooner, then we wouldn't have been left to try and treat the problem ourselves, would we?'

I'd shrunk down under the eiderdown, slightly shocked, but also dead impressed with my mum.

Dr Kingston had huffed and puffed then, and said she was going to talk to the Churchill prior to my appointment on Monday, and would be guided by them on the subject of prescription painkillers. But until then I was not to take any more Feminax. Aspro and hot water bottles, only. Understood?

After Dr Kingston had gone, I told Mum how proud I was of her and we had a little cuddle along with one of the dogs and most of the cats. Then she made me a banana custard and I burst into tears.

The transistor radio beside the bed was tuned to Radio One and was insisting on playing sad songs: The Bee Gees' 'Words', Bobby Goldsboro's 'Honey', The Beatles' dismal 'Hey Jude'...

This really, really wasn't how I thought I'd be spending my birthday.

Stella's Diary
September 30th 1968

This has been the most terrifying day of my life so far. Mr Glendenning, middle-aged, tall, scary, booming voice, loomed above me in the examination room.

Mr Glendenning's clinic didn't have cubicles – there were rooms, a whole corridor of them, and several women and girls all looking as terrified as me, sitting on chairs outside them. Armchairs, mind you, not the usual metal stacking chairs used everywhere else in the hospital. Mr Glendenning was clearly a cut-above.

When my name was called, Mum had to wait outside.

I had the usual naked-under-the-hospital-gown look, but a nurse gave me some paper knickers to put on "for modesty and hygiene purposes, dear".

Oh, the embarrassment.

Mr Glendenning had a team. His team were a mixture of young white-coated male and female students. They all seemed to have notes about me on their clipboards and all smiled at me without actually meeting my eyes.

Mr Glendenning operated – ha! – by remote control, suggesting first one and then another of his acolytes should examine me and ask questions, while he stood back silently and either nodded or shook his head.

It was relentless. The only bright spot came when Mr G asked a very youthful and clearly nervous student what he had first noticed about my stomach.

The boy blushed and stammered and then said, 'it's very flat, sir.'

Everyone laughed.

Mr G harrumphed and said, 'And I'm sure Miss Deacon is delighted about that, but that wasn't what I wanted to know.'

The blushing student looked at me and I looked back. I had

no idea what Mr Glendenning wanted to know either. I just wanted to go home.

'We,' Mr Glendenning boomed down at me, 'are used to dealing with more mature stomachs in here. A flat one is something of a rarity. Now – let's get on...'

***

Ages later – no clock in this room – it was over. Mr G's nurse helped me get dressed, then called Mum in and we sat in front of his desk while the students gathered round behind us.

Mr Glendenning didn't mince his words. 'As suspected, Miss Deacon, you have two major problems. One I believe is irreversible – I suspect your reproductive organs are historically malformed and chronically damaged thus meaning that you possibly have endometriosis among other problems, and this is why menstruation is so painful and prolonged. However, given your age, I'm reluctant to perform a hysterectomy just now.'

Phew, I thought, no operation – what a relief...

Mr Glendenning continued. 'However, the second issue, copious cysts and abscesses, I am practically certain, must be dealt with surgically.'

Surgically...

'You mean...' I whispered as Mum squeezed my hand very tightly. 'I'll have to have an operation?'

'Of course. And the sooner the better.' Mr G peered at me as if I was an imbecile. 'Did you imagine I was going to give you a sticking plaster and some glucose sweets to cure your ills, Miss Deacon?'

The students all laughed dutifully.

I just sat and shook. An operation! Surgery! Nanny Ivy hadn't mentioned surgery in her mumbo-jumbo! I wasn't going to get better – I was going to die!

'I won't know the extent of the damage until I've operated,' Mr Glendenning stood up, gathering his notes and his acolytes as he did so. 'But I fully expect to be able to put an end to your clearly obvious discomfort by surgery. The malformation of your uterus and surrounding organs may be beyond me – nothing much is beyond me though, so we'll have to wait and see. Oh,' he paused and almost smiled, 'and I've been in touch with your general practitioner and suggested she issues you with an ongoing prescription for pethidine tablets until such time as we can get you on the table. Good day, Miss Deacon, you'll be hearing from my secretary forthwith.'

And he and the students sailed outside.

I just clung to Mum's hand in silent misery. I was just 20 years old and I was going to die.

Renza's Diary
November 4th 1968

The last couple of months since I last saw Scott have been sheer hell.

I've missed him so much I haven't been able to eat. I've been surviving on Heinz tomato soup and pumpernickel bread. Mum has given up trying to force food down my throat, and even though I've often cooked the meals, I can't face them. I live for his letters and sometimes there's such a gap in them I've convinced myself he's gone off with one of the many groupies they have hanging around all the time. But not The Bitch however. Scott told me she'd eloped to Gretna Green with a bloke from another band, soon after the Merryhill gig apparently, but that still left so many others.

But when one comes everything is wonderful again and when we manage to talk on the phone in the post room, at the base – not the easiest thing to arrange – I am floating on air again. The cost of the call is always so expensive we hardly get time to say a few words each and we'd have to hang up. It breaks my heart.

A letter came today. It's eleven pages long and it made me cry reading it. Trouble is, I'm not the first to read it.

As usual, Mum managed to get hold of the letter from the post room before I could go down and collect the mail. She's obviously read it, as I'm sure she's read all the others, and that was why she's becoming so anti-Scott. Not that there's anything in them that shouldn't be there, they're not rude or anything.

Scott told me he missed me and loved me more than ever and that his mum was going to write to mine, inviting me over to Jersey for Christmas, Scott would pay my fare. I went to mention it to Mum but she already knew and flew at me like a mad woman because of Scott's undying love and talk of 'wanting' me badly. She isn't happy.

Scott's still in Jersey and has been since October, when the band went over to play the Tropicana. Apparently it didn't work out there and he and Stephan went into St Helier to see the owner of the club, Lords, who is actually a real life Lord! He's booked Narnia's Children until they go to Paris on New Year's Eve.

So apart from a couple of days back in Leighton Buzzard, in early December when they're playing Stonehenge and some other local gigs, they're going to be out of England until the New Year. I can't see me being allowed to go over to Jersey. No way on earth.

Lords is turning out to be a good move for the band apparently. The owner gets drunk with them all the time and even jammed with the band on his organ. A booking agent has seen them playing at Lords and booked them to play the US Airforce bases in England, Scotland and Wales, when they get back from France. The same agent will be booking them into American bases all over Germany sometime in the New Year, and Scott thinks he could get to see me when they're over here. He's going to let me have their schedule when he gets it. I'm so excited I can't sit still!

The band's a bit worried because they might have to work with a girl singer in order to secure the tour – which would wreck their image. Stephan's working on preventing it.

'I'm still not over the shock of you actually going away again and not being here. I miss you so much it hurts, babe', Scott wrote in his spidery hand, hard to read most of the time. *'There just wasn't enough time to tell you all the things I wanted to say. Not just that I love you and always will, and that nothing will ever change that, or how beautiful you looked that last evening – well you're always gorgeous, but that last time, even more than ever.'* I reached for more Kleenex as I read. *'You've made me really happy, more than I ever thought*

possible and more than anyone has ever made me before. Even just walking in the College with you was wonderful, it was and is because I love you – I know you think I'm joking but I'm not, that's the last thing I'd do.' I could hardly read the words through the tears. *'I really wish we were together, just walking and talking again, enjoying ourselves back in the village, but anywhere in the world with you would be great and I'd be happy there, I wouldn't mind where, as long as it was with you.'*

I still couldn't see what he'd written that had got Mum all bent out of shape.

One of his letters mentioned me asking my uncle and his wife if I could visit them and stay with them at some point, and then we could meet up. I think Mum read that one and hadn't got over it yet. She'd hinted at the content of the letter for days before I actually 'received' it from the post sergeant.

I'd written to my uncle and he'd said I could come over anytime. And one of the army blokes, a friend of Dad's, mentioned that he often went back to the UK for a long weekend, driving to Ostend or Rotterdam, getting the ferry from there to Dover, and that I could go along with him whenever I wanted. He could drop me off at Victoria Coach Station so I could get to my uncle's from there.

I'm keeping it in mind and biding my time. But I know I'll try to do this as soon as I can find a way of getting some money together, though Scott said he would try to pay my airfare if I wanted. That wasn't even worth thinking about. Mum would never allow that.

Scott wrote about a new film he'd been to see with Joss and Mo called *The Lost Continent*, which is based on a book by his favourite author, Dennis Wheatley. It was some sort of occult story, but I don't really like stuff like that. I know he reads lots of it. He thought I should see it if it comes to the Mess. I'd much rather read books by John le Carre or Raymond Chandler, and watch crime or spy thrillers, but they never show them in the Mess.

He said there was a big scandal back in London concerning

Mick Jagger and Marianne Faithfull, his girlfriend who went to the school near us at home, and where I might've gone, had I been allowed to stay on to do A Levels. He wouldn't say what it was, but said I should read the papers! Mum and Dad read *The Times* and I haven't seen anything in there about a scandal.

Zak and Scott have written a song called ' Lovin' You,' which is going to be the B side of their single, 'Livin' with You,' which they recorded in London recently and is going to be released in May. Scott says it was written by the writers who have written hits for The Herd and Dave Dee, Dozy, Beaky, Mick, and Titch, and is in the close-harmony style of The Hollies. I can't wait to listen to it! I love all these bands so I'm sure that the song is going to be amazing. Narnia's Children have the most amazing vocal harmonies, they can all take lead singer parts, and they are excellent musicians too. It's going to be a huge hit, I just know it. How exciting. I can't help recalling what Scott said he'd do for me when they made lots of money – he'd pay for me to do a course with The London School of Journalism. Of course I wouldn't be allowed to let him pay for it, but perhaps by then Mum and Dad's opinion wouldn't count because we'd be married and they'd be history. I can dream.

I was at the market the other day trying to make the stall holder understand what I wanted. Talk about frustrating. I kept asking for shallots and she kept giving me ordinary onions. I'd rehearsed the right word all the way from home so I know I wasn't pronouncing it wrongly. The woman ended up throwing the onions at me and shouting so that everyone stared. Thankfully a tall blonde girl came to my rescue and said something to the woman, and then asked me in English if she could help. Thank goodness. Anyway, we got talking and she said her name was Heidi and she taught English and History at one of the local schools. She invited me to Sunday coffee and cake with her and her parents who live just down the hill from where we live. She said she'd love to practise her English with me and could help me with my German. I thought why not and said yes. She gave me her address and I'm going there at 3pm on Sunday after lunch in the Mess.

I was very nervous because Heidi's parents don't speak English and they're quite old. They escaped from East Germany not long after the Berlin Wall went up, hiding under hay in a hay cart and they got shot at and her brother was killed by the guards.

When we next go to NAAFI I'll buy some coffee and something else to take them.

Last time Mum and I went to NAAFI, we went to Iserlohn instead of Dortmund – the Canadian NAAFI is there, used by the Americans as well as Canadians, and they have so much more for sale than we have in ours. The American women are really funny though, they do their shopping in the mornings wearing evening dress, or fur coats with ankle socks and plimsolls, whatever their age, and they go out with their hair in curlers. The Mater was disgusted and never shut up about it the first time we went shopping.

Their NAAFI is what they call a supermarket, I'd never heard of them before, but you go round pushing a huge trolley thing on wheels and help yourself off the shelves to what you want, and pay for it at any one of a long line of tills. It's called self-service. Flipping Henry, those Yanks eat a lot. Their trollies were piled high with food and so much Coca Cola.

I love their music section. They have records by every band imaginable, and so many I've never heard of before. I got another LP by The Association, and by The Beach Boys, who are so groovy and psychedelic – they're too much. I didn't have that much money left from my jobs back home and so have had to be careful what I buy, but I really wanted these. Perhaps they'll sell Narnia's Children – I'll need to save up in case.

We had a snack in the Stomp Club which is a sort of cafe place which sells books and magazines, and the other day I had something called a toasted cheese on rye with tomato and four types of cheese. It was lovely.

The trip to the Canadian NAAFI takes us all along the Ruhr

and the countryside is lovely. So much forest and so many lovely views, sweeping hills and the villages are really cute. All very Hansel and Gretel. I wished I had a camera so I could photograph it all.

At the end of our strasse (street) you can walk to the Harkortsee River which leads off along the Ruhr to the dams which were bombed in the war. Although the area was known for factories and industry, it is still really beautiful. The town hall is called Das Rathaus and is really old and imposing and the base is just down the road from there. All the streets are cobbled, and although most of the homes are flats and in that horrid grey concrete, now and again there are some really lovely buildings, black and white, almost like those in Chester in England.

Heidi and her parents live in an apartment in a grey building, but inside it's really nice. They have the full lacy curtains which are so popular in German homes, and it is all very formal looking. Her parents tried hard to communicate with me and I them, but it was difficult. Thank goodness Heidi's English is so good.

They served me strong black German coffee and cream cakes – I can't stand cream but ate it to be polite – and a delicious Austrian cheese cake which Heidi made especially for me and she gave me the rest to take home for everyone. I met her fiancé, Bernard, who spoke a little English and is also a teacher, but I didn't catch of what. He seemed very nice but so old-fashioned in his dicky-bow tie and check jacket with patches on the elbows, and looked very scholarly with his pebble glasses and short hair. Not my type, and I am surprised he's Heidi's type really, as she wears mini-skirts, false eyelashes and all the mod gear. Bernard looked ancient – about thirty – but I'm sure he couldn't be that old. Heidi is twenty and she said she really likes me and that we should do something together soon. I'd like that.

When I wrote and told Scott about Heidi and Bernard, he

warned me not to get too keen on German men, especially after I told him about the old blokes in the street whistling and shouting at me whenever I go out. I really don't think he has anything to fear from old drunken Germans. They seemed to be drunk from early in the morning onwards. Even the workmen who were doing some repairs on our place had beer and schnapps in the mornings when they started work – at 7am! Scott said he laughed when he read my letter and said that it reminded him of the stewards on the cruises.

Scott's mum hasn't written to my parents yet, so I guess Christmas won't be happening. I didn't really think it would, but I still feel gutted. I'll just have to imagine what it would've been like to be with him in Jersey with his family and to actually sleep under the same roof as him.

When I do the housework I get through it by pretending I'm doing it in *our* house for us, for Scott and me. We're married and he is away on tour but due back soon. I usually play Pythagoras Theorem on my new record player when I'm cleaning – I love 'Our House' – it reminds me of Scott so much.

Music's getting me through the boredom and hell of being here and I'm so glad I got myself a record player and can go to the Canadian NAAFI to buy the latest records. I belong to the English NAAFI library and it's great to have so many books to take out to read. I love reading and every now and again I have a go at writing something, but nothing seems to work. I'd really like to try writing a spy or crime novel, but my head is all over the place and I can't concentrate. One day perhaps.

Everything's so flipping ancient here. The music is all oompah oompah bands and James Last, and don't get me started on their fashions. Dear God! They make Mrs Fowler look like something out of Vogue. If I don't get away soon I'm going to end up looking like a frump without any idea of what's hip any more. When I go back to England they'll think I've stepped out of the dark ages. Scott will die of shame.

Stella's Diary
November 19th 1968

The letter from the Churchill Hospital came today on Mr Glendenning's headed notepaper. I am to go into hospital on Sunday 8th December. My operation will be on Monday 9th.

In 20 days' time. Not even three weeks!

My hands had been shaking as I opened the envelope. They shook even more when I read the letter.

Mr G's secretary had also sent a copy of the letter to Dr Kingston. It was headed Miss S Deacon – Major Surgery. I hoped, especially after the way she spoke to my mum, that she felt bad about it – 'women's troubles' indeed!

Mind you, to give her her due, she'd been pretty damn quick about prescribing the pethidine tablets. And what a difference they'd made! Although, like the Feminax, they also came with dire warnings about overdosing and being habit-forming. But they were so effective that I only needed to take one when the pain started and I was usually fine for the rest of the day. I wished I'd had them months – no years – ago!

So – this is it. I know now – a major operation – on December 9th. The day I die. I won't even be alive for Christmas. Not much time to get well, meet my tall, dark, handsome stranger from over the seas, *and* become Harbury Green's answer to Scarlett O'Hara.

I tried to laugh at my foolishness but only manged to cry. Again.

Renza's Diary
November 20th 1968

I got another letter from Scott today, sent from Leighton Buzzard where they have been staying for a few days whilst they sort out recording and prepare for France on New Year's Eve, though they're going back to Jersey for Christmas first. Apparently Zak and his girlfriend Maureen — not sure which one of the many she was — have broken up and Joss and his girlfriend — don't think I met her, just various groupies — have split as well. Joss found out she'd been two-timing him. What a laugh.

Scott's had his hair cut a little, as it was so long that Stephan said the French might not let them into the country. They get funny about long hair and think everyone with long hair is a hippy and drug addict. The French are weird.

He apologised that his mum's not written to me about Christmas and said she was a bit flaky at times — whatever that means. Anyway it definitely means I won't be going; but I knew that. I'm learning to live with disappointment.

But Scott is going to send me the tapes of their recording sessions. Last Saturday he said they went to London to audition for President Records and they also went into their head offices to sing some of their own songs for them, without music, which was recorded on tape as they did it. Scott thinks it went well. The singer from a band called 'The Action' is sending them some songs he's written for them to consider recording, and Scott thinks if all goes well, they'll be recording for President soon. The company liked Narnia's Children's own material but think it is LP material more than singles. They loved the group image and personalities a lot.

It's all so exciting, I wish I could be with him and enjoy it with them all. Yvette would blow a gasket if she knew what was going on, but she's never answered my letters so I don't know if she even got them. The last I heard when I was home she'd got engaged to an officer cadet and had gone all posh! Her mum will be in seventh heaven, it was her dream that Yvette would marry a 'someone.'

'If I ever did become famous I think my first thought would be to put some money in the bank and also of course spend some, lots, on you' Scott wrote. *'And if Narnia's Children ever broke up, I'm sure I'd find another band because I love this scene, it's far out and too much for me to finish with it'.*

Scott's letter went on to tell me that his father liked me and sent his regards. And apparently Scott had been in touch more since he took me to meet him and Philippa. So something good came of the visit. His dad told him that they'd been a bit sad when I visited because a dear friend, who had been a stewardess and in the Munich air disaster, had died, and they were going to her funeral soon after our visit. This was the flight that Manchester United were on when so many died.

'From Friday we're playing five nights in a row, starting with The Penny Farthing in Leicester, so it is going to be hectic before we go back to Jersey where we're big stars now you know!' I couldn't help laughing at this. *'We were coming back from a gig the other night down the M1 motorway which is groovy, and we stopped off at the Blue Boar which is a very famous group cafe – every group goes there, it's so hip – and we saw Frankie Vaughan and his wife and also Charlie and Inez Foxx, the American brother and sister duo... Cheap thrills!'*

I can't stand Frankie Vaughan, but I've heard of Charles and Inez Foxx... So cool. Scott's so lucky to have such an exciting life when all I have is flipping housework, looking after the kids and hanging out with old people and old blokes who keep trying it on with me in the Mess. I told Scott about a couple of them who had groped me when my dad was in the same room for heaven's sake!

Scott said he'd kill them if he ever got his hands on them. He also said his father had just sold his house and was buying one only about a mile away, and Scott was hoping to pop down

and see them at some point and wished I could go with him. I'll
pass on that I think! I'd love to see Scott – but his father... Oh
no!

I cried (I seemed to do that a lot these days) when I read
the next lines in his letter telling me he loved me and missed
me still.

*'I remember asking you to marry me, of course I do. I
remember feeling like I was floating on air when you said yes. I
hope and pray you'll always feel the same and one day we can
get married. Thanks for those weeks we had together, I hope
we can spend more time together, like the rest of our lives, very
soon. If you did manage to get over to see me I wouldn't let you
out of my sight and I would never stop kissing your lovely
mouth, nibbling your little ears and... Well you come over and
find out!'*

I had a dreadful thought as I read this. What if Mum had
read it already? I was going to be in for it big time if she had. A
feeling of dread swamped me, and the lovely feeling Scott's
letter had filled me with evaporated in a flash.

Stella's Diary
December 7th 1968

In 48 hours I knew I'd be dead.

'So,' Vix, sprawled on my bed, looked across at me, 'what are we going to do tonight?'

I shrugged. 'No idea really. I'm just so scared. I sort of just want to stay in with you and Mum and Dad.'

'*What*?' Vix frowned. 'Stella Deacon – are you mad? You reckon this is going to be your last Saturday night on earth, and you want to *stay in*?'

'Yeah, well, I don't know really. What would you do if you were going to be dead on Monday?'

Vix rolled over on the bed. Her vivid orange mini-dress rose up to groin level and she grinned. 'Oh, I'd run away and marry Mick Jagger and live in a fairy-tale castle on an island in the sun and eat nothing but cherries and chocolate.'

I laughed. 'And that's an awful lot of stuff to pack into 48 hours. No, seriously, Vix... what should I do?'

'Do you hurt today?'

'No. The pethidine is still working well. I can take another one later.'

'Then you should go out,' Vix sat up again. 'Get really, really dolled-up. We'll go out and go mad and have the best night ever. Something to remember.'

'I'll be dead so I won't remember anything anyway.'

'No, but I will.' Vix smiled gently at me. 'I want something lovely and happy to remember you by. We could go into Oxford. There's probably a dance on at the town hall, or there's bound to be some really good bands at the Orchid Rooms or Wheatley Bridge, or – '

The Saturday night trains between Harbury Green and Oxford were lively affairs, always packed with like-minded night-club and dance-hall goers.

I shook my head. 'I've still got to get ready, so it'll be pretty late to get a train into Oxford. Everything'll be half over by the time we get there.'

Vix nodded, scrambling from the bed and heading towards the door. 'True. I know how long it takes you to get ready. So what about going over to St Barnabus? I think I saw in the local paper that they've got a dance on there tonight. Might be a group we've heard of and you can interview them and earn some money from it.'

I shrugged. 'Not much use to me when I'm dead.'

'I'll use the money to put flowers on your grave every Saturday night as a memorial.' Vix grinned. 'Look, hang on – you start making yourself beautiful and I'll go downstairs and nick the paper off your mum.'

'OK. If there's something on at St B's, we'll go. It won't be too far away if I feel ill and need to come home, will it?'

Vix hugged me and rolled off the bed.

I shuddered. Because now I knew it was going to kill me. Well, *it* probably wasn't – but the operation I was having on Monday was. I knew it.

Obviously, I'd never been admitted to hospital before, never had an operation before, but my uncle Maurice had died on the operating table. OK, years and years earlier – but as far as I was concerned that was what hospitals and operations did – killed you.

I was going into hospital tomorrow and the operation was on Monday. I knew I was going to die under the anaesthetic. I'd go to sleep and never wake up again.

With a familiar feeling of dread I started to plaster on my make-up.

'There!' Vix said triumphantly, barging back into the bedroom waving the local paper, 'Told you! Oh, you look great – very glamorous, black suits you now you're so skinny – and there *is* a dance on at St B's. Some group called Narnia's Children – ever heard of them?'

'Nope.' I shook my head carefully, holding my second pair

of false eyelashes in place, waiting for the glue to dry.

'No, me neither. Probably not much use you interviewing them, then. But even if they're rubbish we can still have a good time,' Vix started backcombing her Cilla Black hair in the mirror over my shoulder. 'Oh, my ends won't go right... I need lacquer here – have you got some Sunsilk or something? Ta...'

We both choked in the wild whoosh of sticky hair spray.

'Oh,' Vix wiggled the tail comb and teased her hair upwards, 'and your mum and dad think it's a good idea if we go out tonight. Especially as it's only at St B's. Take your mind off it, they said.'

My poor mum and dad were as worried about the operation as I was, I knew it. I could see it in their eyes however hard they tried not to show it. Being an only child, much-loved and spoiled rotten. I think that made it worse for them. If I'd had brothers or sisters it might not have been so bad if, no *when*, I died on Monday.

'And,' Vix mumbled, pouting as she applied another coat of my Miner's Barely There lipstick, 'they said I've got to make sure you have a good time. So, that's what I'm going to do.'

'Thank you. You're the best friend in the world. Please don't ever forget me.'

'I'd never do that – and now please shut up! I'm not going to cry tonight – and neither are you.'

No, I thought, I wasn't.

My last Saturday night on earth...

I looked at myself in the mirror. I was thin and pale, which I liked. I'd lost loads of weight since the stomach pains started. I couldn't eat much anymore. Still, thin and pale was fashionable, and looked good with my Dusty Springfield heavily-kohled eyes and my blanked-out lips.

Tonight I wore black: a very, very short black silk dress – no more than a tunic really – with long, tight sleeves, and pin-tuck pleats and hundreds of tiny buttons down the front. Because I liked to look different, I usually made my own clothes, but this

199

was an old lady's tea dress I'd bought from the Oxfam shop in Oxford's Broad Street and adapted by slashing several feet from the length and taking in the waist – and tonight I'd added dangly purple earrings, black fishnet tights and long black thigh boots.

Then concentrating hard, I used my eyelash glue to stick a sparkle of silver glitter over my cheekbones, and purple star sequins in arches where my eyebrows had been. Tonight, though, I owed it to myself to pull out all the stops.

I stood back and surveyed the effect. Hmmm – almost as good as Julie Driscoll. Almost...

Just my hair to sort out. I fluffed and combed and flicked and back-combed.

I swooshed Sunsilk everywhere and nodded. Nothing moved. My hair was a mass of rigid spikes and layers. Bernice – bless her little cotton socks – would probably have a fit. It looked OK.

I scrabbled across my cluttered dressing table for the perfume. It was Le Train Bleu this week. Like most of our friends, Vix and I always wore Picot Perfume. Either Le Train Bleu or Akabar or Pagan which we bought in Boots in Oxford on pay days.

'We both look amazingly beautiful and glamorous and fab,' Vix said as she had a liberal dab of scent too, then pulling on her leather coat as I draped my fun fur jacket round my shoulders. 'St B's here we come...'

St Barnabus was our local boys' school. It was only a five-minute walk away from my house – which meant my dad didn't have to come and collect us at the end, which he sometimes did if we went to clubs further afield than Oxford – and they had a huge hall with a stage and hired it out for Saturday night dances about once a month. It was always packed – the groups were usually good, sometimes quite big names – and everyone from our village, and all the other surrounding villages, crowded in.

Vix, bless her, had put Jeff, her long-term boyfriend, on hold to be with me tonight. My last Saturday night alive. Because, to be honest, by now Vix had also decided that Nanny Ivy's predictions had been, as I'd always thought, a load of hokum.

Today I'd been alive for 20 years, 2 months, 1 week and 5 days – and on Monday I was going to die. But tonight I was going to live. For the last time.

Gulping down my prescribed pethidine pill, I kissed Mum and Dad goodbye, patted the dogs and the cats, picked up my homemade shoulder-bag – black beaded taffeta, encrusted with multi-coloured sequins and embellished with hand-sewn satin stars – and Vix and I were off.

Outside, it was a glittering, freezing December night. The sky was clear, velvet black with a zillion stars and everywhere shimmered beneath the layer of heavy frost. No sign of snow, though. I loved snow. I'd hoped I'd see snow again before I died. Not much chance of that now. Not much chance of anything anymore.

Stella's Diary
December 7th 1968 – continued...

After a short walk, we joined the queue outside St Barnabus's hall door, chatting with friends, admiring – or otherwise – each other's outfits – stamping our feet, our breath like smoky plumes in the icy air. After a few minutes of shuffling, we were in, and having paid our money, we dumped our coats in the cloakroom, bought the obligatory beaker of orange squash – there was a no alcohol rule at St B's as it was school premises but it never mattered because everyone just got high on the noise and the music and the excitement – and headed for the hall.

The dusty green curtains were pulled closed across the stage in the gloomy, moody darkness. Tiny lights twinkled in the ceiling and from one of the deepest, darkest corners, the DJ was playing an early Monkees hit. St Barnabus always put on a good night, and certainly knew how to create an atmosphere.

The place was packed. Most people had nabbed one of the chairs that were lined up round the outside of the floor, claiming them with handbags and drinks. A few mini-skirted girls were dancing – always the same ones – in front of the stage. Vix and I grinned at each other. We called them the Dolly Rockers and we knew they'd be the ones trying to get off with the group's singer later – even if he looked like Quasimodo's much uglier cousin. Vix and I found a couple of vacant chairs right at the front to the left of the stage.

'Sit,' Vix said, balancing our beakers of squash. 'We've got ringside seats for when the group – what are they called – oh, yes, Narnia's Children – comes on. And as you're not going to rush off to interview them you can camp here all night if you don't feel up to dancing.'

I nodded. Vix made my journalism sound very grand. It wasn't really. A couple of years ago, I'd been asked by the teenage magazines to contribute pop group interviews as well as my short stories. I loved it.

I'd met and interviewed a lot of really big names and famous chart groups – like the Rolling Stones and The Move and Marmalade, and Amen Corner and The Walker Brothers and Status Quo, and The Crazy World of Arthur Brown and The Herd and Dave Dee, Dozy, Beaky, Mick and Titch – as well as several big-time club acts like The Alan Bown Set and Simon Dupree and The Big Sound and Argent, and many up-and-coming bands too.

The magazines always bought my interviews and the extra money paid for my holidays, make-up, records, books and clothes. Vix always came along with me to these gigs – we'd had some really great adventures on our nights out, been to some top venues and met some fab people.

Of course, whatever Vix thought, the short stories and the pop interviews were really only my pin-money hobby. My proper job was still, and probably always would be – well, until I died on Monday of course – as a civil servant.

I'd been signed off from work indefinitely now, depending on the outcome of the operation and the length of my recuperation period, the personnel lady had said kindly. I could have three months off on full pay, and a further three months after that on half pay, if the hospital thought I needed it.

I hadn't bothered to tell her that it didn't matter too much as I wouldn't be coming back to work when I was dead.

In St B's hall, Vix was fussing round me like a mother hen. 'Now, you don't need to move all night, unless you need the lav of course, if you feel awful. Do you? Feel awful, I mean?'

'No,' I shook my head. 'The pethidine has kicked in nicely – and honestly if this is my last night out I'm going to enjoy every minute of it. It'll be just my luck that the group is rubbish tonight.'

'They won't be,' Vix grinned. 'Last time we were here, it was The Foundations, wasn't it? And you got a really good interview with them – and they were amazing. This lot will be, too. You know they always have good groups here – even the ones we've never heard of like – um – Narnia's Children.'

The DJ – who was actually Mr Fisk, St Barnabus's science teacher, who always played records between the live acts and acted as Master of Ceremonies at the Saturday dances – had replaced the Monkees with the Tremeloes. The Dolly Rocker girls in front of the stage all posed and pouted and pushed each other and danced a bit more wildly.

Then the music stopped, and Mr Fisk left his record deck, and scampered up on the stage, beaming in the spotlight, clapping his hands for silence.

'He really thinks he's Bruce Forsyth,' I giggled. 'And this is Sunday Night at the London Palladium.'

The girls pressed closer to the foot of the stage.

'Ladies and gentlemen, boys and girls!' Mr Fisk yelled into his microphone. 'Lovely to see a full house tonight! Now, let's give a big, big St Barnabus welcome to your sensational band for this evening! All the way from Jersey in the Channel Islands! Let's hear it for – Narnia's Children!!!'

Everyone clapped and cheered and whistled and stamped their feet.

'Blimey,' Vix said. 'No wonder we'd never heard of them. They're foreign.'

The green curtains swished back and the footlights mingled in a smoky haze with the overhead criss-crossing spot-beams. The towers of speakers, slender spikes of microphones and snakes of cables transformed the stage from a school hall to a full-blown rock show and Narnia's Children roared into 'I Get Around' by the Beach Boys.

'Wow...' Vix mouthed, looking at me, wide-eyed. 'Just wow...'

Just wow, indeed...

It was too loud to speak, to say anything, so we just stared at them – and each other.

The four boys – Narnia's Children – on stage weren't just brilliant musicians and sexy movers – they were definitely four of the most devastatingly gorgeous blokes we'd ever seen.

Tall, lean, long-haired and out-of-this-world-stunning, wearing skin-tight, brightly coloured flared trousers, and black skinny-rib sweaters that didn't even attempt to hide their incredible tanned bodies, they rocked into another belting Beach Boys hit, followed by early foot-stomping Beatles, and then The Hollies – all very loud, fast-paced and brilliantly close-harmonied. They could play and they could sing.

West-coast rock-pop at its best.

The Dolly Rockers were no longer dancing in front of the stage. Instead, they were pressed, three deep, against it. Just gazing up in total and complete adoration.

I laughed at Vix, leaning close, my mouth to her ear. 'I think the Dolly Rockers want to eat them.'

'I don't blame them,' she yelled back. 'They're mega, mega cool, totally brilliant – oh, and not to mention the sexiest blokes Harbury Green has ever seen… I'm going to book a holiday in Jersey if that's what the boys are like.'

Me too, I thought, if I wasn't going to be annoyingly dead… because I'd just tumbled instantly and stupidly head-over-heels for the beautiful boy on the guitar, the boy with the long silky black hair falling into the amazingly turquoise eyes.

The most beautiful boy in the world.

'Mine's the singer!' Vix howled in my ear. 'I've always loved a tall blond boy!'

As Jeff, Vix's childhood sweetheart boyfriend, was sort of squat with a lot of gingery hair and even more gingery freckles, I said nothing, just smiled happily to myself, drinking it all in. OK, mainly drinking in the beautiful boy on the guitar. I may not see another Saturday night, I thought, but this one was – so far at least – pretty damn near perfect.

After a couple more numbers, all of which had the St B's crowd dancing and singing along, and the Dolly Rocker girls still staring lustfully at the stage, being watched by their jealous-eyed boyfriends, Narnia's Children stopped playing, and the blond God singer stepped forward.

'Thank you,' he said huskily into the microphone. Golly – even his voice was sexy! 'That's a really great welcome. And before we go any further with our first set, let me introduce you to the boys...'

'Glory be, he's gorgeous...' Vix sighed.

'On drums,' he indicated the fabulous, tall, tanned boy with the Marc Bolan curls, 'we have Mo... And on bass guitar we have Joss...' Joss, darkly, dangerously, gorgeous, looked exactly like a Caravaggio angel – I'd done Art at A level and had been very taken with Caravaggio. 'And on guitar...' Madly, I was holding my breath, 'we have Scott...'

Scott... I rolled the name around in my head. Scott – oh, yes, it suited him...

'And I'm Zak,' he grinned, caressing the microphone. 'And collectively we're Narnia's Children. And now you know who we are, we'd really like to get to know you – so don't forget to come up and say hi when we take our first break.'

This was met by screams and shrieks from the crowd. Mostly the girls.

'Try and stop me,' Vix breathed as the lights dimmed some more, and the St B's glitter-balls revolved and sparkled.

'You're joking? What about Jeff?'

Vix just grinned at me. I shook my head and looked back at the stage, gazing at Scott, as Narnia's Children rocked into The Hollies' 'Just One Look'.

Scott and Zak shared the microphone, harmonising on this one.

The words of the song... Scott was singing the words of the song – 'Just One Look, That's All It Took' – and looking straight at me...

Rubbish! Embarrassed by my own foolishness, I stared

down at the floor in the darkness. He wouldn't even be able to see me from the stage. And even if he could, he wouldn't be interested, and no, of course he couldn't see me, not with the gloom and all those dozens of people dancing and the entire hall only being lit by the shimmering glitter-balls.

Just one look – that's all it took...

Oh, but The Hollies had never sung a truer word, I thought dolefully, realising that falling head over heels for a gorgeous stranger was possibly one of the most ridiculous things I'd ever done in my entire life.

Just one look...

When it ended there was the usual eruption of applause and screams. I just stared at the floor and hoped no one could see me blushing at my foolishness.

'And this next song,' Zak was laughing, 'is for someone who can't be here tonight but who is very special to someone in the band...The words mean a lot...'

The Beach Boys' 'Girl Don't Tell Me'...

Please, please, please, I thought, don't let the someone special be anything to do with Scott.

Again he and Zak were sharing the microphone and the close-harmony vocals: "I met her last summer...." and laughing at one another, sharing a secret joke.

Please, please let the song and the someone be special to Zak...

Then I shook my head at my own stupidity, instinctively knowing both the someone and the song belonged to Scott, and sighed.

Three more songs and Narnia's Children took a break. Mr Fisk was back at his turntable and playing The Turtles.

'You're not really going to talk to him, are you?' I asked as Vix scrambled to her feet and headed towards the curtained-off stage. 'Zak. I mean, not seriously?'

'Course I am. Come on, we're out to have fun tonight, aren't we?'

'Yes, but...' I nodded to the masses of Dolly Rockers in their baby-doll smocks and their Bally button-up shoes, 'look at them. They're practically trampling on one another to get up the steps and round backstage. You don't want to be counted as one of them, do you?'

'No, course not. I'm not joining the groupie hordes. I'm going to use all my feminine wiles to stand out from the crowd... Come on... That Scott is dead dishy...'

Self-preservation kicked-in and I shook my head. 'No, you go. I saw Debbie and Sally from work in the queue earlier. I'll go and chat to them in the break... I'll see you back here.'

'Your loss,' Vix grinned, and sashayed off towards the steps.

I found Debbie and Sally, bought another beaker of orange squash, chatted to some other friends and went to the loo. By the time I got back to our seats, Mr Fisk was playing something by The Shadows, a lot of people were trying to do the Hank Marvin walk and failing, and Vix was sitting on the edge of the stage with Zak on one side of her and Scott on the other.

Some of the Dolly Rockers were standing in front of the stage looking murderous.

'Stella!' Vix beckoned me over. 'Come here – quickly! We've just been talking about you.'

Hoping I wasn't blushing, pretty sure that I was, and knowing that if I refused I was going to look very silly indeed, but cursing Vix silently and violently, I walked across, climbed the shallow steps and sat on the stage beside Scott.

Feeling like a complete fool, and almost unable to look at him because close-to he was even more devastatingly beautiful – if that was possible – I was totally convinced that he could hear my heart thundering under my ribs.

'There,' Vix grinned. 'Stella, this is Zak and Scott, as you probably know if you were listening earlier. Zak and Scott, this is my best friend, Stella.'

We all smiled at one another. Scott's smile was all lovely and wide and lop-sided. Oh my word, he was so gorgeous. All my poise and cool flew out of the window and I knew when I spoke my voice would come out in some sort of strangulated squeak.

'Fab,' Vix smiled. 'Now I just need to powder my nose, so I'll leave you to get to know each other.'

'What?' I glared at her.

'I'll only be a couple of minutes,' she chuckled. Then she leaned forward and whispered. 'Don't waste the opportunity. The rest of the Dolly Rockers are being entertained backstage by Mo and Joss, oh and apparently the roadie, who I think is called Rich. I've captured these two for you to make your evening really special.'

And she was gone.

Zak watched her go, and stood up. 'She's cool. Shame she's spoken for – she told us about her boyfriend... I guess I'd better go and check out the talent backstage and leave you two to it. See you soon, Stella, lovely to meet you – and Scott, 5 minutes, ok?'

Scott nodded, then he smiled at me again. He really had a fabulous smile.

'Hi, Stella.' His voice was deep and warm and well-educated. It did nothing to calm my butterflies. He stared at me and nodded slowly. 'I love the outfit and the sequins... but to be honest, it seems such a waste.'

'Sorry?' I frowned at him. 'I'm not sure...'

'Your operation. Your friend told us all about it.'

'Did she?'

She'd told them – complete strangers – that I had major personal internal medical problems and was going to die? Oh – I knew I'd kill her.

'Sorry, then. She really shouldn't have. I'm sure you didn't want to know all the gory details.'

'She didn't go into any details, just said you were having the

209

operation on Monday. Aren't you scared?'

'Terrified.'

'So don't do it.'

'I don't have a choice.'

This was the most surreal conversation anyone could be having, surely? Especially with someone you'd only been introduced to 30 seconds earlier and who you knew you'd love for the rest of your – obviously – very short life, all played out to a background of The Bonzo Dog Doo Dah Band's 'I'm The Urban Spaceman' blaring from Mr Fisk's turntable.

'Of course you have a choice. I mean, I don't know you or anything about you, but you're definitely a girl and you're very pretty – so why do you want to be a man?'

'*What*???'

'The sex-change operation.' Scott looked at me, his face serious. 'Your friend said you were having a sex-change op and were going to be called Adrian.'

'*What*????' I didn't know whether to laugh or cry. 'She said *what*??? Oh, God in heaven! I'm really going to kill her!!! I'm so, so sorry. That's not why I'm going into hospital.'

'Thank the Lord for that,' Scott grinned at me, the turquoise eyes dancing wickedly. 'I was pretty sure she was lying, and I didn't think you looked much like an Adrian, but she was very convincing and I didn't want to insult you if it was true.'

'No, it isn't, and oh yes, she is very convincing. She can usually manage to pull the wool over most people's eyes. And now I'm really going to throttle her! Anyway, I'm just so sorry – so, yes, I'm going into hospital, yes, I'm having an operation, yes, I'm petrified because I think I'll die under the anaesthetic, and no, I'm definitely not having a sex change or going to be called Adrian. Ever.'

Scott laughed. 'As opening conversations go, this will probably rank as one of the strangest I've ever had.'

'I was just thinking the same thing.'

We smiled at each other. I swear there were fireworks and butterflies and bluebirds and rainbows and celestial trumpets.

'I'd be scared, too,' he said softly. 'And I don't know what you're having done, but you'll be ok. Promise. So was she lying about the other part too?'

'Probably. Depends what it was.'

'That you're a music journalist.'

I laughed. 'Only if she said I worked for *Melody Maker* or the *NME*. I do freelance part-time pop interviews for the teenage magazines – but my real grown-up boring job is as a civil servant.'

'Teenage magazines sound perfect. Just right for us. Will you interview us, then? One day? Seriously?'

'Scott!' Mo, the fabulous Marc Bolan'd-haired drummer, suddenly poked his head through the curtains before I could answer. 'Up here – now! We're ready for the second set.'

Scott nodded. 'Yeah, sure. OK.'

'Now!' Mo snapped, glaring down at me. 'Come on!'

Scott scrambled to his feet and looked at me. 'I hope you'll enjoy the second set. And please – don't run away at the end.'

'Scott!!!!' Mo roared. 'Come on – we're waiting for you!'

'See you later,' Scott smiled, and disappeared through the curtains.

Mo gave me another glare and followed him.

I floated back to my seat, completely and idiotically in love, and only vaguely wondering why Mo didn't seem to like me. Not, I thought, as I sat down, any of it mattered because I'd never see any of them again.

Vix sauntered back and sat down again just as the lights dimmed.

'I will kill you!' I hissed. 'How could you say *that*?'

'It worked, though, didn't it?' she hugged me. 'It was a great ice-breaker. I knew he'd talk to you because he was intrigued.'

'*Intrigued*? He must have thought he'd wandered into a

mad-house. Dear God, Vix – a sex change???? Why on earth-?'

'Because I think he fancies you, and because I saw the way you were looking at him, and because this is going to be a night to remember for you – and I'm guessing that he gets the come-on, and the same boring old chat-up lines, from girls everywhere he goes – so I just used my ingenuity. No, it's ok – no need to thank me. It's what best-friends do.'

I laughed. 'You're crazy. Anyway, of course he doesn't fancy me and even if he did, which he doesn't, what would be the point? He's clearly got someone else, I'm going to die on Monday and he's going to be in Jersey – with the someone else who couldn't be here tonight.'

'But you do fancy him?'

'Yes.'

'There then. Trust Auntie Vix.'

Narnia's Children's second set was just as mind-blowingly amazing as the first had been. Whether they were playing blasting rock'n'roll, full-on complex close-harmony or pure bouncy pop, they were excellent. This time though, I did watch Scott. It didn't matter that he had a special someone or that he'd be a million miles away by the morning and that I'd never see him again because I'd be dead. None of it mattered. I just wanted to soak up as much of him as possible and store it in my memory so that I could drag it out and it would be the last thing I'd see before the anaesthetic killed me.

And then they played The Hollies' 'Stay'. And Scott was singing.

And he was looking at me.

"… please stay… just a little bit longer…"

Vix jabbed me in the ribs. 'Told you!'

And I just smiled. Because it was silly and futile and pointless, not to mention wrong, for so many reasons.

And then, all too soon it was over. To roars of approval and deafening applause and heartbroken screams from the Dolly-Rockers, Narnia's Children finished their set with a flourish and the green curtains swished shut.

I actually felt bereft.

The lights in the hall blazed into life, and immediately the dark, smoochy atmosphere was bleached away. The packed hall no longer looked exciting – it just St B's gym hall. Mr Fisk was busily packing away his records, the Dolly Rockers were still hanging around the stage steps and most other people, blinking blearily, were heading for the cloakroom. I stood up.

'Whoa,' Vix grabbed my arm. 'Where are you going?'

'To get my coat.'

'Not before we've said goodbye to the boys in the band. C'mon...'

'Vix! No! Let's go home.'

But Vix wasn't listening and she hauled me after her, cutting a swathe through the Dolly Rockers, up the steps, and still with me in tow, barged through the curtains on to the stage.

Backstage, it was mayhem.

The boys and a slightly older bloke, presumably Rich the roadie, were winding miles of cables, hefting towers of speakers, packing away guitars, dismantling the drum kit, uncoupling microphone stands.

The stage was littered with discarded T-shirts, coats, drinks cans and bottles, towels and masses of other unrecognisable paraphernalia. Vix and I stood back and watched the organised chaos with fascination. It may have looked like pandemonium, but clearly Narnia's Children, organised by Rich, knew exactly how to clear everything away with the minimum of fuss and in the shortest possible time.

Scott was carefully packing away his guitar on the far side of the stage and he looked up and smiled at me. Warily, I smiled back.

'Go home,' a voice said in my ear. 'Leave him alone. He's got a girlfriend.'

I turned and looked at Mo, his arms full of band gear, and frowned. 'What?'

'He's got a girlfriend. She's gorgeous. Back off. Ok?'

Surprise, surprise. I sighed. 'Oh... er... that's nice...'

'It is. She is,' Mo walked away. 'She's cool. He's not into groupies like you, so clear off.'

'He's right,' Rich, also loaded with band kit, paused beside me. 'Renza's very special to Scott – and to all of us. He's going to marry her. Soon. He never looks at other women and he certainly won't be interested in you. So, stop hanging around. Look, love, putting this very nicely – sod off.'

Renza... pretty name. Italian? She probably looked exactly like Gina Lollobrigida or Sophia Loren. Dark, glamorous, sultry and oh-so-sexy. My imagination went into overdrive as I pictured her and Scott together... Renza... I knew I hated her.

I also knew when I wasn't wanted. You didn't have to tell me twice. Picking my way through the group's muddle, I headed for the gap in the stage curtains.

'Stella!' Scott had put down his guitar case and stepped in front of me. 'Where are you going? You can't just leave. You haven't said goodbye.'

I just stared at him. The most gorgeous, flirty, beautiful, clever, sexy – and engaged-to-be-married – boy I'd ever meet. Then I noticed Mo and Rich, still watching me, glaring at me, standing there, side-by-side behind Scott, like twin Outraged Moral Guardians.

'Go away,' Mo mouthed silently. 'He's got Renza. He's not interested. Go.'

Rich wasn't quite so polite. 'Bugger off!'

I didn't stop to think. I turned back to look at Scott, and without taking my eyes from his, I took a deep breath, balled up my fist, and punched him in the stomach. Hard.

I heard him gasp, heard Vix shriek, but just turned and ran towards the gap in the curtains. Then looking triumphantly over my shoulder at Mo and Rich, I pushed my way through the curtains, slithered down the stairs off the stage and ran out of the hall.

Stella's Diary
December 7th 1968 – continued...

Vix caught up with me in the cloakroom as I was shrugging into my fun-fur jacket.

'Stella! You *punched* him! You-punched-him!'

'Yep.'

'Are you mad?'

'Nope. Come on – let's go home.'

'But... you punched him! You punched Scott! They all saw you! They couldn't believe it! I couldn't believe it!' Vix hurried behind me as we pushed our way through the home-going throng, and emerged into the glittery-dark and bone-numbingly icy night. 'What the hell did you do that for? What did he say to you?'

'Nothing,' I stood outside St B's, surrounded by laughing people, their breath blowing smoky plumes into the air. 'Come on. I want to go home.'

Vix grabbed my arm. 'Did he hurt you? Are you in pain? What – ?'

'It was nothing like that. Please forget it – or don't as it's part of our night to remember...' I sighed as we fought our way through the excited crowd outside St B's. 'But hopefully he now knows I'm not intending to be another one-night-stand groupie – and the rest of them all got the message that I'm well aware about his precious Renza...'

'What? Who?' Vix tried to keep up with me, slipping and slithering across the icy car park.

'Renza. His girlfriend. Fiancée.'

'Oh.'

'Yep. Oh.'

'But you *punched* him! You've never punched anyone ever. Why...?'

'Honestly? I have no idea...' Not true! 'I was just so cross that they all seemed to think – '

'Hang on!' A loud voice shouted from behind us, interrupting me. 'Stella! Hang on!'

'Oooh,' Vix turned to stare, grabbing hold of me, almost falling on the ice. 'It's Mo! The drummer! He's waving at us!'

'Probably making sure we've left the area,' I muttered. 'He warned me off. More than once. Not that it mattered as I'm going to be dead, but...'

Vix stopped walking. 'Stop saying that. And let's see what he's got to say.'

'No thanks.'

I tried to side-step her. I shouldn't have punched Scott. Of course I shouldn't. It was childish and ridiculous. I'd never done anything like it before. But I was just so angry... and hurt... and... scared...? Yes, scared. And not just because of the operation any more. But because of the way I felt about him. I knew I'd made a fool of myself. It really wasn't the way I'd planned my last night out ever, to go.

Mo slid to a halt beside us. 'Please stop... I'm sorry... Stella, Scott's just told us... Sorry, again. It's just that we all love Renza and...'

Renza... I never wanted to hear the name again. I shook my head and snuggled deeper into my fun-fur. My nose and ears were hurting with the cold and I couldn't feel my hands. It was far too icy to stand about talking nonsense. 'Forget it. Have a safe journey back to Jersey. Tell Scott I'm sorry I punched him. Goodbye.'

'Look,' Mo stood in front of us, 'I don't know why you hit him, but Scott's told us that you're a music journalist and he'd asked you to do an interview with us sometime, that's what you were talking about. He also told us you're going into hospital which means you're ill. I'm so sorry – we just jumped to the wrong conclusions.'

'That's fine,' I said, laughing to myself at Scott's tactful interpretation of "music journalist". 'I'm sorry too. Goodnight.'

'The least we can do is give you a lift home,' Mo indicated over his shoulder to where a dark blue transit van was revving up. 'Rich has got us all packed in and we're ready to go. It's a rotten night and you shouldn't be walking anywhere.'

'That's ok.' I shrugged. 'I only live round the – '

'We'd love a lift,' Vix said quickly. 'Thanks so much.'

'No, we wouldn't -' I started.

'Yes we would.' Vix glared at me. 'We really, really would.'

Mo waved towards the transit, and with lights blazing, it crawled through the reluctant home-going crowd towards us.

It drew to a halt, doors were opened, voices shouted above the blaring music on the radio, and Vix and I were pulled inside.

'Where to?' Rich, who was driving, looked over his shoulder.

'Round the corner,' I muttered. I was half-sitting on a guitar case, with a rucksack under my feet and Joss squashed in beside me. I couldn't even see Scott. I guessed he was in the back somewhere. I didn't allow myself the pleasure of turning to look. It was enough to know he was there. 'Seriously. Round the corner. Out of the main gates, right turn, immediate left turn, then the second turning on the left.'

In the darkness, Dusty Springfield was singing 'Son of a Preacher Man'. Oh, those words... so evocative and sexy. I knew I'd remember them for ever and always think of Scott when I heard them. At least until I died on Monday, of course.

'And then where?' Rich said over his shoulder as we left St B's behind.

'Second house on the right,' Vix giggled from the front seat where she was sitting on Zak's lap – by accident or design I wasn't sure.

Rich frowned at me. 'You're kidding? You live here? You could have walked that in two minutes.'

'I know...' I sighed. 'I did say.'

We pulled up outside my house. I slid off the guitar case

and scrabbled for the door handle just as a tall figure loomed out of the darkness.

'Oooh look,' Vix said, slithering from Zak's lap, 'it's your dad, Stella.'

'Christ! Put your foot down, Rich,' Zak chuckled. 'He's a bloody giant – and we don't want any more run-ins with angry dads.'

'Stella's dad isn't like that,' Vix said, helping me scramble from the transit van. 'He's lovely. Oh, look – he's got the dogs with him. He must have been taking them out for their late night walk. Hi, Mr Deacon!'

Dad beamed. 'Hello, Vix. And what's this then? You got a lift home? That's nice... Stella?' He looked anxiously at me. 'You're all right, aren't you, love? You didn't have to be brought home because you felt ill?'

'No, no – I'm fine,' I assured him, bending down to fuss the dogs. 'We've had a wonderful night.'

Understatement.

'The boys in the band gave us a lift home,' Vix said. 'Because it's a cold night. Wasn't that kind of them?'

'Very,' Dad said, nodding towards Rich and Zak in the front seats of the van. 'Thank you, lads. Have you got far to go tonight?'

Jersey, I thought. A million miles away from here.

'Bedfordshire,' Rich said.

Not Jersey? Really?

Dad looked at the transit van. 'It'll take a good couple of hours in that, I reckon. You'd better come in and have a bit of a warm and a hot drink to set you up for the journey.'

Oh God. I closed my eyes. 'Dad – there's no need...'

'There's every need, Stella, love. The boys have been kind enough to see you safely home. It's a bitterly cold night. They've got a long way to go.'

'Yes, and to Bedfordshire *not* Jersey,' Vix giggled, and I kicked her.

Rich leaned out of the van. 'Are you sure? I mean, I could murder a cup of tea – but it's well past midnight – it's very late and...'

Vix laughed. 'Stella's parents are ace. Everyone's welcome. It's my second home – and it's just like an open house for waifs and strays.'

'Hardly that bad,' Dad grinned, 'although we've had our moments. But yes, I think a quick cuppa would be the least we can do. Come along... follow me...'

'Dad!' I grabbed his arm, hearing Narnia's Children leaping out of the transit behind me. 'Please...'

Too late. They were out of the van.

With Dad and the dogs in the lead, Vix still giggling and hugging me, and the group bringing up the rear, we all paraded into the old-fashioned, cluttered and cosy kitchen.

'Visitors, duck,' Dad said to Mum, with her fly-away hair on end and her big glasses on the end of her nose, who was sitting at the kitchen table with two cats and a crossword puzzle. 'I'll get the kettle on...'

It was surreal. Seriously. Amidst all the kitchen clutter and the animals and the ancient dusty coke boiler pouring out heat and my parents both talking at the same time, were Narnia's Children.

Sexy, knock-out, famous, drop dead gorgeous, Narnia's Children.

In my home.

A few hours ago Vix and I had been lustfully staring at them in the spotlights, on the stage, rocking St B's as it had never been rocked before. And now they were here.

'Take your coats off, girls, and go on through to the living room all of you,' Mum said once introductions and explanations had been made. 'It's warmer in there. Tea or coffee or hot chocolate?'

Everyone opted delightedly for hot chocolate. I didn't. I was still shell-shocked.

Somehow we all moved through to the living room, all lamplight and big old-fashioned lop-sided sofas and huge scruffy chairs and a coal fire roaring up the chimney.

'Wow!' Rich grinned. 'Paradise.'

Zak, Mo and Joss nodded in agreement.

They all plonked themselves down round the fire, stretching out their long legs, holding their hands out to the flames. Vix, the dogs and three of the cats joined them. I just stood in the doorway looking at them and wanted to laugh hysterically. It was all too bizarre for words. Still, I'd wanted a last-Saturday-night-on-earth to remember, hadn't I? I certainly hadn't bargained on this, though.

Scott had stopped to stroke one of the cats in the kitchen. He smiled at me. 'Fab home... and parents... you're so lucky.'

'I know...' I took a deep breath. 'I'm so sorry. About hitting you. It was unforgiveable.'

'It was a shock,' he laughed softly. 'You pack quite a punch. Want to tell me why?'

I shook my head. 'I shouldn't have done it. Put it down to insanity. I'm just sorry. That's all.'

'Here we are,' Mum bustled in then with a tray loaded with mis-matched cups and mugs and started handing them round to murmurs of thanks and appreciation. 'Now, I bet you boys haven't had anything to eat tonight, have you?'

'Oh my God...' I shook my head. 'Mum, honestly, they're ok...'

As one, Narnia's Children, who were so skinny they looked like they hadn't eaten a decent meal for months, looked at her expectantly.

'Will beans on toast be ok? If I'd known Stella and Vix were going to bring friends home I'd have popped some potatoes to cook under the fire. Nothing like a baked potato for supper on a night like this.'

Again, the boys all raved ecstatically about beans on toast

and Mum bustled out happily.

Oh, I loved my mum – but her need to feed the world was sometimes so embarrassing.

Scott, who was perched on the arm of one of the sofas patted the seat beside him. I sat down.

'Are you cold?' He looked down at me. 'You're shaking. Oh – do you feel ill?'

I shook my head. The reason for my shakes was exactly the same as the reason for the punch, and had absolutely nothing to do with my illness – but I wasn't going to tell him that. Never. Ever.

'Good – oh, and does your mum need a hand with anything? It's the middle of the night. We really shouldn't take advantage like this and...'

I turned away from him. I couldn't look at him. He'd know how I felt. And because of Renza, there was absolutely no point in it, was there? And, of course, the fact that I wasn't going to be alive for much longer anyway didn't help.

'Mum's fine – she's never happier than when she has a houseful of people to feed – and we'll just get in her way. I'll help her with the washing-up later.'

'We could do that,' Scott grinned. 'Not that we're much good at it. But it'd be the least we could do.'

'Believe me, she wouldn't let you. You're guests. In my mum's rules, guests don't do the washing up.'

I knew he was looking at me. I stared at the carpet. It really was very old and worn and covered in dogs' hairs. I wondered if Scott had a posh house in Jersey. Of course he did. Everyone in Jersey was fabulously rich. Even I knew that.

What a lame conversation! But what else could I say? He belonged to Renza and would soon walk out of my life forever. He'd disappear back to the delights of the sultry Renza in Bedfordshire or Jersey or wherever she lived. There was absolutely no point in pretending it was going to be any different.

'Stella,' Scott's voice was low. 'I need to say so many things – but, about the interview...'

'Probably not a good idea. Not right now.'

'No, of course not. But maybe in the future. When you're better. You can let me know when the time's right. Look, if you give me your phone number now and...'

'We're not on the phone.'

'Oh, right...'

And I'm not going to survive the operation and you have a fiancée and I really, really want to cry now, I thought.

Dad made his entrance at that point, carrying a massive pile of sliced bread and several toasting forks. 'Make yourself useful, lads. Grab a fork... beans are bubbling... Supper won't be long...'

There was a lot of vying for the best position in front of the fire as Narnia's Children knelt on our faded, tatty hearth rug and duelled with toasting forks, much to the delight of the over-excited dogs. It was growing more and more wacky by the minute.

The television, sharing its battered two-tiered table in the corner with the wireless, was long-silent, given the time, so Vix, still grinning at me, turned the radio on to Luxembourg and danced around the living room. Judy Clay and William Bell were singing 'Private Number'.

Scott had asked for my private number. Some hopes!

I let the sexy, sultry voices and the words of the song seep into my brain, staring at Scott's black hair gleaming in the firelight as he attempted to turn his slice of bread on the toasting fork without burning himself, knowing again it was a song that would always mean the world to me.

'How we doing, boys?' Dad stuck his head into the room. 'Ah, looking good. Right here's some more bread to toast. I'll butter this lot. Ta.'

Within moments, plates were piled high with beans on toast, Vix joined the boys eating their mountainous supper –

Mum never did things by half – while Dad asked them endless questions about the group and about Jersey and about them now living somewhere in Bedfordshire... Leighton Buzzard I thought I heard them say... I wasn't absolutely sure where it was but I'd heard about it because of the Great Train Robbery. And then Rich was saying they wouldn't be living in Leighton Buzzard properly again until January as they were going home to Jersey for Christmas and then had gigs in France for the New Year.

Leaving them all eating, drinking, talking and laughing at Dad's outrageous stories, and because I wasn't able to eat anything, I went into the kitchen and hugged Mum. 'Thank you. They love it. And sorry to have dumped this lot on you so late.'

She hugged me back. 'Don't apologise. Dad says they were kind enough to see you home, and he invited them in – not you. They're a lovely crowd of boys, too. So polite – and very handsome. Actually, I saw you and the very good-looking boy with the black hair, Scott – is that his name? – chatting just now. You seemed to be getting on well together. I thought, maybe...?'

'Oh, yes, he's gorgeous.' Understatement again. 'But he's got a fiancée.'

'Ah. Shame. Anyway, having them here into the early hours is definitely a good thing,' she looked at me, her eyes sad behind the glasses. 'I doubt if any of us would have slept much tonight, would we? What with you going into hospital tomorrow...'

'Today.' I gulped. 'It's today, Mum. Now it's Sunday. The operation is tomorrow.'

'Oh, Stella.' Mum hugged me a bit more. 'It'll be ok. You'll be alright. They'll sort everything out and you'll feel so much better again.'

'I'm so scared, Mum.'

'I know, love. I know.'

***

Half an hour later, having said their goodbyes and thanks and offered a million times to do the washing-up, and having shaken Dad's hand and kissed Mum, Narnia's Children filed back outside into the bitter, glittery, icy night.

Joss and Mo, already yawning, scrambled back into the van. Zak, shivering, lingered behind and asked Vix if she wanted a lift home and was most put-out when she said she was sleeping at my house, so he kissed her briefly and leapt into the van. Vix hugged herself, said it was far too cold to hang about and hurried back inside as Rich swung himself into the driving seat.

Which left Scott. He paused beside me.

'Goodnight. Have a safe journey.' I said through chattering teeth. 'And I'm sorry.'

'For punching me?'

'No — well, yes, that of course — but... I know about Renza.'

'Ah, yes. I thought you might. They told you?'

'They did. And they also told me that you love her and you're going to marry her.'

'Both true.'

We stared at one another in the black, diamond-frosty night.

He took my hands in his. I shivered. Not with the cold. His hands were icy and burned my skin like fire.

He moved closer. 'Take care of yourself. Don't die. Please. I'll be thinking of you, Twinkle.'

'Twinkle?' My voice was only a whisper. '*Twinkle*?'

He smiled that lovely lop-sided smile. 'Stella means star — I've had an education, you know. So — twinkle, twinkle little star...'

I giggled.

'That's better.' He smiled some more. 'I mean it, Twinkle. Don't die. You're too special. Goodbye.'

He let go of my hands, kissed my cheek very, very gently

and swung himself into the van.

'Goodbye...' I whispered to the tall, dark, handsome stranger from over the sea. 'Goodbye...'

And I stood there, in the freezing diamond darkness long, long after the red tail lights had disappeared into the distance with my tears crystallizing on my cheeks.

Stella's Diary
December 9ᵗʰ 1968

'Wakey-wakey...'

The voice echoed from the depths of a long, long, dark red corridor. I was warm and deeply asleep. I really didn't want to open my eyes. My head felt heavy and I couldn't move.

I couldn't move...

I tried opening one eye and that didn't work either.

'Stella! Wakey-wakey! Come on, love!'

I felt very sick. And I still couldn't move or open my eyes. Was I dead?

'Time to wake up, Stella!' The voice was close to my ear, loud and irritatingly cheerful.

Somehow, fighting the urge to be sick, I dragged myself out of the dizzying, dark red, roaring pit I appeared to be stuck in.

'Hello,' the cheerful voice said even more loudly. 'You're back with us, then.'

'I'm going to be sick,' I croaked. And was.

There was a lot of bustling round and mopping and reassuring noises.

'There. All done. No, don't try to move. I'll give you something for the nausea. Stay still — it's just a small injection — it'll make you feel much better... there...'

I felt something cold jab into my arm.

'Am I dead?' My voice crackled weakly.

'Bless you. Of course not. You're in recovery. We'll have you back up on the ward in a jiffy.'

I tried to let this sink into my swirling brain. 'Recovery? Back? Is it over? The operation?'

'Of course it is, love.' The nurse came into view then, very blurry and smiley. 'You're just coming round, so you'll feel a bit groggy.'

'But — so, I didn't die? I'm still alive?'

The nurse laughed. 'No you didn't and yes you are.' She was

226

plump and the stripes on her uniform dress danced in zig-zags. 'Now, just one thing – don't try to move your arms, there's a good girl. OK?'

'Okay...' My arms felt like lead weights. I'd have agreed to anything. Anything at all. I was alive! I hadn't died under the anaesthetic!

I smiled. Or tried to. I didn't care how sick I felt, or how much I ached, or how weird any of this was – I was alive! Still!

'Right, Stella, love – we'll get the porters to whizz you back up to the ward as soon as poss. You'll feel a bit sore I expect, but the ward nurses will give you something for that. Good girl, try to stay awake at the moment – you'll feel so much better if you do – and mind those arms.'

'Yes...' I croaked obediently, wishing my head would stop spinning. 'But my throat's a bit sore... and my mouth's dry...'

'You can have a sip of water back up on the ward. Bound to be a bit dry – you've had tubes and whatnots down your throat and your mouth's been taped open for ages.'

Somewhere in my still-swirling brain I realised this should shock me but somehow none of it mattered. Not anymore. It was over. I didn't die!

'Good girl.' The nurse patted my shoulder and stuck a thermometer in my mouth. 'Ok. Temperature a bit high – I'll get them to sort that out on the ward.' There was a tight sensation in my upper arm. 'Ah, blood pressure a bit low... we'll have to see to that. But you've done really well. Oh, good, here's the porters.'

***

I have no idea how long it took to trundle me along miles of green-painted corridors, through umpteen sets of swishy plastic doors, past various lights in the ceiling. I was vaguely aware of the reassuring alive hospital smell of disinfectant and heat and municipal catering and hoped I wouldn't be sick again while I was lying flat on my back.

227

We crashed into the dimly-lit ward, through yet more swishy doors, and there was a lot of lifting and moving and shifting as the porters and nurses transferred me to a bed. My bed? The one I'd been in previously? I had no idea.

'Right, Stella,' a very pretty nurse who I'd never seen before and who honestly didn't look much older than me, busied herself checking all my vital signs again. 'I'm Mary and I'll be here all night if you need me. Do you feel sick?'

'No. Not anymore. Just thirsty. And a bit sore. And tired.'

'Right. We'll give you a pain-killing injection. Sister Wolstenholme will see to that. She's in charge of the ward — and me. And you can have a sip of water. Then sleep. And you'll feel much better in the morning.'

Sister Wolstenholme — big and kindly — bustled up. Another injection. A mouthful of luke-warm water that tasted stale and was the loveliest drink I'd ever had. Then I realised why I couldn't move my arms. I squinted at them. They were both supported by splints wrapped in bandages, with large cannulas attached to my veins with intravenous drip bottles suspended on either side.

I watched with interest as blood dripped slowly into my right arm and a clear fluid into my left.

'Saline solution,' Mary said. 'And a blood transfusion. You lost quite a lot of fluids according to the notes. We'll have to top them up during the night, but you'll get rid of them in the morning, hopefully.'

'I can't move. What if I need to –um – wee?'

'Catheter, love.' Sister Wolstenholme said cheerfully. 'All draining out of you and tucked away under the bed as we speak. No need for you to worry. That won't be in for long, either.'

'Thanks.' I honestly didn't care. I was alive. I worked some saliva into my mouth. 'What time is it?'

'Almost 11.30,' Mary checked her watch and grinned. 'Past your bedtime.'

11.30? At night? Crikey. I'd gone – happily floating on pre-med – down to the operating theatre at 3.30 in the afternoon. That was ages ago. The operation must have taken hours. I didn't care about that, either. Because I wasn't dead.

'Right,' Mary said. 'I'll leave you now. Try to sleep. I'll pop over to you during the night – I'll have to wake you up, I'm afraid, to check your temperature and blood pressure and change the drips.'

'That's OK,' I mumbled, suddenly desperately tired. 'I don't mind. I'm just glad I'm not dead.'

Mary and Sister Wolstenholme laughed. I think they thought I was joking. I'd never been more serious in my life.

Stella's Diary
December 10th 1968

My consultant – Mr Glendenning – who I'd only ever seen at that final outpatient appointment, rattled the faded floral curtains closed and loomed over my bed. He was still tall, balding, stern-faced and terrifying. He had an extremely posh voice, half-moon spectacles, scared me witless, and had never, ever smiled. A small red-haired woman stood beside him, and they were flanked, as ever, by several youthful, white-coated boys and girls. Everyone was staring at me. And again they all had stethoscopes and clipboards.

'You still have no objection to the students, I hope, Miss Deacon?' Mr Glendenning boomed. 'I believe you understand this is a teaching hospital.'

Terrified, I shook my head. Then nodded. It covered everything.

'Good.' He consulted the chart from the bottom of the bed. 'As I'd suspected. Laparotomy. Investigative. Ah, yes. You had – and have had – numerous neglected cysts and subsequent abscesses on your ovary – did you know you only have one ovary, Miss Deacon? No? Fascinating. Also on your uterus and surrounding pelvic sites. Some of these cysts and abscesses were geriatric and had become severely infected. We removed them all. We cleaned you up. A further course of intravenous antibiotics while in hospital, and oral on your discharge, should mean the tissue and organs stay contamination-free and heal naturally. Understand so far?'

I nodded. It sounded like I'd been in a heck of a mess and now I wasn't. It meant the pains would stop. It was all I needed to know, really. And I hadn't died.

He checked my pulse, looked again at my notes and nodded at the drips. 'You lost a lot of blood. The operation took far longer than we'd anticipated. I will advise the nurses to remove the blood-transfusion bottle at lunchtime.

The saline drip must stay for another 24 hours.'

I nodded again. The students were scribbling on their clipboards.

'Good.' Mr Glendenning boomed even more loudly. 'Are you married, Miss Deacon? I'm assuming not.'

'Er... no....'

'Planning on marrying in the near future?'

'No.'

'Right. But you have had sexual intercourse?'

Oh my God. I turned my head away. I just wanted to die with embarrassment. What sort of question was that? In front of all those people? Strangers?

Yes, of course I had... once. Just once. That hideously embarrassing once. Ages ago – in that caravan – with Mike, the one-and-only boyfriend.

Crimson-faced, I nodded and muttered something. The students smirked. I saw the small red-haired woman look at me with deep sympathy.

Mr Glendenning showed no such emotion. 'Very well. Please refrain from repeating the process for at least eight weeks. You need time to heal.'

'I haven't even got a boyfriend...' I mumbled.

'Well, that will help,' Mr Glendenning snapped, 'but is of no interest to me. I will need to book you outpatients appointments once we've discharged you as there are a few issues looming. I will tell you this – although I don't want you to assume it's a green-light to promiscuity – but given the condition of your reproductive system, the chances of you ever becoming pregnant would be about as miraculous as the Raising of Lazarus.'

Still desperately humiliated by the sex question, I seriously didn't care. I didn't care if I never had sex again. Ever. And, my mangled and mashed-up innards meant I may never be able to have children? I was 20. Single. No boyfriend. Never having sex again. It wasn't a problem. Truly.

Again the red-haired woman shot me a sympathetic smile.

'I will leave you with Miss Edwards here to examine you, explain more about your operation, what the next stages of the treatment will be, and the implications.' Mr Glendenning indicated the red-haired woman. 'But, Miss Deacon, to reiterate, as you appear to have been born with a pretty useless reproductive system which, if I'm not mistaken, is already showing signs of advanced endometriosis, I doubt there will be very much good news she will be able to impart. Good day.'

I had absolutely no idea what he was talking about. I just wanted him and the smirking students to go away so that I could bury my burning face in my pillow.

'Er... goodbye... and – um – thank you...' I muttered.

'Oh, don't thank me,' Mr Glendenning paused in pulling the curtains. 'Miss Edwards was your surgeon. Not me. I simply oversaw the process.'

He stomped away, mercifully followed by the students.

Miss Edwards, my tiny red-haired surgeon, smiled kindly at me. 'I'm so, so sorry.'

'It's ok,' I wriggled uncomfortably on my rubber sheet. I still couldn't sit up. 'I don't think I want children. I've never thought about it. I'll think about it later.'

'Like Scarlett O'Hara,' Miss Edwards smiled kindly. 'But actually I was apologising for the excruciating questions. He's an amazingly talented and enlightened man – there still aren't many women surgeons and he pushed for me to be on his team – but his bed-side manner leaves a lot to be desired. I know how embarrassing that must have been for you.'

I nodded. I really didn't want to think about it. 'I didn't think there were lady surgeons, actually. And thank you for sorting me out and making me better. I was so scared. I thought I'd die on the operating table.'

Miss Edwards chuckled and perched on the foot of the bed.

'Oh, I wouldn't have let that happen. It would look so bad on my curriculum vitae. Now, Stella, as you'll have gathered, you were in a pretty appalling mess, and I'm confident that I've cleared everything out. However, you will have to have follow-up appointments and some possible heat treatment on the scar tissue, then further investigations... oh, and I'm afraid the information about infertility was very accurate. Still, as this isn't a problem at the moment, let's be positive and deal with the current issues. Have you looked at your operation area yet?'

'God no!'

Miss Edwards laughed. 'Not that there's anything to see – I've used metal butterfly clips, not stitches, so it might feel a little funny when you're brave enough to touch it – and it's well-covered up so there's nothing gory to see, I promise you.'

'Clips? Like bulldog clips?'

'More or less, I suppose. Only smaller. More efficient than stiches for such a large wound.'

I winced.

She carried on, 'I've also, bearing in mind that you're so young, tried hard to keep the scar as low as possible. You should still be able to wear a bikini without it showing, and it will eventually fade even if it never completely disappears – but, a word of warning, it does go from hip to hip.'

Hip to hip? Dear Lord! I'd been sawn in half! I'd never be able to move again in case my innards spilled out.

Miss Edwards pulled back the covers and lifted my hospital gown and gently prodded my stomach. 'Yes, very good. It all feels fine. I'm not hurting you?'

'No. I still can't feel anything. I mean, I had a bad stomach ache earlier and they gave me another injection.'

'It's a shame you've still got those drips in, otherwise you could have sat up and had a look. It's quite psychedelic, actually.' She chuckled. 'Your stomach was painted with iodine pre-op, so it's now a delightful orangey yellow, and I've used bright blue adhesive tape to cover the clips. Very colourful.'

I closed my eyes. I really didn't want to know. I knew I'd never be able to look at it or touch it anyway. I'd probably never be able to laugh or dance or swim or cry or cough... and I'd definitely never have a bath again in case it split open and I was left sitting in my own offal.

'The clips should come out in 10 days. And if you're doing well, with everything healing and returning to normal, you should be discharged within 48 hours after that.' Miss Edwards grinned as she straightened my gown and the sheet. 'Hopefully, we'll have you home in time for Christmas yet.

Stella's Diary
December 20th 1968

I had my bulldog clips out today. I didn't look. They gave the job to Mary, who, I'd found out was one of the really young SENs, watched carefully by Sister Wolstenholme. I don't know which one of us – me or Mary – was the most terrified. But Mary did a grand job, and I listened to her sigh of relief as she dropped yet another clip successfully into the kidney dish with a metallic clang.

'There. Last one done,' she looked at me. 'I didn't hurt you, did I?'

'No. Not at all. Thank you.'

Both Mary and Sister Wolstenholme peered at the scar tissue and seemed happy.

Mary handed me a mirror. 'Have a look. Go on. Honestly. It's ok.'

I looked. I wasn't scared of it any longer, but heavens above – it didn't look ok to me. Miss Edwards' "hip to hip" hadn't been an exaggeration. I was bright orange from my waist downwards. The massive scar was raised, livid red and blobbed with congealed blood, and the clips had left two rows of scarlet teeth marks on either side of it.

I looked like I zipped up.

'Wonderful job,' Sister Wolstenholme enthused. 'You're a lucky girl, Stella. The physiotherapist is delighted with you too, so you just need to get that temperature to stay down and the blood pressure to stay up, and we'll be waving goodbye to you really soon.'

I propped myself back up on my pillows once they'd gone and thought about things. Mainly about that horrendous gash right across my stomach. Just as well I didn't have a boyfriend, I thought. That was enough to put anyone off.

Even Scott. Especially Scott.

Oh, yes, especially Scott. Scott, who had the obviously un-scarred perfect Renza.

I'd thought about Scott quite a bit. I knew it was daft, but it had helped to while away some of the more scary hours. I re-lived every minute of the night we'd met. Over and over again. I'd never forget him, I knew that. I wondered where he was... Leighton Buzzard? No, they'd probably left for Jersey now to spend Christmas, and then France for the New Year. And no doubt the glorious sultry Renza would be anchored to his side.

Ah, well.... water under the bridge, as my nan always said – or ships that pass in the night? Whichever it was, I knew I'd never see Scott again.

I gingerly touched my scar and smiled. He'd made me promise not to die – and I hadn't. I hoped, not that he'd ever know, that he'd be pleased.

In fact, once I'd realised that I hadn't died, and once the soreness had lessened and I'd had all the drips and tubes removed, I'd quite enjoyed my stay in hospital so far. It was like a little closed-in world. Like anything on the outside had ceased to exist.

There were 12 beds in the ward, 6 on each side, and we'd all been admitted at much the same time for all manner of "women's problems" and become good friends. With no regard to emotional clashes regarding treatment, we were a mixed bunch: Joan and Maureen on either side of me were about the same age as my mum and had had hysterectomies, then there were the four girls on the other side of the ward who were having abortions for various reasons, two ladies having fertility treatment, and another two expectant mums who were having to stay in hospital for the duration of their confinements.

And then there was The Woman in the End Bed.

She didn't belong to our chummy club. She refused to speak to us. None of knew why she was in – unlike the rest of us, obviously, she hadn't shared the most intimate details of her treatment – but she looked really old and had long straggly hair and she roared all night long, having awful nightmares, and then got up and walked the ward chain-smoking.

I didn't smoke, but those who did were allowed to smoke in the day room, but I think the nurses, who all smoked in their nurses station room – it was like a pea-souper when you went past it if you got up in the night for wee – were scared of her, so they turned a blind eye.

I felt sorry for The Woman in the End Bed.

Mr Glendenning, accompanied by Miss Edwards and the students, made his daily round, and seemed increasingly happy with my progress. All in all, once I'd stopped feeling ill, it was almost like being on holiday. Dad had bought me two massive doorstopper books: *The Foxes of Harrow* by Frank Yerby, and *Mr Britling Sees It Through* by H. G. Wells. I lost myself in them. I read anything and everything – and these long, long stories were absolutely perfect to while away the hours.

Maureen and Joan were both a bit shocked that I read so much and so avidly. They both said the serial in their *Woman's Weekly* was enough for them.

And despite what everyone had said, the food wasn't bad, and now I didn't have a constant stomach ache I'd regained my appetite and ate everything that was put in front of me. Then, at night, when the trolley came round, we had a choice of drinks – milky ones like Horlicks, or either a small tipple of spirits or a glass of stout. I had stout because Sister Wolstenholme said it would help my low iron levels. I'd never had Guinness before, not being much of a drinker, and it tasted a bit odd, but mixed with my various pills, it always sent me off to sleep very nicely.

I'd even had my hair done by the hospital hairdresser when she came round the ward. We all had. It was odd to have your hair washed and set (she only did one style but I wasn't out to impress anyone so I didn't care) sitting on the bed, but lovely to have clean hair again even if my fringe was a bit frizzier than I'd have liked.

And we had hospital radio on headphones. I loved this and sang along happily. Whoever played or requested the records seemed to like the Paper Dolls and the Caravelles a lot... And The

237

Love Affair's 'Everlasting Love'. Yes, I loved this one and dreamed foolishly of Scott. Just more music, more lyrics, I thought, that would never leave me.

At visiting time, the ward was like one big noisy party. Everyone had visitors at the same time – except The Woman In The End Bed – no one ever came to see her. She just sat there, in bed, glaring, watching everyone else being hugged and chatted to. I felt really sorry for her, but when Maureen, Joan and I had tried to talk to her she'd told us all to piss off and spat on the floor. We gave her a wide berth after that. So sad.

Mum and Dad visited every evening, Vix and Jeff, and the girls from work, and other friends popped in, and my bed was surrounded by flowers and grapes and Get Well Soon cards. Now I hadn't died, I thought being in hospital wasn't too bad at all.

Stella's Diary

December 23rd 1968 – morning

'Right,' Sister Wolstenholme beamed at me after Mr Glendenning and his entourage had left the ward following his morning rounds. 'We're getting rid of you at last, Stella. You're being discharged.'

It seemed everyone on our ward – except the long-term confinement ladies and The Woman In The End Bed – was also being discharged.

'They like a clear-out before Christmas,' Joan said knowledgeably, as we all sat on our beds, surrounded by our clothes and outdoor coats and boots and bags, and clutching our large sealed envelopes containing the letter for our local doctor, details of further outpatients appointments and prescriptions. 'Makes sense. Them poor nurses need a Christmas, too.'

I was so excited to be going home. Yes, ok, I'd been a bit homesick. And I'd missed the dogs and cats and my nans and grandpas. And having a proper giggle with Vix. And I wanted to talk to someone about Scott. And she was the only person who knew and who would understand.

We'd all had to make arrangements for being picked up: mine, because we weren't on the phone at home, meant one of the nurses leaving a message for my dad at the transport depot where he was a lorry driver, and he and Mum would come and get me as soon as they could. I knew I might have a long wait, as I sadly waved goodbye to Joan and Maureen and the other women who had become the only inhabitants of my world for so long.

'Have they spoken to my dad?' I asked Mary. 'Do you know what time they'll be here? Can I get dressed yet?'

I hadn't been out of my Marks and Spencer's white cotton Victoriana nighties and pink silk 1920s wrap and fluffy slippers since I'd graduated from the hospital gowns. I knew I had to wear something loose – and very big knickers – so that nothing touched the scar. I'd brought one of the short floaty frocks I'd made last year and a pair of pull-on wide-legged black Biba trousers I'd found at a jumble sale, and couldn't wait to wear proper clothes again.

'Ah... um....' Mary mumbled. 'You're not exactly going home...'

'Yes I am.' I laughed. 'Look – I've got all my papers and medicines and things.'

'Yes, you're leaving here, but,' Mary bustled round tidying the top of my empty locker and not looking at me, 'you're not going home. Because you need daily heat treatment, you're going into Harbury Green Cottage Hospital. They have the right heat machine there. Your dad has been phoned. Your parents know what's happening. The ambulance will take you in about half an hour.'

I stared at her. She had to be joking. The Cottage Hospital, on the outskirts of our village, was only about fifteen minutes' walk from my home. It was where old people, with no families to care for them in Harbury Green, went to die.

'I'm not going there.'

'You are.' Mary stared me down from under her neat cap. 'You have to.'

'I'm not going. It's where people die.'

'It's a very good Cottage Hospital and Convalescent Home. That's why you're going there. For convalescence. You're fit enough to not need us anymore, but not well enough to go home.'

I felt fine. I didn't need to convalesce – and if I did, I'd do it at home. With my mum and dad and the animals.

I knew I was going to cry. I bit my lips really, really hard. 'You mean – I'll be so nearly home, but in the bloody Cottage Hospital *over Christmas*?'

'Yes... and don't swear. We don't have swearing on the ward.'

'I know. Sorry... but it's Christmas Eve tomorrow. I want to be at home for Christmas.'

Mary pulled a face. 'I know. So do I. But I've got to work and my family all live in Sunderland.'

I sighed heavily. 'That's rotten, but you don't have a choice. I do.'

'You don't, you know,' Mary said firmly as she whisked away the curtains round my bed. 'You've had major surgery. You still need medical attention. The ambulance will be here in about ten minutes. Don't bother to get dressed, they'll take you in your nightie and pop you straight into a bed at the Cottage Hospital.'

'Over my dead body.'

'And it probably will be,' Mary said darkly, 'if you don't do what you're told.'

Renza's Diary
December 23rd 1968

It's been a fun time for the kids who are really excited about Christmas. All throughout the month there have been pantomimes and special events laid on for them. There've been various entertainments in the Mess and a military dance band came to play several nights in a row. I was allowed to go a couple of times. The music was good but I hated having to dance with some of the old fogies from Dad's office. I wrote and told Scott he'd better watch out because one of the fat policeman seemed to have a 'thing' for me according to one of the wives who is friends with Mum.

The Mess held a Christmas dinner for the families and some specially invited Germans — mostly the Police chief and other important people from the area. The tables were all decorated in red, gold and green and a huge Christmas tree stood in the main ballroom with lots of real lighted candles, baubles and chocolate ornaments which the kids got to take home with gingerbread men and huge heart shaped pretzels.

The kids were all on tables together and had smaller versions of what we were having. Crackers were being pulled constantly and paper hats worn and the noise from them was unbelievable but someone else had to supervise all the children for a change, leaving me to enjoy myself.

We had turkey, roast pork and lamb — such a nice change as it's hard to get lamb in Germany — and all the trimmings and every kind of vegetable imaginable and some of the best roast spuds I've ever had. Every table had champagne and wine to drink and I was allowed to have whatever I wanted — and I did.

Magicians entertained the kids and Father Christmas came and handed out presents for them. They were taken in to watch a movie a bit later when the grown-ups had coffee and Christmas cake with mince pies, served in the bar. I crept into a corner out of sight of the fat policeman who'd spotted me at dinner, and tried to hide.

German men in traditional costumes – lederhosen and silly hats – started jumping around, thigh slapping, shouting, playing accordions and blowing horns, and everyone got up to dance. Zillions of miles away from a Narnia's Children gig, I told Scott when I wrote; I bet he laughed. How the heck you're supposed to dance to oompah oompah I've no idea, but by this time nearly everyone was a bit the worse for wear, including me. When he eventually found me I even let the fat policeman tread on my toes for two dances; my resistance was low.

Stella's Diary
December 23rd 1968 – afternoon

The ambulance driver had locked the doors! He'd laughed and said he'd been warned I might try to escape! We'd bundled off from the hospital – me and half a dozen other discharged patients – round Oxford, dropping the lucky ones off at their homes. Each time one was let out of the ambulance, the driver kept a careful eye on me. Exasperated, I fleetingly glimpsed bleak, grey daylight and smelled fresh air for the first time in ages. Still in my nightie and flimsy dressing gown, I shivered. It was very, very cold.

Then it was just me left. The ambulance man laughed some more as he locked me in for the last time and we headed off through the icy gunmetal countryside, en route for Harbury Green.

We arrived all too soon.

The convalescent ward at the Cottage Hospital was tropically hot and smelled of wee and biscuits and Dettol. It was in semi-darkness and hand-made paperchains looped sadly from the ceiling. An unlit Christmas tree lurked in a shadowy corner. I could hear snores and gentle snuffles from the half a dozen beds.

More depressed than I could ever remember being, I stood at the nurses' desk clutching my paperwork in one hand and my bag in the other.

'Right, dearie,' the elderly nurse whispered. 'You'll be over there. In the bed in the corner. We'll be waking everyone up for afternoon tea in a minute. You pop yourself into bed and I'll have a look at your notes.'

'No.'

'I beg your pardon?'

'I'm not getting into bed because I'm not stopping here. Sorry.'

'Of course you're stopping here,' she hissed so as not to

disturb the other slumbering patients. 'I need to check your notes from Oxford but we already know you're here to convalesce and have 10 days of heat treatment to heal your internal surgical damage and mend your severed stomach muscles. With bed rest and everything, we'll probably need to have you here for about a month.'

A month! I'd be stark, staring crazy within a month.

'I want to go home. I want to discharge myself.'

'Don't be silly. Anyway, you can't. You're under 21.'

I deflated. And tried again. 'How can I be discharged, then? Look, I'm not being awkward or anything – but I don't live very far away, my mum will make sure I stay in bed or whatever I'm supposed to do, and I promise I'll turn up here every day for my treatment. Is there anyone I can talk to? Someone in charge?'

The nurse bridled. She looked about as old as my nan. 'We don't have doctors in situ, as you no doubt know, being a local. Everyone's family doctor pops in each day. We have a matron. And an almoner.'

'And could either of those discharge me?'

'No,' she tried smiling kindly. 'You're too young. I know it must seem very frustrating, being so close to home, but the Churchill said you needed to convalesce – and that's what you're going to do. Look, why don't you wait for your parents to arrive. They've been told you're here, I gather. You'll feel better when you see them. Shall I make you a cup of tea?'

I nodded. I felt very tired and my legs hurt and my back ached and I thought I was probably going to cry.

Half an hour later, I was sitting in the high-backed chair beside my allocated-but-untouched bed with a cup of tea and two custard creams, when my mum and dad arrived. The nurse got to them first, and I could tell by the body language that she was explaining why I wasn't in bed and clearly what an ungrateful little madam I was.

The rest of the ward had woken up and, wrapped in fluffy bed jackets, were watching the floor show with interest.

It took another half an hour for me to explain to Mum and Dad why I wasn't stopping at the Cottage Hospital and persuade them to sign the discharge forms on my behalf, and a further rather frosty encounter with the almoner and the matron – both of whom looked like they'd been dragged away from something far more vital and thought I was simply beyond the pale.

With dire medical warnings ringing in my ears, strict instructions that – in the unlikely event that I hadn't died or at least deteriorated and needed urgent hospital re-admission in the intervening days – I'd be collected by ambulance early on December 27th for my first 9 a.m. outpatients heat treatment session, and being told in no uncertain terms that any further medical emergencies caused by my stupidity would be dealt with by Oxford and *not* the Cottage Hospital, I stepped out into the bitterly cold December night with Mum and Dad.

Stella's Diary
December 1968 23rd – evening

I was home at last! Bliss!

Because I still couldn't walk upstairs very well, I was in bed in my downstairs room. It was really supposed to be the dining room, but as we always ate in the kitchen, I'd made it my den while I was studying for O levels – and now, as well as my desk, it had a lovely big and cosy studio couch which turned into a bed, masses of rugs and floor cushions, two standard lamps, my radio and record player, posters and photos all over the walls and a huge bookcase. It was where Vix – or any other visitors – slept if they stayed over.

A fire crackled in the grate, the dogs were sprawled out on the floor in front of it and the cats were snuggled into my eiderdown as Radio Luxembourg played softly.

I was home.

Mum and Dad, at first desperately worried about me insisting that I wasn't staying at the Cottage Hospital, and frankly a bit angry with me for causing so much fuss, had doled out my medication, more or less forgiven me, made me a mug of hot chocolate and a plate of cheese and pickle sandwiches, and had tucked me up in bed like I was 10 years old. It was lovely.

Oh, but Luxembourg was being a bit cruel...

'Son of a Preacher Man'... 'Private Number'... 'Everlasting Love'...

I flicked through the pages of *Boyfriend* and *Rave* – Vix had left them for me along with a note saying she'd see me on Christmas Eve – and leaned back on my pillows and daydreamed foolishly.

'Still awake, Stella?' Mum popped her head round the door. 'All ok?'

I nodded. 'Yes. I feel great. Thank you. And I'm sorry...'

'No need,' Mum smiled and perched on the edge of the bed, trying not to dislodge the cats. 'I'd be the same. And to be

247

honest, I know I can look after you as well, if not better, than those semi-retired nurses up at the Cottage. We're just glad to have you home and getting well again. Now... there are a few more Christmas cards for you here. Are you too tired to look at them? Do you want me to save them until tomorrow?'

'Yes please. Tomorrow,' I said sleepily. 'Can you just leave them on the bed?'

Mum straightened her glasses and nodded. 'Um – there's one you might want to open...'

'No, it's ok. I'll do them all tomorrow.'

Mum smiled gently at me. 'It's got a Jersey stamp on it...'

My hands were shaking as I opened the envelope. The writing was sloping and spiky, in black ink. The card was an Alpine scene – all brilliant blue skies, glistening snow and glossy fir trees.

I fumbled with the card. I could hardly breathe...

'*To Stella* – Merry Christmas and a Happy New Year – *with love, Scott x*'.

And then, on left hand side of the card....

'*My dear Twinkle, I'm sending this to wish you a happy Xmas and because I hope you're out of hospital now and feeling much better. If you're reading this then you're still alive! And I told you you wouldn't die, didn't I? I've thought about you a lot. I've hoped that the operation wasn't too painful. I know you didn't give me your address but the name of the road was on the sign outside and I noted your house number – and of course I knew it was in Harbury Green – if I fail as a musician I might get a new job as a detective! I've put our Leighton Buzzard address on here and the telephone number. I know you're not on the phone – but there's a phone box at the end of your road – I saw it! We'll be back in England straight after New Year, so if you'd like to get in touch with me, I'd love to hear from you. Take care of yourself and get well soon. Love, Scott xxx*'

I read it and re-read it. My grin was from ear-to-ear and I

hugged the card.

Mum carried on smiling, stood up and pulled the curtains open. 'Your face says it all, Stell. I'm saying nothing... and – just to make you even happier... look...'

Outside, in the faint orange glow of the street light, against the deep blackness of the winter sky, huge fat goose-feather snowflakes were tumbling and dancing.

Renza's Diary
December 25th 1968

Christmas day. I shouldn't be here, I should be with Scott. I know I've had time to get used to the idea of not being with him but deep down I've been hoping something would turn up and we'd spend Christmas together after all. The disappointment is crippling. I know it's self-torment, but I can't stop imagining what it would be like to spend Christmas Eve with him.

I've been imagining the farm house in Jersey, a huge decorated tree in the sitting room, with gifts around its base and every room decorated and filled with the scent of nutmeg and cinnamon, with big open fireplaces where we could snuggle under blankets on the hearth and watch the fire dying before curling up in bed, excited about spending Christmas day together, as part of Eva's family. Christmas afternoon the band would arrive and we'd give gifts and play silly games and sing songs and just have fun.

Or perhaps Narnia's Children would be gigging in St Helier Christmas Eve with all the rich and trendy people specially invited and, as if by magic, I'd have something really far out and amazing to wear and all the girls would be wrung out with envy at the sight of me with Scott – two of the 'beautiful' people – as they watched our every move at the lavish after gig party. I'd enjoy seeing them watch the ring on my finger flashing as the crystal chandeliers caught its diamonds when we announced our surprise, but 'official' engagement. Fans would be crying – wishing it were them – and Scott would scoop me up in his arms and drive me home along one of the coast roads, stopping off at one of the many beautiful bays he's told me about, where we'd run barefoot in the waves, hand in hand, kissing under the moonlight and, and... well that's just it. And what? I need my head read, dreaming such nonsense. I'm losing the plot. He's in Jersey up to goodness knows what – and with whom I wonder – and I'm here, about to go downstairs and help prepare our Christmas dinner, miserable, lonely and fed-up.

Oh Scott, if only you'd be more reliable, and your mum too. Always promising and rarely delivering. Marjorie Proops would advise me to forget you and find someone else should I ever write a letter to her agony column. She'd most probably be right. But I can't. I can't forget you. You're an excruciating pain deep within my soul that nothing will cure. Something's got to give. I can't stay here. It's not fair.

I'd better go down and start the dinner before Mum gives me grief.

Downstairs the sitting room floor's covered in wrapping paper, cardboard boxes and toys where the kids have ripped their presents open in a frenzy of excitement. Lucy is pedalling up and down on a tricycle, Crispin is bashing hell out of a drum kit – whoever gave it to him is on my death list – and Jasper is kicking a ball around the room. I'm just waiting for Mum to come in and find him. Let's hope he doesn't break anything beforehand. No one is taking any notice of my cries to stop. Sophia and Simon are kneeling beside the coffee table making an Airfix model, the smell of the glue is overwhelming. I'll have to open the windows – Airfix glue and Simon are not a good mix, God only knows what he might end up doing.

Mum and Dad are in the kitchen drinking sherry with someone who has dropped in for drinks, I can hear voices, but I'm not interested in who it is. As soon as I'm needed to peel spuds and veg someone will shout. I'll head back to my room until then. I have a small tape recording of some songs Narnia's Children has recorded and I think I'll play it on the reel-to-reel for a while. Scott at least kept his promise to send me them.

I can hear Scott's voice so clearly, it is just like being with him, as he sings some of the songs he's written with Zak. These are the songs I remember getting demo recordings and the

251

sheet music for when we went to Tin Pan Alley – a lifetime ago. I really miss being with him and the band, it was so exciting and so different to my life here. I miss talking about books and movies and going for walks and just, well, everything. He's my only real friend, let alone the love of my life. I wish I knew what I really am to him. When I'm with him I totally believe all he says, I can feel his love for me, but as soon as we're apart, well, it all disintegrates into uncertainty, suspicion and anxiety. I know he says not to read anything into his irregular, sparse letters, and infrequent phone calls, and he keeps apologising for promising to see me and, when it all falls through, he's mortified and gutted, he says. But it's all right for him, he's got a life, an exciting life. What have I got? A houseful of lunatics, a few trips out with the Wives' Club, or a trip to the shops in Dusseldorf with Heidi. Not quite the same.

Shopping with her is a nightmare sometimes. She loves to try several sizes on when clothes shopping and she'll mix up the tops and bottoms of suits, for example, as she isn't a standard size top and bottom, so nothing fits; swopping sizes she can get a perfect fit. I'm always on the verge of a nervous breakdown in case she gets caught.

Heidi can be mean too. She loves sending me in to shops to try my German out, telling me I have to speak the language and not to expect everyone to speak English. Trouble is she'll tell me the word for something, shoes for instance, and when I go in and ask for what I think are shoes, the shop assistant nearly has a seizure because Heidi has given me a rude word to say. She'll wander off in hysterics laughing.

Mum always takes one of the kids shopping to the local farmer's market because the first time she went on her own, shopping for potatoes and strawberries, she came back with about a ton of spuds and an ironing board! Her German isn't as good as the little ones.

'Renza, I thought you were supposed to be peeling the spuds, get down here now.' Mum's on the war-path, I knew she would be at some point. Christmas wouldn't be Christmas unless she lost it with me at least once. The guests must've gone.

'Coming. I came down before but you had company.' I shouted back, racing down the stairs.

'They've gone,' she said. She and Dad had their coats on. 'We'll be back in about an hour, we've been invited for drinks with the Brigadier and his wife. I've prepared most of the veg – just do the carrots and spuds – the turkey is in the oven, put the spuds in to boil for a while before adding them to the roast.' They headed towards the front door, 'Oh, and stop the kids making that racket, the neighbours will be complaining, and don't forget to tidy up the mess they've made.' The front door slammed.

'Happy Christmas to you too.' I shouted just as one of the kids turned the radio up. Bing Crosby was singing 'White Christmas' for the millionth time. Not quite the Christmas I've been dreaming about, thanks very much Scott.

He didn't even send a Christmas card – I wonder if he's even thinking of me.

Renza's Diary
December 27th 1968

The post sergeant called in this morning with a Christmas card from Scott which had come before Christmas apparently, but for some reason no one had given it to my dad. My heart jumped as I read his lovely words, and I felt bad for all my horrid suspicious thoughts. My resentment towards him evaporated instantly. He'd put his new telephone number at the top and said he couldn't afford to call me, but perhaps when I'd some spare cash I'd call him. He wished me happy New Year and hoped the family was well and that we would see each other soon. Life was as hectic as ever and he was feeling shattered. He said he loved me and drew a huge heart with four kisses.

After lunch I told Mum I needed to get some things from the Apotheke – chemist – in the village as an excuse to go to the post room to use the phone. I needed to hear Scott's voice.

'Do you want anything from the Apotheke, I've got to get some things?' I asked her, hoping she wouldn't ask what.

'Can't it wait until we go to NAAFI?'

'No, I've got to get some 'you-know-what' and it can't wait.' I lied. 'Do you need anything?'

'No, but don't take all day, we're going to the Lovetts for drinks later on, you'll have to get the kids their tea.'

I shot out the door and ran almost all the way to the base, hoping the post room was open and I could use the phone.

One of Dad's colleagues, Bob James, was on the phone when I arrived, and I waited outside whilst he finished his call, but I overheard his conversation. He was arranging to go home on the Dover ferry either the 5th or 6th of January for a very quick visit, back on or about the 9th, and when he'd finished, I smiled sweetly at him, my heart racing, terrified at what I was about to ask. Sometimes I amaze myself. I don't know where I get the nerve, but sometimes I just go for it.

'I couldn't help overhearing you'll be going back to England in a few days. I wondered if you might find room for me, I need a lift to the ferry and back here again around the same time as you? I'd pay my share of the petrol.' Keith Moon was back inside my brain. What the hell was I doing?

'Of course, Renza, I've got to confirm the sailing date and time, and my return date, but yes, of course, I've told you before you're welcome to cadge a lift any time.' He smiled and added, 'I'll give Katie the details and you can sort it all out with her, just pop over to her tomorrow lunch-time, I should know for sure by then.' Katie was his wife, they both lived in the street next to ours.

'Oh thanks so much, you're a life saver,' I said, wondering how the hell I'd tell Mum and Dad, but first I had to ask Scott if it was all right to come at such short notice. I hoped they weren't away gigging. Plans often changed so fast, I knew.

Joss answered the phone. 'Hi Renza, Happy Crimble and all that jazz, how's it hanging?'

'Yes good, same to you thanks.'

'Scott's in the bath, shall I get him?'

'Oh, no, better not, this call is costing the earth as it is, can you give him a message please?' The phone was eating up coins like some sort of hungry beast.

'Of course, but he'll be pissed he's missed you.'

'Tell him I'm home on either the 5th or 6th of January – if you're not gigging, you're not are you? If it's convenient that is, I can come and stay a couple of days, but I'll need a lift from Victoria, I can't pay the fare to Leighton Buzzard. Do you think it's all right, for me to come, then?' The line wasn't clear and I had to shout.

'Yeah we're here then, I'll tell him, just ring to let us know the time and he'll be there, or one of us will be. Hang out by the taxi rank, because they've put parking meters everywhere and it'll be a flying pick up.' Joss shouted back. 'It'll be cool seeing you.'

'Thanks Joss, I'll ring back as soon as I know which day and the time the boat train arrives at Victoria. Can someone ring me and leave a message with the post sergeant here if things change, so I don't come over for nothing? Though I can visit my uncle I suppose, if it's not all right. Just don't tell the post bloke any details or names. I'll know who it's from.'

No point wasting money on the ferry and train if they had to take off somewhere at short notice. We said goodbye. I rang my uncle and asked if it was all right to say I was coming to stay with him. He said anytime, and I ran to the Apotheke and purchased some supplies, then legged it home as fast as I could.

Renza Diary
December 28th 1968

Dad hit the roof when I told him I'd got a lift back to England for a few days staying with my uncle. He was cross I'd sprung it on him, but I said I'd not planned it. I told him I wanted to see one of my school friends who'd written and told me she was going to live in France, and wanted to say goodbye to me, and my uncle said I could stay for a few days. Dad was cross I'd called my uncle before asking him but never questioned me having a close friend. I brazened it out, I've no idea how. Mum had a migraine so missed most of the row, which the kids enjoyed no end.

I'd seen Katie earlier that afternoon and she'd confirmed the 6th and the overnight sailing times, and I'd raced to the post room to call Scott who was out apparently. Mo took the call this time. I asked where Scott was but he said he'd gone shopping, Stephan dropped in with some money for food earlier. I suppose it was true. I was disappointed I'd missed him again, but at least the band is expecting me.

'See you soon Renza, I'm – we're – all looking forward to seeing you, have a safe trip and don't worry you won't be stranded, I'll come for you if I have to.' Mo laughed, knowing I'd get anxious if I thought I'd been forgotten. 'I'll remind Scott, he's always singing 'Gotta See Jane,' and now he can see Renza instead.'

My heart skipped, Scott has been singing one of my favourite songs by R. Dean Taylor. I hummed it for hours afterwards.

Mum and Dad gave me the cool treatment for the next couple of days, but I didn't care. I was going to see Scott and everything was going to be fantastic.

Stella's Diary
January 6th 1969

Scott and I met in Oxford today.

It was bitterly cold and the remaining Christmas snow had frozen solid. I didn't notice the cold. I didn't notice anything except him. He met me from the early-afternoon Harbury Green train at Oxford railway station and was wearing a black coat over his sweater and jeans. I was in my fun fur, a pink velvet smock dress and – by necessity – the baggy black Biba trousers tucked into my long pink boots.

We didn't speak and we didn't touch. We simply looked and looked and then smiled at each other. We were surrounded by noise and bustle, but no one else in the world existed.

I thought we were exactly like a 1960s version of *Brief Encounter*.

However, there was a bit more to fill in...

***

I'd written to Scott, at the Leighton Buzzard address, on Christmas Day. After several attempts, I'd made the letter light-hearted, funny, not at all personal – just in case Renza opened his mail or was reading over his shoulder – and thanked him for the Christmas card, hoped the French gigs had gone well, and told him all about the hospital and that I'd discharged myself from the Cottage – and I drew little cartoons in the margins to illustrate each paragraph. I finished up with a mention of interviewing Narnia's Children for one of the teenage magazines – which made it sound, if anyone else should read it, that it was more or less a business letter.

Mum posted it for me on the day after Boxing Day.

Both she and Vix had said much the same things about it: you're doing exactly what Bernice did to you and Mike... he's got a fiancée... you can't even think about splitting them up – you're not that sort of girl... he's in a group, he must have girls everywhere... you're going to get very hurt... he probably only wants you to do the interviews for the group's publicity, anyway... don't go getting any daft ideas, Stell...

Of course I knew they were right. And I knew – even if there was the slightest chance of it – that I'd never, ever be "the other woman" in his life. Even before Mike two-timed me with Bernice, I'd always thought girls who went after someone else's bloke were the lowest of the low... but I couldn't forget him... and there was always the interview... so it surely wouldn't hurt to keep in touch, would it? Just from a distance... it would be something, and something was better than nothing...

We could be just friends.

On the day Mum posted the letter to Scott, I started my 10 days of intensive heat treatment. The Cottage sent an ambulance to collect me each morning at 8.30. The driver was a cheerful lady called Pearl who knew my nans, and because I was the only patient she let me sit up front with her. We bowled along Harbury Green's frozen roads and Pearl chattered away while I just dreamed about Scott until we reached the hospital.

Mercifully, I didn't see any of the nurses, the matron or the almoner – simply the physiotherapist who operated the rather innovative heat machine. And she didn't speak much, so I spent the daily hour I was stretched out, practically naked and supine, while this massive wheel, filled with criss-crossed wires and a million red-hot filaments, circled slowly over and round my middle, wondering if I'd ever see Scott again.

'You're doing nicely,' the physiotherapist barked after the first week. 'You'll only need a couple more treatments. The scar is drying beautifully and, from my examinations, you're healing well internally. Everything is knitting together perfectly. You're lucky, you're young and fit – you'll make a full recovery. Are the muscles feeling better now? Sit up properly? Stand? Can you walk? Climb stairs?'

'Yes, thank you. All of those. A bit slow, but I'm almost back to normal.'

'Good.' She gave a rare smile. 'Just don't go mad. Don't rush yourself to get better. Don't do anything too energetic. Take your time. A few nice bracing walks will do you the power of good. Oh, and I'm sure you were told this at the Churchill, but no sexual intercourse for another six weeks at least.'

Oh! The shame! Again!

I buried my face as I got dressed, cheeks flaming. I wished I could just shrink into nothing and creep away. The physiotherapist didn't seem to notice my discomfiture as she switched off the heat machine and packed her equipment away. She clearly thought anyone under 21 with spiky hair and heavy eye-make-up was into the Swinging Sixties bed-hopping non-stop. Thank heavens I'd never have to see her again once I'd finished my treatment.

Although, I thought, there was no need for anyone to keep reminding me not to make love – the fact that my stomach looked like someone had run amok with a chainsaw, and I was still wearing knickers bigger than my nan's bloomers, was going to make sure I stayed celibate for the rest of my life.

As well as the heat treatment, I'd been walking each day with Mum, or Dad, if he was home, and the dogs, and a couple of times with Vix. The paths were still a bit slippery and I felt like Bambi on ice... my legs were a bit wobbly, but I got stronger each day.

And on January 3rd I'd made a solo trip to the phone box.

I told no one. I wasn't even sure I'd be brave enough to make the call. I certainly didn't want Vix and Mum telling me gently that I was wasting my time.

I was sure they'd be able to hear my heart thudding at the end of the road as I closed the telephone box door behind me, piled my stash of sixpences and shillings on the shelf above the phone directory, and wiped my sweaty palms down my baggy black trousers.

I looked at Scott's Christmas card with the phone number on – not that I needed to, I knew it off by heart, I'd looked at it that many times – and lifted the heavy black Bakelite receiver. It almost slipped from my grasp, my hands were shaking that much, and I closed my eyes and counted to ten to calm myself down a bit.

Oh, but what if Renza answered...? Or what if Scott didn't really want to talk to me and was being polite in his card...? Or what if Scott answered and Renza was there and he pretended he didn't know me...? Or...?

I dialled the number.

Three rings, then it connected and I fed money in, my fingers trembling....

'Hello...?'

'Hi, babe,' a male voice said cheerfully, 'who are you?'

'Um – Stella... er, can I speak to Scott, please?'

'Yeah, sure... Stella? Stella? Hey – are you the chick from Salisbury?'

'No.'

Oh, God. He gave his phone number to millions of girls... I should have listened to my mum and Vix.

He laughed. 'Good – because she was all over *me*. I'm Zak, by the way... You're Stella...? *Stella*? Stone me! Not the chick from that boys' school gig with the really cool parents and the sexy friend? The one who's been in hospital? Are you that Stella? Really? Oh, shit, he'll go insane!!! Hold on – don't go away – I'll get him...'

And he did.

Scott's voice, after all those weeks of dreaming about him, made me go weak at the knees. At that moment, I knew whatever my mum or Vix or anyone said, I'd do anything – anything at all – to see him again.

Anyway, we talked. And laughed. And talked some more. About everything. Except Renza. Neither of us mentioned Renza. And when my pile of coins had run out, he asked me for the phone box's number and rang me back and we talked again for over an hour.

And we arranged to meet in Oxford on January 6th – when he said Narnia's Children had their first couple of gig-free days since New Year so he'd be around, and I'd have had my final heat treatment. I said I'd pop down into the village, look up the train times on the board outside the vicarage – the one that gave up trains and down trains – and ring him straight back from the phone box outside the post office opposite.

Which I did – eventually, although it was my first longish solo trek – and with my hands shaking and my heart racing (although for completely different reasons this time) – I called him back and he picked the phone up at the first ring. I wondered if he could *hear* the soppy ear-to-ear grin on my face.

***

So, we did our *Brief Encounter* re-enactment three days later.

Seeing him again took my breath away. The long black hair, those amazing turquoise eyes, the sheer beauty of him – the reality was far, far more mind-blowingly incredible than anything I'd conjured up in my wildest dreams.

And yes, I knew what I was doing was wrong, he belonged to someone else, he was engaged to be married and this was a very dangerous game, but again, I knew there was nothing on this earth that would have made me stop meeting him.

We walked away from the railway station, through Oxford, not looking at the glorious golden-stone architecture; oblivious to the cold, north-easterly wind; unaware of the shoppers or tourists or of anything but each other.

People stared at us – because he was simply the most beautiful boy in the world? Or because of my weird clothes and pink and purple sequins? Or just because we were so obviously smitten?

He mesmerised me.

We kept looking at one another and grinning like idiots.

It was lovely. We didn't touch. We walked closely together, his coat sleeve occasionally brushing against my fun-fur arm, and talked and laughed. He made me laugh. A lot.

He told me about being very, very sick with food poisoning in France and how he'd nearly been killed in Stephan's car – Stephan, I was told, was Narnia's Children's manager – when it had skidded on ice after a night out. Neither of these events were remotely funny, but, in retrospect, he made them so. He was a great story-teller.

In return, I repeated and slightly embellished some of the more amusing times in hospital – and especially the discharging myself from the Cottage.

'It was a bit of a shock, even to me. I just felt so fierce about it,' I said as we crossed Carfax and headed up the High Street. 'I'm usually pretty law-abiding. I just couldn't stay there when I wanted to go home so much.'

He nodded. 'I think it's completely understandable, feeling like that. You've got a lovely home and great parents. And, once you felt better, you must have wanted to get as far away from hospitals as possible. And you must have been very homesick...'

'I was, I think.' I looked at him. 'Do you get homesick? You must do. Being away from home with the group all the time?'

'Not really. No, in fact. I don't really feel as though I have a home. My parents are divorced and both remarried – my mum and stepfather live in Jersey with my very young step-sister – my father and his new, also very young, wife live here on the mainland on the south coast. I don't really feel as though I belong in either place... although, probably Jersey is the closest thing I have to calling anywhere home. And with the band, we're always on the move – we never stay anywhere for long.'

I thought that was very sad. I linked my hand through his arm and squeezed it.

He grinned down at me. 'Thanks. That's why you're so lucky – having the home and family that you do. Hey, sorry – I'm not walking too fast for you, am I?'

I shook my head and giggled. 'No – walking is about the one thing I *can* do...'

We stopped on Magdalen Bridge and watched the turgid grey river slowly wend its way beneath us towards the stark winter beauty of Christ Church Meadow.

I wondered about the home thing. I wondered if Renza was "at home", wherever that was. I wondered again if Renza was in Jersey or if she travelled about with him. I wondered about when they got married if they'd live in some glitzy rock'n'roll apartment in a trendy part of London. I wondered where she thought he was today.

I didn't wonder any of this out loud.

We carried on walking and reached The Plain, Oxford's famous roundabout, linking all the main city routes, with the gothic folly in the middle.

'Shall we have a cup of tea?' I said. 'It's getting colder than ever – and I could do with a rest.'

'See,' Scott looked at me anxiously, 'I knew all this walking wasn't good for you. You're hardly out of hospital... are you ok? And yes, a cup of tea would be great... but where on earth are we going to get one round here?'

'Follow me,' I chuckled. 'And as long as you're not too fussy.'

Daft! He was bound to be fussy! He was posh!

He followed me anyway. And laughed.

'Seriously?'

'Yep,' I nodded, walking into the narrow, scrubby gap between two long-established shops and along an untidy gravel path, heading towards the long rather dilapidated building. 'It used to be The British Restaurant in the war – they had them in every town – you know, government funded, providing basic hot cooked meals, so that everyone got something decent to eat while rationing was on... the council took it over a few years back. It's the cheapest place in Oxford. And the warmest.'

It was. Inside, we were surrounded by other people, mostly

old age pensioners who'd also come in from the cold, and who beamed at us kindly and whispered "ah, bless..." "love 'em..." and "oooh look – hippies".

Trying not to laugh, we queued at the counter and bought dark brown tea in thick white china cups, and toasted currant buns. The transistor radio on the counter was playing The Foundations' 'Build Me Up Buttercup'.

Finding a secluded corner, we sat opposite one another on trestles at a long wooden table – like a works canteen.

Again, nothing and no one else existed. Just us.

I leaned my elbows on the table. 'When are you playing again?'

'Tomorrow night. The California Ballroom in Dunstable – practically next door to Leighton Buzzard. We're supporting Doc Holliday and the Cards.

'Wow. Impressive.'

Scott shrugged. 'We share the same management. Stephan has pulled strings. As usual. He's an ace string-puller. We've got a few more local-ish gigs – then we're off to Scotland for a while at the end of February, staying in B&Bs while we're on the road. And it looks as though we've got a longish German residency in a club in either Frankfurt or Kaiserslautern, or both, in April. If that comes off, according to Stephan, we're being put up in a swish hotel, which should be ok.'

I stared into my tea cup. He was telling me that he wasn't going to be around. That he and Renza were going to be on the road, playing venues I'd never seen or heard of. Staying in exotic locations, in hotels. He was telling me that this, today, was all there was going to be. All there could be.

I sighed. 'It sounds really exciting. In April I'll be back at work... processing claims forms. It's hardly the same.'

'But before that? You don't have to go back to work?'

'No. I'm signed off for three months – on full pay, luckily. I've got various out-patients appointments at both the Radcliffe and the Churchill, but no – apart from those, I'm as free as a bird until April.' I looked at my watch. 'Oh, the time has flown! Do you have to catch the train or bus or something to get back to Leighton Buzzard? Should we be heading back now?'

'Not yet, no.' He smiled slowly. 'I'm not going back to Leighton Buzzard tonight – I'm going to catch the Paddington train and stay with Stephan in London overnight. I have some things to sort out.'

'Ok,' I smiled. 'We can walk back to the station together then.'

It was all I was going to have. I'd cling on to every minute with him.

'Sounds cool. Look, I need to ask you something. Oh, don't look like that – it's not personal – it's to do with the band. With Narnia's Children.'

'Oh. Of course. The interview.' Clearly this was the whole point of today's meeting – I should have guessed. 'Well, I'm sure I could send you the questions and you could post the answers back to me and -'

He laughed. 'It's nothing to do with the interview, actually. Although, that would be fab if you could tie that in with the record's release.'

'Record?'

'We recorded it some time back. It's called "Livin' With You". It was written by the guys who write for Dave Dee and The Herd and loads of others. Zak and I have written the B side though.'

A record. I was very, very impressed but tried not to show it. Narnia's Children were no small-time outfit. They were recording stars. Big time. I pushed crumbs around my plate and hoped I didn't look like a besotted fan. I'd been warned off. Told where I stood. This was clearly a business meeting after all.

'Really? That's cool. Do you write a lot of your own stuff?'

'Loads. We used to play all original music at our gigs but we soon worked out that to get the crowd going, people really want to hear familiar tunes – so we might put one or two of our own songs into a set, but mostly we keep to the tried and tested – rock, west coast pop, close harmonies, chart stuff...like The Beach Boys and The Beatles and The Hollies.'

I grinned. 'Mmm. I noticed. So, when's your record coming out?' Was that the right term? 'Er – being released?'

He shrugged. 'The release date keeps being delayed. I think it'll be out in May – but we're clearly the last to know.'

'It would certainly make sense for publicity if I did the interview to tie in with that – and the magazines need a six week lead time, so – if I interviewed you sometime in March...?'

'Sounds perfect. OK, we'll go for that. No, but what I really wanted to ask you – and please say no if you don't want to – but would you be our fan club secretary?'

I wanted to laugh. I honestly wanted to laugh. He was asking me to be part of the Narnia's Children team? A small bit player, but still involved with the band. Could I do that? Stand on the side-lines being efficient and watch him with Renza?

Of course I damn well could! It would be better than nothing. I knew I should say no...

I clattered my spoon in my thick, white saucer. 'What? Me? Why?'

'Because you're a writer, and clever, and because we're getting a lot of fan letters sent mainly to Stephan at the moment and we need someone to do it and help us build up and maintain a fan base – and if it's you then it means I'll be able to see you again.'

I blinked and swallowed. Had he really said that? Did he really mean it? And what about Renza...? I stared at him. I was sure he could hear my heart thundering somewhere beneath the fun fur.

He leaned across the table. 'Hopefully the fan club stuff wouldn't take up very much time. You'd still be able to do your short stories and interviews. Stephan will pay all the expenses if you invoice him. We'd just need you to set-up and send out membership forms and then answer all our fan letters – we'd have to give them your address so they all come straight to you, if that's ok – oh, and send out a newsletter every month – with photos and things... but if you don't want to...'

I didn't even try to play it cool. 'Of course I want to. I'd love to. I'll get it sorted out as soon as I go home. I've got a friend who's just set up his own printing business... he'll really welcome the work. I can get headed notepaper – with the Narnia's Children logo at the top... and he can print copies of the monthly newsletter and – wow! Yes...'

We grinned at one another.

'And the other thing...' he reached across the scruffy, scrubbed table and held my hand... it was like an electric shock. He took a deep breath. 'While you're signed off sick, come and stay in Leighton Buzzard. With me. Please.'

268

Renza's Diary
January 20th 1969

I don't know what to think anymore. I've been back in Germany for almost two weeks now and apart from a quick phone call – which I made – I haven't had a letter or any word from Scott.

My trip home to see him, which was going to be so wonderful, was a disaster. I can't stop thinking about it

Bob James was as good as his word and was kind enough to give me a lift with him to Ostend, on the 5th of January where we got the overnight ferry to Dover. Scott arranged for Rich to pick me up from Victoria Station when I got off the boat train from Dover on the 6th of January. My aunt and uncle seemed happy to cover for me, otherwise Mum would never have let me go. Bob would meet me off the boat train in Dover, on the 9th for the return journey with him on the day ferry.

I should have known right away it would all go wrong. First no one was at the station when I arrived, cold and wet because the ferry had got caught in a force 9 gale in the channel, and everyone was so sick, even the crew. Bob and I spent the whole night sitting up the top of the boat trying to get away from the smell and sight of vomit. Plus the boat seemed less rocky up there, but with the wind and rain we got drenched to the skin.

Eventually Rich turned up and said the band had been gigging non-stop since France, where they'd had a great time. Spending New Year's Eve in Paris with all the cars honking at midnight and people dancing in the streets was a blast he said, but Toulouse was hell. The van broke down and they were put up in a posh hotel by the local police and had to wait for Stephan to fly out and pay for it all. Meantime they all got food poisoning and had been really ill.

Rich told me Scott was nearly killed when Stephan's Rover skidded on ice in Leighton Buzzard when coming back from a late night out together. He seemed surprised I knew none of this and raised his eyebrows when I said Scott had not been in touch that much since early December.

There was no sign of Scott when we got to the house in Leighton Buzzard; the others were there but didn't seem to know where he had gone.

'I told Joss I'd be here on the 6th. Do you think he thought I meant the 5th because when I rang the first time I wasn't sure which date?' I asked Rich.

'Could be, I've no idea, Joss says he told Scott the 6th. It's possible Scott's forgotten or got the date muddled.' Rich looked uncomfortable. It all seemed highly unlikely to me, how could he forget, I'd even told Mo.

I overheard Joss and Mo whispering something about him still being in Harbury Green, wherever that was. Rich said he was sure Scott would be back soon and made me tea and showed me to Scott's room which he usually shared with Mo, but as I was staying, Mo had bunked in with Rich.

I honestly hadn't thought about sleeping arrangements when I agreed to stay for a few days. Now I was filled with panic at the thought of actually sharing a bed with him. What on earth was I to do?

Not that it mattered, because Scott didn't appear at all the day I arrived and I couldn't really get much sense out of the band or Rich. They seemed to be a bit cagey I thought, saying he must be visiting friends or family, as they'd had a couple of gig-free nights, and weren't playing again until the next night when they were at The California Ballroom in Dunstable, just down the road. So I got his bed to myself.

The band assured me Scott knew I was coming today, and anyway Rich had collected me, so of course he knew. No one could tell me why he wasn't there to meet me and why he hadn't come home. I was so unhappy and disappointed – we were wasting so much valuable time.

The doubts started to fill my head again. I'd come all this way, and at considerable expense, and he couldn't even be there to see me. I cried myself to sleep.

The following afternoon Scott graced us with his presence and made things worse because he couldn't really explain where he had been or what he'd been doing.

'Hi babe, great to see you,' he said, pulling me close and kissing me. Something felt different. He didn't look me in the eye once.

'Hello,' I said, trying not to let my eyes well up in front of him. Disappointment flooded my whole body, like a cold water shower. 'Missed you too.'

He mumbled something and disappeared into the bathroom and I heard the bath running. Great. I sat on the lumpy bed in his room and tried not to cry. This isn't how it's meant to be.

My detective-like brain went into overload and I made my mind up he'd been with a girl. Cross examining him made him angry and sullen, and asking the others just resulted in vague, non-committal answers – which meant I knew I was right.

So, if he'd found someone else, what the hell was I doing there, then? Why let me come home to see only him, if he had someone new?

After his bath he got changed and made me some tea and toast. 'I need to run through the songs with the guys, so why don't you check out some of the books we've been given by Stephan, there's Dennis Wheatley and a couple of those Spy thriller ones you like. Won't be long.' And he was gone. I heard them in the back bedroom soon after, harmonising, and it was sheer bliss. I looked through the pile of books on the coffee table and picked a Frederick Forsyth novel, but I couldn't concentrate enough to read and retain any of it. How could anyone read when their life had just ended. Scott was avoiding being alone with me.

We all went to the California Ballroom later in the afternoon to set the gear up and run through the songs before the audience came in about 7pm. Rich managed to shut my fingers in the van door and I nearly passed out with the pain, not that Scott seemed overly bothered. He seemed pre-occupied all the time, we'd hardly spoken since he arrived back from Harbury Green or wherever.

I felt miserable, so lonely and unwanted.

We spent most of the time in the dressing room with the other band on the bill that night, Doc Holliday and The Cards. It should have been so exciting meeting such a famous singer whose song, 'The Egyptians,' I loved. But all I could think about was that Scott didn't love me anymore, didn't want me around... it was like a nightmare.

Apparently Doc Holliday and The Cards were on the same record label as Narnia's Children and also shared the same management now. Stephan has become the band's 'Personal Manager' whatever that is. I thought he was anyway.

Doc was a funny sort of bloke really, his band didn't seem to like him much and they argued the whole time. I discovered Doc had several wives and loads of kids and his band kept mentioning them when they had a shouting match about anything – from the songs not being sung right in rehearsal, to the way the microphones were situated. It was mayhem.

Still, I would love to tell Yvette and Selina all about this – their faces would be a sight worth seeing! The venue was heaving; people were still trying to get in when the show started.

Doc's band were terrible to him on stage, in front of everyone, not just in rehearsals. They deliberately turned his mic off so that when they started their song, no one could hear him. It took him a while to realise that he was not being heard by the audience. Doc's band fell about laughing but I thought it was cruel.

Backstage, afterwards, they had a massive fight, and I mean a real brawling fight. We thought the police might have to be called as they looked as if they meant him real harm.

Narnia's Children were amazing as usual and I loved watching them. Zak was so sexy, a bit like Mick Jagger in the way he moved, and he had the girls eating out of his hand from the get-go. Scott had his usual moody stance on stage which really turns me on, and it also seemed to turn all the other girls on too. Some screamed his name out and a couple tried to get on the stage.

Everyone sang along to the songs too, which was groovy. Sadly, though, there was nearly a fight at one point – and this one was nothing to do with Doc Holliday and The Cards. Some weird skin-head blokes dressed in big boots, braces and with really cropped hair got up on the stage and tried to thump Scott and Zak, and accused them of looking at their girlfriends, but seriously, I thought it was the girls who were doing the looking.

And I couldn't see how the band could help looking at someone at some point since they were facing the audience. But it was nasty, and in the end Zak smacked one of them on the back with the mic stand and twirled it round and round until the skin-heads got off the stage, and some big black guys came and shoved them out of the Ballroom.

After the gig, when we got back to the house, everyone had Spam sandwiches, tea or coffee before they all went to bed. Scott and I went to his room and it was awful. I didn't know what to do and felt so uncomfortable about it all. He still wasn't that friendly, and I felt so hurt and confused and disappointed about everything I wasn't much joy to be with, either.

He went into the bathroom while I got undressed and he was gone so long, and I was so cold – it was a funny house, all dark and dreary, freezing cold and not very homely – I decided to get into one of the double beds in the room – the only one with any bed-clothes, and go to the bathroom when he came back. He was gone so long, almost like he was putting it off, that I was almost asleep by the time he appeared.

After I'd been to the bathroom, I got back into bed and lay

there hardly daring to breathe, wondering if he was asleep or not.

'Scott...' I whispered after a while.

He never moved or spoke and I didn't know what to say anyway. My hopes and dreams of a moment like this had all come crashing down and the reality was a bitter pill to swallow.

Here we were, in bed together at last, and it was all so very wrong. We didn't touch each other at all, and I soon realised he had gone to sleep and I turned my back and silently wept into my pillow.

The next morning he apologised for being off with me, saying he was tired but he still didn't want to tell me where he had been and why he had not been there when I arrived. He tried to make it up to me by chatting about the band and their plans and the tour of Germany which was coming up after a trip back to Scotland, but something had changed and it killed me.

'I just don't understand why you can't be honest with me and tell me if you've found someone else.' I tried again when we had a few moments alone, which was difficult in a house full of musicians, always walking into Scott's room asking for new song lyrics, picks, or to borrow an LP.

'There's nothing to tell, you're being paranoid. I told you I don't know how many times, I'm tired, and when I get tired I'm quiet. Sorry, but that's how I am.' He looked cross and I don't blame him, I can't stand it when Mum gives me the third degree. But I'm usually innocent, he, I'm afraid, was not. I could feel it.

'I love you, I want to marry you, nothing has changed, really, stop worrying.'

'Why can't you say where you were, it's not a state secret or anything is it?' I know I'm like a dog with a bone when I get started but who could blame me? He's always grilling me about Germany and whether I've met anyone or not, every time I go back home after a visit, he brings it up in his letters; who have you seen? Where have you been? Are there any blokes at the base who are after you? Like an interrogation and here I am doing the same to him.

'Trust me, it's nothing to do with you and me or how I feel about you, it's, well, it's something I have to work out and I'd rather not discuss it with you or anyone.' He snapped at me.

'Fine, I won't ask again. Sorry to be such a nag.' I snapped back. We'd never ever had a row, and now I know what falling out would be like. Me wanting to clear the air and Scott wanting to sulk and keep his feelings to himself.

I softened my voice, 'I just thought that when you love someone and you're close to them, you'd want to share everything with them, no secrets. I just want us to be happy, to share everything like you always said we would. I can try and understand whatever is worrying you. I might be able to help.'

'I've told you Renza, it is nothing to do with you. Stop bloody asking me all the time. You and me, we're good, we're fine, nothing has changed. There's just no need to keep asking me.' He shouted crossly and stomped off into the sitting room and I ran into his bedroom, tears streaming down my face, my throat tight and my chest fit to burst. I didn't believe him.

I knew I couldn't stay there any longer with him, remembering how it had been, how insanely in love we had been – and I still was – feeling hurt and resentful I decided to go and stay with my uncle after all, and when I told him, Scott didn't even ask me to stay!

I asked Rich to drive me to Victoria so I could get the coach to my uncle's – it stops in the town where he lives. He looked shocked but agreed, he even made me some cheese and Branston pickle sandwiches to eat on the way. Not that I would ever eat again. The band didn't seem shocked to see me leave earlier than planned and they all rather solemnly kissed me goodbye for the last time, I was sure. Mo hugged me tightly and said not to worry, Scott loved me and it'll all be sorted soon, he was sure. I'm glad someone was, I wish I knew what needed to be sorted soon.

I waved to them – choked up with emotion – as the van pulled out of the drive. I'd never see them again. My dear friends whom I'd come to love like family. The feeling of loss was overwhelming. I physically ached with grief.

When Scott and Rich dropped me off at Victoria coach station later, Scott hardly bothered to look at me as the coach left the bay. He waved once and walked away. I watched him until he was out of sight, tears streaming down my face, convinced I would never see him again. Peter, Paul and Mary's song, 'Leaving on a Jet Plane,' kept playing in my head all the way to my uncle's.

***

And now I'm back in Germany and watching for the post sergeant every day like a stupid idiot, convinced that there's going to be a miracle and Scott will be his old self and I'll get one of his delicious letters full of undying love, but it hasn't come.

The one phone call on my return was brief and paid for by me. I rang to give him a chance to explain himself, I thought the time and distance between us might have cleared his thinking. And he was almost, but only almost, like his old self, confusing the hell out of me. He seemed pleased to hear from me, not at all surprised in fact. That annoyed me for a start. I'm a push-over obviously.

He chatted about the band and their plans and told me they were going back to Elgin at the end of February and then on to Germany – Frankfurt and Kaiserslautern – which he said wasn't far from me, if I felt like meeting up. But I've looked on the map and he's wrong. There are several places with the same name as here, and one is not far from Kaiserslautern, but it's not my village, so I doubt if I shall be going to visit him after all. Part of me wonders what's the point anyway?

I'm so confused by everything. He hasn't said it's over, but I'm convinced he's acting as if it is – and I've given him several chances to tell me – I've asked him outright, but he said he loved me and everything was fine. For him perhaps.

We left it that he'd write when he can and if I find a way to get to Kaiserslautern I should let him know. He gave me the name of the hotel Stephan had booked and the address, and told me to ask directory enquiries for the number, he didn't have it.

The Lovin' Spoonful are on the wireless with 'You Didn't Have To Be So Nice'. Scott loves this song as well – he's sung it to me on our walks round the village which seem a lifetime ago now. Talk about rubbing it in.

I'm determined to get on with life and just see where it takes me. I'm exhausted by all this emotion, and what with Mum and her craziness, I've got to make plans regardless, even with a broken heart, or I'll end up in the loony bin.

I've got an interview for a job at the base the next week, as a sort of secretary or something, so I hope to use my short-hand and typing (at last) before I forget it all. Even better, it means no more kids and housework, well, except evenings and weekends so Mum says. Dad says the job is in Personnel and I will be dealing with Germans as well as Squaddies. I wish I felt more interested and excited, but I don't. I'm terrified. My first job – well, if I get it, that is.

Me, Mum, and the Wives' Club will be going on a trip to Holland at the weekend, to the Keuchkenhoff, where they grow all the tulips and flowers. I'd look forward to it if I wasn't going with a load of old women and catty young wives.

Still, Holland is supposed to be ultra-cool and Heidi said you can get drugs in shops there, out in the open. Not that I want any of course. She told me there are shops where you can buy sex things and somewhere where prostitutes sit in windows, like goods for sale, waiting for clients. Mum will just love that! I must admit I'm curious; anything for a laugh after all. I hope Narnia's Children never visit Amsterdam on tour.

Stella's Diary
January 23rd 1969

Today I went to Leighton Buzzard with all my worldly belongings – well, almost all, well, ok, enough for the couple of days I'd be there – in two pink and orange psychedelic paper tote bags, and dire warnings from my mum and Vix ringing in my ears.

I was wearing the fun fur and my long white boots and the vivid, tight, and thigh-high rainbow-striped jersey dress I'd adapted from another Oxfam-shop-find. I'd at last been able to dump the baggy Biba trousers and wear tights and mini dresses again as Mum had found some flesh-coloured tights in Woolworths with *knickers attached* where tights usually had the ugly see-through gussetty thing.

Vix and I were very excited about this – me even more so because the pants part, while not being at all sexy, at least came up to the waist – thus missing my mutilated stomach and not sitting on the not-yet-healed scar – and were in black or white and I'd bought loads of them to go with my short skirts and boots.

So, with my tote bags filled with tights and boots and dresses, I caught the lunchtime bus from Gloucester Green in Oxford to Aylesbury, counting the miles as we rumbled through Wheatley, Thame, Haddenham... stopping and starting...

Then, after waiting in Aylesbury's freezing, wind-swept market square, I caught another bus to Leighton Buzzard. This time the villages along the route were unfamiliar and pretty, and I memorised the sequence of names as a mantra – each one taking me closer to Scott: Bierton, Wingrave, Aston Abbotts, Cublington, Wing, Linslade – and I enjoyed people-watching as the passengers got on and off – but the journey seemed to take forever. I just wanted to be there.

Impatiently, I settled back in my seat, watching the bare winter countryside trundle slowly by, and had no doubts at all about what I was doing.

My mum and Vix had every doubt under the sun!

'And you haven't asked him anything about Renza?' Vix had sprawled on my bed in her usual spot, and glared at me. 'You don't know any more about her now than you did the night we met him?'

'No. I haven't mentioned her and neither has he.'

'So she could be living at Leighton Buzzard?'

I'd shrugged. 'She could be, I suppose. But I doubt it. I don't think he's setting us up as a *ménage-a-trois* or anything.'

'And, after what Mike and Bernice did to you – you still think it's ok to cheat on this Renza – who is a *fiancée* not just a girlfriend – do you? Really, Stella – you can't – you just can't!'

'I'm not cheating on anyone – neither is Scott. We're just friends – and anyway, remember what I said – if I survived the operation and stopped feeling ill and stopped being miffed about being dumped by Mike, then I was going to do something different... have an adventure – and that's exactly what I'm doing.'

'Are you mad? You have no idea what you're getting into!' Vix had sat up, looking really angry. 'And don't keep giving me that nonsense from Nanny Ivy's – you know as well as I do that it's all baloney – tall, dark stranger be blowed! He could be a murderer or anything.'

'Of course he isn't – and I like him.' Understatement – but it didn't seem the right time to say exactly how I felt about Scott. 'We get on well together. We make each other laugh and we can talk about everything and he likes reading as much as I do, and we like the same music. He's a really nice boy and –'

'Oh, yes, he's Mr Wonderful! He's engaged to be married and he's inviting you to go and live with him? That makes him a cheat and a liar in my book.'

I winced. Put like that...

'And,' Vix continued, 'you know full well what girls who do

what you're doing are called, don't you? I thought you had higher principles than that!'

'I'm not a tart and I'm not going to be living with him! I'm going to be staying – for a couple of days – in a house with a lot of other people. I might not ever see him again after this.' I decided not to tell her about the fan club thing. Not then. It would probably be a step too far.

'And,' Vix clearly hadn't finished, 'how old is he?'

'Eighteen.'

'And you're twenty one this year. That makes you a cradle snatcher as well! Honestly, Stella – I'm really worried about you.'

'Well, don't be. There's no need. And his age is immaterial. He could be twenty eight or ninety eight and I'd still feel the same way about him. Anyway, this is all your fault. If you hadn't introduced me to him....'

'Because I thought you were going to die! You said you were going to die! I thought it was your last night out! I wanted you to be happy! I didn't expect you to – '

'To what? Fall in love with him? Go on – say it! You might as well – because it's too damn late!'

We stared at one another.

'Stella? Are you serious?' Vix shook her head. 'Oh, glory... you are, aren't you? You haven't *told* him, have you?'

'Don't be daft,' I sighed. 'I haven't even kissed him.'

'Really? Then you're even more crazy than I thought. And trust me, once he's got you at Leighton Buzzard, he'll be wanting far more than kisses. You *can't* love him – you hardly know him!'

'I know enough.'

Vix swung her legs to the floor and tugged at her very short tartan kilt. 'Rubbish! You're talking like one of your stories now! But I'm still your best friend even if I do think you're doing the wrong thing for all the wrong reasons. When he's broken your heart in a million pieces you'll know where to come for a shoulder to cry on, won't you?'

Mum was far more pragmatic. "He's a nice boy, but..." "He's in a pop group and he's got a girlfriend... a fiancée..." "You've had major surgery – you're hardly fit enough to walk down the road..." "You still have out-patient appointments to go to in a few days..." "Please don't do anything silly...."

Which all boiled down to "I hope you're not going to sleep with him" – I knew it and so did she, but there was no way on earth that either of us would ever mention it.

I just hugged her and told her Scott and I were just friends, it was only for a couple of days, to sort out the fan club stuff and the interview and there'd be loads of other people in the house and I really needed a couple of days away after the operation and everything.

Eventually, it was Dad who made it ok.

Mind you, as Dad had run away from his very happy home and with the approval of his very loving parents, to become a circus clown at the tender age of 15, I suppose me going to stay for a couple of days with a rock group was probably pretty small beer.

'Oh, let her go.' He'd chuckled. 'Let her have a bit of fun. Heaven knows, we thought we were going to lose her, didn't we? Six months ago we'd have given anything to let her have her freedom. She's been so ill for so long. If this makes her happy and brings her sparkle back, then where's the harm?' He'd winked at me. 'Mind you, Stell – you tell him if he hurts you I'll break every bone in his body. OK?'

'OK. But he won't.'

'All right – I suppose it will be all right. But what do we tell people?' Mum, always aware of her local social standing as a teacher, had looked over the top of her glasses. 'You know what they're like round here – they'll see her going – they'll want to know where and why and when and what and – '

Dad laughed. 'Oh, we'll just tell 'em she's living in sin in Leighton Buzzard. That should keep 'em happy for ages.'

The short January afternoon was rapidly disappearing into darkness as the bus eventually reached Leighton Buzzard. There was a garage on the left-hand corner as we swayed into the curve of the High Street and I caught a glimpse of attractive grey-stone buildings and old inns and pretty little shops ablaze with lights.

I held my breath. Scott had told me to ask the bus driver to be dropped at the Heath and Reach end of the town. I'd laughed and said Heath and Reach sounded like a firm of solicitors. He'd said it was a lovely village and we'd walk there one day.

The bus continued to crawl through the darkness.

'Your stop coming up, love,' the conductor called along the bus to me, with a nod to the driver. 'Just before the bridge, bottom of the hill here.'

'Er… ' I tried to sound normal but my mouth was dry and my heart was about to thunder out of my chest, 'oh, right – yes – um – thank you…'

The bus juddered to a halt. I stood up, gathered up my bags and walked forward. Slowly. Very slowly. Because…. w*hat if he wasn't there?*

It honestly hadn't occurred to me before. Yes, I knew the address of course, but I had no idea how to find the house. I was in a strange town, in the dark – and possibly alone…

He was there.

At the bus stop. Under the street lamp. As he'd promised.

He was wearing the black coat and his long dark hair fell into his eyes and he pushed it away impatiently as he looked up as the bus arrived.

My heart melted. I practically flew off the bus, my smile was ear-to-ear. The bus driver and the conductor were both laughing to themselves as they rumbled away.

Scott stepped forward and pulled me into his arms. I

dropped my bags and slid my arms round his neck.

'Hello.'

'Hello, yourself.'

Our breath mingled in clouds in the freezing air. We just grinned at one another.

And then he kissed me.

And right then it didn't matter if I was a cradle-snatching, man-stealing, groupie tart. It didn't matter about Renza. Nothing mattered but being with him.

Ages later, holding hands, we walked away from the bus stop, up the hill, round the sharp right hand bend – to the house. It was detached, bay-windowed, sitting back from the road in an oasis of long gravelled drives and pathways. Narnia's Children's Transit van was parked in front of the steps.

'Scott...' I stopped at the gate. 'Is Renza here?'

'No.'

'But you're still together?'

'Yes.'

'And do the others – well, Mo and Rich mainly, know I'm staying?'

'Yes.'

It was enigmatic and not really what I wanted to hear, but it'd have to do.

I grinned at him. 'You'd be rubbish on the *Yes, No Interlude*... it's a game show... don't look like that... oh...'

He laughed and kissed me again then opened the front door.

The house was very cold, and dark, all the lights seemed to be dimmed, I got the impression of high ceilings, several doors leading off a long narrow hall, music – the *Sergeant Pepper* LP – booming from a room on the left, and delicious smells floating from the kitchen straight ahead.

'Mo's cooking dinner. He always does. He's our chef – well, he's like our mother-hen really... him and Rich. Let me show you your room, you can leave your bags and things... upstairs...'

I followed him up the dimly lit staircase. Neither of us had taken our coats off, the house had a really chilly feel to it. No cosy roaring crackling home fires here.

'Bathroom is there... and this is us...' Scott pushed open a door and flicked on another dim light. 'I usually share with Mo, but he's gone in with Rich while you're here.'

Us? *Us*?

There were two double beds in the room, one haphazardly covered with sheets, blankets and a paisley eiderdown, the other stripped bare to a scruffy ticking mattress. There were dark green curtains at the window. A sort of tall dressing table thing stood to the right of the room and a bedside cabinet with a transistor radio to the left.

It was bitterly cold.

I dropped my tote bags inside the door. I honestly hadn't thought about the sleeping arrangements at all. I just assumed I'd have a little spare room or something. I seriously hadn't considered that Scott and I would be *sharing*...

I knew I'd have to tackle the subject later – but not now.

'If you want to use the bathroom... freshen up or anything... I'll go downstairs and tell Mo you're here and there's one extra for dinner...' Scott said. 'Come down when you're ready.'

'Ok. Thanks. But if there's not enough food to go round I'll be fine.'

'I'm sure there'll be plenty – as long as you're not fussy.'

I wasn't a fussy eater. Eating was currently the least of my problems.

'You have no idea how happy I am that you're here.' He hugged me. 'I wasn't sure that you'd come. Don't be long...'

By the time I'd visited the bathroom, which was utilitarian but very clean considering all those boys in the house, and re-negotiated the gloomy staircase – and kept my coat on because I'd never been in such a cold house – the scents from the kitchen were stronger than ever and I really hoped there'd be enough food to go around.

'Stella!' Zak appeared from the door on the left, with *Sergeant Pepper* still playing, just as I reached the bottom of the stairs. 'Wow! Hi!' He grabbed me and kissed me on the cheek. 'Great to see you again. Are you better now?'

'Yes, thanks.'

'Cool. And you haven't brought your sexy and "hands off – I've got a boyfriend" friend with you by any chance?'

'No,' I smiled. 'Sadly not.'

'Bugger,' Zak said good naturedly, drifting off into a room to the right. 'See you later.'

I stood in the hallway for a moment, not knowing which room I should be in, then I just headed for the kitchen because I could see it and I hoped it was warm. Mo, with his glorious Marc Bolan hair, was standing with his back to me at the stove, stirring a massive pot of something which smelled like a really spicy curry. A second huge pot bubbled and hissed beside it. Rice? I seriously hoped so.

The kitchen was blissfully warm and properly lit, although it did seem a bit basic and unloved. Like the rest of the house. There were no personal touches, nothing to warm it up and make it homely. Maybe the owners just let it out all the time?

I shrugged off my fun fur and moved closer to the cooker. 'Hello…'

Mo spun round. 'Oh – it's you. Hi… Scott said you'd arrived.' And he turned away again.

A bit of a slap in the face – and possibly deserved – I took a deep breath. 'Can I help? Is there anything I can do?'

'For the cooking? No.' He didn't look at me. 'For Scott? Yes. Once you've done the interview and got the fan club stuff up and running, leave him alone.'

Stung, I recoiled a bit then took a deep breath. 'I thought we'd got over all this? Called a truce? And if Scott wants to see me, then I honestly don't see what business it is of yours.'

Mo turned round. 'Thanks to you, Scott doesn't know what he wants any more. He's completely messed up now. But he loves Renza and she loves him and they will get married – and you won't stop that.'

'I don't want to! Anyway...' I tried smiling, it didn't really work. 'If she loves him so much, then why isn't she here? Why doesn't she live with him? Why aren't they together? Why am I here and she isn't?'

'You really don't know? He hasn't told you anything about her?'

I shook my head. 'No. Nothing. And I haven't asked. It's like she's in a different compartment of his life. I'm in one box and she's in another – and as long as no one gets the lids muddled we'll all be ok.'

'Her name's Renza – not Pandora.' Mo almost smiled. Almost. He checked his two massive pots, then looked at me. 'Renza lived next door to us when we rented a flat last summer. That's how and when they met. It was special between them – instantly – we all knew that. Love at first sight for them both. Renza is like no one else I've ever met. Funny, clever – and very beautiful. Scott worshipped her – still worships her. Always will.'

Each word was like a punch in the stomach – apt, given what I'd done to Scott at our first meeting – but I needed to know. To understand.

'OK. So she's the love of his life – he's told me that much himself. But that still doesn't explain why they're not living together.'

'She lives in Germany now. She moved there in August. It broke his heart.'

Right... ok... Germany explained some, but not all. I could see her – this super-cool business woman, still Italian-looking in my imagination – but now in some natty business suit, running an international organisation...

'So,' Mo continued, 'until she's able to get back to the UK again permanently, Scott has to make do with letters and phone calls. What you are, if you're anything at all in his life, is merely a stop-gap.'

Ouch! Still, to be in his life, I'd happily be a stop-gap – and as long as Renza stayed ruling her business empire in Germany, I'd be a stop-gap for as long as possible.

I didn't say any of this.

'Is she going to move her business to the UK, then? Is that the plan?'

Mo looked at me as if I was mad. 'What the heck are you talking about? Business? Renza doesn't have a business. She had to go to Germany with her parents – her dad's in the army or something – she's 16.'

Oh my God – Renza was a *child*! I was speechless.

Mo sort of grinned. 'Now you understand? They're made for each other. Young love. First love. There will never be anyone else for either of them.'

'But they're engaged? She's so *young*...'

'What does that matter? Renza is absolutely gorgeous – and the sweetest girl we've ever known. So – back off.'

Stella's Diary
January 23rd 1969 – later

We ate Mo's huge plates of curry and rice, with a mountain of sliced bread on the side, and bottles of cola and beer, in the sitting room. This was the room on the right, which was large and a bit gloomy although a couple of standard lamps in the corners cast something of a rosy glow, again with those miserable dark green curtains and with no heating whatsoever.

As far as I could see there was an old-fashioned radiogram in the window alcove, and a lot of books on the inglenook shelves, but no television, or any other furniture. Just several sofas and cushions on the floor.

I didn't tell Scott about my Renza-conversation with Mo. Like the sleeping arrangements, I decided I'd do that later. Right now, it was just out of this world to be there, with him, sharing his life.

Using my bunched-up coat as a tray, I sat on the sofa and he was on a cushion at my feet, leaning back against my legs as we ate. Joss, who had said hi and kissed me, and Zak were also sitting on the floor, while Mo and Rich – who had welcomed me with only slightly less enthusiasm than Mo – were on the other sofa. I'd thought there'd be other people there – maybe Stephan, and definitely girlfriends – but not that night it seemed.

The radiogram was tuned to Luxembourg, and added more unforgettable tunes to my musical memory box: 'Eloise' by Barry Ryan, 'Montague Terrace in Blue' by Scott Walker, the weird and wonderful 'MacArthur Park', and Gun's 'Race with the Devil'.

The conversation rose and fell as we ate, with the music as a background: they talked about gigs and music and people I didn't know and the occult and books and films.

I couldn't remember when I was last happier.

When everyone had finished eating, I stood up and started to collect the empty plates. 'Thank you, Mo, that was fab. I'll do the washing up and earn my keep.'

Mo just shrugged. 'Fine by me.'

Scott scrambled to his feet to help me, and once we were in the kitchen and all the dirty dishes were piled in the sink, he hugged me. 'Sorry about Mo – he and Rich do have an ongoing agenda.'

'I know,' I looked up at him. 'About Renza. And now I understand why. I didn't realise she was so young...' I sighed. 'She's who you need here – not me. You should be with someone young and carefree and sweet – and if she's slim and very pretty with long blonde hair and endless legs, then so much the better. You'd look like the perfect, ideal couple.'

Scott frowned. 'I had no idea Mo had told you so much.'

'He hasn't. He didn't... you mean – that's what she looks like?'

He nodded. 'Yep – and now let's do the washing up...'

I tried to push the image of young, blonde and beautiful out of my head and plunged my hands into the hot soapy water – there must be an immersion heater somewhere to get hot water, which meant I'd volunteer to do the washing up all the time to keep warm. Think about immersion heaters; don't think about Renza.

As we clattered the dishes from the sink to the draining board and Scott flapped around them with a grubby tea-towel, I knew that this was going to be a very temporary thing – he and Renza belonged together. I was just, as Mo had said, a stop-gap.

'I'm Twinkle Stop-Gap,' I said out loud in a mock-upper-class voice. 'One of the Berkshire Stop-Gaps, don't you know.'

'What?' Scott stopped drying a plate and stared at me.

'My new role and title,' I grinned at him and flicked soap suds. 'I think I'll get used to it in time.'

'Crazy,' he grinned at me.

Crazy? Probably, but I also knew that I'd be a stop-gap for as long as possible. When and if Renza came to stay, I'd just disappear and stay out of the way until he wanted me back again. Until he didn't want me anymore.

Pride? What pride? I loved him.

We went to bed at midnight.

At home, since the operation, I'd been sleeping in baggy T-shirts and the big knickers. It was what I'd brought to sleep in here, too. Shivering, teeth chattering, and not just because of the cold, I changed in the bathroom and walked slowly into the bedroom.

Scott, still fully dressed, was sitting on the edge of the bed.

I sat beside him. I didn't look at him. 'I can't sleep with you.'

He stood up, saying nothing, and with his back to me started piling up the small change from his jeans' pockets on to the tall dressing table thing.

I giggled. 'Did you used to work in a bank?'

'What?'

'You're piling them all up in order – pennies, threepenny bits, sixpences – all neatly...'

'So, you can't sleep with me but you can question my – um – quirks?'

'Yep.'

'Do you mean sleeping with me as in making love or as in sharing a bed?'

I shrugged. 'A bit of both really.'

He stopped piling up the coins and looked at me. 'You can't sleep with me because of the moral issue? Or because of Renza? Because you don't want to? Or because – ?'

Embarrassed, I took a deep breath and stared at the floor. 'All of those. And because the doctors say I can't. Because my insides are a mess. And because of this.' I yanked up the T-shirt and pulled down the top of my baggy pants to my hip bones. 'Because of this.'

He looked at the scar – still massive, still livid, still scabbed, still with the delightful double row of vivid puncture marks from the clips – and then at me. 'Christ. You poor thing. I had no idea that it would look like that... I'm so sorry...'

'Oh, it's much better than it was,' I said, hiding it away again. 'And as I'm medically off-limits and the scar has no doubt revolted you beyond words, I'll just pack my bags and leave, shall I?'

'Yes. Clear off.'

We stared at one another, then laughed.

He leaned down and kissed me gently. 'I didn't just want you to be here to sleep with you.'

'Liar,' I smiled. 'But no, physically I can't sleep with you – morally... well, we both know the answer to that one.'

'So?' He looked at me. 'What are we going to do?'

There was only one thing to do...

'I don't know about you,' I slid to the bottom of the bed and sat with my legs dangling over the footboard, flicking at imaginary reins and clicking my tongue at imaginary horses, 'but I'm going to drive the wagon train – you can fight off the Indians...'

Only hesitating for a moment, Scott leapt on to the bed, sat cross-legged on the pillows, and started firing an imaginary but very noisy rifle.

We exploded with laughter.

'What the hell is going on in here?' The door flew open and Zak stared at us. 'Jesus! Why can't you two just have sex and fight like normal couples?'

The door slammed shut again and our laughter rocked that cold, grim house.

Stella's Diary
January 24th 1969

Today has been just perfect. I woke up at about 10 o'clock, curled in Scott's arms and it seemed the most natural thing in the world. And I didn't feel guilty. Should I feel guilty? After all, we'd just fallen asleep together after talking for hours about everything under the sun, laughing some more, followed by a rather chaste goodnight kiss. Nothing else. Yes... ok, I probably should feel guilty – but I honestly didn't care.

I just stared at him as he slept. Oh God, he was so beautiful and it didn't seem even the slightest bit wrong to be there with him like this.

I stroked his hair away from his face, smiled to myself and stretched my legs down the bed – then quickly withdrew them. The sheets were icy. And although I was warm and cosy from the neck down, my face felt cold, my breath was hovering in clouds, and my nose was frozen. Just for one treacherous moment I thought about home: snug, cosy, warm from the coke boiler in the kitchen and the coal fires in the grates.

Then, shivering, I pulled the eiderdown up a bit further and squinted at the windows. The dark green curtains seemed to be backlit in an odd sort of way and without disturbing Scott, I slid out of bed and tiptoed towards the window.

Hell! It was cold!

I pulled my coat on over the T-shirt and tried to open the curtains. They were stuck solid. Frozen to the windows. I peeled back a corner – the windows were covered in the most amazing intricate frost patterns. I was amazed that we hadn't frozen to death overnight. Scraping some of the ice from the window I peered out. Everywhere was covered in a heavy hoar frost. It looked like fairyland.

While he was still sleeping, I nipped to the bathroom,

holding my breath and being as quick as possible – it was even more like an ice box – dressed, in my warmest mini frock, a brown and green and cream paisley wool with massively ballooning sleeves, then tiptoed downstairs in search of tea or coffee.

No one else was up. The house was silent and freezing and gloomy. The white light from the frost brightened it a bit though, as barefoot – well, ok, I had tights but they were hardly warm – I mooched around in the kitchen wishing I'd brought a pair of slippers. Well, ok maybe not – slippers weren't very rock'n'roll after all, but they'd probably be better than frostbitten toes.

I put the kettle on to boil, found two clean mugs, a jar of coffee and a bag of sugar but after a long search – including checking the ice-covered doorstep – no milk. So I made my way back upstairs with black coffee with two sugars for two.

Scott was awake and dressed and sitting on the bed.

'Good morning. I thought you'd left me,' he grinned. 'Then I thought you were in the bathroom – and you weren't – oh, wow... coffee... ta. Luxury. ' He wrapped his hands round the mug and inhaled the steam. 'Aah, warmth...'

'Goodness knows how you all survive here in this weather.' I sat carefully beside him. 'And sorry it's black. No milk to be found.'

'Rich and Mo will go shopping later. Stephan gives us an allowance for food.' He looked at me. 'Did you sleep in those sequins?'

'Not these, no. I put them on just now. I slept in the old ones – which are probably all over the pillows – and kept the eyelashes on, though. In case you woke up and I scared you. I look like a swede on a stick without the eyelashes.'

Scott laughed, hugged me, kissed me, spilled his coffee on the bed.

'Ooops.'

We attempted to mop it up with a corner of the eiderdown

and laughed again.

'Bloody hell!' Zak, on his way to the bathroom and looking a bit naked, shoved the door open. 'Are you *still* laughing? And fully dressed? You're weird.'

And slammed the door again. Then he opened it. He was definitely naked. 'Have you got coffee? Can I have some?'

Embarrassed, I didn't look at him. 'If you promise to be downstairs and dressed by the time I've made it, yes.'

He was. And so were Rich, Mo and Joss. I made coffee for all of them. Rich and Mo even said thank you and smiled at me.

I'd hoped someone might suggest a late breakfast or dinner or something, but it appeared that Narnia's Children only ate one meal a day. It seemed Stephan's food allowance didn't stretch to any more than that.

After I'd explored the rest of the house and discovered that the room opposite the sitting room was huge, empty of all furniture except a record player, a small sofa and a sideboard, and was used by Narnia's Children as their practice room when they needed to try out new songs, Scott suggested we went for a walk.

'Mo and Rich are taking the Transit into town to stock up on food,' he said, pulling on his black coat. 'And tonight we've got a gig.'

I paused in zipping up my boots. My heart sank. That meant he'd be gone soon, back to being Scott the sex-god guitarist in Narnia's Children – and no longer Scott, the most beautiful boy in the world who made me laugh and who I'd love forever – and I had to go home tomorrow for the next hospital appointment and a return to reality. This visit was going to be over before it had begun... and I didn't even know if there'd be another one.

'Don't look so miserable,' Scott frowned at me. 'I thought you'd enjoy it.'

'The walk? Yes, of course... but...'

'And the gig. You don't think I'm leaving you here, do

you?'

'Um – well – yes, actually. No one else has girls with them, do they? I mean – it's your job. If you worked in an office you wouldn't take me with you, would you?'

'Probably not. But I don't. Now grab your coat – it's still freezing out there.'

Hand-in-hand, we walked along the quiet, undulating road towards Heath and Reach, talking and laughing. I tried not to skip with happiness.

The early-morning frost had melted away, and the afternoon was grey and bitterly cold. The surrounding hills were the colour of slate, and the skeletal trees were black-outlined against the pewter sky. It was stark and brutally beautiful. I knew it was an image that would stay with me always. Something else to squirrel away in my memory box.

We played I-spy and had kisses as forfeits and somehow never got to Heath and Reach. By the time we returned to the house it was late afternoon and already growing dark, and Mo was unloading the Transit van with shopping while Rich was reloading it with the group's gear.

The shopping seemed to consist of huge sacks of potatoes, onions and rice; dozens of boxes of Vesta beef curry; and piled-high tins of Fray Bentos steak and kidney pies and Heinz baked beans.

'This is our basic larder. We live on this stuff all the time.' Scott grinned. 'Mo gets it cheap in bulk and works miracles.'

As Scott disappeared inside the house, Rich paused in heaving a speaker into the van and beckoned me over. 'You're coming to the gig with us tonight?'

I nodded slowly, waiting for the harsh words.

He smiled. 'That's good. No, really. We've talked about it, me and Mo, and we're ok with you. We're pretty sure you're not a threat to Renza. Scott loves Renza – not you. In fact,' he winked, 'we reckon that while Scott's hanging with you he won't be tempted to stray with anyone else, so you'll be doing Renza a favour.'

It was a bit of a back-handed compliment – but as a peace-offering it was probably as good as it was going to get.

'Thanks – I think. Er – are we leaving soon?'

Rich laughed. 'About an hour if they all get ready in time. They're worse than you girls – primping and preening. Still, it's only local tonight, thank goodness – practically the next village along... Milton Keynes. We should be home not long after midnight.'

'Sounds great... um – are we going to eat before we go? Shall I help Mo with tea or anything?'

'God, no!' Rich hefted another speaker. 'No time for food. We'll eat when we get home. Oh – it looks like Scott's trying to attract your attention.'

Scott was standing in the doorway waving my pink boots. 'Stella – are you wearing these tonight?'

'No. I'm wearing the pale blue ones with my blue and white dress. Why?'

'Cool – so can I borrow these for the gig?'

'*What*? They're girls' boots!' I laughed. 'They'll never fit you! Your feet are much bigger than mine!'

Scott grinned. 'I reckon if I just shove my toes in and don't zip them up and don't put them on until we go on stage they'll be OK. They'll look so cool with my black trousers.'

'Pink? Pink ladies boots? Really? Of course you can borrow them, but I still think they'll cripple you.'

'You're a star, Twinkle,' Scott laughed, and disappeared back indoors.

***

Milton Keynes looked like a really pretty little place, and the village hall was fabulous. Smaller than St B's, but with the same dimly-lit, exciting atmosphere. It was packed with teenagers, and I was amused to see that there were plenty of Dolly Rockers already positioned in front of the stage — clearly the groupie scene was universal. The brief journey through the icy darkness had been like a re-run of the last time I was in the Transit, except this time I sat on Scott's lap and he kissed my neck a lot and it all got a bit steamy. I absolutely loved it.

I left Narnia's Children and Rich to set-up behind the dark red curtains and found the bar and bought bottles of beer and Coke and as many packets of crisps and peanuts as I could load on to a tray and stuff into my sequinned shoulder bag, then staggered backstage.

'Oh my God!' Joss paused in tuning up his bass guitar and relieved me of the tray and the armfuls I'd disgorged from my bag. 'You're one cool chick! Scott can sod off with Renza. I'm going to marry you!'

As they all abandoned their gear and the setting-up, and fell on the food and drinks, Scott winked at me.

Then they all said thank you nicely and laughed, and I just stared at them. They'd been transformed. No longer the four bone-thin scruffy boys who lounged around in that cold, bleak house... now dressed in their skin-tight flares and tight short skinny-rib sweaters, with their glossy hair falling to their shoulders, they were Narnia's Children: super-sexy, super-talented, close-harmony rock band.

I was in heaven.

Narnia's Children were stupendous. They were so talented. They went down a storm. I sat to one side, halfway down the hall in the darkness, and just soaked up every fab moment. The music was much the same as it had been at St B's and I re-lived every wonderful minute. Whether they were playing hard, throbbing rock'n'roll, or perfect west coast pop, they were simply fantastic.

Zak growled and posed sexily, striding about with the microphone like Mick Jagger; Mo was a frenzy of drumsticks and wild air; Joss pouted and preened; and Scott just stood there, his guitar slung low, his superb body still and oh-so-wanton, simply oozing sex appeal.

The dance-floor was packed, the Dolly Rockers screamed loudly at the foot of the stage, everyone yelled for more at the end of each set, the hall vibrated.

And I sat there, smiling, because drop-dead-gorgeous Scott was wearing my pink boots – well, almost because he hadn't quite managed to get his feet into them or zipped up however hard we'd tried – and, amazingly, because I'd woken up with him and would be sleeping with him when we went home after the gig. It was the most addictive feeling in the world.

Scott, I realised, was going to be a very hard habit to break.

Stella's Diary
February 1st 1969

I read *The Ka of Gifford Hillary* on the bus all the way to Leighton Buzzard. I'd spoken to Scott on the phone the night before and he was a chapter ahead of me, so I had some catching up to do.

Just before I'd left the Leighton Buzzard house, a week ago, Scott and I had found two battered copies of the Dennis Wheatley book in one of the tall bookcases, and as neither of us had read it, we decided to make it a shared experience. Scott, apparently, was a massive Wheatley fan, and I'd never read any of his books before, so I was really looking forward to it.

It was like nothing I'd ever read and it had me gripped. It was about a man being buried alive by his love rival and how his "ka" or spirit managed to escape from his coffin and pursue justice on the astral plain: weird, terrifying and exciting in equal measure, I knew I'd read more of his books in the future. So, the book, and the mantra of the villages, helped to pass the time as I returned to Leighton Buzzard.

And this time, because I'd had my post-op out-patient's appointment and didn't have another one until the end of the month when Narnia's Children were off to tour Scotland, I was going to stay with Scott for nearly three weeks.

This time the warnings from Mum and Vix were even more loudly voiced, but this time I simply wasn't listening. I knew that Scott loved Renza and that Renza loved him. I knew he didn't love me. I knew one day Renza would come home and he'd marry her. I also knew that Rich and Mo were right – I *was* a stop-gap, and my being around probably did mean he wouldn't be tempted to cheat on Renza while they were apart, however cock-eyed that reasoning might be. I knew all this.

I also knew I loved him.

The weather was still bitterly cold, with a north-easterly wind and a low, yellow sky. I'd not only got practically my entire wardrobe in my tote bags, but also the first lot of paperwork for Narnia's Children's fan club.

My school-friend, Barry, had set up a small printing business in Harbury Green, and was delighted when I told him what I wanted. He'd made an ace job of it. We'd agreed on 100 copies of everything to start with, just to see how it went, and then he'd have the templates to do some more as needed.

I'd given him the Narnia's Children logo, and he'd used it as a vivid red header on each piece of A4 paperwork: the fan club application forms, the page with my carefully typed potted biogs of each member of the band, and sheets of blank paper, with Stella Deacon: Fan Club Secretary and my address on the top, for me to write answering letters to all the girls who joined the club. It looked so professional, and was all very exciting.

I'd paid Barry and kept his invoice to give to Stephan when – if – I saw him.

Scott was at the bus stop again. My heart went into overdrive when I saw him under the street lamp, my smile was ear-to-ear. It was a different bus driver and conductor but they too grinned as I hurtled off the bus into Scott's arms, my tote bags flying everywhere.

'I've missed you,' I laughed up at him.

'I've missed you, too.'

We walked back to the house in the icy cold darkness, the wind whipping our hair round our faces, and talked about the week we'd been apart as if it had been a year –despite the fact that I'd rung him from the phone box every day and he'd called me back and we'd chatted for hours. I'd wondered who paid the phone bill; maybe it was Stephan, or perhaps there was a box somewhere for the phone call money like Mrs Palmer, our vicar's wife, had. One thing was for sure – it wasn't Narnia's Children. They were constantly broke.

And I knew the group had been working hard, playing nearly every night for the last week – small venues like the

Milton Keynes village hall one – and big ballroom and club gigs – but they never seemed to be paid much. I guessed Stephan, as their manager, arranged the bookings, got the money, and dished it out to them as and when.

We reached the house, and it still looked a bit grim and unwelcoming, but my heart leapt at the sight of it because it was something I shared with Scott. A special place.

After I'd dumped my luggage in the still freezing bedroom I followed Scott into the kitchen, where it was lovely and warm and where Mo was cooking again. This time he greeted me with a smile and actually welcomed my offer to help him peel a mountain of potatoes. It was a huge step forward. So, while I peeled, Scott made coffee for everyone, the music – a Simon and Garfunkel LP this time – echoed from the radiogram in the sitting room and the rest of the band drifted in and out and chatted. I was blissfully happy.

That evening's meal was tinned steak and kidney pies, mashed potatoes and baked beans. Mo had allowed half a pie per person and each plate was piled high with mash and beans. We again ate in the big sitting room with music in the background and the group talked about gigs as they ravenously shovelled down the food. I ate only slightly more slowly – it was fab comfort food – again with Scott leaning against my legs.

The rest of the evening drifted by in a happy haze of conversation, music and laughter. Only one thing jolted me slightly from my bliss: apparently Mo's steady girlfriend, Cassie, might be coming over from Jersey to stay for a while. That sort of made sense. Of course, Mo seemed the type to have a long-term girlfriend. I wondered if Cassie and Renza had ever met. I guessed they might have done, and made a mental note *not* to be in Leighton Buzzard at the same time as Cassie. It also explained why Mo didn't slope off outside with a local groupie Dolly Rocker "to look at the van" in the break at Milton Keynes. Zak and Joss had, and their giggling conquests had returned for the second half with undone tops, love bites and messed-up make-up.

Rich never seemed to bother with girls either, although I was absolutely sure he wasn't homosexual. Maybe he too had a steady girlfriend tucked away somewhere. And maybe she too was friends with Renza. I decided not to ask.

Zak put The Beach Boys' *Pet Sounds* LP on the radiogram, Mo fetched bottles of beer from the kitchen, and Scott stretched out beside me on the sofa, his long legs across my lap.

The conversation and laughter rose and fell, the boys occasionally sang along with one of the tracks, and I knew I'd remember it forever.

And then we went to bed.

Stella's Diary
February 2nd 1969

It was daylight when I woke up. I squinted at the bedside clock. Almost mid-day. An icy white glow came from behind the green curtains. The radio beside the bed was burbling quietly. We'd left it on when we'd eventually fallen asleep. It had been on Luxembourg playing soul, but was now emitting odd foreign squeaks. I reached across Scott, who was deeply asleep, and turned the dial to Radio One. Then I kissed his cheek, shivered, and slid from the bed.

My goodness – it was colder than ever!

As I had no idea where exactly my clothes were after I'd hurled them off the night before, I grabbed Scott's discarded T-shirt and hurried into the mercifully vacant bathroom. I grinned knowingly at my reflection in the tiny mirror over the sink.

It was proper now; a real proper grown-up relationship. And making love with Scott had been nothing on earth like that one previous embarrassing fumbled experience with Mike.

Absolutely nothing on earth.

I hugged myself in delight. Then stopped, because now I was really, truly "the other woman". I tried to feel ashamed, guilty, all the things I knew I should be feeling – but I didn't. I didn't care how wrong it was. I really didn't care. I loved Scott more than life. Ok, I was the stop-gap, the substitute – but until Renza was back permanently, I was more than happy to live with it.

No wonder, I thought as I cleaned my teeth, re-did my sequins and eyelashes and spiked my hair, that the rather sweet junior houseman at my out-patients appointment, had said what he'd said – not exactly meeting my eyes.

"... Although the cysts and abscesses are gone and the wounds are healing nicely, I'm afraid the internal scarring is irreversible and severely damaging to your reproductive organs, which were, according to your notes, rather – um – malformed. You'll probably not menstruate – do you understand what that means? Good — for months. And I'm afraid you'll never be able to have a baby."

The nurse who had been attending to me had pulled a horrified face at the brutal sentence. I'd smiled reassuringly at her. It was hardly news to me. It was OK.

"Not," the houseman had looked at me then, blushing a little, "that this is the green-light to promiscuity, you understand. I'm not — er — suggesting that your infertility should mean that you — um — assume you have in-built contraception. Post-operation, you may now safely have — well — um — sexual intercourse, but I'm advising against it on moral rather than medical grounds."

The nurse had hissed a bit and then winked at me. I'd grinned at her. And I was still grinning now as I hurried back to the bedroom.

I pulled the curtains back a little, managing to unstick them from the frozen windows, and yelped with delight. It was snowing! It must have been snowing all night! Everywhere was covered in a glorious white eiderdown, and the fat goose-feather flakes were still tumbling from the ochre sky.

'Scott!' I leapt into bed and dived under the covers. 'Scott! Wake up! It's snowing!'

He opened the gorgeous turquoise eyes, pushed his long black hair away from his face, then smiled lazily. 'Hi... is it? Good...' Then closed his eyes again.

I giggled and snuggled closer to him, watching the snowflakes dance against the window. He sighed sleepily and pulled me towards him. Amen Corner were singing 'Half As Nice' on the radio. Paradise, I thought, dreamily, is here, now, in bed with Scott and watching the snow.

The bedroom door flew open. Zak, dressed for once, peered in. 'Scott! Ah — sorry...' he grinned. 'Well, at least you're behaving like a normal couple at last... um — Stephan's on the phone for you... I think he wants to meet up. Shall I tell him you're otherwise engaged?'

'No,' Scott kissed me and swung himself out of bed. 'I need to talk to him. We need to know where we're playing... And if I don't catch him now he'll disappear for weeks.' He looked at me. 'Don't go anywhere. I'll be back.'

***

Stephan arrived at the house later that afternoon, just as Scott and I, having built a lop-sided snowman, were shoving handfuls of snow down each other's necks in the front garden and shrieking with cold and laughter.

Having ploughed through the snow from London in his latest model automatic white Rover, Stephan surveyed us with grave doubt, said he needed to talk to Scott pronto and marched into the house. He was younger than I'd imagined; very suave and quite elegant in a grown-up businessman sort of way.

Still grinning and dripping snow, we trailed indoors after him. It was only slightly warmer inside than out. So, once Scott and I had shed wet coats and boots, and Scott and Stephan had disappeared into the "practice room", I changed into the rainbow jersey dress, and using my coat as a blanket, snuggled up on the sofa with *The Ka of Gifford Hillary*.

It was dark when Stephan and Scott emerged, and Mo was busy in the kitchen preparing tonight's dinner — curry again — Rich, Zak and Joss were reading various music papers, and I was completely gripped by Dennis Wheatley's spooky story.

'Stella,' Stephan held out his hand. 'Maybe I should have introduced myself earlier — but I never like to interrupt children at play. It's very nice to meet you. Scott's told me a lot about you, you sound like a well-connected young lady.'

Slightly intimidated, after all he was a big-name music mogul, I put down the book and shook his hand. Scott was laughing behind Stephan and I raised my sequinned eyebrows at him questioningly. He just shook his head and smiled that wicked smile.

'We've been through the fan club stuff,' Stephan continued,

'and I'm impressed. Extremely professional. I've brought a box file of all the letters we've received from fans so far – so you're going to be busy sending out the application forms – and I've included stamps for postage. If you run out, let me have invoices for everything next time we meet. And – yes – Scott's also told me about your teen magazine connections. All very good news for us.'

'Um – thank you… I'm really looking forward to running the fan club – and – er – I think we've already decided to do the interview for the magazines to tie in with the record coming out – er – being released…'

'Ideal. Right, if one of you could get me some coffee, I'll be on my way. It's a sod of a night out there, the roads are crazy mad, and I need to be back in London tonight.'

Everyone, including Scott, rapidly disappeared towards the kitchen.

Stephan laughed and slumped on the other end of the sofa. 'They're good boys. Have you known them long?'

'No. Just a few months.' Oh, God, I thought. He's going to ask me about Renza or something.

He didn't.

'They're very talented – and certainly getting their name known, but it's a jungle out there. Cut-throat. I'm doing my best for them but every lad and his dog wants to be a pop star these days. So, you and Scott….?'

'Are friends,' I said, hoping my voice wasn't wobbling.

'Of course,' Stephan nodded, smiling a bit. 'He's the only one I can talk business with. He's got a great business brain, that boy. The way he plays guitar would make the angels weep, but he'd be ace in management. Mo and Rich hold them together in a sort of parental way, and Zak and Joss are just a pair of mad kids making the most of the available chicks and the freedom. But Scott's got a sensible head on his shoulders. You'll make a good team. Ah – coffee… thanks, Rich.'

A good team? I sighed to myself. If only….

Stella's Diary
February 10th 1969

I'd had an interesting week in Leighton Buzzard. It'd snowed every day, and the wind had whipped it into drifts, so the road outside the house was covered almost to the tops of the hedges. We'd still managed to get out though. I think Scott loved the snow almost as much as I did, and because we both liked walking, we'd slipped and slithered our way into the town, playing snowballs and window-shopping, on most days.

Stephan had apparently left a list of bookings with Scott – keeping Narnia's Children busy until they leave for Scotland at the end of the month, and maybe, I hoped, with some sort of money coming in – and they'd had three gigs in the last week: two reasonably local in dance-halls, and one at a club near London.

I'd gone with the band to both the local ones – the roads were tightly-packed with snow and resembled bob-sleigh-runs, but Rich drove carefully and we made it one piece – and had a great time. It seemed that this had always been my life... being with Scott, travelling in the van, curled against him, his arms round me, his guitar case under my knees, the stack of speakers wobbling precariously behind my head, the radio blaring, everyone else laughing, talking, singing, smoking... watching them be brilliantly talented and stupendously sexy on stage, so very proud to be part of it all, buying them beer and crisps in the break, and then going home in the early hours of the morning and falling into bed with Scott and making love and sleeping until the afternoon.

I never wanted it to end.

I'd stayed in the house alone for the third gig. It was quite scary once they'd all gone, but I locked all the doors, switched all the lights on and turned Luxembourg up really loud on the radiogram in the sitting room and worked. Yes, worked!

Well, sort of. I started sifting through the mountain of fan club mail Stephan had left, addressing envelopes and popping fan club application forms into them, then keeping the original letters to type up the contact names and addresses so that when I got home I could send out the monthly newsletters. There were, as Stephan had said, masses of them, from all over the country, and lots of them from girls who seemed to have met Narnia's Children on some Mediterranean cruises they'd done the previous summer, and most of them declaring undying love for one or other or all of the group. I tried really, really hard not to feel jealous about the ones who said they'd love Scott forever.

Then, I came across a beautifully written letter postmarked Germany and signed *Renza Rossi*.

I stared at it. At the perfect writing in pale blue ink – fountain pen, not ballpoint – Renza... in Germany... Renza Rossi... what a beautifully exotic name that was. A beautiful name for my beautiful 16 year-old rival. No, there was no rivalry... there never would or could be... Renza would win every time. I shivered and it had nothing to do with the cold.

She'd written to Stephan saying Scott had told her recently that there was a fan club being set up and as a laugh she'd like to join and so would one of her brothers and a sister – Jasper and Sophia.

I exhaled heavily and, with trembling hands, folded three application forms into an envelope and wrote the German address on the envelope. Then I pushed it to the bottom of the pile and tried to forget it. But I couldn't. It seemed so very wrong to be writing to Renza, to be sending her fan club stuff, when I was sleeping with her fiancé.

Maybe Vix had been right all along – maybe I was a man-stealing, groupie tart. I shoved the fan club stuff away, turned the radio up even louder, tried dancing round the sitting room to 'Build Me Up Buttercup', but it didn't work. For the first time I felt horribly guilty and I didn't like it at all.

I abandoned the fan club stuff and the futile dancing, and

concentrated on finishing Scott's birthday card instead in the hope that it might make the guilt go away. His birthday was on the 14th, and I'd decided to make him a massive card, using all my art A level skills (Miss Loxley would be so proud, I thought), with cut-outs and sketches and cartoons – all relevant to him and his life. It was my secret labour of love and I'd worked on it when the band was practising and hidden the card under the bed (no one seemed to clean under the beds ever) when Scott was around. It was all mad hippy stuff, and rock'n'roll, and guitars and books and astrology and sci-fi, and everything else I thought he might like. The colours were clashing and shocking and probably glowed in the dark. I really hoped he'd like it.

By 1 in the morning I was falling asleep, but I'd finally finished it, and after careful deliberation, wrote *'Happy Birthday Superstar, with all my love always and forever, Twinkle XXXXX'*. Then, turning off all the lights and the radiogram, and taking the chain off the door, I took it upstairs and carefully wrapped it in "happy birthday" paper before hiding it again. After that I quickly got ready for bed and slipped under the covers.

Oh my Lord! The bed was freezing! I pulled the eiderdown up over my nose, closed my eyes and tried really, really hard not to think about Renza.

I must have fallen asleep despite the guilt and the ice-box temperatures because the next thing I knew was Scott sliding into bed beside me – even colder than I was.

'What time is it?' I asked, trying hard to keep his icy feet away from mine. 'Is it time to get up?'

'4.30-ish... You been ok?'

'Fine, thanks. Good gig?'

'Great.'

'Good.'

I curled against him. 'Scott... tell me about Renza – no, listen...' and I told him about the fan club applications.

He laughed in the darkness. 'Sorry, I should have forewarned you. She'd told me that the kids wanted to join –

309

they're smashing, those two... She's got a lot of younger brothers and sisters, and her mother – who's a dragon, believe me – uses Renza as an unpaid nursemaid and skivvy.'

I swallowed. It was like Cinderella only real. I'd had such a cushy life in comparison. 'I've put a form in for her, too. Because she asked for one. Shall I take it out?'

'No, don't. She says she's our number one fan – which she is – so she deserves to be an honorary member at least.'

'Okay. I'll make her number one on the list. And this way she'll know what you're all doing when you don't write or ring her often enough?'

'Ouch.'

'Do you have a photo?'

'Yes.'

'Can I see it?'

'Now? Seriously?'

'Yep. Scott... I have this picture in my head, I'd love to know what she's really like... I know it's all wrong, and rubbish timing, but...'

He sighed, swung himself out of bed and felt his way round to the dressing table-wardrobe thing. 'There...'

He pushed the black and white photo into my hand and switched on the bedside light.

I stared at it. At Renza. At last. She wasn't just beautiful – she was stunning. It looked like a posed studio photo, and she was looking wistfully over her shoulder: so slim, gorgeous complexion, perfect features, huge eyes, a waterfall of straight blonde hair tumbling out of sight.

I handed it back. 'Thank you. She's very, very lovely.'

'She is. And special. Like no one I've ever known in my life. Sweet, innocent, unworldly, funny, tells amazing stories, knows so much, could do anything she wanted but isn't allowed to, and has a really terrible time at home.' He put the photo back on the shelf, closed the door, switched off the light and slid into bed. 'I love her very much. I promised her I'd sleep with that photo under my pillow – and I always do – until now. But I'll never hurt her.'

'No...' I turned away from him, my words muffled by my pillow. 'I know.'

Renza's Diary
February 14th 1969 – Valentine's Day

Some St. Valentine's Day this is turning out to be. No card from Scott even though I sent him one with a birthday card included over a week ago to ensure he got it in time. I've been pestering the post sergeant and it's embarrassing. He's forgotten me.

There's a do in the Mess tonight, a German band is going to be playing and there is a formal dinner with all the big-wigs from the Town Hall and Police invited. I'm babysitting for Mum and Dad and I'll have a couple of babies from the families opposite to keep an eye on too. What a romantic way to spend the evening; snotty-nosed kids and nappies. Still, it beats listening to yet another oompah band.

I wonder what Scott is doing – gigging I guess – and somewhere romantic I bet, with lots of girls done-up-to-the-nines gazing adoringly at him on stage. Zak and Joss will be picking off groupies and getting drunk and Mo and Rich will be the sensible ones, keeping everyone organised. I wish I could be with them, having a laugh and a life. Scott has no idea what my life's like and how much I miss him. I can't stand the thought of him being so accessible to all that female talent. Who could resist him when I can't.

Oh well, time to change another nappy and give the youngest baby his bottle. Good practice Mum says. To hell with that.

Stella's Diary

February 14th 1969 – Valentine's Day

Scott's birthday. And Narnia's Children surprisingly didn't have a Valentine's Day booking. The snow continued to tumble fitfully from the yellow sky. It was bitterly cold, inside the house and out.

If Scott had received birthday cards – or Valentine cards – from anyone else I had no idea. I knew Renza must have sent him one of each, but he'd been discreet enough not to let me know. It seemed like a pretty dismal birthday to me: no presents, no cards displayed on the mantelpiece, no one getting excited and shouting and kissing and sneaking around with secret gifts like they always did for me at home. The rest of the band did wish him a happy birthday, but it seemed they didn't do anything special for any of their birthdays, ever.

However, he loved my card. He seemed genuinely amazed that I'd thought of him, remembered his birthday, secretly made him the card-cum-present. It made him laugh at first, then smile as he noticed each little relevant cartoon or picture. He pulled me to him, and kissed me and said ruefully that I clearly knew him very well indeed and it was the best card he'd ever had and he'd treasure it for ever.

Or, I thought, at least until Renza moved in.

We walked into Leighton Buzzard that afternoon, hand-in-hand, sliding on the hard-packed snow, hurling snowballs at one another, laughing.

We stopped at a small stationer's shop on the outskirts of the town centre.

'I've got to buy a card,' Scott said, pushing his hair away from his eyes.

'A bit late for Valentine's Day,' I grinned at him, 'but I'll take a late offering.'

'It's for Renza's birthday.'

'Ah.'

I wondered then if he'd sent her a Valentine's card. I hoped so.

We nudged our way inside, between the crowded shelves, and stared at the ranks of cards. I found one with a gorgeous doe-eyed cartoon girl on the front, she had long blonde hair and was dressed in jeans and a striped T-shirt.

'This looks like Renza,' I waved the card at Scott. 'So pretty. She'd love it.'

He shook his head. 'I can't send something like that. I want something – well – you know... special.'

I blinked. Of course he did. He wanted a lovely romantic birthday card for her. She was his fiancée. He loved her. I had absolutely no right to be involved in this.

I turned away. 'Ok, look – I've got the fan club stuff to post, so I'll pop into the shop next door and meet you outside.'

'Stella...?'

'It's ok. Really. Take as long as you need. Find the loveliest card in the world. She deserves it. I'll go and play in the snow to pass the time.'

I didn't. I went into the equally tiny general post office stores next door, posted all the fan club forms, including the ones to Germany, and, remembering something Vix and I had done once for a Valentine's Day party, bought the most exotic thing I could find – a pineapple. And a small bottle of cochineal. And tried hard not to think about the hearts and flowers and promises of undying love that Scott was choosing for Renza.

When we got home – home, hark at me! – it was dark and Scott disappeared into the sitting room to finish writing to Renza so that he could post her card, and I made myself scarce. As Mo wasn't in the kitchen I went to town with the pineapple, hacking it into slices, then carefully cutting it into bite-sized heart shapes and dunking them in the cochineal and arranging them on a couple of big plates. It was fiddly and time-consuming and took my mind away from

Scott and Renza as a couple.

'That looks cool,' Joss stuck his head into the kitchen. 'What is it?'

'Valentine's Day hearts,' I showed him. 'It's a birthday tea present for Scott.'

Joss's beautiful wicked-angel face fell. 'Not for the rest of us?'

'It's only pineapple soaked in red food colouring. But I'm sure Scott won't mind sharing. Anyway, Mo'll be in here soon to cook dinner, won't he?'

'Doubt it,' Joss pulled a face. 'We've only got rice left, he says. Until Stephan gives him some more money, we're going to starve.'

I stared at him. 'Really? I wish I'd known, I could have bought some stuff in town. The shops are all shut now.'

'We'll be ok. Mo says there'll be some money tomorrow. We can just have rice tonight – and maybe onions.'

'But you can't not eat!' I really was my mother's daughter! 'Isn't there a chip shop or something?'

'Nope. Don't think so. And even if there was, we're all broke.'

'I've got money,' I said. 'I'm staying here for nothing – I'll happily buy you some food.'

'Cool,' Joss grinned. 'But you don't have to do that.'

'I do if we're all going to starve.'

'But all the shops are shut.'

'I know,' I said. 'I'll buy some basics tomorrow. Promise.'

Rich joined Joss in the doorway and looked at the plates of red pineapple hearts. 'Oh, pudding! If only we had dinner... However, I have a plan...'

Two hours later, looking like a bedraggled band of refugees, Narnia's Children and I, led by Rich, trudged through the snow, sliding unsteadily down the hills in the darkness, hurling snowballs, singing very off-key, to the far side of Leighton Buzzard. The snow, frozen solid, sparkled and danced like a million spangles under the street lights.

It was extremely pretty, but bone-numbingly cold, and my fun-fur, already saturated from our earlier outing, now looked like a drowned rat.

'Where are we going?' I asked Scott who was holding my icy hand very tightly as the pavements were now like skating rinks.

'No idea,' he chuckled in the darkness, 'but it seems like a pretty groovy way to be spending my birthday even if I do think I've got frostbite. It's been fab so far.'

And he didn't even know about the pineapple hearts. I'd taken them upstairs and hidden them in the bedroom. I knew they'd be ok. There was no need for a refrigerator in that house.

'Why aren't we going in the van?' I puffed, my breath spiralling into the white night.

'Same reason as we haven't eaten,' Mo said. 'No money. No petrol. Thank goodness we get paid tomorrow.'

'Jam tomorrow,' I muttered. 'Like Alice in Wonderland.'

Eventually, frozen stiff and with Zak and Joss swearing and complaining loudly, we reached a long, low corrugated iron building, with lights spilling out across the frozen wilderness like a welcoming beacon.

'This is it. In we go,' Rich said through chattering teeth.

In we went. I laughed. Narnia's Children simply looked stunned.

It was the Salvation Army.

And it was delightfully warm and cosy. Various elderly and not-so-elderly, cold, very-wrapped-up people were dotted around as smiley men and women in uniform dished out bowls of soup with hunks of bread, mugs of hot chocolate and plates of biscuits.

They welcomed Rich like an old friend.

Zak eyed him suspiciously. 'You been here before?'

'Once or twice,' Rich said shortly.

'When you go out at night to get petrol in the van?' Scott

grinned at him.

Rich nodded just as we were gathered together by a motherly-looking Sally Army lady who ushered us towards the coke stove and started ladling out soup. The regulars stared at us with suspicion. I wasn't surprised. We looked like a gaggle of long-haired hippie guttersnipes.

Joss looked around with horror. 'Oh, very cool,' he said sarcastically. 'So bloody rock'n'roll. It's a bloody soup kitchen.'

'It's warm and we get fed,' Mo snapped, clearly a bit rattled. 'What were you expecting? The Ritz? Stop moaning.'

'This is a whole new experience for me,' I muttered through numbed lips.

'And me,' Scott agreed, 'but still very welcome and another part of a birthday I'm never going to forget.'

The Salvation Army soldiers were lovely. They chatted to us, seemingly knowing from Rich that the band lived in an unheated house with very little money, and didn't seem to mind that we weren't exactly homeless or destitute.

'We help all those who need a friend and a warm meal,' our motherly-lady said, comfortingly. 'We don't ask questions. We never judge. Young or old. And in weather like this we're simply delighted to be able to help. Now settle yourselves down, eat, drink and get warm.'

We did. It was fabulous.

***

We were much happier, warmer, and fuller and hardly noticed the sub-zero temperatures on the way home. Home! That cold, unwelcoming house *was* home to me – albeit temporarily. The mood had lifted sky-high.

I gave Scott the pineapple hearts when we eventually went to bed. Loudly joining in with Stevie Wonder warbling 'For Once In My Life' on Luxembourg, we attempted to feed one another with them. It was very messy. And funny.

Zak hurled the bedroom door open. 'For Christ's sake shut-up! Some of us need to sleep – sodding hell! Is that blood on your hands? God – you two are so bloody scary weird... goodnight!'

The door slammed shut again and I managed not to choke on a piece of pineapple. I grinned at Scott. 'Happy birthday...'

Stella's Diary
February 20th 1969

A sad day. I left Leighton Buzzard and went home to Harbury Green. Tomorrow, Narnia's Children were off on their tour of Scotland. It had stopped snowing a few days earlier but was still very cold, and the snow had frozen in big billowy ruts everywhere. I hoped and prayed they'd get to Scotland safely. And stay safe.

Scott came with me on the bus as far as Aylesbury. We were supposed to have parted company in Leighton Buzzard, at the bus stop at the bottom of the Heath and Reach hill, but neither of us seemed to be able to say goodbye, so we sat upstairs, at the front, amongst the heavy smokers – even though neither of us did – and watched the bleak countryside vanish through a swirling haze.

We played a whispered "put a name and life" to our fellow passengers. It got a bit rude and ridiculously funny, and my laughter masked the fact that in a few short moments I'd leave Scott and not know when – or even if – I'd ever see him again.

'I'll write and let you know when we're due back from Scotland,' he whispered against my hair as we clung together at the bus-stop in Aylesbury's dismal late-afternoon market place. 'Then you'll come back, won't you? Straight away?'

'Yes,' I nodded sadly, thinking that three weeks without him now was going to be almost impossible to bear. 'Of course. You go and have a fab time and enjoy Scotland and be superstars everywhere you go.'

'I'm going to miss you.'

'No you won't,' I smiled. 'You won't give me a second thought – oh, here's my bus... goodbye...'

We kissed for the last time then, totally wrapped up in one another, but I was vaguely aware of people watching us, probably thinking we were a living embodiment of all that was wrong with the Youth of Today. The clothes! The hair! The brazen behaviour!

I jumped on the bus and waved to Scott until he vanished from sight as we turned the corner, then cried all the way home.

Renza's Diary
March 10th 1969

Two days before my 17th birthday and a letter at last. I've received a couple of postcards from Scott and we've chatted a few times on the phone in the last month, but apart from Fan Club membership forms coming for us all, courtesy of the band's new Fan Club Secretary, Stella Deacon, he hasn't written.

'As you can see by the address, we are in Elgin, Scotland, again and we're having a great time playing-wise.' he wrote. *'We've been topping the bill everywhere we've played and the audience reactions have been great.'*

Big deal, I thought, as I looked at the birthday card he'd sent me. At least he hadn't forgotten that. It was a lovely card, and the words nice and he'd signed it *'All my love,'* with seventeen kisses.

'Thanks for the request on Luxembourg, we all heard it and were totally knocked out. Not just me, but the band were too. Great for publicity and words just can't express what I felt when I heard it, it was a fantastic feeling, thanks very much.'

He went on to apologise for not sending a Valentine's Day card – it being his birthday, he said he never sends cards to anyone, and didn't even think of me.

Well, thanks for nothing. I *loved* that bit.

'Don't get me wrong, I do care, and I do love you very much. I didn't send anyone else a card either.' He wrote in his spidery hand. *'I'm sorry if I seemed off when you came over to stay. I was just going through a bad time, feeling so tired and shattered. <u>Please forgive me.</u> Remembering the way we were together before you went to Germany, emotionally, when we got very close to making love and how it felt, I'm sorry about how it was when you came to Leighton Buzzard, and how it should have been.'* He wrote as I cried. *'Anyway, next time I won't have any excuse. Even though I was tired I should have been more loving*

towards you. I'm sorry.'

I read on and cried some more. Next time? Would there be a next time I wondered.

He went on to describe the Guest House they were staying in and the lady who ran it, who made them flasks of tea to take up to bed in the middle of the night when they got in. They've been gigging in somewhere called Wick and another place called Buckie, as well as Elgin and Aberdeen, where there was a circular ballroom; as they played on stage the audience lined the walls walking round and round watching them, which he said was really weird.

Wick was like being on the moon, apparently, with nothing for miles. They even drove over very high mountains in the snow, ending up near lochs where American submarines were moored, and they were chased away by American Military Police just for driving in the area.

The record is now supposed to be coming out this week, on the President label for Creole Records, and the plugger from President who made The Equals record a hit is raving about it and is going all out to push it.

Scott ended with declarations of undying love and how much he missed me. I just feel confused, thrilled, happy, miserable and desolate. He's messing with my head big time. And my heart.

***

I've been working at the base for about a month and it's horrid. I've cried every day because I hate it so much. No one speaks English in my office and apart from Frau Neuhaus and Frau Keppler, who are so old it's unreal, there's only one other female, called Hannah, who is a bit older than me. The rest are old German men, about ten of them, and they do nothing but drink and smoke and try and make me look at disgustingly rude photos of naked women and men doing stuff, and sometimes not just with men and women! Dad would go mental if I'd told him. They've got photos on the backs of cupboard doors that

322

would make your hair stand on end.

We start work at 7am — seriously, half way through the night! I walk to the base every morning, and the same German policeman has caught me, each time, crossing the road before the little sign tells me I can. But I stand for ages and nothing comes, if I didn't cross I'd be late. He always hides behind the wall and when I think it's clear, getting half way across the road, he steps out and starts *'Guten morgen Fraulein...'* and tells me off, threatening to fine me about 20 Marks. So funny, I don't think! I just played dumb. So far it's working. I only earn 9 Marks a week, so how could I pay the fine? Mum has most of my money anyway, the rest I'm saving for visits home and my food and clothes.

The office work is weird. I spend all my time typing endless forms and work sheets for engineering repairs, reconditioning and stripping down of engines, tanks and scout cars for the British Army on the Rhine. I'm becoming an expert on guns and shell sizes, plus we cover all aspects of leave, sick leave and the usual personnel stuff for the German civilian staff. Squaddies, delivering vehicles for repair and collecting them afterwards, come into the office and I do their paperwork. Some of them are about the same age as me, it's really embarrassing and not just for me, they blush as badly as I do when we do the paperwork together. I've got to do everything in English and in German, but as I know very little German it's a painful affair. The men yell at me all the time as if shouting's going to make me understand what they want me to do. There's a woman, Fraulein Carpentier, who's seven feet tall, seriously, and has a deep voice. She's in charge and keeps telling me, in German, what she wants me to type or do, which is nuts. I don't understand German, especially technical stuff. They're all losing their cool with me. I can't take much more of it.

Not only that, but they start on the vodka and schnapps at 7am when the hot bread roll man comes with breakfast: raw minced pork and onion with pepper on hot bread rolls. It's called

Mette, and it's gross. They have a fridge in the office where they keep their drinks and cream cakes. Every afternoon we have glasses of wine with strawberries in the bottom and if it's someone's birthday we have *huge* cream cakes. I am sent to the nearby dairy to buy more cream which they pile on top of the cream cakes, all washed down with wine.

I haven't arrived home sober since I started working there. By 4pm I'm as high as a kite. So far the S.S. hasn't noticed, but give her time.

I've started wearing hipsters to work too, because they're always sending me over to my dad's building, a huge engineering workshop (hangar) with hundreds of Germans working there and Dad's office is up a spiral staircase. The first few times I went up there, I managed to stop everything dead; and they shouted and whistled so loud the army colonel came out of his office and yelled at them and me. Apparently my short skirts are too much for them all and I have to dress *decently* in future, but they didn't allow trousers usually, and as my midi and maxi lengths are not allowed either – and not possessing any old frump clothes – I've been given permission to wear trousers to work, so as not to *inflame the passions* of the Germans, so Dad said. Blimey.

Plus Dad says the squaddies have been fighting over who should come up to our office to have their paperwork seen to by me and it's apparently causing 'bad morale' amongst the young soldiers. Sad devils.

Dad's introduced me to a young German bloke from his office, a bit older than me, called Klaus, who wants to practise his English with me. He's all right, he dresses a bit straight but so do most Germans I've seen, but he's quite good looking. Anyway, we've been out to a disco a few times, in Dortmund, Dusseldorf, and Koln so we can chat socially. It's all right I guess, but the music is so out of date it would be embarrassing if anyone I know had seen me there. Klaus is nice, very polite and proper, but a couple of times recently, he's tried to kiss me and put my hand somewhere unmentionable. Mum and Dad like him, so that's all right then. I've mentioned him in my letters to Scott, just to see what he says. So far, silence on the matter.

Holland was interesting and the Red Light District was a great laugh, well I laughed, Mum and the Catty Wives all pulled suitably shocked faces. We went up the river in Amsterdam in a glass-roofed boat so we could see the buildings, all tall and thin, and we saw the narrowest building in Holland and a few houses of 'ill repute' en route. My entertainment these days.

There were buildings called 'sex shops' but none of the ladies would go near enough to look properly, and Mum wasn't about to let me go inside to look. Some cafes sold 'special' cakes which our driver said meant they had drugs inside them and it was all very legal and above board. Imagine. A hippy paradise. Zak would be in heaven.

Amsterdam was very modern, not like Germany at all, and everyone seemed to speak English and were friendly and wore hip clothes as well. All the shops played English pop and rock music and it was like being in London really. The Rolling Stones and The Who seemed really popular and you could hear them a lot. Also Jimi Hendrix was being played in the cafes and bars as we passed.

I really liked Holland.

Renza's Diary
March 12th 1969

Happy birthday to me, happy birthday to me. I'm 17 today. 17 and stuck in the back of beyond while my former school mates are probably having birthday parties when they turn 17, and going out to celebrate with boyfriends and generally having a life. Life! Ha, that's a laugh. I don't have a life, on my birthday or any other day, unless you call going the NAAFI and the Stomp Club living, or crawling round a dance floor to really old music with Klaus now and again. Deep flipping joy!

I'm not even going to mention Scott, well...no, I am not. I can't stand the ache and stress attached to thoughts of him during the daytime – night-time is bad enough. I look at the moon – when I can see it – as we agreed to do every night, and wonder what he is doing. I wonder if he is wondering what I am doing – probably not. I kiss his photo every night and then try to go to sleep, but he won't let me. He fills my head as I try to drift off, then haunts my dreams when I sleep. So I'm not going to think of him. I got a card from Mum and Dad and 20 Marks to spend on something sensible they insisted, but I am going to save half of it towards a trip home next time I am able to arrange one. Nan always gave me a card and something nice on my birthday, and of course now she is gone, it reminds me of how much I miss her. If I'd stayed with her and gone to college, she might still be alive. Gosh this is depressing the hell out of me. Some happy birthday. There's a movie on in the Mess tonight, a World War Two movie, so I shan't be going. Mum and Dad are going to go since I'm not. I shall babysit and play my records and think about Scott – I know, I said I wouldn't. I lied. Happy birthday to me...

Stella's Diary
March 13th 1969

Today it was three weeks since I'd seen Scott and it's driven me almost insane. Oh, it was nice to have been back home again with Mum and Dad and the dogs and cats in a really warm house with proper food; and to see Vix and my other friends and go out with them, but it wasn't *real*. Not anymore. My real life was wrapped up with Scott, and Narnia's Children and living and loving in that cold, bleak house.

I thought about him all the time. I played all the records that reminded me of him. I read every Dennis Wheatley book I could find in the library. And I missed him more than words could say. He'd sent me a couple of postcards from Scotland, where they seemed to be having a great time and topping the bill everywhere they went and having massive sell-out audiences, which I'd propped up on my bedside table, but I needed to be with him, to see him, to hear his voice...

I'd tried to keep myself busy. I'd done masses of work for the fan club, getting tons of extra stuff printed, and Stephan had sent me 500 publicity photos of the group to send out with my ever-growing list of membership forms and monthly newsletters. As I didn't have a picture of Scott I pinched two of them – one with the whole band and then cutting him out on his own – and framed them and again had them beside my bed. And I'd written several short stories – all heartbreakingly sad – and sent them off to *Jackie* and *Romeo*, and I'd written up the Narnia's Children interview – cobbled together from everything I knew plus the answers to the various questions I'd asked them while I'd been at Leighton Buzzard – and sent it to Stephan for his ok.

He'd loved it and said to get it out there as soon as possible, to as many magazines as possible, along with one of the publicity photos, because it looked as if Narnia's

Children's record – 'Livin' With You' – would now be released on May 1st, so they'd need as much topical publicity as possible. He also asked me to do a sort of spoof press-release for future use, which was fun.

So, yes, I'd done all this. I'd immersed myself in all things Narnia's Children and practically lived at the post office, sending things hither and thither, but I actually ached from missing Scott. My heart ached. Living without him was a physical pain. And one, I kept telling myself, that I was going to have to get used to.

Because, far worse than any of this was the fact that I'd had another hospital appointment.

And they'd declared me fully recovered from the operation, and the endometriosis was, they said, not showing any signs of flaring up at the moment, and all the other tests had come back clear, and the rest of my internal problems would be monitored closely during future out-patients appointments – so – they said – I was to be signed-off as fit to return to work on April 1st.

April Fool's Day! How appropriate that was!

I'd be back at work in the office, 9 to 5, Monday to Friday, dealing with boring, boring claims forms while Scott was travelling all over the place – never at home long enough for us to get together – and it was obviously the end of everything.

I was devastated. Heartbroken. It was like the end of the world. No, it *was* the end of the world. My life was over.

Stella's Diary
March 17th 1969

Narnia's Children are home from Scotland! I'd had a postcard from Scott saying they'd be back in Leighton Buzzard over the weekend of the 15th and 16th and he couldn't wait to see me and would I be there on the Monday?

He didn't need to ask twice.

This time, as the bus trundled through the sleepy lamp-lit dusk of Leighton Buzzard High Street, there was no snow. The snow was long gone. People were looking forward to Spring. I wasn't.

Grabbing my tote bags, I stood up as we reached the stop. Then I blinked. Scott wasn't there. There was no tall, slender figure in a black coat, with long black hair flopping into his eyes as he looked up for the bus. He wasn't there!

Instead there was a shorter, stockier figure in a suede jacket standing at the stop.

Rich.

I didn't move as the bus juddered to a halt. It could only mean one thing. Renza had arrived unexpectedly at Leighton Buzzard and Rich had been sent to tell me and to pack me back off to Harbury Green immediately.

I felt very, very sick.

'You getting off or stopping on, love?' The conductor beamed at me. 'Only, make your mind up, see, we've got a way to go yet and we'd like to get home sometime this year.'

'What? Oh, yes, sorry...'

I stepped slowly from the bus, my heart somewhere in my boots, and looked at Rich.

'I know what you're going to say.'

'Do you?' He frowned at me. 'Are you psychic or something?'

'Obviously.'

He grinned. 'Okay then, you tell me what I'm going to say?'

I told him. He laughed.

'Wrong! It's far worse than that.'

'What? Hell's teeth, Rich – what's happened?'

'Scott's not very well.' Rich picked up one of my bags. 'In fact he's pretty ill. Came on worse overnight... he's got a heck of a fever, and...'

Oh my God! Scott was going to die! And it was all my fault for being a man-stealing, cradle-snatching, groupie tart! God had declared retribution!

I grabbed Rich's arm. 'Where is he? In hospital? What's wrong with him? Come on!'

'He's at home,' Rich panted trying to keep up with me as we rounded the corner and started to climb the hilly road towards the house. 'He's not dying or anything... he just wasn't well enough to come and meet you. Although he wanted to – and he did try, but -'

I tore up the gravelled drive and waited impatiently for Rich to unlock the front door. Then I flew towards the stairs.

'He's in the sitting room,' Rich chuckled. 'He'd die of hypothermia in that bedroom.'

It was true – despite the rise in the outside temperature, the house still felt like an ice-box.

I pushed open the sitting room door.

Scott was sitting on the sofa. The rest of Narnia's Children were dotted around, eating curry, listening to *Pet Sounds*, looking relatively unconcerned.

'Hi,' Scott smiled at me, melting my heart. 'Thanks for coming. I've missed you.'

'Oh, you have no idea how much I've missed you,' I sat beside him. He looked very pale. 'Rich told me you weren't well. What's wrong? How are you?'

He shrugged. 'Ok, I think. I just keep going hot and cold... and falling asleep and my arm hurts.'

It didn't sound ok to me.

'You've hurt your arm?'

'It was just a scratch and it's gone a bit funny.'

I took his hand. It was cold and clammy. 'Let me see... bloody hell! That's not right!'

There was a line of vivid red snaking along the vein from Scott's wrist right up his arm.

'That's what I said,' Mo nodded. 'It shouldn't look like that.'

'I think you've got blood poisoning.' I gulped. 'That's gone septic. You need to see a doctor.'

'We haven't got a doctor,' Zak said. 'Well, at home in Jersey, but not here.'

I looked at Scott again. His face was grey and his eyes were closing. 'Then he should be seen at Casualty. Is it far to Leighton Buzzard hospital? Oh, God – is there petrol in the van?'

'Yes to petrol,' Rich said. 'No to a hospital – well, not one that would be able to help tonight.'

'The nearest big one is in Luton,' Joss said. 'They've got a Casualty Department.'

Mo looked at Scott, then at me. 'I think you're right, Stella. I think he needs to see a doctor and sooner rather than later. He wasn't this bad earlier. Let's go.'

Scott shook his head. 'I'll be ok. I'll put some more Germolene on it. It'll be better in the morning.'

'The way you look now,' Rich said worriedly, 'you'll probably be dead in the morning. Come on – I'll go and get the van started.'

We all piled into the van. My heart was thudding with panic but I kept smiling cheerfully. I didn't want Scott to know how scared I was. He sat beside me, his head on my shoulder and went to sleep.

***

Luton Hospital's Casualty Department was dimly lit and fairly quiet, and had that universal hospital smell: heat, fear, disinfectant and over-boiled cabbage. Once Rich and Mo had explained about Scott to the receptionist and Zak and Joss had eyed up all the nurses, Scott and I sat on the grey metal chairs in the waiting area and watched people in various stages of pain and distress disappear into the corridors and cubicles. I held his good hand. He smiled sleepily at me. We didn't speak. We didn't need to.

The rest of Narnia's Children sat down too. It caused a bit of a stir among the younger nurses who kept popping out from the corridors and cubicles, taking sneaky peeks, nudging one another, and then sashaying away again. I grinned to myself. Even Rich was dead good looking, so I guessed an entire line of gorgeous blokes would liven up anyone's night-shift.

After about ten minutes a very pretty nurse, with huge green eyes and tendrils of auburn hair escaping from under her cap, called Scott's name.

'Lucky sod!' Zak said. 'She's one cute chick.'

I glared at him.

Scott, looking petrified and very ill, staggered to his feet.

'Good luck,' I whispered as he followed the red-haired sex bomb out of sight.

Don't let him die, I whispered inside my head, *please, please don't let him die.*

'We've done the right thing,' Mo said comfortingly. 'He needed to get that seen to. If it had got worse we'd have had to cancel our gigs.'

'Yeah,' Zak nodded. 'Could have turned to gangrene and been amputated.'

'And,' Joss added, 'a one-armed guitarist is pretty useless really. Mind you, one-armed drummers are ok – perhaps he could play drums... Mo could learn bass and I'd play guitar, and – '

'Shut up!' I hissed. 'Just shut up!'

I closed my eyes and prayed silently. *'Dear God, I know this is all my fault, everything I've done has been wrong, I've behaved really badly, I know that — but if this is my punishment then it's not fair. Not for him. So if you could just let him be ok I promise I'll never see him again and he and Renza can live happily ever after. Just let him be ok. Thank you, God. Amen.'*

Joss peered at me. 'You alright, Stella?'

'Fine,' I muttered. 'Just fine.'

There was a bit of a stir then from the cubicles and two of the young nurses appeared and shimmied across.

'We were just wondering,' the blonde one said, 'if you were a pop group... only, we went to see Doc Holliday in Dunstable and...'

'We reckon you were the support act,' the darker one giggled. 'Dead sexy you were — and tons better than Doc Holliday and he was ace.'

'We tried to see you afterwards but the bouncers wouldn't let us get near you.'

Joss and Zak immediately perked up.

'That was us,' Joss beamed. 'And I'm gutted that you couldn't meet us after the gig. We could have given you — um — autographs.'

'We can still do autographs,' Zak grinned, 'in exchange for phone numbers.'

The nurses giggled and there was scribbling and exchanges of bits of paper before they undulated back into the cubicles. I shook my head.

The time dragged.

'Here he is,' Rich said suddenly, as Scott, accompanied by the auburn haired nurse and an equally young and weary-looking doctor, re-appeared, his arm in a sling.

'I'll leave you to sort out the paperwork,' the doctor said, glancing at us all and not focusing on anyone in particular. 'We've done a basic clean-up and administered antibiotics and pain-killers, however, we need to do a minor operation to drain

333

the poison and clean the wound, which will then require stitches – but we can't do it tonight, obviously. We have a day surgery slot tomorrow morning and we've booked him in at 8.30. So, take him home, nil by mouth from now on, and be back here by 8 sharp.'

An operation! I swallowed. Scott simply looked too ill to care.

'Only one problem,' the nurse said cheerfully. 'As the patient is under age and the procedure will require a light general anaesthetic, we need next of kin to sign the surgical consent forms.'

'Oh, no. Really?' Mo sighed. 'That's impossible. His mother is in Jersey... and his dad's somewhere on the south coast... and...'

'But his wife's here,' Zak said quickly. 'Isn't she?'

I jolted in my seat. Was she? His *wife*? Renza? Was Scott secretly *married*? Had someone phoned her and got her to fly over from Germany?

'Ah, yes,' Joss nodded, nudging me. 'You're here, aren't you, wifey?'

'*What*?'

Zak nodded, beaming at the nurse. 'He's married to Stella, here. I think she's a bit upset about all this, and didn't quite understand. But she's his next of kin, being his wife, isn't she?'

The nurse and the doctor looked slightly askance at me – taking in the very short black dress, the fishnet tights, the fur coat, the long pink boots, the pantomime cow eyelashes and the sequins. And the absence of a wedding ring.

I glared at Zak. He glared back.

Rich nudged me. 'He needs the operation. Just do it.'

'Er – um – yes... of course...' I muttered at the doctor. 'I'm – um – married to Scott – er – where do I sign?'

I then looked quickly at Scott who was clinging on to the nearest table, clearly in pain, but trying valiantly not to laugh.

My hand shook as I signed the surgical consent forms, only

just remembering at the last minute to put Scott's surname after Stella instead of Deacon. I looked at it for a moment. It looked pretty good to me.

'Right, we'll see you in the morning,' the doctor said as the nurse whisked the forms away. 'Don't be late.'

We all crowded out of Casualty then. I slid my arm round Scott's skinny waist and he leaned heavily on me.

'As every bit of that was illegal, you'd better hope,' Rich chuckled at me as he unlocked the van, 'that he doesn't die on the operating table tomorrow. God knows what we'd tell Stephan.'

'Sod Stephan,' Mo frowned. 'How the hell would we ever explain it to Renza?'

Stella's Diary
March 18th 1969

It was a beautiful, warm sunny Spring morning in Luton. Scott, flanked by two nurses, emerged from his day surgery at around 11.30. Given my still-held belief that people died under anaesthetic, I had never been so pleased to see anyone in my life. He looked totally spaced out, but the sling had gone and instead there was a dressing and a small bandage on his injured arm. Again, Narnia's Children had turned out en masse to escort him back to the hospital and again had caused something of a stir in the waiting area.

We hadn't gone to bed the night before when we went home. As none of us possessed an alarm clock it seemed safer to stay awake in case we missed the – for the band at least – ridiculously early start. We'd spent the night in the lamp-lit sitting room, listening to Luxembourg and drinking coffee and talking about everything under the sun all night to keep awake. Scott didn't even try. He'd simply slumped against me on the sofa and slept his drug-induced sleep.

I'd shifted his head on to my shoulder and thought about my signature on that consent form. For a few short glorious moments I was his wife... well, almost... and as long as he survived the operation, I'd never regret it, and no one except me and Narnia's Children would ever know. Would they?

At some point in the early hours, when the conversation was flagging and the house was growing colder, the Luxembourg DJ played Glen Campbell's latest record, 'Wichita Lineman'...

Wow.

I was transfixed by the words. The hairs on the back of my neck stood up. I shivered. I had goose-bumps. I wiped away unbidden tears. Glen Campbell's lonely lovesick lineman was sharing my deepest heartfelt thoughts and emotions.

He needed his woman more than wanting her, and he'd

want her for all time...

What fabulous, evocative, heart-rending, oh-so-true words. And ones I'd never, ever forget – or where I'd first heard them.

I'd looked at Scott, sleeping, and prayed he'd never know exactly how I felt about him.

***

We left Luton hospital in buoyant mood. Scott, still floating from the anaesthetic, and I sat in the front of the van beside Rich.

'Wish I had some of what he's had,' Zak said enviously. 'He's so far out of it.'

'Lucky bugger,' Joss grinned. 'I'm knackered and starving.'

We drove away from the hospital and I was just so relieved that Scott had survived that I didn't worry too much about the deal I'd done with God. Nor that in a couple of weeks this would all be over and I'd be back at work. I'd think about all that later.

'Is there a Trustees Savings Bank anywhere round here, do you know?' I leaned across to Rich.

'Not a clue,' Rich shrugged, 'but I'll trawl round and we can look. Why?'

'Because I've got my bank book, I'm still getting paid from work, and if you can find a café, I think we should go and get something to eat to celebrate.'

They all perked up then and we found the bank quite quickly and then decamped to a small backstreet café where Rich – who seemed to always know exactly where to get food – said they did great fry-ups, for a late breakfast.

Scott was still far too drowsy to move, so I stayed in the van with him, and Mo brought us out bacon sandwiches and big mugs of tea. Scott couldn't eat much but he drank both mugs of tea thirstily. We had our picnic with the sun streaming through the windscreen, watching billowing white clouds chase across the blue sky. It was glorious. Almost like summer.

I wasn't looking forward to summer one little bit.

Scott smiled his lovely sexy sleepy smile. His voice was still a bit slurred but his eyes had lost most of the glazed look. 'Stella... thank you.'

'For lying? For forging information on an official document? For risking your life?'

'Well, now you come to mention it...'

'I was more scared than I've ever been in my life. If you'd died...'

'But I didn't. I was pretty scared myself. And anyway, we'll be able to compare scars now.'

I giggled. 'How many stiches did you have?'

'Three or four, I think.'

'No contest then! I'll win hands down.'

He laughed. Then closed his eyes. 'God, I'm so tired.'

I took a deep breath. 'Before you go to sleep... At my last outpatients appointment, they told me I'm fully recovered now and I've got to go back to work at the beginning of April.'

He opened his eyes and looked at me, smiling. 'That's great.'

'No it isn't!'

'Isn't it?'

'No.'

'But it's really cool that you're better. And,' he looked at me with those gorgeous drowsy turquoise eyes, 'we won't be here after the end of March either. We've got a month in Germany – clubs in Frankfurt and Kaiserslautern – and then, well.... who knows?'

I turned my head away, my heart sinking. A month in Germany... with Renza. Of course...

Scott stretched his legs out. 'We'll work something out. Promise. Don't look so sad.'

But I wasn't just sad. I was desolate. Devastated. I knew it would have to come to an end sometime – but I wasn't ready for it. Not yet. Not ever.

Stella's Diary
March 21st 1969 – afternoon

Scott's arm was better, the wound was covered with a plaster, and he could play the guitar again! Which was just as well as they had a big London gig tonight.

We hadn't mentioned the end-of-March parting of the ways thing again. I knew there was no point. He'd be in Germany with Renza, as he should be, it was going to be over for us, and there was no way on earth I was going to spoil the last days we had together.

Earlier, Scott and I had been in the front room – amongst all the speakers and cases and instruments – and listened to Simon and Garfunkel's *Bookends* LP. I stood looking out of the window, and when 'America' came on, he stood behind me and slid his arms round my waist.

'This track always reminds me of us,' he whispered into my hair. 'You know, when we were on the bus, making up mad stories about the other passengers... I'll always think of you when I hear it.'

I leaned back against him, knowing I'd always remember it too, long, long after we were no longer together, and tried not to cry.

'It's a great story song,' I said, hoping my voice wasn't wobbling. 'It really paints a picture. And America always looks so glamourous and exciting in the films. I'd love to go there – but as I've never been out of England yet, I doubt if that'll ever happen.'

Scott kissed my neck. 'I'd love to go there too. One day. It's a big dream of mine. But who knows what will happen in the future? Where we'll go? What we'll do?'

I took a deep breath. 'Mmm – who knows...'

Now Narnia's Children were practising in the front room so I decided to walk into Leighton Buzzard and buy some food to help stock Mo's larder. I left a note for Scott to tell him where

I'd gone, pulled on my ancient faded Levis that I'd lived in during A level year and had worn to second-skin-softness, and a lemon angora sweater and the white boots. Out for the first time this year without a coat – I laughed to myself – I was sounding like my nan!

The afternoon weather was still lovely – perfect spring – warm and gentle – and as I walked down the hill away from the house I could hear the group belting out their rendition of The Hollies's latest 'Sorry Suzanne' . It sounded amazing – exactly like the real thing... I could hear Zak and Scott singing the chorus together and their harmonies were pitch-perfect. I smiled to myself, proud to be part of it – they were so very talented. And soon they'd have a record out and everything.

And it would be over...

'Stella!' Rich caught me up as I reached the end of the road. 'Don't go too far! We're leaving in about an hour as soon as they've got a few numbers sorted and I can get the stuff in the van.'

'Leave the front door key and I'll let myself in, then.'

'You're coming with us.'

'What? But I never go to the London gigs.'

'Scott wants you to come to this one. It's our first booking there – and could lead to more. It's at the Café des Artistes in the Fulham Road – where all the beautiful people, not to mention producers and agents, hang-out – and Stephan has booked us as support to The Equals tonight.'

Wowee! Big time! I loved The Equals! I wondered if I could manage to interview them.

'So get a move on – Scott wants you to be there. He says you'll enjoy it.'

Wow! I looked at him, wide-eyed. 'Really? Fab – but what about the rest of you? Don't you get fed up with me always being around? Always tagging along?'

Rich shook his head. 'We're kind of used to you being around now. You're like part of the gang. No – I know it's not right, and we all love Renza, and this is a bloody mess – but, hell – we kinda like you.'

I hugged him. 'Thank you. Rich – why haven't you got a girlfriend? You're so lovely.'

'Oh, I've got a steady girl back home. Like Mo. Only mine's in London, not Jersey. Julie. She's a nurse. One day we'll settle down – but this is no life for her.'

I hugged him again. I was glad for him. Zak and Joss made the most of the groupies, Mo and Rich had steady girlfriends, and Scott...

I decided not to think about that.

Rich wriggled free. 'How long will it take you to get ready?'

'Ages,' I grinned happily. Wow! A posh London nightclub gig! With The Equals! 'Mo's larder will have to stay empty. Race you back to the house.'

Stella's Diary
March 21st 1969 – evening

I was entranced by night-time London: all the lights dancing in the darkness, and the buzz of the traffic, and shops and restaurants open for business, and crowds of people walking about as if it was the middle of the day. It was a million light-years away from Harbury Green. Rich manoeuvred the transit van along the busy Fulham Road and I almost jigged up and down with excitement. As usual, I was sitting on Scott's lap, with his guitar case under my feet, and as usual the radio was blaring and everyone was singing along.

'Here we are,' Rich said, pulling up outside some railings. 'I'll just go down and tell them we're here... it looks like we'll be humping the gear down a lot of steps – trust Stephan not to mention it was a bloody basement club... you lot had better start unloading the van.'

He disappeared down some winding, dimly-lit stone steps. Mo opened the van's back doors, and cursing, Zak and Joss climbed over us and started dragging out the equipment. I slid off Scott's lap, and he pulled his guitar case out from under my feet. I grinned at him. He was wearing my fun fur coat over his skin-tight black flares and a black skinny jumper that hardly covered his rib cage. He'd also borrowed my pale blue boots and my black floppy hippy Hendrix hat. With his shoulder length black hair he looked every inch the rock god.

'You look very cool, and very sexy,' I smiled. 'The girls are going to love you tonight.'

'They always do,' Zak laughed, appearing at the side of the van and hefting various bits of microphone stand and part of an amplifier. 'But not as much as they love me. Haven't you noticed? Right – Rich is waving to us so I guess they're ready... Shift yourself, Scott. Give us a hand here. And no excuses about having stitches in your arm. Stella, you can grab his guitar and Joss's. We'll be back in a bit.'

I watched them go, organised as ever by Mo and Rich, disappearing down the steps to set up the gear on stage.

Tonight, because it was a London club and obviously pretty special, I'd made a real effort with everything, especially my clothes. I always used the same Style pattern for my home-made dresses: top-of-the-thigh-high, low-cut, straight down, with a band of contrasting satin or ribbon under the bustline. The only variations were the sleeves. Some I made tight-fitting, some ballooned into long cuffs, some were leg-o-mutton, and others, like tonight's, were long, wide and flowing – using more material than the frock.

My dress tonight was white, the band under the bust was pink rosebuds on a paler-pink velvet ribbon and the sleeves were lined with the same pattern. I'd added the pink boots, my eye-sequins were pearly pink above two pairs of false eyelashes, and as well as a swooshing scented cocktail of Sunsilk, Body Mist and Picot's Le Train Bleu, I'd sprinkled some pink glitter powder in my hair.

Scott had been very complimentary.

Narnia's Children reappeared en-masse to take the next lot of equipment.

'It's really cool in there,' Scott grinned. 'Mind-blowing. Like a cavern with cloisters and little caves snaking off all over the place with stone tables and benches – and the DJ plays records from a sort of glass-fronted cave half way up the wall – and there's a bar and an eating area too.'

'Wow... and the stage?'

'Is at the far end. The club must hold hundreds and hundreds of people – but they'll all be able to see us. It's going to be ace. You ok out here?'

'Fine, thanks. I can't wait to see it all though.'

'Patience!' Mo laughed from behind a stack of cymbals. 'We're nearly done. Probably one more trip then we can lock the van. Grab the guitar cases from Stella, Scott...'

I was still sitting in the van and handed him the first case.

The radio was still playing: Diana Ross and The Supremes and The Temptations "I'm Gonna Make You Love Me".

I sang along with Diana, agreeing that I'd try every trick in the book and try to make him love me...

'You don't have to try.' Scott stared at me.

I stared back.

'There's no need,' he smiled gently at me. 'I love you.'

I think my mouth was open. My heart thundered in my ears. Eventually I managed to speak.

'You can't... you love Renza...'

'Yes. And you.'

'You can't love two people at the same time.'

'I can and I do.'

'But....'

'But nothing.' He leaned into the van and kissed me. 'This wasn't supposed to happen, was it?'

'No.'

'But it has. You do love me, don't you?'

'Yes.'

He smiled. 'That's all right then.'

It was far from all right – it was absolutely all wrong – but I honestly didn't care. It was the happiest moment of my life. I held his face between my hands and kissed him and said the words I'd wanted to say for months. 'I love you.'

'Oh, for God's sake!' Zak yelled, appearing at the top of the club steps. 'Put him down! Get those guitars, Scott, and let's do a sound check and then maybe eat something before we go on – although you two look like you've already started on each other.'

Laughing, we grabbed the guitar cases, locked the van and walked hand-in-hand down the steep stone stairs. I swear my feet didn't touch one of them. I was floating. I knew I was grinning like a loon. I wanted to laugh out loud and turn cartwheels. Scott loved me – and I wanted to tell the whole wide world.

Stella's Diary
March 21st 1969 – later

The Café des Artistes was unbelievable. It was exactly how Scott had described it – and more. But, to be honest, it could have been a tin shed in a deserted rain-soaked field and it would have still seemed the most magical place on earth – because he loved me!

I watched Narnia's Children set up their gear on the stage, alongside that of The Equals – who were nowhere to be seen, and I guessed they were being wined and dined somewhere as befitted the stars of the show. It was all very exciting.

'We're on at 11 for an hour,' Rich said. 'Then the Equals from midnight. Then us again at 1 – and then they play their last set at 2. Which means we're not going to be able to pack our stuff up until at least 3...'

'And it'll be daylight before we get home,' Joss sighed.

'Which means we can stay in bed all day tomorrow,' Scott said cheerfully, discarding my fun fur and floppy hat, and winking at me.

'All right for some,' Zak grizzled, but he was laughing as he said it.

As the little red candles flickered and danced in multi-faceted glass jars on the tables, the DJ in the glass-fronted suspended booth was warming up, playing all sorts of smoochy, classy pop music – Mason Williams, Herb Alpert, Paul Mauriat, Dean Martin... and then the crowds started to arrive.

There was a sudden tidal wave of every beautiful, fashionable person in London – or so it seemed to me. The girls – and the boys – all had long silky hair, gloriously coloured exotic clothes, amazing make-up (boys and girls!), and a mass of flowers and beads and jangling bangles. It was like seeing the fashion pages of *Rave* and *Honey* come to life.

I doubted that any of them had made their own clothes on their mum's ancient Singer sewing machine or had dyed their boots with Lady Esquire. But it didn't matter – I was happy with my clothes and the way I looked tonight, and more importantly, I was with Scott – and he loved me!

It was like a mantra going round and round in my head and I didn't think I'd ever stop smiling. It didn't matter that the stunningly gorgeous London girls – no Dolly Rockers here – were watching Narnia's Children with hungry eyes. It simply didn't matter. They could look all they liked – *he* loved *me*!

The girls all greeted each other with kisses and high-class squeals and swooshing waterfalls of hair. The air was filled with expensive perfumes – definitely not several squirts of Le Train Bleu and Body Mist – and even more high-class shrieks of laughter.

While Rich put the group through their sound checks, I wandered round the dark nooks and crannies of the nightclub, watching as the girls danced sinuously beneath the DJ, moving with grace and perfect rhythm, but careful not to disturb their make-up, hair or clothes. Several of the boys – long-haired and pretty but not a patch on any one of Narnia's Children – eyed me up as I passed. I smiled to myself. Not a chance, lads, I thought – not a chance...

I found the bar and the eating area. It was like a massive cave, with little stars studded in the roof and thick white candles in fat wine bottles flickering on the tables and the scents wafting from behind the counter made my stomach rumble. Of course, as usual, we hadn't eaten all day.

I looked at my watch, then at the blackboard behind the bar. There were two meals chalked up: beef goulash or chicken curry – both with rice. I reckoned Narnia's Children deserved a change from Mo's cobbled-together Vesta curry – so, even though I had no idea what goulash was, I ordered six portions plus five pints of beer and a Coke for me.

'For the band,' I shouted at the chap behind the bar. 'Narnia's Children! They'll be ready in about 15 minutes I guess.'

'Gotcha,' he grinned at me and handed me a bucket with cutlery and a numbered wooden spoon in it. ' Stick this on your table. You paying?'

I paid. And found a table in one of the darker corners. I was amused by the bucket and the spoon. They didn't do things like that back home.

Mind you, we didn't have restaurants like this back home, either. And we never ate out, no one I knew did, it was deemed a waste of good money. Well, maybe Mum and I would have lunch at the Cadena, or I'd share a hippy salad and frothy coffee with Vix in The Fantasia, on our shopping trips to Oxford, and sometimes we all went to the Chinese in Summertown if it was someone's birthday, and rather daringly one of the local Harbury Green pubs had recently started doing chicken in a basket but I'd never tried it.

This, tonight, was something else entirely.

I managed to weave my way back through the glamorous crowds. The DJ had upped his game to more poppy chart music – The Casuals, The Box Tops, Amen Corner – and the beautiful people still danced with the same elegant grace, the girls making sure that their long Dunhill cigarettes didn't ruin their carefully-applied pale pink pouts.

You'd think I'd just given the band the keys to Paradise when I told them there was food ready for them. Zak and Joss dropped what they were doing and jumped off the stage. Scott laughed and followed them. Rich and Mo both said thanks and then joined the charge.

Goulash, it turned out, was very much like my mum's beef stew, only a bit more spicy and with a dollop of sour cream on top – which I found a bit odd but didn't say – and served on a mountain of rice. The portions were enormous – which went down really well with Narnia's Children – and everyone scraped their bowls clean and Joss and Zak helped me to finish mine as well.

After that the evening passed in a blur of music and colours and noise. Narnia's Children's first set went down a storm. I sat to one side of the stage with Rich, and watched. They were so good, playing all the songs that had become part of my life, so talented. And so very, very sexy.

The beautiful girls clearly thought so too as they pressed round the foot of the stage and stared lustfully. Scott looked across at me – they were playing their Hollies medley: 'Just One Look', 'Stay', 'I'll Be True To You' – and gave me the slow, knowing smile. Dear God, I loved him so much... and he played the guitar like a dream and sang – sometimes alone – sometimes harmonising with Zak – brilliantly. He was a superstar. Oh – and he loved me!

Still staying with the Hollies, they roared into 'Here I Go Again'. Scott took lead vocals and sang it to me. Just to me. He stood at the mic, staring at me, smiling, and sang every word to me. Oh, those words!

I was on cloud nine – and I just laughed and blew him a kiss. The beautiful girls all glared at me so I smiled at them and blew them a kiss too.

At some point towards the end of the first set, in the midst of my delirium, I was aware that Stephan had arrived. He nodded at me and sat next to Rich. They had a brief shouted conversation then Stephan disappeared off into the crowd.

'Talking to A&R men...' Rich yelled in my ear. 'Always wheeling and dealing...'

The Equals burst on to the stage at midnight. They opened with their big hit of the previous year – 'Baby, Come Back' – and Eddy Grant was absolutely fantastic. Again I sat at the side of the stage, this time with all of Narnia's Children, and with Scott's arms round me. The Equals were amazing – but I still thought Narnia's Children were better.

The Equals closed their first set with the stonking 'Michael and the Slipper Tree' and I was practically bouncing up and down.

Scott kissed me as Rich and the group stood up ready to

take the stage again. 'Stay there, Twinkle, so that I can see you and letch.' He laughed. 'I love you.'

'I love you, too.'

Almost straight away, Stephan plonked down beside me. 'That was a good catch-up just now – very lucrative – a nice bit of schmoozing with some guys I've been trying to tie-down for a while. All went well. Should reap dividends for the boys. They're going great tonight and it's been noticed. It is really nice to see you again, Stella. And thanks for all the Fan Club and PR stuff. Damn good work, love. Shame you won't be around for much longer, you've done the band proud. They're gonna miss you.'

Stunned, I blinked at him wordlessly. On stage, the boys were taking their places. Zak was doing the "one-two one-two" thing into the microphone.

Stephan shrugged. 'Well, they're off to Germany for several weeks and then I've got them signed up for a summer season in Jersey – it'll be Autumn at the earliest before they're back over here, and...'

Of course I knew about Narnia's Children going to Germany, which was bad enough, but *Jersey*? For the *whole* summer? Why hadn't Scott told me? Why?

My glorious golden bubble burst with a sad plop.

And wherever they were, I wouldn't be with them. And Scott would be with Renza and I'd never see him again.

I knew exactly what Stephan was saying.

And I wanted to cry because I knew it was true.

Stella's Diary
April 1st 1969

Lunchtime. My first day back at work. It was to be a short re-introduction to the world of Subsistence Claims as it was Easter Week and we finished for the holiday break at lunchtime on Maundy Thursday.

So far every hour had seemed like a lifetime.

Everyone in the office had been really kind to me: Debbie and Sally – the clerical assistants and my friends – because of course they knew all about Scott; Mrs Everton our Executive Officer because she was very motherly anyway but also because she'd probably been briefed by Personnel to be nice to me after such a serious illness and long absence; even Nicholas, my fellow CO, who wore cardigans and sucked bullseyes and never talked much and still lived with his mum even though he was very ancient.

I hated it.

I hated being away from Scott and the band and the crazy life that had become my reality for the last few months. I hated the pointlessness of shuffling piles of paper. I hated the feeling of being trapped here for ever. I hated the fact that I had to dress reasonably sensibly again. I hated the fact that I'd never see Leighton Buzzard or the house again. I hated that right now Scott was in Kaiserslautern with Renza. Oh, God – how I hated that.

But most of all I hated the fact that it was over. Really all over.

It felt like a bereavement. An aching, tearing loss that would never, ever go away.

Oh, yes, it was lovely to be back home with Mum and Dad and the dogs and cats again – it was lovely to have my mum's home-cooking and to see my grandparents again, and catch up with Vix and my other friends... but, because this was all there was ever going to be from now on, it made me want to cry. This time there'd be no dashing back to Leighton Buzzard; this time there'd be no happy reunion with Scott – this time I was home, on my own, for ever.

My parents had been great about it. I'd written to them regularly while I was away so they knew most of it anyway. Neither of them had asked too many questions. Dad had hugged me a lot and said I needed feeding up. Mum had wisely said nothing about my tear-stained face each morning or made any remarks along the lines of "plenty more fish in the sea". They'd both welcomed me home quietly and warmly and with love – and I knew I was lucky to have them.

But none of this helped to heal my broken heart.

So, at lunchtime on my first day back, I was sitting on the grass outside the office in the sunshine – the glorious spring weather had continued – with Debbie and Sally, eating lemon mousse from the shop. It was one of the plusses of working for the Atomic Energy Research Establishment – it was like a large village with beautifully landscaped grounds and gardens, shops and social clubs, each of the buildings situated on wide roads lined with trees.

'… but why don't you just ask him to finish with this Renza?' Debbie frowned, hoiking her skirt up to get the sun on her legs. 'If you love him that much why don't you fight for him?'

'There's no contest,' I sighed. 'Their relationship is different. Special. He loves Renza. He's *in love* with Renza. He's going to marry Renza. I was always just a stop-gap. If I asked him to choose then I know he wouldn't choose me – which is why I never asked. And never will.'

Sally looked shocked. 'But that makes you sound so cheap. And feeble.'

'Thanks,' I laughed.

'No, but you know what I mean, Stella.'

I tried to keep the wobble out of my voice. 'Yes. But

that's how it is. How I knew it would be.'

'So, when you left Leighton Buzzard, how did he end it?'

'He didn't.' I pushed the unfinished mousse away. I had no appetite. 'He just said it'd be ok and he'd write to me.'

'And has he?'

'No.'

Sally and Debbie looked at one another and pulled faces.

'He probably can't,' I said, 'even if he wants to. Because he's in Germany. With Renza.'

'Does she know about you?' Sally frowned. 'Like you know about her?'

'I don't know. I've never asked. We don't talk about Renza. Probably... oh, I don't know! All I know is that he's in Germany with her now and not with me and it's over.'

'So you'll never see him again?' Debbie rolled over on to her stomach. 'He's gone – out of your life – just like that.'

'Exactly like that.'

'But you love him?'

'More than life.'

'Blimey...' Sally shook her head. 'It's bloomin' tragic.'

Bloomin' tragic – yes, that's exactly what it was. And I wasn't at all sure I'd be able to cope with it. Not now – not for the rest of my life without him.

Debbie frowned. 'And he loved you?'

'So he said.'

'And yet he still loved – loves – this Renza?' Sally squinted against the sun.

'Yes, he said that too.'

'Well, that's just plain wrong,' Debbie asserted. 'He's got it made, hasn't he? You're both in love with him and he's making the most of it by being with the one who's handiest at the time. Bet he doesn't really love either of you. He's just messing you both about. I know he's gorgeous and all that, but I'd forget all about him if I were you. Plenty more fish in the sea.'

I winced. Ok, maybe there were, I thought, staring up at the cornflower blue sky. Maybe somewhere out there was a boy who might just take Scott's place in my heart... maybe one day I'd meet someone else who would love me and make me fall madly, giddily, insanely head-over-heels in love with them too...

But I doubted it.

I scrambled to my feet. 'Come on. Lunchtime's over. Let's get back to the joyous world of subsistence claims.'

Stella's Diary

April 3rd 1969 – Maundy Thursday

How life can change in just a few short days!

Coming home from work at mid-day – it was still scorchingly hot, more like July than April – I plodded slowly from the bus towards our house, carrying a massive box of Swiss chocolates – the traditional Easter gift to everyone in the office from our Higher Executive Officer, Mr Williams – wondering how on earth I was going to get through the next few days of not only missing Scott to the point of insanity, but also the enforced holiday.

At least at work there was the mundane routine and office chat to while away the hours. Now there'd be nothing but being alone to torment myself about Scott all over Easter.

Good Friday was always pretty awful anyway: apart from the early morning queue at the baker's to buy the hot-cross-buns, and then a further queue in the middle of the day for fish from the chip shop, no one ventured out, and everything, everywhere, was closed. It was a long dreary day of quiet reflection.

Easter Saturday was a bit more normal and the only day of the four when the shops opened, and Vix and I and the rest of the gang always went into Oxford; then on Easter Sunday Mum and I went to church and then Dad joined us for dinner and tea at my nan's; and Easter Monday was the village fete which anyone with any sense avoided like the plague.

Oh, joy...

Mum was sitting in the back garden in an ancient deck chair under the apple trees, surrounded by the dogs and cats all sprawled out in the dappled shade, and she jumped to her feet when I walked miserably down the path.

'Thank goodness you're home, I've got some ginger beer on the go,' she said, smiling broadly. 'I thought we could have it out here as it's so hot and... ooh, chocolates!'

'Have them.' I handed her the ornate box. 'They're probably already melting and I don't feel much like chocolates at the moment.'

'Oooh, thanks, and I'll save you some, promise,' Mum smiled kindly. 'You might feel differently later... shall I get the ginger beer?'

'Please. That'd be lovely.' My mum's home-made ginger beer was legendary. She had a ginger beer plant continuously fermenting in the larder and single-handedly supplied the village. 'I'll just go and get changed.'

'OK,' Mum stopped smiling and looked a bit put out. 'But don't be long. I've got a surprise for you.'

Oh, please, I thought as I trudged upstairs to put on my faded Levis and a T-shirt, don't let her have cooked me something. Eating was the last thing I wanted to do.

By the time I got back to the garden, Mum had pulled out our rickety wicker-work table and another deck chair for me. The massive jug of cloudy ginger beer, jingling with ice-cubes, and two glasses stood on the table – and mercifully there was no food.

'Sit down,' she indicated the chair. 'Go on, Stell. Sit.'

I sat.

She poured out a glass of ginger beer and pushed it towards me, then she scrabbled in the pocket of her apron and handed me a postcard. A picture postcard. Of a very beautiful foreign-looking chalet covered in tumbling purple flowers. Addressed to me in oh-so-familiar spiky writing. With a German stamp. Postmarked Kaiserslautern.

'There you go, my love,' she beamed at me. 'Happy Easter.'

I knew she'd already read it – it was a postcard after all – and it didn't matter. Nothing mattered.

He said he really missed me. He said things were going ok but that the club they played in wasn't the best place they'd ever been, and he couldn't wait to leave and see me again. He asked me to write to him asap – and gave me the hotel address

– and that he had a suggestion for us meeting up in the summer. He ended with love and kisses.

I hugged the postcard, hugged Mum, couldn't wipe the smile from my face and ignoring the heat and the ginger beer, grabbed my purse and my shoulder bag and headed into the village.

***

I bought a pale pink airmail writing pad and envelopes from WH Smith. I didn't even wonder if Renza had watched him write the postcard. I didn't even care that she may wonder about the pale pink airmail letter that would arrive for him as soon as I could get it there. I didn't wonder about Renza at all. In fact, I realised as I got home, sitting in the garden under the apple trees with Radio One playing softly, and writing to Scott, that I honestly didn't care about sharing him. It was far, far better than never seeing him again. I could only hope that Renza felt the same.

As I'd done before, I was careful to make the letter funny and fairly non-committal. Something a good friend and fan club secretary would write to a member of the band. Just in case Renza read his mail. Yes, OK, I cared that much – I didn't want to hurt her. After the Mike and Bernice episode, I'd never do that to anyone else – especially not to someone as young and in love as Renza clearly was.

I drew little pictures in the margins and managed to stick some of the pretty and quirky wrappers from my Easter Swiss chocolates on as well, which proved a bit tricky on the flimsy paper. Then, still playing it very cool although I actually wanted to pour out my heart, I finished with a bit about being intrigued about meeting up for the summer, hoped the rest of the group were well, and couldn't wait to hear from him again. I too ended with – rather reckless under the circumstances – love and kisses.

I read it through quickly, then, because if he replied, the post – even by airmail – would take ages, I added my work

356

phone number and office extension just in case he was able – or wanted – to ring me. Then I sealed the envelope and dashed off back into the village to the post office before they closed for the interminably long Easter holiday.

'This for your young man in the rock'n'roll group?' Mrs Norris in the post office peered at me as she weighed the pink envelope and studied the address. 'In Germany now is he? You been writing him a love letter, have you? Your nan said you and him was living over the brush somewhere. Left you now, has he? Taken up with some foreign gel, I'll be bound. I know you've been ill young Stella, and always been spoiled rotten, but honest to God, what your parents are thinking of letting you go and live in sin with someone who plays a guitar I have no idea. You've got a bad name for yourself now, my lady, and you'll never shake that off – you mark my words.'

I just smiled sweetly and tried hard not to laugh. No one could ever keep a secret in Harbury Green, and Mrs Norris heard and saw everything, made it a million times worse than it really was, and couldn't wait to pass it on, richly deserving her nickname of Nosey Norris I always thought.

I paid the postage, watched as Mrs Norris thumped both the stamps and the blue "par avion" sticker on, and made sure she finally dropped the pink envelope into the sack behind her. My letter to Scott was on its way.

Then, still smiling, I practically skipped all the way home.

Renza's Diary
April 17th 1969

Scott has written! Halleluiah and pass the gravy!

They're in Kaisterslautern, staying at The Hotel Garni, which Scott says isn't too bad. He wants to see me but doesn't think he can spare time to come here, and there's no way I can get to him, even though he's offered to pay my fare and hotel bill. It's way too far – as if Mum and Dad would allow me to go! Besides, I'm not sure I'd get time off work and what a flipping nerve anyway, expecting me to be at his beck and call. I ached to go.

Scott says the record is now being released on 23rd April and on 1st May in Europe. I just wish it would come out; so much faffing about, it's beyond me.

Frankfurt is a bit of a dump apparently, and so is the club they're playing at, and they aren't keen on it. There are a lot of American GIs hanging out there and some of them are seriously screwed-up and start fights with everyone, getting drunk and abusive, he said the Germans hate them.

Scott said a couple of the soldiers have taken a shine to the band and hang around them all the time, some have been in Vietnam and are psychopaths, whatever that is. They told stories about taking Viet Cong up in helicopters to question them and when they did or didn't 'talk' they threw them out of the helicopters without any parachutes. He said they're sickening and so boastful about the atrocities they committed against the Vietnamese, even those supposedly on their side! Scott wouldn't tell me all of it, because it was like a scene from a horror film. So I'm not too bothered about going to Frankfurt or Kaiserslautern to visit him if there are people like that there.

When they go back to England they probably won't be going back to Leighton Buzzard because Stephan has to find them another place, so they'll be in Jersey for a while. He thinks they'll be headed back to Jersey for the summer, if everything works to plan. Bully for him! He's never mentioned me going to Jersey again, so I suppose it's never going to happen and I'm not going to mention it. I feel gutted and disappointed with him messing me around all the time. I just don't get it. I wish he'd stop making promises and asking me to go here, there, and goodness knows where, when he knows he doesn't mean it and I can't go anyway. .

They're going to be on TV next week, on a famous show called, *Beat Club*. Lots of famous bands, even The Beatles, have appeared on it. I'm excited for him, of course I am, but it's all so distant to me, I feel so uninvolved and for the life of me I can't understand why he's keeping me hanging on, just like that damn song 'You Keep me Hanging On,' by The Supremes, which has been on the radio a lot this week. Marjorie Proops would say he's covering his bets, having his cake and eating it. I saw her reply to a letter someone in a similar situation had written to her in her latest agony column. She's right of course. I don't understand why I'm still hanging on either, but I am.

Renza's Diary

May 3rd 1969 – 4:30pm

The post room was quiet, so thankfully my call to Scott was private. I didn't have much money so it had to be quick. He'd sent a card from Jersey, asking me to ring him today. I hoped nothing was wrong.

'Hi babe, how's it hanging?'

'OK thanks, how is it, er, hanging with you?' I've never quite worked out what that means, but the band always ask.

Scott burst out laughing. 'Yeah, good, everything's good. Sorry we never hooked up when we were over, it was mental. TV and Radio stuff going on and playing the club every night, well you know how it is.'

'Oh, that's all right, I never really expected to see you,' I lied. 'I'm glad it went well.'

'Yeah, it was cool, but if we could've got together it would've been better.'

'Why did you ask me to ring? Is anything wrong?' My body shook with worry at what he might say.

'No, nothing's wrong, except that you're there and I'm here. I just wanted to hear your voice again. I miss you so much it hurts.' He lowered his voice and it's tone sent shivers of delight through me.

'Thank goodness,' I said. 'I mean, that nothing's wrong.'

Scott went quiet so I quickly added, 'I really miss you too.'

'Cool,' he said and then went quiet again.

Conscious of the money running out I said, 'Is that all?' Stupid bitch! I kicked myself as soon as the words left my lips.

'Well, I guess so, sorry for bothering you.' Scott snapped back.

'No, no I didn't mean that, it's just I haven't any more money if the operator comes on.'

'I'm sorry I can't afford to ring you. Stephan hasn't paid us yet, and you know how things are...'

'I know, I didn't mean how it came out.'

'I'll write and let you know what's going on. Perhaps you could come over?'

'I'd like that but I don't know, what with work and Mum and Dad, and the cost of it all...'

'We'll sort something.' Scott shouted as the pips started to go. 'Love you.'

Stella's Diary
May 6th 1969

It had all been a bit of a whirlwind in the weeks since Easter.

Scott – back from Germany and now living at home in Jersey – had been phoning me at work! And I'd been phoning him back! It was amazing! We'd talked for ages and ages several times every day, and when Mrs Everton peered across the office and said 'Do you have a problem there, Stella? That phone call seems to be taking an awfully long time.' I'd just shrugged and sighed and said things like 'Oh, it's those ferry receipts for Ben Becula. They seem to have gone missing. I'm just chasing them up.' Or 'The hotel in Belgium has muddled the payments for last month, I'm just sorting it out.'

I was, sadly, becoming quite adept at not telling the truth.

In fact, I wasn't telling the truth to anyone. Even my parents.

Because I was going to Jersey.

To stay with Scott and his family – well, his mum and step-dad and small step-sister (Holly, as she was born at Christmas, he said) – for the summer.

Narnia's Children were already in their nightly residency on the island at the club called Lords and expected to be there until the end of July at least – and Scott had asked me to go and stay. This was his "suggestion for us meeting up in the summer" and it was way beyond my wildest dreams.

I'd even spoken to his mum – 'call me, Eva' – on the phone, and she'd said as long as I could pay my way and maybe cook – 'I loathe cooking, Stella' – she'd be really happy for me to come for a visit. Having assured her that I had money and loved cooking, she said she and Dan – who I guessed was the step-father – would welcome me, as a friend of Scott's, for as long as I wanted to stay.

Neither Eva nor I mentioned Renza, but I guessed that as I

was classed as a "friend" and not a "girlfriend", and she obviously knew that Scott and Renza were engaged, she therefore had been told by Scott that I was the fan club secretary and a good mate to everyone in Narnia's Children.

Actually I *had* asked Scott about Renza during one of our phone calls. I'd wondered, just casually, why she wasn't going to be spending the summer with him in Jersey. After all, I knew she was only 17, so I assumed she'd have long school holidays and I simply couldn't imagine why she wouldn't want to spend them with him.

'Renza is working now,' Scott had said. 'But even if she could get leave, her parents wouldn't allow it.'

'So you've asked her? Invited her?'

'Yes.'

I'd sighed. 'And because she said no, or won't be allowed to go, you're asking me? As second best?'

'No.' He'd laughed. 'You've never been that. I want you to come over. I want you to spend the summer with me. I miss you so much.'

'But you also love and miss Renza very much?'

He'd laughed again. 'Yes.'

'But because she's still ruled by her strict parents and I'm a bit of a free bird, if you can't have one of us, you'll have the other?'

'Something like that...'

Of course I probably should have told him to go to hell at that point and spent my summer sobbing broken-heartedly in my bedroom – but to be honest, I loved him, he said he loved me, and whatever else I was in Scott's life, if it meant we could be together, then none of the Renza stuff bothered me at all.

I'd told him he was a letch – and a lucky one at that – and that I'd buy him the Lovin' Spoonful LP so that he could carefully listen to the words of 'A Younger Girl' and 'Did You Ever Have To Make Up Your Mind?', and we'd both laughed because we both knew the score, then changed the subject, and Renza wasn't mentioned again in that or any further phone calls.

So far so good. But of course there was one other huge problem. Much, much huger than Renza.

Going to Jersey indefinitely would mean leaving work. Leaving work would involve handing in my notice and working for at least another month. And there was no way I was going to be able to do that. Waste a month when I could be in Jersey with Scott! Not a chance. And I couldn't take leave – even unpaid – because I'd already had so much time off sick.

So, I simply made my plans and didn't tell anyone what I was going to do.

I wrote an extra-long fan club letter and got Barry to print out the hundreds of copies needed – telling everyone that the boys were back from Germany, and were playing in Lords in Jersey for the summer, and that 'Livin' With You' had just been released and was getting masses of airplays on Radio One and Luxembourg (I hadn't actually heard it yet but I didn't say so!) so they must all rush out and buy it and request it on the radio shows, and that as soon as Narnia's Children were back on the mainland I'd write again and let everyone know the next exciting instalment in the group's life.

I added the usual snippets (some of them made-up!) about each of the boys, and promised to send a new group photograph after the summer season. Then I posted them all out (including copies to Renza and her brother and sister), using Stephan's supply of stamps and various post boxes in Harbury Green to avoid the inquisition from Mrs Norris, and reckoned that would keep everyone happy until I got back from Jersey.

Next, I went to the railway station and bought an open-ended return ticket on British Rail's morning ferry from Weymouth to Jersey. I'd catch the train from Harbury Green to Reading, change there for Basingstoke, then on to Weymouth. I'd arranged this with Scott during our phone calls and would be sailing on May 17th.

Not long to go…

Then I sorted out my wardrobe. As I had no idea how long I'd be staying, and as I assumed Jersey was practically tropical, I managed to get most of my tiny mini-dresses washed and ironed and folded away in my orange and pink tote bags.

I bought a very daring black bikini – my lovely surgeon had been right, even though the pants were tiny they *just* covered my still-massive and livid scar – and a floaty chiffon turquoise and lilac shirt to wear over the top. Shoes…? No shoes… but definitely three pairs of long boots – white, pale blue and pink; and my going-out sandals, flat, toe-post, made up of tiny silver rings.

All my underwear I squished up into the bottom of the largest bag; and my all new make-up (Mary Quant's Make-Up To Make Love In, because Scott hadn't yet seen me totally *au naturelle* and never would if I could help it) and Cosmedin cleanser and Oil of Olay face cream and my trusty Body Mist deodorant and every other cosmetic-aid I could possibly need went in the bottom of the other one; oh, and perfume – I bought Yardley's new Sea Jade specially. And the matching talc and bath foam and the body lotion too. Because it smelled gorgeous and because it was like a turquoise sea and looked fab. And because it would always, always remind me of Scott and Jersey.

All this I squirreled away and hid in the bottom of my wardrobe.

Then I withdrew everything from my Trustees Savings Bank – just over £100 – and hid that, along with my train and ferry tickets, in various bags and pockets too.

I was almost ready to go and counting the hours.

Stella's Diary
May 16th 1969

I left work today. I still hadn't said a word to anyone, and Sally, Debbie and I joined the massive crowds filing out through the main gates, all excitedly chattering about the hot weather and what they'd be doing on the weekend ahead.

Oh, if only they knew!

I really, really hoped I wouldn't get stopped by one of the security guards for a random search because I'd emptied my desk drawers and stuffed everything in my shoulder bag at the last minute. I'd got all sorts of handbooks and information packs which we were all given when we started work, and I'd slotted Scott's letters and photos into them and simply didn't have time to sort them out without anyone noticing. So they were all in my bag to be dealt with when I got home, and I knew there'd be very awkward questions if I was searched.

I held my breath as we neared the gates, but thankfully the guards just glanced at our passes, smiled as they waved us through and wished us a lovely weekend.

Phew.

It wasn't quite so "phew" when I got home though.

Mum and Dad were in the living room – and so were all my bags from the wardrobe! Mum looked as if she'd been crying and Dad just looked cross. In all my nearly twenty one years they'd never raised a hand to me and, only very rarely, their voices.

'When were you going to tell us?' Mum said, sniffing a bit. 'I mean, running away from home... why, Stella? Why?'

'I'm not!' I said quickly, hugging her. 'I'd never do that! But – oh...'

And then I told them. Well, almost all of it. I managed to fudge the truth again about work because I knew they'd be really cross about that – so I sort of hinted that I was merely taking unpaid leave.

Dad nodded. 'Well, that all sounds so much better than we'd feared, Stell. I just wished you'd told us sooner – we could have helped you sort things out – given you a lift down to Weymouth... you know we're not too sure about what you're doing with Scott – but you're a grown-up and he seems like a nice well-brought-up lad and he makes you happy, and it's a wonderful opportunity to go to Jersey.'

'And very kind of his mum and dad, too,' Mum had brightened up considerably. 'I must write and thank them. I do know how much you've missed him... you're a lucky girl, Stella – it's a holiday we could never afford to give you, and you don't have another hospital appointment for ages so I think it'll do you all the good in the world.'

Yes, I felt horribly guilty. I loved them so much. They were the best parents anyone could wish for.

'And we weren't snooping in your wardrobe,' Mum nodded towards the collection of tote bags. 'I was just putting some of your washing away... but actually, it's all worked out rather well.'

Dad chuckled. 'We'll have to give you one of your birthday presents a bit early. We'd managed to pay off the last bit to the tally man... here, Stell... what do you think?'

He stood up and took a big bag from behind the sofa. 'I know it's not your 21st til September, but I think you'll find this useful now.'

I scrabbled at the paper and could hardly see through my tears.

They'd bought me one of the brand new Samsonite suitcases!

Lightweight, with zipped compartments and lots of pockets and masses of space inside both the shells, it was in a gorgeous pale turquoise green colour. It was absolutely perfect!

I couldn't speak. I just hugged and kissed them.

'Thank you so much...' I eventually managed to gulp. 'It's the best present ever. And I know you can't afford it – and I'm so grateful. I will make it up to you – promise. And I know I should have told you sooner, but...'

Mum kissed me. 'We've always given you your freedom, Stella. And you've always used it wisely. And, if – no, let's be realistic, probably when – this relationship with Scott comes to an end, you know we'll be here to pick up the pieces.'

By then we were all in tears and Dad hurried out into the kitchen, followed by the dogs, to put the kettle on.

***

After we'd finished re-packing my things in the Samsonite case (I still needed one tote bag for "essentials I'd need on the voyage" – Mum's words even though none of us had actually ever been on a voyage and had no idea what to expect), and I'd given them Scott's address and phone number in Jersey – for emergencies only of course – I made two brief visits to both sets of grandparents to say goodbye. They were shocked and pleased and a bit anxious in equal measure but I promised to send them a postcard every week and both my grandpas pressed a five pound note into my hand as I was leaving.

I honestly didn't deserve my family!

When I got back home again, Vix was pacing up and down the living room.

'Yep – your mum and dad have filled me in. And just when did you intend to tell *me*?' She nodded angrily at the case and bag. 'Bloody hell, Stella! We've been best friends since infants school! We've shared everything! Were you really just going to bugger off and not say a word?'

'No, course not. I was going to come round to see you tonight and... Look, let's go up to my bedroom – we can talk there.'

We did. We sprawled on my bed as we always did, and I told her everything. Even about work – and about Scott having suggested to Renza about going to Jersey first – and well, everything.

'God, I wish I'd never persuaded you to go to St B's dance that night...' Vix shook her head. 'I wish you'd never met him.'

'I don't. I'm loving every minute of it.'

Vix glared at me. 'He's changed you.'

'No he hasn't.'

'He has. You used to be nice and gentle and kind and honest – and well, trustworthy. Now you've become totally selfish – no, listen to me. You'd never have dreamed of doing half the things you've done since you met him. Bunking off work, lying to your mum and dad, being devious, discharging yourself from hospital, behaving like a proper little madam.'

She was probably right. I knew I'd become bolder, more confident, happier – and yes, far more daring – since meeting Scott. Selfish, yes, that too, probably. There was no way I intended to justify it though. Not to Vix. Not to anyone.

'And I told you that after Mike and Bernice and if I didn't die having the operation then I'd go mad and have an adventure. Enjoy living. Life.' I sighed. 'I love him. Madly, insanely, desperately. I just want to be with him. Now. And I'll do whatever it takes.'

'And the future? When he's gone and you don't have a job and no one believes a word you say anymore?'

'Jesus – it's not going to be that bad! Anyway, I don't think about the future. No point in worrying about things that may never happen – I'll deal with them when I have to. Right now I'll just enjoy the present. And the present is pretty fab.'

'Oh, I give up. You're mad,' Vix grinned at me. 'I've told you that before. And whatever romantic hearts and flowers nonsense you've got in your head, we both know this is all going to end in tears – and I've said that before, too. But I'll give you one thing – I didn't expect it to last this long – and you're getting a holiday in Jersey – and yes, Scott is definitely a cheating, two-timing scum-bag – but also the sexiest bloke I've ever set eyes on – well, apart from Zak and my Jeff, of course –

and I'm maybe just the teeniest bit jealous.'

I laughed. 'I'll send you a postcard. But promise me one thing – you won't breathe a word about work to anyone. Especially not to Debbie and Sally – don't tell them where I am. Or Mum and Dad. They know where I'm going of course, but I don't want them to know that I've just walked out.'

'They'll find out soon enough, but, ok, my lips are sealed. At a price, of course.' Vix giggled. 'Oh, Stella – I'm going to miss you – and I really hope you know what you're doing.'

That made two of us.

Stella's Diary

May 17ᵗʰ 1969 – going to Jersey, part 1

The ship, The Sarnia (I loved that because it sounded like Narnia!), was absolutely enormous! I don't know what I was expecting – but it certainly wasn't the massive three-storey monster that filled the Weymouth dock as far as the eye could see.

Shuffling through the vast dimly-lit quay-side customs shed lined with long trestle tables prior to boarding, in line with hundreds of others, and having my tickets and papers and luggage – thank goodness for the lovely Samsonite case! – inspected, I felt a mixture of very excited and not a little scared. I'd never been on a boat other than the Isle of Wight ferry before, and I'd certainly never travelled away from home on my own. However, as I climbed the gangplank (trying not to think of how deep the water was under me or how much the whole thing wobbled) I knew that for Scott I would have flown to the moon without wings.

Mum and Dad and the dogs had taken me to Harbury Green railway station in the car, bought platform tickets and waved me off on my adventure. Mum had given me two paperback books and a pound note "for essentials", and Dad handed me a tinfoil packet of sandwiches: 'Pink salmon and salad, Stell. At least then when you're seasick it'll look pretty.'

The rail journey had been lovely: once we'd left Reading it was all pastures new, and I'd settled into my window seat drinking in the early morning scenery, and we'd arrived at Weymouth ahead of time. Now I was really on my way. I hadn't booked a seat on the ship or anything, so along with everyone else I just wandered up and down the staircases, trying to remember the deck numbers and where all the doors led, exploring. I was very grateful I'd worn my Levis and pale pink T-shirt for travelling – climbing those staircases in my short dresses would have probably given some of the more elderly passengers a heart-attack!

When The Sarnia's engines started, deep down beneath my feet, I nearly jumped out of my skin. Everything vibrated and roared. The deck appeared to be moving before the ship was. It was all very disorientating. At dead-on 11 o'clock, there was an ear-splitting blast of the ship's siren, a change in the engine noise, a further throbbing lurch of the floor, a big cheer all around me, and The Sarnia set sail for Jersey. I tried not to jump up and down with excitement. I was on my way to see Scott again! After so many long, lonely weeks! Before the day was over, I was actually going to be with him again!

It took me ages to get used to the noise and vibrations from the depths of the ship. And walking straight was a bit of a problem. And it was very, very hot. I started to feel queasy, so lugging my case and tote bag, I headed for the upper deck. It was very crowded with everyone sitting on their suitcases and I wriggled my way through to a gap on the left-hand side of the deck where I could lean back against something solid but have a good view of the sea. The sea! It stretched forever. There was nothing to see except the blue sky and this dark green rolling, churning ocean. The movement of the ship and the motion of the sea didn't help my slight feeling of nausea and I sat back on my case and took some deep breaths. I only had to endure 152 miles of sea, I told myself. I'd looked up the distances in the library: it was 220 miles from Harbury Green to Jersey and I'd already done 68 of those by the time I boarded the ship. And every rather giddying minute was a step closer to Scott.

I closed my eyes. Then, because everything was going round, I opened them very quickly.

'Excuse me,' a middle-aged sandy-haired man next to me, leaned over. 'Could you keep an eye on my children while I go and get some drinks, please?'

'Err,' I'd noticed the four rather unruly red-haired children running up and down the deck, screaming and laughing and getting in people's way. 'Um – yes, ok...'

I really hoped they wouldn't keep climbing on the rails. I wasn't going to dive in and save them if they fell over.

'Thank you,' the sandy man said. 'They're a bit over-excited. Oh, can I get you something to drink?'

'Lemonade would be lovely.' My mouth was really dry but I didn't think my stomach would be able to cope with anything more exotic. I started to scrabble in my bag for my purse.

'No, no – my treat – you deserve it for keeping an eye on that lot! I won't be long.'

He wasn't. Mercifully all his out-of-control brood were still alive.

He handed me a glass of lemonade and dished some out to his children, then sank down beside me again. 'Thank you. My wife left me. Ran off with the insurance man. Didn't take the kids. It's the devil's own job trying to keep them under control. I hoped the holiday in Jersey would be a good thing – I hadn't really reckoned on the voyage. Look, you're very pretty. Are you single?'

'What?' I spluttered into my lemonade.

'Single? You're not married or engaged or anything?'

'No.'

'Then if I paid you £500 would you marry me and look after my kids?'

I stared at him and laughed – because it had to be a joke. It wasn't. He was deadly serious.

'Oh, my God.' I struggled to my feet and handed him my half-drunk lemonade. 'No way on earth. Leave me alone.'

'I've got a good job. You'd never be short of money or anything. Just think about it.'

'No! You're weird. Sorry...'

I grabbed my luggage and staggered off as fast as I could on the rolling deck, round the other side of the ship, as far away from my would-be suitor and his kids as it was possible to get.

Settling down between two elderly couples, neither of whom looked as if they were in the white-slave-trade, I could almost see the funny side. Almost. I sighed and looked at my watch. How much longer of this rolling, churning, nothing-to-see-but-the-sea, was there going to be? How much longer before Scott and I were together again? I groaned. Hours. We were due to dock in Jersey at 7 p.m. It wasn't even 3.

I thought about the two books Mum had given me at the station: Daphne du Maurier's *Frenchman's Creek* and Edna O'Brien's *August Is a Wicked Month* — but I'd really wanted to hang on to them to read in Jersey and anyway, trying to read while the ship was rising and falling would probably make my queasiness a million times worse. I sighed and settled back and watched the sea.

'Land ahoy!'

I jumped and opened my eyes. I must have dozed off in the sunshine. Heck — I felt sick... one of the elderly couples beside me was pointing towards a just-visible rocky outcrop in the distance.

I blinked. 'Is that...? Are we here...?'

They nodded excitedly.

Wow! I scrambled to my feet, asked them if they'd mind keeping an eye on my luggage, and staggered down two flights of stairs to the Ladies. We were nearly there! I had to go to the loo and re-do my hair and my make-up.

I closed the cubicle door and wished I hadn't. With no windows and no air, the roaring and lurching and stifling heat was even worse than before. Never had a loo-visit and face-repair been done so quickly!

By the time I emerged, The Sarnia was slowing down, and people were on the move, heading up the stairs towards the deck for disembarking. I wriggled my way through, headed back upstairs and found my luggage.

'We're early,' I said happily to one of the elderly ladies. 'I thought we didn't get to Jersey until 7.'

'We don't,' she said. 'This is Guernsey. We're here for an hour.'

Stella's Diary
May 17th 1969 – going to Jersey, part 2

The Sarnia stayed docked in St Peter Port in Guernsey for *hours*! Well, maybe a little over an hour – but it was driving me insane with impatience. I leaned over the side and watched the people coming and going. Oh, hurry up! How long did it take to get on and off a boat for heaven's sake?!

Admittedly, what I could see of St Peter Port looked very pretty under the wall-to-wall blue sky and hot afternoon sun: all ancient granite buildings and narrow streets leading away from the quayside – but it wasn't Jersey!

Eventually we chugged off again, rocking and rolling, and almost immediately I could smell the heat from the ship's engines. I sank back on to my suitcase, watched the churning waves as we ploughed away from Guernsey, and wondered how anyone could ever find a cruise enjoyable.

But eventually, miraculously, Jersey was in sight!

I stood up, leaning over the rails, no longer feeling sick, just staring as Scott's island took shape. I could see rocks and flower-sprigged cliffs and little white sandy bays... and then, as The Sarnia slowed towards St Helier, the imposing sight of Fort Regent high up on its granite hill, towering into the sky. He'd told me that when I saw Fort Regent I was there. I practically jumped up and down with excited anticipation. I'd made it! I was in Jersey! Almost...

Of course, even once it had manoeuvred and docked, actually getting off The Sarnia took absolutely ages. It was past 8 o'clock when I wobbled unsteadily towards dry land. And also, of course, I knew Scott wasn't going to be there to meet me. Narnia's Children would be playing at Lords. Dan, Scott's step-father, was going to collect me.

'How will he recognise me?' I'd asked Scott on the phone.

He'd laughed. 'He's seen a photo.'

Oh... I knew Scott had some photos of me. I had no idea

he'd shown them to anyone. 'Oh, Lord... Which one...?'

'The one in the white dress.'

The white dress I'd worn to The Café des Artistes the night Scott told me he loved me! The photo had been quite revealing...

I'd gulped. 'Oh, help...'

'He said, thanks to that, he'd be able to recognise you easily,' Scott had laughed again. 'Just walk off the ship, follow the herd, he'll be parked somewhere on the left and will make himself known, trust me. See you soon, Twinkle.'

So, armed with my case and tote bag and shoulder bag and not a little intimidated, I staggered in amidst the mass of humanity, hoping that Dan would be there to meet me, for my first taste of Jersey.

It was exhilarating – the air was warm, the evening sky was clear, deep blue, and the sun still shone. I only wished I didn't feel quite so exhausted, wobbly, slightly sick, and rather hot and scruffy and travel-worn, peering hopefully for someone who looked as if they might recognise me. I felt Dan wasn't going to see me at my best.

'Stella! Stella! Over here!'

I'd shuffled, in line, almost to the end of the quay. I glanced up and saw this wiry, sun-tanned man in jeans and faded T-shirt, with a mass of fair-streaked hair, waving at me from behind the railings.

I stopped. 'Er – Dan? Are you Dan?'

He nodded. 'Get yourself over here. I've got the car.'

Getting myself "over there" was far more difficult than I'd anticipated due to the crowds of people and the fact that the ground was still dipping and swaying under my feet and I felt pretty groggy. However I eventually managed it.

Dan, laughing at my lack of co-ordination, skilfully managed to get me and my luggage into his car and we whirled away from St Helier's quayside in a small dust storm.

'You're wasting your time with Scott,' he grinned across at me as we waited for the harbour-side traffic to move at a junction. 'My opinion of course – but you do know he's engaged, don't you?'

Wow! That was some introduction! Don't beat about the bush, Dan, I thought.

'Yes. I do. I know all about Renza.'

'Really? Have you met her?'

'No.'

'No, neither have I. I think he's invited her out here but she couldn't make it and we got you instead.'

Wham, again!

I took a deep breath. 'He told me Renza couldn't be here, yes...'

'So are you a girlfriend or what? Scott said *friend* and I know you run the group's fan club, so what's the score?'

'Exactly that.'

Dan laughed. 'Yeah – maybe... anyway, he seems very keen to have you out here,' he looked across at me, 'and I can see why... just don't expect any sort of happy ever after with him.'

'I'm not,' I said shortly, thinking this wasn't exactly the sort of welcome I'd expected.

'Oh, don't look like that. I always say what I think. It's probably never what anyone wants to hear, but no point in gilding the lily, is there? Now – hang on – I need to get back to work. Time's money.'

I already knew that Dan ran various businesses, that he was highly skilled and qualified in some sort of engineering capacity, and now knew that I didn't actually like him very much.

I studied him as he drove like a demon. He was younger than I'd imagined, talked quickly with a biting sense of humour and had very shrewd intelligent eyes. I was more than slightly intimidated now, and carefully answered each of his probing questions in monosyllables.

'Hang on again,' he shot at me. 'I'm going to whizz across here.'

I hung as he whizzed, and the urban surroundings of St Helier disappeared as the car purred up a gorgeous long hill called Le Mont Felard.

I knew that the Jersey road names were all in French, and was enchanted by the tall granite walls, all dripping with brightly coloured flowers as we span upwards at some sort of breakneck speed.

Scott had told me how low the Jersey speed limits were compared to the mainland but this didn't seem to bother Dan. Maybe, I thought as we roared into a mass of glorious narrow, high-banked lanes, he couldn't wait to get rid of me. He must have thought I was pretty dumb anyway as I simply couldn't say more than a couple of words in reply to his non-stop questions.

Now the high-banked twisty lanes we tore along were hardly wide enough for bicycles, but the speed didn't drop. I assumed Dan knew these roads really well. I hoped so. I caught glimpses of stone cottages, and farmland and miles of glorious countryside through the towering trees that formed deep green arches above us. We slowed slightly at a place called Carrefour Selous – it had a small garage on one side and what looked like a shop on the other – but before I could actually take it in Dan had pressed his foot to the floor and we'd torn away again.

Then suddenly, we slowed properly as we rounded a bend. I saw the name of the lane, half-hidden by long grass and flowers – Les Chanolles des Six Rues – and thought how amazing the island was – exactly like being abroad – then minutes later Dan drove into a wide shingle drive, with stones spraying everywhere.

'This is it.' He looked at me. 'I'll get your stuff out of the boot. Eva's around somewhere – I've got to be somewhere else. Nice to meet you. Goodbye.'

As Dan and the car disappeared, I stood outside the large

detached centuries-old granite farmhouse, golden in the evening sun, surrounded by a large walled garden at the front and snaking lanes at the back, with nothing but fields and trees as far as the eye could see, and thought how very different it was from my own red-brick, semi-detached council house. And suddenly felt violently homesick.

What the hell was I doing here?

Stella's Diary
May 17th 1969 – going to Jersey, part 3

'Hi!'

Just as I was wondering if I could somehow find my way back to the harbour and catch the next ferry home, the door opened and someone – Eva? – waved and called cheerfully.

I squinted against the sun. 'Er – hello.'

'Stella? Has Dan dropped you off and gone already? Trust him... Hello – I'm Eva – and this...' she walked towards me and indicated the small blonde child beside her, 'is Holly. Did you have a good trip?'

'Er – yes... thank you...'

I just gawped at Eva. Young, tall, slender, and totally gorgeous, she had tousled tawny hair, high cheekbones and the same stunning turquoise eyes as Scott. She looked like Ursula Andress. Scott's parents were about as far removed from mine as it was possible to get!

Holly smiled prettily and showed me her toy tractor.

'She takes after Dan,' Eva said. 'Loves tractors, cars, lorries – not even slightly interested in dolls or teddy bears. Anyway, it's nice to meet you.'

'It's very kind of you to – er – invite me...'

'You're welcome. Scott uses this place like a hotel and so do his friends. As I said on the phone, as long as you're willing to pay your way and can cook, I'm fine with you staying as long as you want. Come along in...'

I grabbed the suitcase and tote bag and followed Eva and Holly into the house.

It was exactly as I'd guessed it would be: all flagged floors, with heavy doors leading to many and various rooms, high ceilings, a wide staircase ahead. Massive, ancient and imposing.

'Kitchen through here,' Eva pushed open a door. 'Sitting room... family room... dining room... sort of study-cum-officecum-junk-room... you'll soon find your way around I'm sure. Now – upstairs... Holly will show you your bedroom.'

In a bit of a daze I followed them both up the wide, curving wooden curving staircase.

'This is yours,' Eva indicated a door at the end of a corridor on the second floor as Holly scampered on ahead into the room.

The whole place was like a hotel! I was sure I'd get lost! And I knew I was very, very out of my depth there.

'There's a bathroom next door. We're on the floor above. So's Holly. Scott has a room downstairs so he can come and go as he pleases, entertain friends, eat, drink, sleep, play music, whatever, without disturbing the rest of us.'

I stepped into the bedroom. It was huge, and very lovely with a massive quilted bed and ancient oak furniture and double sash windows overlooking the front of the house and the fields beyond.

'Thank you...' I smiled at Eva. 'This is wonderful.'

'And yours for the duration of your stay. Yours. Not yours and Scott's. I'm well aware that your relationship has gone far beyond holding hands, but under the circumstances...'

'Um...' I blushed. This was so embarrassing. 'No, I understand...'

'Good. And the stairs creak and so do the floorboards so please don't imagine he'll be doing any nocturnal visiting.'

'Um...' I blushed. 'No, I...'

'I'm not old-fashioned in any way, and your morals are your own concern, and I know you practically lived together in Leighton Buzzard, and what you do together away from here is fine by me, but as Scott is engaged to someone else I just think...'

'Er... yes...'

'Out of interest, if he stayed in your home would your parents allow you to share a bed?'

'God, no!'

'Exactly. I'm so glad we understand one another.' Eva smiled at me. 'OK, now I'm going to get Holly to bed. I'll leave you to unpack – oh, and Scott won't be home until the early hours so there's no point in waiting up for him. I'll probably see you in the morning if I'm around.'

And she whisked Holly away and they disappeared along the corridor.

Leaving me alone. No offer of food or drink. No suggestion that I should come downstairs for the rest of the evening, when I was ready. No nothing.

I liked Eva, first impressions were that she was open and friendly, but I simply couldn't imagine my mum not making sure any visitor had a cup of tea, or ginger beer – depending on the time of year – and more food than anyone could possibly need. I was exhausted, homesick, and very lonely. And I hadn't eaten all day or had anything to drink since the lemonade on The Sarnia...

I sat on the edge of the big downy double bed and wanted to cry.

Stella's Diary
May 17th 1969 – going to Jersey, part 4

It was still daylight. Just. The sun had set across the tops of the distant trees but it was still very warm and stiflingly humid. I'd unpacked and put my clothes away, put my toiletries in the bathroom – and then, because I was tired and sweaty and scruffy and there was nothing else to do, I'd washed my hair and had a bath.

By now I was far too tired to be hungry, but really needed a drink, so I filled a glass in the bathroom with water from the tap several times. It wasn't exactly how I'd imagined my first night in paradise was going to be.

Back in the bedroom, utterly exhausted and scarily homesick, I put on my new-for-Jersey baby-doll pyjamas, threw up the sash windows to try and get some air, and, knowing there was no way I'd ever get to sleep, climbed into bed. I must have read all of two pages of *Frenchman's Creek* before I sank into oblivion.

***

The knock on the door woke me. For a moment I had absolutely no idea where I was and, panicking, heart-racing, blinked in the darkness. Where on earth...? Oh, yes – I was in Jersey – I must have dropped off for a moment... had I been dreaming? Was the knocking on the door part of the dream?

'Twinkle?'

The one whispered word made me shoot out of bed and hurtle across the unfamiliar room, cannoning into things as I did so.

I opened the door.

I just stared at him: at the long black hair and the gorgeous turquoise eyes and the slow, sexy smile – then I hurled myself into his arms.

'Oh, my God, I've missed you so much...' I muttered into his neck, trembling from the nearness of him after so long, drinking in the warmth and feel of him, loving the scent of him.

'I've missed you too,' he whispered, holding me so close, and kissing me over and over again. 'I've been thinking about you all night – couldn't wait to get back here. Oh, Twinkle I'm so glad you're here.'

I suddenly pulled away from him. 'Argh – nooo... you can't see me like this!'

'What?' he stared at me. 'Like what?'

'I haven't done my hair and my eyelashes are on the dressing table.'

Scott laughed, then clamped his hand over his mouth. 'You crack me up! No – hush – don't make me laugh – we mustn't make a noise. Listen, your hair is very Hendrix and your eyes are like a panda and you're gorgeous and I love you. Now – keep quiet... However...'

My heart sank. 'Yes?'

He looked me up and down, grinning at the rose-sprigged, lacy, baby-dolls. 'You're very – um – overdressed. I'm not used to you being so well covered at bedtime.'

'You are too,' I retorted. 'And you have a short memory – surely you haven't forgotten the massive granny knickers and the big-top T-shirts?'

'Ah, yes. How could I forget,' he chuckled. 'One of my favourite things about you.'

I poked my tongue out at him and we both giggled again.

He held out his hand. 'Come on – and shush...'

'What? Where?'

'Downstairs... my room. We have loads to catch up on – but we can't talk up here... they'll overhear us or we'll wake Holly or something and we wouldn't want that, would we?' He grinned at me. 'Shush – don't giggle...'

I giggled happily. 'What time is it?'

'Two-ish.'

I'd slept for ages then... odd.

He grabbed my hand, and both trying hard not to laugh

as we avoided the squeakiest floorboards, we tiptoed downstairs.

Scott's ground-floor room, at the front of the house overlooking the garden, was like a massive bed-sit. It had everything necessary to make it self-contained. That much I took in before he grabbed me and pulled me down on to the bed...

Ages – blissful ages – later, I sat up in bed. 'Um – weren't we going to talk?'

He rolled over and looked at me. 'Oh, yes... I somehow forgot that bit... can't imagine how that happened. Go on, then – talk – tell me about the journey and everything...'

While Scott put the Moody Blues' latest LP – *On the Threshold of a Dream* – on the stereogram, I told him the highlights. He was highly amused by the man wanting to buy me as a wife, resigned to Dan's comments about us, laughed about Eva's being adamant that we shouldn't be sharing a bed, and slightly apologetic about her lack of hospitality.

'I'm sorry you didn't get anything to eat or drink. Mum really isn't very interested in that sort of thing – she and Dan eat out most of the time, with or without Holly – and there's rarely much food here. I think that was why she was so delighted that you could and would cook. You must be starving – I know I am – and I'd kill for a cup of tea.'

I slid off the bed. 'You go and make the tea – I've just remembered I've got some sandwiches upstairs – Dad made them for me, there's masses of them, and they're still in my bag.'

'They'll be a bit worse for wear, surely?'

'No – they're in tinfoil in a sandwich box. Practically hermetically sealed. They'll be fine, trust me.' I headed for the door. 'Go on –you make the tea – I'll get the food.'

'Stella!'

'What?'

'You're naked.'

'So are you.'

'Yes, but I'm staying down here to make tea. You're going upstairs. Where my mother and Dan and Holly are and where you're supposed to be.'

'Ah, yes...'

I retraced my steps and pulled on the baby-dolls.

The sandwiches were still more than edible and we had a picnic in bed as the dawn broke. While we were eating, Scott told me about Lords, and about the airplays for 'Livin' with You' and the sales and progress, and about the rest of the band — and how Rich hadn't come over with them as there was no travelling or setting up or any need for a roadie and that he was going to spend the summer in London with his mum and his girlfriend. I hoped he'd be happy — it was going to be weird without him.

'And I've got a present for you,' Scott handed me a 45 rpm record, then took it back again. 'No, hang on — I'll just put it on the turntable so you can hear it.'

'Livin' With You!' Narnia's Children's record! At last! Oh, my word! Right from the opening bars I got goosebumps! God — they were so talented! What a heart-breaking, gorgeous, melodic, clever song... and so very sad... a lament for lost love, never to be reclaimed...

I sat on the bed, transfixed. It was even more amazing than I'd imagined. Oh, I hoped Stephan was pulling out all the publicity shots like he had for Doc Dekker. 'Livin' with You' deserved to be Number One all over the world. We played it another three times before Scott replaced it with *On the Threshold of a Dream* again.

'Thank you.' I hugged my copy of 'Livin' with You' to me. 'I'll treasure it for ever and play it every day for the rest of my life and remember now... this moment...'

And I had a sad and scary premonition that the lyrics would come to mean so much more to me in the future.

As the grey light turned to daylight, we just lay there,

listening to the Moody Blues. It was magical. Floating, drowsy, I decided that the words to 'To Share Our Love', 'So Deep Within You', 'Lovely to See You' and 'Never Comes the Day', could have been written for us... And I knew they'd not only be added to my eternal musical memory box, but also – along with 'Livin' With You' – be the theme tunes for my stay in Jersey.

I was totally, blissfully, idyllically happy.

'Oh, I suppose I'll have to go...' I stretched lazily. 'Before anyone realises I'm not where I should be.'

'Stay...'

'No – you're already half-asleep and it's nearly daylight now. Oh, and "Stay" was the song that got us into this mess to start with, remember?'

'Uh-huh...' Scott sighed. 'Never liked it much... joke. Night, Twinkle – see you later...'

I kissed him but he was already asleep, and I made it back upstairs and into bed just in time for Holly to come rushing into my room to show me her tractor collection.

Stella's Diary
May 18th 1969

Tonight I went to Lords with Narnia's Children. I'd had a really fab day and this just rounded it off perfectly.

This morning, once Holly had "entertained" me with her tractors and told me Mummy was still in bed and Daddy was going to work, there was no chance of me getting any sleep, so I dressed and followed her downstairs. It was Sunday so I knew there would be no way of stocking up the apparently sparse food supply in the kitchen. I found some eggs and milk, and as there was no sign of Eva and Scott was still asleep, I made scrambled eggs for Holly and me, hoping they hadn't been ear-marked for something else.

Eva, looking stunning in white shorts and a sleeveless linen top, drifted in just as we were finishing, beamed at me, kissed Holly, didn't mention the eggs, made herself some coffee and drifted out again.

'Mummy will be sunbathing,' Holly informed me as she slid from her chair. 'She sunbathes a lot. You can sunbathe if you want. I've got a sandpit. Goodbye.'

I sunbathed.

I changed into the black bikini with the floaty turquoise shirt over the top, took *Frenchman's Creek,* my Ambre Solaire and a towel, and joined Eva and Holly in the walled garden. Goodness it was hot! I shed the shirt and lay on my back and squinted up at the azure blue sky. What luxurious lazy bliss this was.

Sometime later, Eva lifted her sunglasses and leaned across from her deckchair. 'Sounds as if Scott's awake. I can hear music. Go and see if he's going to join us, Stella. After all, you must be dying to say hello to him having not seen him for so long...'

Eva's eyebrows were raised. I looked away – did she *know* about last night or was she merely fishing?

I didn't wait to find out, I scrambled to my feet and rushed into the house.

Scott was indeed awake, and dressed, and sitting on his bed writing. The Beatles were rocking from the stereo.

'Hi,' he looked up. 'And wow – nice bikini. Does it -?'

'Cover the scars, as promised?' I sat beside him, loving him for remembering. 'Yep. Just.'

'So it does.' He leaned across and kissed me. 'And you smell fab.'

'Ambre Solaire and Sea Jade,' I kissed him back. 'My summer scent – blimey... are you writing a book?'

He pushed the pages away quickly. 'No – but you should.'

'No way! I'm ok with the short stories and interviews and stuff – but you have to be a proper grown-up, intelligent, posh person to write books. So what are you writing...? Ah... ok... I'll leave you to it.'

'Stella...'

'No, honestly. I'm outside with your mum and Holly. It's really hot. I'll see you later...'

I rushed back into the garden.

'That was quick.' Eva lifted the sunglasses again and looked at me. 'Is he joining us?'

'Um...' I buried myself in *Frenchman's Creek,* 'Later, I think. He's – um – writing a letter at the moment.'

'Is he?' She did the eyebrow-raise again and let the sunglasses slide back over her eyes. 'That's pretty bad timing... men, eh?'

I said nothing. There wasn't much to say.

I read on. Holly chugged various small mechanical toys through the sand-pit.

Eva leaned across again. 'Thank you for giving Holly breakfast. Kind of you and saved me a job – I'd never have thought of scrambled eggs. Actually, for late lunch or early supper tonight I've got some kidneys somewhere and a cabbage and a few early Royals we were given by the neighbouring farm... I don't suppose you could concoct something edible from those?'

Not my first choice in ingredients, I thought, guessing that the early Royals were potatoes and not some sort of Channel Islands nobility. But, heck, I was my mother's daughter and could surely manage to make *something?*

'I'll certainly try. Maybe a sort of casserole with thick gravy?' That might mask the taste of the kidneys if I could add onions... surely there were onions? 'Do you want me to make it for all of us?'

'If it'll stretch. That sounds good, though. I'm impressed. We'll go food shopping tomorrow – you can buy what you like then.'

Thanks, I thought. But then, I was staying practically rent-free in her house, wasn't I? Earning my keep by buying food and cooking wasn't the worst thing I could be asked to do.

'OK. I enjoy food shopping.'

Eva shuddered. 'Each to their own.'

I laughed. 'You'll have to let me know what Holly will eat, though.'

'She'll eat anything,' Eva settled back in her deckchair with a happy sigh. 'As long as I don't have to cook it.'

I smiled at her honesty, tried not to think about Scott declaring undying love to Renza in his letter, and resumed reading.

The peace was shattered by the arrival of a rather scruffy van on the gravel drive. I looked up from *Frenchman's Creek* – if it was Dan coming home then I'd wrap myself in the turquoise shirt and cover up. I really didn't want those sardonic eyes skimming my beach-wear and finding it wanting.

'Oh!' Eva waved. 'Hi, Mo!'

'Hello, Eva!'

Mo? I sat up, watching as he uncurled his long legs from the driving seat and wandered towards us. It was lovely to see him.

I grinned at him. He was wearing cut-off jeans and

nothing else. His muscular body was really brown and his wild Bolan-curls were even longer and wilder. He looked like a proper rock god crossed with a surfer boy.

'Stella!' He smiled broadly. 'Great to see you again. Glad you got here safely. Where's Scott?'

'Writing to Renza.'

'Ah.'

Ah, indeed.

He dropped down beside me. 'Do you hate her?'

'Renza? No of course not. Nothing's changed. She's part of Scott's life, not mine. If she could be here, she would be and I wouldn't. But I am, and she's still in her box.'

Mo laughed. I knew Eva was listening. I didn't want to talk about Renza.

Mo luckily changed the subject and chatted about how he'd come over to let Scott know he'd pick him up as usual tonight for the Lords gig, and explained to me that he lived quite close by with his parents, while both Zak and Joss lived in St Helier near the club.

Scott, also stripped to the waist like Mo and equally brown and muscular, but even more devastating, wandered out into the garden then, carrying bottles of something called Oranjeboom and a glass of squash for Holly.

He handed round the drinks and sat beside me on the beach towel. I wanted to touch him but didn't. Eva took her beer and gave him a hard stare but said nothing.

'Just been telling Stella that I'll pick you up at 7 tonight,' Mo said. 'Thought she'd need a bit of advance warning. Cassie always takes ages to get ready when we're going out.'

I frowned. 'Me? Getting ready? Am I going out?'

Scott and Mo both laughed.

'You thought I'd be leaving you behind?' Scott shook his head. 'Sorry, Twinkle – this is how your evenings are going to be from now on – Lords every night.'

Wow! 'Really? I thought... well, I just thought...'

'Don't think,' Scott hugged me. 'I want you to be there. OK?'

More than OK. I looked at Mo. 'Er – will Cassie be there too?'

Mo shook his head. 'No, she's not that into the band to be honest. She turns up some nights with her friends but I think she finds it a bit boring after a while. And Joss and Zak are still playing the field with the holiday-makers so you'll be our sole resident cheer leader.'

I wanted to laugh out loud but decided that would be far too juvenile, so I just smiled to myself. Lords! With Scott! Every night! Wow!

Stella's Diary
May 18th 1969 – Lords

We arrived at Lords, in the middle of St Helier, at about 7.30. Like most clubs I'd been to, it looked like nothing from outside: just a door in a building in a side street, with a rather over-embellished name sign above it that would probably glow garishly neon-bright in the dark.

Lords didn't open until 8, and Scott held my hand as we, with Mo, walked inside, past the currently empty payment booth and cloakroom hatch, and into the club-proper. It was a bit of a shock, stepping into the cool, dim club straight from the still-scorching blue-sky-and-sunshine outside.

I was bubbling with excitement – the "I'm with the group" thing still entranced me – and gazed around at the dark, gothic interior.

I'd never seen a totally empty club before, and as I'd guessed it was like walking into Dr Who's Tardis. It was huge, and looked like a massive cave hewn from the local granite but probably wasn't. Millions of tiny pinpricks of light flickered from crevices in the uneven walls and ceiling giving it a constantly moving iridescence.

The stage – already set-up with Narnia's Children's equipment – was straight ahead, with a low-lit curved bar area with tables and chairs to the right, and a very impressive DJ's glass-fronted booth half-way along the far wall. Dark red chairs and benches lined the walls all around, the dance-floor was wooden and glittery with resin, and the atmosphere practically sizzled with anticipation.

Mo and Scott were dressed in their stage gear – new for Lords apparently – skin-tight black flares and equally tight-fitting very short black skinny-rib sweaters. They looked amazingly sexy. Scott had, once again, crammed his feet into my pink boots much to Eva's amusement.

I'd worn the second-skin pale blue and grey silk mini dress

and my silver sandals and added silver sequins and glitter to my eyes. Dan had laughed at my eyes, but Eva and Holly had been very impressed.

Apart from us, there were a few other early-comers in the club: the six tall and stunningly beautiful girls in their white flared hipsters and brief white bikini tops who worked the bar area as hostesses; the DJ, who was called Jonno; the doorman, Reggie and his side-kick, Norm; and Pat and Doreen who'd run the cloakroom since the club first opened. Scott had filled me in on all this and much more on our journey into town in Mo's van as we sailed dizzily down the slalom of Le Mont Cochon and via First Tower, into St Helier.

So, I already knew that Narnia's Children had added several new songs to their stage repertoire since I'd last been with them, that they did three hourly sets, 9 til 10, 11 til midnight and 1 til 2 when the club closed. I'd also been informed that I'd sit at the band's table, next to the stage on the left-hand side and that I wasn't to talk to anyone and definitely not accept offers of a dance! Scott had laughed when he'd said this, and I knew he was joking but it didn't matter, he needn't have worried: there was only one person in the world I was going to be with – tonight and every night.

Zak and Joss – also looking very tanned and drop dead sexy in the all-black clothes – arrived together and greeted me with whoops and hugs – it was lovely. It was fab being back with them all again after so long.

Once Narnia's Children started their tune-ups and sound checks, I settled back in my seat and just drank it all in. Oh, they looked and sounded so sensational – I'd missed this so much – I just loved it!

Then, as the doors opened, and the crowds started arriving, the group came and sat round the table with me, and Jonno, the DJ, boomed into action. Most records I knew, a couple were new to me, but cool tune after cool tune bounced off the walls: Bob and Earl's 'Harlem Shuffle', The Beach Boys' 'Darlin', The

Foundations' 'Build Me Up Buttercup', The Herd's 'I Don't Want Our Lovin' to Die', Crazy Elephant's 'Gimme, Gimme Good Loving', Max Romeo's 'Wet Dream', Herman's Hermits's 'My Sentimental Friend', Creedence Clearwater Revival's 'Proud Mary' and Doc Holliday's 'The Egyptians' – this last one brought a mocking cheer from Narnia's Children.

It was so exciting and noisy and colourful – the club was soon packed, presumably with a mix of locals and holiday makers, and the dance-floor was jammed.

Mo fetched us all drinks – I was daring and asked for a gin and orange – then, after Scott had suggested it, I had a rye and dry like the rest of the band – rye whisky and dry ginger – wow! I loved it – and knew this would be my drink of choice from now on. The mix of drinks – I really didn't drink much alcohol – had made me even more giggly than before, so by the time it came for Narnia's Children to start their first set, I was buzzing!

I don't think I can describe how amazing it was to see them on stage again. They slammed into their opening set with The Beatles' 'Back in the USSR' – and within seconds, the local Dolly Rockers were pressed three deep against the stage. I looked at Scott and grinned. He winked at me. God – he was so cool. The most beautiful boy in the world. Standing there, making the guitar sing, so still, so damn sexy...

The set was a mixture of songs they'd always played, and some new numbers including 'Get Back', 'Don't Let Me Down', 'Lady Madonna', 'Loving Things', and a very, very funny version of 'Ob-La-Di, Ob-La-Da'. I just sat there and stared and sang and tapped my feet and loved every single fantastic second of it.

The first hour flew by and I went up to the bar and re-ordered drinks all round – I bought beers as well as rye and drys because I guessed they'd be thirsty – and was back in my seat just as they came off stage and were mobbed by the waiting girls.

I wasn't jealous of the would-be groupie girls, or of the

gorgeous Lords's hostesses who clearly were very friendly with the group. I wasn't even jealous of Renza. This all came as a bit of a shock as I watched Scott disentangle himself from the clutches of a rather chubby girl with a bad perm.

What Scott did, and who he did it with, when he wasn't with me, really didn't bother me. It was a revelation – and maybe something to do with the alcohol – but as long as he was with me, loved me, was mine when we were together and still wanted to be with me whenever possible, nothing else mattered.

I decided I wouldn't tell him this.

Jonno was back DJ-ing like a mad thing and once again the floor was packed.

In Narnia's Children's second set they slotted some real hard rock in amongst some of the more melodic Beach Boys, Hollies and Moody Blues hits. 'Go Now', 'Wouldn't It Be Nice?', 'California Girls', 'Bus Stop', 'Ride My See-Saw', 'When I Grow Up', 'We're Through' – all these and so many more. All absolutely fab and brilliant.

Whether they played rock'n'roll or close harmony – they were a sensation. The atmosphere was ramped up even higher, the dancing was even more wild, and the Dolly Rockers even more vocally adoring.

I was asked to dance several times but just shook my head. One boy was a bit insistent so I yelled above the sound of the band that I had a boyfriend. He yelled back that he must be the Invisible Man. I yelled back even more loudly, and pointed out that it was Scott. He swore and wandered off. I laughed.

The group's third and final set, in the early hours, was even more incredible. They played all the music that they'd played when we first met, all the songs that meant so much to me, then – with a fanfare and an announcement from Zak – they played 'Livin' with You'. Wow! It brought the place to a standstill – perfect for a slow dance too – those gorgeous, haunting, heart-breaking words and that sad, melancholic tune. I got goosebumps and blinked away tears.

Narnia's Children got a standing ovation and Zak said thank you and announced that copies of the record would be on sale – along with fan club flyers – from Jonno at the end of the evening.

Clever, I thought. Very clever.

They then lifted the mood by roaring into a west coast and Beatles rock'n'roll medley to finish the show.

Almost immediately, once the cheers and applause and foot-stamping had died down, Jonno said it was time to go – that he'd be happy to take everyone's hard-earned cash for copies of 'Livin' With You' and to form an orderly queue. The queue was far from orderly and I guessed I'd have a lot more fan club applications when I got home.

I decided not to think about going home.

Jonno's 'Last Three' – a trio of discs played every night to indicate it was your last chance for a slow dance and that the show really was over – were 'Aquarius (Let the Sun Shine In)' by the Fifth Dimension, 'Goodmorning Starshine' by Oliver, and finally 'Isn't This a Lovely Way to Say Goodnight?' by the For Evers.

Three more tunes stored in my musical memory box for the rest of my life.

Once the band were happy that all the equipment was switched off and secure and safe and ready for a repeat performance tomorrow, we all had a final drink as the lights were dimmed and the last stragglers left the club.

High as a kite, madly in love and not a little inebriated, I laughed with Mo and Zak and Joss, kissed Scott a lot and knew that I'd be more than happy for my first night at Lords to be repeated night after night after blissful night for as long as my Jersey sojourn lasted.

Renza's Diary
May 19th 1969

Mum and Dad have gone to dinner with someone from the base who has a huge estate not far from Wuppertal. Mum will be in her element, I can just imagine. Apparently he has a deer park with acres and acres of forest, lakes, and a huge schloss, which was seized from a rich family by the Nazis in the war, and a lot of the works of art were sacked. The man who now owns it works as a civilian big-wig at the base and apparently, so the story goes, after the war when he was a still a soldier, he was part of a team from London responsible for recovering missing pieces of art and restoring them to their rightful owners. Dad said the story is that he somehow 'forgot' to restore most of it and had managed to 'acquire' an estate as well. I don't know what to make of it, surely he'd be in prison if it were true.

The parentals won't be back for hours and I managed to get the kids to bed early for once. They've been swimming which always knocks them out, and that means I can have a 'Scott' evening.

I keep all his letters in a long wooden box hidden under the last drawer in the upstairs kitchen, which is never used. I've spread them out on the carpet. I'm going to sit on the floor to read them through from the very first to the latest one. I've put the reel to reel tape player on and I'm having a great time playing the Chart Show which I've taped off Radio Luxemburg.

Back in April Rich sent me a tape recording of a song from the latest Led Zeppelin LP, called 'Communication Breakdown.' Apparently Narnia's Children had to learn some of it so they could incorporate it in part of their set when they played American bases. They needed more material than usual, because on the bases they had two long sets a night.

It was nice of him to write telling me about books he'd read, and I should read – we like the same authors – and he said he thought he'd send me the LP because he knew I'd have to wait ages for it to become available in the NAAFI. I'm a huge rock fan and adore Zeppelin and The Who and, well, music. I adore music.

It was so kind of him and I was thrilled. He didn't mention anything about Scott or the band. I don't know if I should read anything in to it.

One great thing about living in converted flats is that the distance from the kids and my room is quite big and so I can turn the music up and bop happily without upsetting anyone. And I can read Scott's letters to the music. It's the next best thing to being with him sometimes.

Renza's Diary
May 20th 1969

I got a post card from Scott today with a lovely photo of Elizabeth Castle in Jersey on the front. He's missing me and wishes I could be with him. He said his mum thought I'd be over this summer. Yeah, me too.

He said he was lonely but writing some really cool songs. I'm his inspiration and sometimes the words just spill onto his notebook so fast he doesn't know where they're coming from. He'll sing them to me next time we speak on the phone.

Scott hoped I wasn't too lonely without him and that I missed him as much as he missed me.

He sent lots of love and kisses and even Holly had drawn a heart on it for me with her name underneath, printed by Scott I guessed.

It made me feel really guilty reading it because Klaus had taken me to see the Mohnesee Dam yesterday, as a surprise. We walked all over the dam which was one of those the Dam Busters blew up in the war, and we went through the woods to a funny little shop, for cake and coffee – tea wasn't available, so I suffered coffee. It was all very nice and a bit old fashioned but I really enjoyed it. The scenery was out of this world. I wish I'd had dad's camera, but I forgot to ask. Klaus took my photo by the dam which was nice of him. We had a lovely time and I even let Klaus kiss me when he said goodbye to me afterwards. That's why I'm feeling guilty. I hate leading Klaus on and I feel as if I've betrayed Scott. Scott is by far the better kisser too.

Stella's Diary
May 23rd 1969

My days and nights in Jersey with Scott had quickly fallen into a pattern. The days – long, scorching hot days, this truly was a fabulous summer with not a cloud in the sky so far – were spent sunbathing, reading, listening to music, walking, exploring the island, swimming, talking – sometimes with others, mostly just us. We were very, very happy together. We laughed a lot and never seemed to run out of things to say.

Occasionally we took Holly with us on our walks round the sun-dappled lanes near Scott's house, along sandy tracks between miles and miles of glasshouses where the famous Jersey tomatoes were grown in their thousands. I was amazed at how tall they were – the arched roofs, reflecting the sun in dazzling prisms, towered above us – and how many of them there were, and how gorgeous they smelled in their special hot-house environment.

Or across to the flower fields – rainbows of carnations as far as the eye could see, all destined for the Flying Flower market – with a hot, wafting scent that filled the air and made you giddy. We'd even plodded through the rutted potato fields, picking up stray Jersey royals and taking them home to add to my vegetable stash in Eva's larder.

And all the time I'd been discovering new things about this amazing island. Scott told me it's only 5 miles by 9! Tiny! An entire country *that* small! And it's divided into 12 parishes, each one named after the saint to which their parish church is dedicated, and each parish has its own law-keepers: their Honorary Police – the constables and the centeniers and vignteniers – it's truly another world. Quaint – almost feudal.

And when we ventured further afield into one of the northern parishes, some of the really old women were wearing Breton black and nearly all the older generation spoke in a French-Jersey patois. I'd stored all this up to tell Mum and Dad and Vix.

I'd sent them – and my grandparents – postcards, of course, letting them know I was there and safe and very happy. I actually sent them all a postcard with the same gorgeous picture on: Mont Orgueil Castle at night, illuminated by multi-coloured lights spilling across Gory Harbour in Grouville. It looked amazingly beautiful. Scott promised we'd go there one night and see it for real!

Other afternoons we'd just sprawl on the grass, or on Scott's bed, and listen to music and read and doze – at least Scott got to sleep in in the mornings and rarely woke before mid-day – I, thanks to Holly, wasn't so lucky!

And the nights. Well, the nights, (after I'd cooked for everyone – if Eva and Dan and Holly weren't eating out – and so far they'd eaten everything I'd cooked and seemed to enjoy it – cannelloni was the current favourite! – and then had a bath and got all gussied up in a micro-mini frock and boots or the silver sandals and, of course, done my hair and eye make-up) were all about Lords of course.

But after Lords, before going home, in those still and stifling early mornings, the band and I would all drift out into the lush, warm night and buy fish and chips and sit on the sea wall and watch the moon dance across the waves, while Narnia's Children dissected the night's performance and Joss and Zak decided which of the Dolly Rockers was the next on their hit-list.

I loved those moments too. Just me and the band. Together again while the rest of the world slept. Like it had been at the start.

And then, after Mo had dropped us off, we'd go to Scott's room, drink tea using Eva's dainty glass cups and saucers, and play music and just be together. And so far I'd woken up in time to get out of his bed and back to my room before Holly's early morning alarm call.

I was in paradise and I never wanted it to end.

Stella's Diary
May 25th 1969 – Whitsunday

Today Narnia's Children were taking part in a live two hour Radio One Show being broadcast from St Helier.

Having got all their equipment from Lords and set up really early that morning, they played live. I was really nervous for them but needn't have worried – they were, as always, so professional and mind-blowing.

And they were interviewed afterwards by the hugely famous Radio One DJ Stuart Henry. I could hardly hear what he was saying because the non-stop cheers and screams and applause for the band practically drowned him out.

The place was a massive entertainment venue on the island, and it was absolutely packed. Hardly surprising as Radio One had shipped out a fair few very famous chart-topping musicians to be there, as well as Narnia's Children (who are Jersey's top pop group and superstars in their own right!). I'd wondered if I might be able to interview anyone – we'd been told The Move and The Kinks, among others, were going to be there – but it was far, far too crowded and hectic for anyone to get anywhere near them.

The whole place was awash with cameras and lighting and recording equipment, and wires and cables snaked everywhere, and men and women wearing headphones and carrying sound equipment weaved in and out of the excited audience.

This was a major coup for the band: huge coverage on Radio One who already had 'Livin' With You' on their playlist and gave it a lot of air-time. I had half expected Stephan to be there too – but I guessed he must still be in London making millions with Doc Holliday. Such a shame he didn't seem to recognise or appreciate the talent and brilliance – and potential money-making ability – of Narnia's Children with the same enthusiasm.

I spotted Carl Wayne, The Move's vocalist, in the crowd beside the stage. I'd interviewed The Move several times for the teenage magazines and they were all really lovely blokes and friendly and down-to-earth, and their PR company had been delighted with my coverage – but again, it was impossible to fight my way through the hundreds – maybe thousands – of people in the hall.

So I just hung around at the back, enjoying all the acts, loving the music and feeling ridiculously proud of Scott and the rest of the band – especially as he was not only wearing my pink boots (I don't think they'll ever fit me properly again!) but also my black skinny-rib sweater as his Lords stage one had been washed and not dried.

There! The domestic secrets of a rock'n'roll superstar!

Today, not for the first time, I had to pinch myself to make sure this wasn't all a dream. That I was actually here, with Scott, with Narnia's Children. Sometimes this year has seemed like one big amazing mind-blowing hippy trip! So many things have happened! My life has been turned upside down and inside out. From that night in St B's – oh, so long ago now – to this... and Scott and I, still together, still happy, still in love.

I stood there, watching the programme being made, and knew how very, very lucky I was.

After the show and the interviews there were loads of reporters crowding on to the stage and flash-bulbs going off all over the place. I was so proud to be part of this. So proud of Scott and the rest of the band. So proud – that for now at any rate – he was my boyfriend and he loved me.

Fingers crossed that somehow I'll be able to get hold of a copy of the photo of Scott and Stuart Henry together.

Another amazing day.

Stella's Diary
June 4ᵗʰ 1969

This morning, after Eva, Holly and I had been to the supermarket, Eva wanted to go clothes shopping. On the days that Scott went to Lords during daylight hours for band practice and to rehearse new songs with Narnia's Children, Eva and I went out together.

I liked going to the little supermarket in St Helier – straddling two parishes and almost in St Aubin, according to Eva – at the foot of Mont Felard, with its sea-views and lovely villagey feel. It was like being back home, everyone knew everyone else and there was lots of gossiping about everyone's business and local scandals.

They'd got used to me being with Eva. I was "one of Scott's girlfriends over from the mainland". At first, everyone had stared at my very short dresses and way-out eye-make up and wild hair – but I think they were getting used to it, and me, now.

Today all the talk was about Narnia's Children being "live on the wireless". Eva said she was very proud.

There *had* been a picture of Scott with Stuart Henry in the *Jersey Evening Post*. It was fab – and I'd cut it out and put it under my pillow. I didn't tell him – he was big-headed enough as it was!

Once everyone had finished congratulating Eva on her talented boy, we bought food, and an iced-lolly for Holly, and were packing it in the car when Eva said she needed a new top or dress for a function she and Dan were going to and she'd welcome my input.

As Eva and I were poles apart in fashion and practically everything else, I was actually ridiculously flattered. We did get on well, though, so of course I said yes.

The food shopping had been easy and Eva and I had worked out what we needed and were organised enough to have a list. I didn't cook every night because now there was plenty of food in the house, Eva had become really clever at chucking together left-overs even though she said she still hated it – but as she hated waste more, she managed to come up with some really nice meals.

'We'll go to Red Houses,' Eva said as we pulled recklessly out into the traffic. 'There's a fabulous shop there that sells the most divine things. You might find something you like, too.'

I somehow doubted that they'd sell anything that would a) suit me or b) I could afford, but I just nodded and smiled as Holly dripped ice-lolly and trundled her newest lorry across the back of my head.

Red Houses, it turned out, wasn't a row of houses or anything like. It was a small L-shaped collection of shops in St Brelade, and as we parked haphazardly outside, it was clear which one Eva was heading for.

It was the sort of expensive ladieswear shop that Vix and I always hurried past in Oxford and Reading because we knew we'd never be grown-up enough to wear those sort of clothes.

However, it clearly suited Eva down to the ground. She was obviously a regular customer, and was soon surrounded by assistants offering advice and producing frock after frock. Eva disappeared into the fitting room and kept reappearing wearing yet another stunning creation. Honestly, she looked like a model – and far too young to be Scott's mum. She looked amazing in all of them and I unhelpfully told her so.

She seemed to agree with me, as the pile of gorgeous dresses heaped on the chair by the counter was growing rapidly. I kept one eye on that and the other on Holly in case she drove her now-sticky mechanical fleet across something that cost a fortune!

Having decided on three cocktail dresses and a shirt in shimmering turquoise silk that matched her eyes, Eva beamed at me as she paid for her purchases and they were being swathed in pale grey tissue paper.

'Have you seen anything you like, Stella?'

Well, yes actually – loads, surprisingly – but nothing that I'd ever wear in this lifetime or could afford.

'No – not really... I mean, they're all beautiful, but I don't go to the sort of places to wear them, and I've already got lots of clothes and...'

'All hand-made, though,' Eva looked a bit disparaging. 'Don't you fancy something off-the-peg for once?'

'Honestly... they're all a bit grown-up for me... but I do love those black evening trousers...'

Without another word, Eva had swept across the shop and returned brandishing a pair of fine black silk flared hipsters, so soft and tight-fitting to the knee and then falling in swirling folds to the floor.

I'd made a very similar pair to go with my Julie Driscoll-style floppy top – but these were incredible.

'Go on – try them... oh, and while you're at it – try these, too. You never wear shorts – and this perfect weather looks set to stay – and these would fit you I'm sure, and you're already really brown, and they're really cute...' Eva flourished a pair of very, very short white shorts.

I took both, wincing at the price tickets, and vanished into the sumptuous fitting room.

Yes, I bought them. Both of them. And for the first time in my life walked out of a posh frock shop with two expensive-looking boxy carrier bags.

Eva was delighted. All the way home I hoped Scott would like them when he got back from rehearsals. Not that I dressed to please him, of course, I'd always had my own style – but I'd noticed night after night that the competition at Lords was very fierce and I didn't want him to think I'd gone frumpy.

He didn't. He was amused that Eva had bought so many clothes and said she'd have already hidden them in her wardrobe to be brought out with the "What? This old thing? I've had it for ages!" line when Dan noticed.

He was listening to Radio One – and I think probably writing to Renza – when we'd got home, but broke off to insist on me giving him a preview of my new clothes. To the background of Clodagh Rodgers singing "Come Back and Shake Me" and Vanity Fare's "Early in the Morning" (both songs that will whisk me back to that exact moment no matter how old I get) I tried on the trousers then the shorts – and he wolf-whistled and said I looked fab.

Maybe I should buy "proper clothes" more often!

Stella's Diary
June 6th 1969

I have to write about today. It was so funny. Well, not immediately – not for either of us – but looking back I know I'll always laugh about it.

It was really late when we got home from Lords last night. Even later than usual, and such a hot night – ridiculously humid – honestly, Jersey is like a tropical island! Anyway, because Zak had taken a fancy to one of the Dolly Rockers and had gone "outside to talk to her" during Narnia's Children's second break, no one could find him for ages. This meant their third set was very late starting so we – Scott and I – were equally very late being dropped off by an extremely hot, irritable and tired Mo.

As soon as we'd got in, Scott had fetched two beers from the kitchen and we'd opened all the windows in his room as wide as possible and stripped off and just collapsed on to the bed.

Which was where Eva found us when she burst into his room at around 8.30 this morning!

'Scott – sorry to disturb you – but just to let you know – I'm taking Holly out to Bonne Nuit for the day. Dan's already left for work – but he's meeting us there later and we're eating at the hotel. If you could just let Stella know we won't be around and won't need feeding and – oh!'

Oh, indeed!

I sat up and clutched the discarded sheet to my nakedness. Eva and I stared at each other. Scott, of course, slept blissfully on.

Eva shook her head. 'Knowing him, I really should have guessed. Mind you, you've been very clever at being back in your own room in time for Holly's wake-up visit, I must say. Right, let's get one thing clear – if this is how it is, then please make sure you're back in your bedroom before the rest of the house is up, ok?'

I nodded, very, very embarrassed. I'd abused her hospitality – ok, and she'd just found me in bed with her son!

'Yes – sorry... we were late back last night and it was stifling and we just fell asleep – look...' I indicated the two un-drunk bottles of beer beside the bed. 'We didn't even...'

Eva held up her hand. 'I don't want details, thank you. There's no need to explain. Believe me – none of this comes as a surprise. And I'd have no objection to him sleeping with his girlfriends – in fact, I'd be amazed if he didn't. But – there is Renza...'

'I know. But...'

Eva shook her head. 'It's ok. I like you. You're a nice girl. Of course it's not going to last, but – oh, I just wish he'd stop getting engaged!'

And she left the room.

I blinked my wonky eyelashes, still embarrassed. What the heck did that mean? How many times had Scott been engaged for heaven's sake?

I prodded him sharply in the ribs.

'Ouch! Don't! I'm awake.'

'Really?'

'Yep,' he pushed his hair out of his eyes. 'But there was no way I was going to get involved in that.' He laughed. 'You handled it really, well, Twinkle. I'm proud of you.'

'Shut up! I could have died from embarrassment there! And what did she mean about you keep getting engaged? How many other fiancées do you have hidden away?'

'None,' he laughed again. 'Seriously. Ok, yes, I was engaged to someone else before I met Renza – but I broke it off when I met her, and she – the girlfriend here – kicked up a bit of a fuss. Mum, being on the spot, got the worst of it I think, and...'

'Dear God!' I punched him. 'You have a fiancée here, too? In Jersey?'

'Ex-fiancée.'

'Oh, that makes all the difference! You must have still been in junior school! Am I likely to run into her? Will she come running at me with sharpened talons because she thinks I'm Renza?'

He grinned. 'No, of course not. You're so funny. I think I love you.'

'You,' I swung my legs out of bed, 'are incorrigible!'

'Twinkle! Come back to bed!'

'Not a chance!' I gathered up my discarded clothes. 'Go and find a fiancée to take my place!'

He laughed. 'No idea where to find one at this time of the morning. You'll just have to do.'

I grinned at him. 'Is that the best offer I'm going to get?'

'Crikey – yes! What more could you want? I'm a sexy rock-god superstar and I'm inviting you into my bed. There are ladies who would kill for that opportunity!'

'Go and find one, then,' I retorted, giggling, hurling my sandals at him. 'I'm going to make a cup of tea.'

'Ah, tea! Better than sex! Two sugars in mine, Twinkle!'

And we were both still laughing as I headed for the kitchen.

Renza's Diary
June 12th 1969

Today there was a letter from Jersey – they've been there over four weeks so far – 13 pages long! They're booked every night at Lords where they'd had a huge celebration for the release of 'Livin' with You' at the beginning of May. It seems they've been drunk a lot. Big deal!

Scott said they've had a lot of coverage in the national press and on TV and radio and they've been on a programme called *Scene and Heard* on Radio One several times, and also on *What's New* a lot, because the DJ loves them so much.

On Whitsunday they were on Radio One again, on a two hour long programme with Stuart Henry, who is a famous DJ even I've heard of, and he'd interviewed them live. Scott is going to send me a photo of the band with him being interviewed. I love Stuart Henry so I'm looking forward to it.

Apparently there were thousands of people watching the show being recorded live. They were on the show with Ray and Dave Davies from The 'The Kinks and Carl Wayne from The Move, Jess Conrad, Solomon King and Malcolm Roberts, plus lots of others. I'm more than a bit envious. I adore 'The Kinks' and 'The Move,' and I've got all their records which I play to death. I'll never forget when Radio One first started, the very first record they played was 'Flowers in the Rain' by The Move and I'd just bought it, so I was really hip; it was so groovy and unreal.

'"Get Back" by The Beatles is playing as I write this, have you heard it? I prefer the B side actually. I got "Time of the Season" when I was in Germany but it hasn't been released here yet, have you heard it? I love both sides, it's great. I love The Zombies. I long for you to come over here and be with me. I love and miss you so much it hurts.'

I'd read his letter a dozen times, trying to read between the lines I suppose. I love The Zombies, I've got their record which I got from the Canadian NAAFI. I put it on as I read his letter again, bringing him closer somehow.

Declaring his undying love for me, again, and how the memories of our first date and the weeks we spent together keep him going, he said. The whole band thought it was a magical time last year in the village, their favourite place to live so far.

He wants me to ask my friends to send request cards into the radio stations and TV shows so they can get enough fans to help them get the exposure.

I'll ask my new German friends and I'll write to a couple of former class-mates from school whose addresses I know, telling them all about Narnia's children in the hope they'll be interested, but I don't have anyone else to ask. I'll hint that they should buy the record too, because Scott says that sales and radio air-play helps with getting into the Charts.

I hope it'll happen – Narnia's Children in the Top 20 would be so cool! – and that they get lots of publicity. When I last wrote to him, I told him I'd read a piece about them in the *Record Mirror* and he said they were all so thrilled.

On the 14th it will be a year since our first date and he only briefly referred to it. What does that mean? He wants me to come over, but dare I risk another rejection like last time? I do have time due to me and could go over for a long weekend, my Uncle is still happy to cover for me, but should I? Since starting work I've got to know some of Heidi's friends, and another German girl, Isolde, who lives behind us in the strasse. In many ways Mum seems a lot easier about me going out – but she makes me pay for it later with moodiness and being horrid at every opportunity – so I've not been stuck indoors as much as before. And there's Klaus to go to the odd disco and dance with. Mum and Dad think he's the bees knees, but he's getting all serious and lately he's always trying to get me into bed. He knows about Scott, but chooses to ignore it. I shouldn't have kissed him. It's so intense all the time.

In my last letter to Scott I told him about Hannah, in the office, who it turns out is English, and married to a German who won't allow her to speak any English. She told me everyone in my office speaks perfect English, they have to because of their jobs. Some have even been there since the end of the war. So what's all this, 'We no speak English' rubbish all about? I'm so fed-up. I told him I've been saving like mad and I've been looking in *The Lady* magazine for jobs in England. Even a post as a live-in nanny or something would be good. I told Scott I've been babysitting for the families here, and have even taken on a young German girl whose dad works with mine, teaching her English, to help earn towards my savings. He never mentioned any of this in his reply I noticed.

He never took the bait about me going to discos with Klaus or out with Heidi and Isolde either, perhaps I've got him rattled.

He said it was cool I'd seen *Guess Who's Coming To Dinner,* with Spencer Tracey and Katherine Hepburn, and hoped I'd enjoyed seeing *The Anniversary,* at the Mess. It wasn't his kind of film. Can't say it's mine, but it's something else to do. Beggars can't be choosers.

I know Zak had his 18th birthday in early May and hoped they all got drunk and had a laugh. Knowing them I bet they did. I expect they went bowling and to a pub or to some clubs or something after they'd finished at Lords. Scott didn't say anything about it in his letter.

I can't help feeling annoyed at Scott having such a fab life whilst I'm stuck out here. I try not to let it show in my letters. And I don't want him knowing I'm worried about him and all the girls who hang around the band. It wouldn't be cool.

Marmalade were playing 'Baby Make It Soon' on the radio as I finished writing to Scott, and just before I sealed the envelope I asked him if he'd heard it yet and also if he likes 'Chicken Shack'. I added a note asking where they might move to when they go back to the mainland. And another PS saying that a BBC Film Unit is at the base and to look out for anything on TV about the base. Not that I expect to be seen on film or anything, but you never know.

I've also written to Rich, suggesting he read 'My Bed Is Not For Sleeping,' written by Gerty Agoston which I've recently read. He must think I'm a sad bugger as I have hardly anything interesting to write about. I try not to go on about Scott, blokes don't like that sort of thing.

Mo's written to me again, suggesting I read Jean Plaidy's books. He enjoys historical novels and he is writing one of his own. He's always encouraging me to write as well. When I write back I'll tell him I've had a dabble at writing some funny stories about the Gypsies back home. I think it's all rubbish really, so perhaps I won't. I don't know, it's just nice to correspond with like-minded people.

Scott thinks Mo has a soft spot for me, so he said last time he saw me, and given half a chance would try it on, but I think he's got it wrong, Mo is just a nice boy looking out for a friend, and that's all he is and ever will be to me. I know Scott was unconvinced – yes, some jealousy at last!

Stella's Diary
June 26ᵗʰ 1969

The weeks have flown by. I felt as though I'd lived here with Scott and his family forever. Today, after Dan had left for work and Eva had taken Holly to visit friends, Scott and I sat on the floor in the sitting room – the room with the television in it which made me realise I have watched no television at all since I got here! Not even *Coronation Street*! Vix won't believe it! – and played records on Dan's much-prized hi-fi system.

We were going to meet the rest of the band on the beach at St Helier this afternoon for a sort of picnic/party and then going further along the coast to meet up with Eva for a lift home in time to get ready for Lords.

Scott had the new Zombies LP, *Odessey and Oracle* and played 'Time of the Season', one track that he loved, over and over again. He said he'd bought the record in Germany and the track had been released as a single everywhere else but not in Britain.

Goodness knows why not – it was fabulous. It gave me goose-bumps – and the words seemed very apt... I loved it! When I read the sleeve notes I realised it had been written by Rod Argent who I'd interviewed for *Romeo* a couple of years previously. He was another lovely bloke and a very accomplished musician – and now he'd written this wonderful, evocative and sexy song that would definitely find its way into my musical memory box.

Coincidentally, the next record was The Who's 'Magic Bus' with Jess Roden, The Alan Bown's singer, adding his brilliant raucous blue-eyed soul vocals. I'd interviewed The Alan Bown, too – and again they were really down-to-earth and friendly and helpful and I loved their music and had bought all their records.

I told Scott all this and that I'd also interviewed the wildly original and far-out World of Oz on the same night as Argent.

He said it must be nice to be a groupie *and* get paid for it. I hit him.

We met the rest of Narnia's Children — and Mo's girlfriend Cassie, who was gorgeous and looked like Cher, and some of her friends — at Havre des Pas. This was a really popular beach in St Helier and it had a swimming pool. *On the beach*! How cool was that? Well, apparently sometimes on the beach, other times actually out in the sea depending on the tide. This afternoon the tide was out and the swimming pool was packed.

We had a fab time. I wore the black bikini under my new white shorts and with the floaty shirt on top. I even got brave enough to strip down just to the bikini and join everyone splashing about on the edge of the pool. Joss had brought a beach ball and we all played a mad kind of football match — boys versus girls. Of course the boys won — but it was really good fun — if hot and exhausting so we all had to go in the sea to cool off.

The sea was warm! I mean, really warm! Zak teased me about not being daring enough to actually swim because of my false eyelashes and spiky back-combed hair. He bet me as many rye and drys as I could drink that I wouldn't do it.

I soon showed him — even if I did get a bit bedraggled and almost lose an eyelash — and told him he'd be buying the drinks at Lords later!

When we'd eaten the sandwiches that Mo had brought — his mum made them and there were loads — and washed them down with bottles of Oranjeboom, we all went our separate ways. It was cool knowing that I'd be seeing them again in a few hours at Lords — and yes, I loved the way the holiday-making girls on the beach recognised Narnia's Children and stared at them and clearly envied me.

I am so lucky!

Hand-in-hand, Scott and I walked for ages through the sea as far as we could, then still barefoot, along the scorching sandy pavement. We were meeting Eva at somewhere called Quaisne – Scott said it was another beach, around the coast from St Aubin. I was really glad when we got there – I think we must have walked miles!

We climbed up on to the rocks and waited for Eva who'd been visiting one of her very rich friends who had a sea-front house. Scott said he'd been there once and it was like a Spanish villa. It seemed that everyone in Jersey lived in luxury detached houses – not like our streets and streets of red-brick rented semis at home.

Today, sitting here on the scorching granite, watching the sea's diamonds dance in the sun, with Scott's arm round my shoulders and feeling the heat prickling gently on my salty, sandy skin, home seemed a million miles away.

I knew I'd have to go home one day – but hoped and prayed it wouldn't be any time soon.

Stella's Diary

July 1st 1969 – a day of two halves, part 1

This has been a real Oh My God sort of day! Honestly!

I'd finished reading both *Frenchman's Creek* and the Edna O'Brien book Mum had given me and had raided Scott's Dennis Wheatley collection. I was sprawled out in the garden in the morning sun scaring myself silly with *The Devil Rides Out* when Eva appeared in the doorway.

'Stella – phone call for you. It's your dad.'

Honestly, my heart stopped beating. My mouth was dry. I felt violently sick. Dad? On the phone? From the phone box? Or work? I knew he'd only phone in the direst emergency.

Oh goodness – it must mean something awful had happened to Mum, or my grandparents, or Vix, or one of the animals... It had to be bad news.

I stood up and my legs were shaking. The sun, scorching from a cloudless sky, suddenly drenched me in icy cold fear.

I hurried into the hall. Eva had left the receiver on the phone table at the foot of the stairs and I picked it up and nearly dropped it my hands were so clammy.

'Hello? Dad?'

'Stell?'

'Dad? Where are you ringing from? It's not a hospital or anything?'

'No. I'm ringing from my boss's office. I've got to pay for the call too. Tight wad, he is.'

I'd never spoken to Dad on the phone before. I was surprised how Berkshire-gruff his voice was.

'Oh, but Dad – what's wrong. What's happened? Is it Mum? Is it...?'

'Nothing like that, Stell. Don't panic, love. Everyone's ok here. But we have got a bit of trouble.'

I gulped in relief – it didn't matter what it was – as long as everyone was ok. But I still knew if something awful had

419

happened it was my fault – it was karma – retribution for me so silly and headstrong and selfish and wanting adventures and telling so many lies this year.

'What sort of trouble?'

'We've had the police here, Stell. At home. Well, not the real police, but the security people from the Atomic... they want to know where you are.'

'What? Why?'

'Because they say you've broken The Official Secrets Act.'

Oh my God! I'd go to prison for that!

'What? How? Dad – I don't understand...'

'Well, neither did we at first because of course you'd told us that you'd taken unpaid leave to go to Jersey.'

The accusation hung unspoken in the air. I *knew* I should have been honest with them.

'Yes, sorry. I'm really sorry. I should have told you the truth – but I knew you'd be cross with me.'

'Not half as cross as we are right now.'

'No – sorry – I've been so stupid. But, Dad, how could I break the Official Secrets Act? I only did subsistence claims – I didn't deal with anything classified... I don't know any Russians or anything... I've never told anyone anything about work because I only worked in an office moving paper around and -'

'Stell! Listen. They gave you the benefit of the doubt for some time because Personnel said you'd been ill – but when you didn't come back – they had to act. You vanished and no one knew where you'd gone.'

'Well, yes – I mean, no – I didn't tell *anyone*...' Well, apart from Vix and presumably they hadn't got hold of her yet. 'But I only walked out of a job – I didn't steal state secrets.'

Dad sighed. 'No, love – but what you did do is sign the Official Secrets Act when you started working there – it's standard if you remember, being a government establishment.'

'Oh... yes... right, and...?

'That means, if you leave, you give notice, you have a debrief and a signing-off session and hand everything over. You don't just disappear – with all your handbooks, certificates, classified employee information and, more importantly, your security pass. And you apparently did, didn't you?'

Oh God! All those documents! All those things in my desk that I'd swept up and stuffed in my tote bag on the last day! I hadn't even *thought*...

'Yes. Oh, blimey...'

'Blimey isn't what we said here, Stell, I can tell you. Your mum was very angry – very angry indeed. They seem to think you could have passed all this, particularly the pass, on to – well – people who would love to infiltrate a secure government establishment. You can see how serious this is, can't you?'

Oh Lord yes!

'Dad – you didn't tell them where I was, did you?' I had visions of all of Jersey's Honorary Police Force storming Scott's home with battering rams and Alsatians, arresting me and throwing me into some Dickensian-type prison. 'Oh, Dad – what did you say?'

'What could we say, Stell? They wanted to search the house! We told them you'd gone on holiday – because you'd been ill – and we didn't know exactly where you were.'

'Oh, Dad! You lied for me!'

'Yes,' he was very gruff. 'We did. And we know we shouldn't have done. Anyway, they want us to let them know when you get in touch and they want to know where all the official paperwork – and the security pass – is. Where is it, Stell?'

'Upstairs. Here. In my bag – where I shoved it all the day I left. Oh – what do I do now?'

Dad sighed heavily. 'Nothing, Stella. Nothing. The last thing we want is for the real police to get involved – which they might do if they think you've left the country with government information. We'll tell them you've phoned us, but we still don't know where you are, that you understand the severity of the situation, but it was an oversight on your part. We'll tell them all the security things are safe and with you.'

'Thank you – oh, thank you...'

'It's been a proper to-do here and no mistake. Look, love, when you know when you're coming home let us know. We have a phone number to contact the security people and tell them. They'll want you to go back to work immediately for the dressing down and everything – and of course handing over all the papers and signing off your pass. It won't be pleasant.'

Understatement!

'Ok. I promise I'll let you know the minute I'm coming home. And, Dad – I'm really, really sorry.'

Dad almost chuckled. 'I'm sure you are, love. I just hope it's all been worth it. Are you having a good time?'

'Fab – the best time ever. But – oh, God – I'm so sorry.'

'No point crying over spilt milk, Stell. What's done is done and we'll just have to make the best of it. I'm sure it'll be all right once we tell them it was all a big mistake and you'll be happy to sort it out when you're back.'

I wanted to kiss him. I didn't deserve my wonderful mum and dad. 'Dad – please, please say sorry to Mum – and give her all my love – and oh, now I miss you so much.'

'We miss you, too, Stell. Look, give our best to young Scott and his parents – and we'll say no more about this until you get home. We love you, Stell – don't forget that.'

As if I could!

'I love you too, Dad. So much. And Mum. And I'm really sorry.'

'I've got to go, love. The boss is looking daggers. But as long as I've got something to tell the security people it'll be all right. You enjoy the rest of your holiday and we'll see you soon. Bye, Stell – bye.'

'Bye Dad – I'm so very sorry...'

But he'd already hung up.

Stella's Diary

July 1st 1969 – a day of two halves, part 2

I knew I'd never mention the content of Dad's phone call to Eva – I was pretty sure she'd make me pack my bags and clear off straight away. And I wouldn't blame her. She certainly wouldn't want that sort of trouble on her doorstep.

When she asked if everything was ok, I lied – I'm getting so good at it! – and said, yes, it was all fine and he was just wondering if there was anything I'd really like for my 21st birthday in September.

Yes, I know – it sounded pathetic even to me – but if she disbelieved me, she didn't say so.

I was very, very scared – and dreading what I'd have to face when I went home – but as going home wasn't even on the horizon yet, I decided to do yet another Scarlett O'Hara and "think about it tomorrow".

Oh, I was getting really good at this head-in-the-sand stuff!

I told Scott though, swearing him to secrecy, and he was alternately shocked, impressed, worried, admiring, and finally amused and called me Mata Hari for the rest of the day.

***

That night, at Lords, after a rather fraught day, I was still a bit on edge, and as I tried to relax by people-watching, I noticed a new girl in the ever-growing mob of Dolly Rockers. She was small and slim and had very "done" blonde hair, all curls and swirls, and was wearing a neat little beige dress and matching shoes.

I noticed her particularly because she stood, on her own, right in front of Zak and never took her eyes off him. He – strutting across the stage in his sexy Mick Jagger mode – didn't seem to have noticed her – yet. I thought she really wasn't the type of girl he usually went for, but admired her persistence.

In Narnia's Children's first break, while we sitting round our table, she perched on one of the bar stools and stared across at us – or rather, at Zak. By the second break, while Scott was at the bar getting the drinks and chatting to a broad-shouldered man in a tuxedo, she'd introduced herself to Zak – 'she's called Sue or Lou or Prue or something,' he said. 'I couldn't hear her properly. She's over here to work for the summer season I think. She's dead pretty, though. I've said I'll see her after the gig.'

We all exchanged "here we go again" looks. Sue/Lou/Prue really wasn't Zak's usual type at all and I wondered what would happen after the show was over.

But all thoughts of Zak's latest conquest went right out of my head when, half way through their final set, Narnia's Children started playing 'Time of the Season'.

Oh my Lord! It was a phenomenal version – so cool! My goosebumps had goosebumps. Scott was looking over at me and laughed. He'd told me they'd been rehearsing some new numbers but not which ones – which was why I really, really wasn't prepared for the next bit.

They swept from 'Time of the Season' straight into 'Nights in White Satin'.

Scott took lead vocals – and, without taking his eyes off me, sang them to me. Just to me…

The club-going dancers in Lords wouldn't have noticed – they'd all taken the opportunity to cling together for a slow dance – but it was as if there was just Scott and me and those beautiful lyrics, alone in the world.

'I love you … oh, how I love you…'

I just sat there, watching him, completely swamped by a million emotions.

Wow! Just wow! I loved him so, so much. No one in the history of the world had ever been as much in love as I was at that moment.

Zak was doing the harmonies and he grinned from Scott to me and back again.

I was in heaven. Floating on cloud nine. The happiest girl in the world. It was a perfect end to a day that had started so badly and I never wanted it to end.

But this day of highs and lows wasn't over yet.

When we'd all piled out of Lords into the hot, humid night, and Zak had, as promised, whisked his Dolly Rocker — who turned out to be called Prue — away to "look at the sea", and Joss had taken Prue's friend "for a walk", Scott, Mo and I climbed into the van.

'This isn't the way home. We're going the wrong way,' I frowned at Mo.

'We're not,' he grinned. 'Hold on tight for the magical mystery tour.'

I wriggled round on Scott's lap and looked at him. 'Do you know where we're going?'

'Yes.'

'And?'

'Wait and see.'

'Are you being enigmatic?'

'Yes.'

'I hate you.'

'I know.'

After what seemed like ages, leaving St Helier behind, climbing a switchback hill, and driving past rows of darkened houses and cottages, then through somewhere called Five Oaks which reminded me of *Gone With The Wind*, and round dozens of twisty-turny bends and very narrow roads, we slowed down.

Mo stopped the van. 'I'll wait here for you. You have ten minutes.'

We got out of the van and I looked around me. I had no idea where we were.

'Come on... just along here.' Scott took my hand.

Mystified, I clung on to his hand, as we walked along a narrow pavement in the steamy night. Buildings in total darkness loomed along one side and I could hear the sea.

Then, as we rounded a bend, ahead of us, I saw it!

Mont Orgueil Castle! In all its glory!

It was enormous – a proper, crenelated centuries-old castle, exactly like the postcards only a hundred million times better! Illuminated with white spotlights from the base, it towered up into the black sky, with the multi-coloured rainbow lights sweeping over the huge walls and lofty battlements and dropping down into the sea and then spreading out across the water, rippling gently with the tide.

We sat on the sea wall, close together and I wanted to cry with happiness.

The castle and the lights were breathtakingly spectacular and one of the most beautiful things I'd ever seen. I stared and stared at it, knowing I'd never forget this moment.

'Thank you.' I kissed Scott. 'Just thank you.'

'I know how much you wanted to see it. And as there won't be many more opportunities, I knew it'd have to be tonight.'

It took a few moments for the implication of those words to sink in

'What...?'

He sighed. 'Stephan has been in touch with the owner of Lords. He told me tonight – we've got to cut our residency short. We're coming back again apparently to finish the season later, but Stephan has got us a lot of gigs on the mainland and wants us to promo "Livin' With You" to a wider audience.'

'The guy in the dinner jacket that you were talking to tonight? Was that him...? Was that when...?'

'Yeah.'

My heart sank. All the happiness seeped away in the cold, painful realisation. 'So – I'll be going home? And you...?'

'I've been told that Stephan has arranged for us to go back to Leighton Buzzard to start with while we fulfil the bookings, then back here for a short time to finish the season. He's currently looking for a permanent place for us to live in London. London is where it's all happening, of course.'

Oh, of course.

'And – when...?'

'I'm not sure. Soon, I guess. Apparently Stephan's going to ring me sometime with all the details. Don't worry, Twinkle. It'll be ok.'

But it wouldn't – I just knew it wouldn't. I'd be leaving Jersey, and Scott – and I'd have to go home and face an entirely different kind of music...

Stella's Diary
July 10th 1969

Oh, cruel fate! Or karma! Or whoever is up there pulling the strings! Just when I thought things couldn't get any worse...

It was late morning, and we were all sitting in the garden, waiting for Stephan's phone call which still hadn't come – well, Scott and I were waiting – Eva was immersed in a glossy magazine and Holly was tunnelling under the sandpit with a miniature excavator.

I'd long given up hoping that Stephan had changed his mind and cancelled the mainland gigs and we'd all stay here for ever. I just wished he'd make the damn phone call and get it over.

And I'd kept telling myself that if Narnia's Children were going back to the mainland at the same time as I was, and would be living at Leighton Buzzard – at least for a while – then there'd be nothing to stop me going back there. We could re-live those happy-go-lucky days from the start of the year... yes, I'd be leaving Jersey – but it would be ok... Scott and I could still be together. Maybe it would be ok, as he'd said.

The phone rang.

Eva went to answer it. Scott and I looked at one another. I held my breath. It had to be Stephan. I'd soon know how long I had left.

Eva re-appeared in the doorway. 'Scott! Call for you! Your girlfriend's on the phone!'

He leapt up bit too quickly for my liking, then looked at me, and hurried indoors.

I just groaned and sank further down into my deckchair. Renza! That was all I needed.

Eva stood beside me. 'Do you fancy going out to lunch?'

'Me?'

'Yes, you. I'm going to lunch with some friends. I think it would do you good to come along as well...' she indicated the house. 'Leave him alone for a while, maybe? Try not to think about it. Oh, damn him – this is so awkward – come on, let's leave them to it.'

'But,' I looked down at my shorts and the floaty shirt. 'I'm not dressed for going out to lunch. I'll need to get changed.'

'Believe me, you're perfectly dressed for lunch with Francoise and Marcel – as you'll discover.'

'But won't they mind? An extra person – a stranger – turning up?'

'Not at all – they're very laid-back. Come on, grab your bag and whatever else you need and let's go.'

We went. Without saying anything to Scott. I glanced in through the open doorway as we were climbing into Eva's car, and he was sitting on the bottom stair, talking and smiling.

Oh, hell! Hell! Hell!

We drove, with Holly as ever playing with her fleet on the back seat, through what seemed like dozens and dozens of narrow frondy lanes which were about wide enough for a careful bicycle. I felt sick. Lunch with strangers was the absolutely last thing I wanted to be doing – but I certainly didn't want to have stayed behind either and listened to Scott sweet-talking to Renza.

'I have no idea what to say to you about this,' Eva looked across at me. 'Except, as you've always known about Renza, then the fact that they're still in touch can't be that much of a shock. Although I suppose him writing letters is one thing, actually talking to her in front of you is quite another. I'm assuming Renza has no idea that you're here?'

'I don't know. I shouldn't think so. We never talk about her. It wouldn't be fair.'

Eva laughed. 'Ok – then it's all a bit odd, isn't it? His relationship with you. I honestly think he means to marry her and...'

'Oh, so do I,' I said bitterly. 'I've never been in any doubt about that. The difference is that he loves me but he's *in love* with Renza.'

'Subtle,' Eva changed gear abruptly as we started to chug more slowly across a field. 'Sorry. Yes, I suppose that would make a difference.'

'It does. It always has. I think he met me at the wrong time in one way – but at the right time in another. He and Renza were going to have to be apart, and I kind of filled the gap until they could be together again. I do know that if Renza hadn't gone to Germany then Scott and I would never have happened.'

'You have no illusions about my son, have you?' Eva stopped the car in what seemed like a small wood.

'None whatsoever.'

We got out of the car and Holly ran on ahead.

'After you've gone home – when all this is over, I hope we can stay in touch,' Eva said. 'I'd like that.'

'So would I. But not because...'

'I'm Scott's mother? No, simply because we like one another.'

I nodded. It didn't matter. I'd never come back to Jersey, we didn't have a phone at home, and I somehow couldn't see Eva and me exchanging chatty letters when Renza was her daughter-in-law.

However, it was nice of her to say it.

Marcel and Francoise lived in a sort of prefabricated chalet in the middle of nowhere. They may have had French names but they had Jersey accents. They wore very hippie clothes and dreadlocks and had a brood of tanned, scruffy, happy children.

They welcomed me with open arms.

They obviously knew all about me, and didn't seem to mind me squashing up round their tiny table while all the children, including Holly, ate bread and cheese and fruit outside in the dusty garden.

Eva and Francoise did all the talking. Marcel smoked a joint – yes, I was shocked! – and picked at some meat from a large platter. I had no idea what half the things were and wasn't hungry anyway, so I just ate some bread and some very runny cheese and what I thought was a gherkin but wasn't and drank every glass of wine that was poured for me.

I'd rarely had wine. At home, we always had a bottle of Sauternes with Christmas dinner – just the one bottle – and I didn't like it at all. I didn't like this wine much either. I did however like the warm, hazy, drowsy numbing sensation it gave me. As no one talked to me, I just sat and drank and smiled.

It was the happiest I'd been all day.

Stella's Diary
July 11th 1969

So now I knew. And it was far, far worse than I'd imagined.

The eventual phone call from Stephan to Scott this morning confirmed that Narnia's Children would be returning to the mainland and Leighton Buzzard within days.

A second phone call from Renza to Scott this morning confirmed that – obviously Scott had mentioned the change in plans to her during the previous day's call – she'd checked and would be able to join them there.

Oh joy!

Scott, to give him his due, managed to break all this to me in the briefest and kindest way possible.

I knew I had to accept it. All of it. But I didn't want to. I wanted to stuff my fingers in my ears and close my eyes until it had all gone away.

Instead I asked Eva to run me to St Helier so I could use my return ticket to book a seat on the next ferry leaving as soon as possible. She did. It was going to be on Monday. Early. On Monday, in three days' time, I'd be home in Harbury Green and I'd never see Scott again.

I can't put into words how desolate any of this was. I had never, ever felt so unhappy, so heartbroken, so torn apart. So bloody awful!

I rang Mum at the school – they had to go and fetch her out of the classroom and into the office, something I knew was frowned on – and told her when the ship would dock at Weymouth and to ask Dad to pick me up. She was quite short with me – clearly not having forgiven me for bringing the wrath of the Official Secrets Act to her door. She also said she'd let the Atomic know when I'd be home too as they'd promised to do so.

She did soften a bit at the end and say she'd missed me and would be so happy to have me home safe and sound. This

made me cry and she said she'd have to go before she cried
and made a show of herself in front of the headmistress.

It was over – truly over – and the knowledge was really
killing me now.

Stella's Diary
July 14th 1969

The end of Jersey. The end of the mad, insane, perfect, incredible dream.

In the beautiful golden light of a Jersey morning, I went home on The Caesarea, The Sarnia's sister-ship. Narnia's Children and all their band gear would be flying back to the mainland and then on to Leighton Buzzard tomorrow. I had no idea what Renza's travel plans were.

I'd thanked Dan and Eva for their hospitality and for making me feel so welcome and so at home, and kissed Holly goodbye. And I'd cried as we drove away from the house that had become my second home for the last two months.

Scott had come to see me off. I didn't want him to. There was no point.

He tenderly kissed me goodbye on the quayside and, falling apart, I pulled away, turned round and didn't look back.

'Stella – listen – I'll let you know what's happening as soon as I can,' he shouted as I reached the gangplank. 'I'll write. I promise.'

I turned then and shook my head. 'Ok. Thank you for everything... I've had a fab time – oh, and be happy...'

'Stella...'

But I got barged and bumped up and on to The Caesarea's deck and was out of sight and earshot within minutes.

I'd booked a seat on one of the lower decks, and just sat there amidst a crowd of strangers, hugging my Samsonite suitcase and my tote bag and my memories.

It was nothing like the exciting, exhilarating, joyous journey out. This voyage was slow and sick-making and suited my mood. And to make it worse, someone had a transistor radio and 'Proud Mary' was playing. The owner of the radio said how appropriate it was as we were on a big ship too and he and all his companions kept singing the

434

damn song over and over again. All it did was make me remember Lords and Jonno playing it and the memory hurt so much that I cried.

Dad was there at Weymouth when I eventually emerged. I knew it must have been hard for him to get a day off at such short notice. I hugged him and he hugged me and said I was as brown as a berry and he hoped I'd had a great time and how much they'd missed me.

He carried on chattering as we left Weymouth but when I didn't answer him, he looked at me, squeezed my hand and stopped talking. Bless him, he never even mentioned the Official Secrets Act thing at all.

All too soon we were back in Harbury Green. It was a glorious summer evening and if I'd still been in Jersey I'd have been getting ready to leave for Lords. The thought just killed me. I hurt so much I could hardly breathe.

I just managed to stroke the over-excited dogs and cats, and hug and kiss Mum and say no I didn't want anything to eat, before flying upstairs, hurling myself on my bed and sobbing as if my heart would break.

Renza's Diary
July 16th 1969

I've been thinking a lot lately about Scott and me ever since reading about long-distance relationships in one of Mum's magazine Agony Aunt columns; well, thinking about it in a more determined way. This cannot continue. I have to know what's really going on. I can't stand the long wait for letters and the feeling that there is unfinished business between us. It's horrid being a suspicious, moaning misery, and I can't stand it here any longer. I need to begin making serious plans to get back to England and to get a proper job so I can feel alive and part of the real world again. I've sent out dozens of job applications and it's taking them forever to respond.

I need to be around people of my own age, working and having a social life, not babysitting and working in a place I hate, with a lot of old fogies getting drunk before 4pm every working day. Life is passing me by. No one cares. All they want is what they want, not what I want or is best for me. A whole year has gone past and I'm going nowhere fast.

Scott will either be with me or not. I want to be with him but if he doesn't want me, then I'll have to get over it and move on. Getting a proper job and meeting new people should take my mind off things if he dumps me. It's not the end of the world. There're plenty of fish in the sea. Trouble is I don't want another fish, I want Scott. Oh, what am I to do, someone tell me?

Renza's Diary
July 17ᵗʰ 1969

The BBC film crew have been and gone and I hardly saw any of them. They set up cameras in the various workshops and filmed interviews with some of the longest serving German civilian staff, the local police and Rathaus officials, as well as the army and MoD bigwigs, and there was a demonstration of a Centurion tank being serviced and then a Saracen scout car guns were fired a few times. All too flipping exciting for words. The film crew came into the office but I was kept out of the way in case they discovered I was English. Apparently the base wasn't supposed to employ 'dependents' family members. Nepotism and all that. So I watched everything from afar. Not that I cared. All in all there was nothing worth telling Scott about. I don't even know if or when it will be broadcast. No-one seemed to know. Dad said they were a right bunch of camp 'luvvies,' whatever that meant.

Renza's Diary
July 18th 1969

I got a lift back to England with John Barry from the base. He works with my dad and offered to take me back for a long weekend. We drove to somewhere in Holland, near Rotterdam, and hitched with an RAF transport plane full of squaddies going home on leave to Heathrow. We had to sit on the floor and I was the only female on the flight, but it only cost me £3. It was cold and uncomfortable but I got home faster than via the ferry.

I got a train to Leighton Buzzard and Rich collected me from the station. I was very cold, and very tired, but just so happy to be seeing Scott again. It had all been so rushed and when I'd rung him I was terrified he would say no or they'd be away or something. But he'd sounded as excited as I was.

Dad's friend, John, arranged to meet me again at Victoria Station on the 23rd to travel back to Germany, we'd catch the boat train to Dover and across to Holland from there. He'd said he'd drive me back to the base so I wouldn't have to pay for much except a couple of train fares.

When I got to Leighton Buzzard, Scott was there and we fell into each other's arms and I cried. Scott was all choked up as well and it was the most wonderful kiss in the whole world ever. Eat your heart out Juliet.

It was as if we'd never been apart, as if the last time we met had never happened.

Otis Redding was on the radio in the kitchen, singing 'I've been Loving You so Long.' Scott hummed along to it as he made me a cup of tea and some toast to warm me. the house was freezing inside even though it was warm outside.

The band have been gigging at some important venues locally and in London, with bigger crowds, which the Music Press now covered regularly, so Scott said. He told me to wear my glad-rags so he could show me off at the gig that night,

438

which was at The New Penny Watford. I made sure I wouldn't let Scott down and wore my new purple trouser suit with my favourite, really high heeled black boots. I haven't been going flat out with the Dusty look for a while, so just lined my eyes with purple eyeliner and put lots of black mascara and eye-shadow on, with deep grey shading in the sockets. I left my lips pale. I used the last of the perfume my auntie sent from America last year.

'You look gorgeous, good enough to eat,' he said when I came downstairs ready to leave. I couldn't help grinning from ear to ear. That's just what I intended.

The gig was ace, with lots of journalists and photographers there, especially to see Narnia's Children, and they were made a huge fuss of. The band's set had changed a lot from when I last heard them but their harmonies and their playing was just amazing. Everyone was mesmerised, including me, by the sheer electricity they gave off. Zak was a brilliant front man, even better than I remembered and I couldn't take my eyes off Scott for long, with his guitar slung low, and the way he moved...he was sex on legs. After the gig the band nearly disappeared into a sea of screaming girls, all waving autograph books and photos they wanted signed. It was so exciting. Very different to Merryhill. Rich kept an eye on me – he knew I was nervous after what happened on the Army Base.

On the way back Thunderclap Newman's song, 'Something in the Air,' played and we all sang along, and then Jane Birkin and Serge Gainsbourg sang, 'Je T'Aime,' which I found embarrassing, not that my school French helped with the lyrics, but all that heavy breathing...

But most of the time Scott and I were able to be alone and it was magic. We talked and talked and managed to sort ourselves out, I think. He said he still wanted to get married and we will one day, but not for a while. I'll try and get a job in England and come home – but he said he wasn't sure we should live together, not sure what that meant, so we shall have to see about that later.

'Just because I take ages to write, don't think the worst.' Scott said as he held me close while I tried to make us all a cup of tea.

'I won't, but it's hard and sometimes you seem so cool towards me in your letters and on the phone.'

I handed him his cup. A little reassured. But not much.

But that night I shared his room and this time there was nothing in the way of being together in every sense of the word. At last. Indescribable. Magic. Groovy and like soaring above the clouds... All those things and more. So wonderful and tender and so moving – we both cried.

Stella's Diary
July 18th 1969

I deserved today. I'll gloss over the finer details here I think. You can probably imagine how it went.

I went back to work for the dressing down – and it was a zillion times worse than I could ever have imagined.

However, as I hadn't slept properly since being back from Jersey, I was a gibbering wreck long before I entered "The Room". They'd sent a car and an escort for me and I had to be security checked at the gate – and no one spoke or smiled.

There were four of them – two in uniform – behind a long table and they, quite rightly, read me the riot act. They asked why I'd done it, where I'd been and what I'd been doing and who I'd met.

Scared stiff, I managed to gabble and give them a sort of outline about an extended holiday and just having been thoughtless and that none of the documents had ever left my possession and that I was very, very sorry.

One of the non-uniform ones was clearly from Personnel and had my file and read out bits about my illness and operation, which helped a bit, I think. I smiled at her. She froze me with a glare.

I was then told that I was reckless and feckless and childish and dishonest. I was told I was a disgrace and had let so many people down. I was told how lucky I was that this hadn't gone outside The Establishment.

I was told disappearing with my security pass was a breach of every Authority rule and law *and* breaking the Official Secrets Act. I was reminded that I'd signed legally-binding contracts to this effect. It could – if taken further – involve a prison sentence.

By this time I was more than terrified.

I then had to hand over each and every one of my documents to have them verified and signed off.

Then I was sacked. And told I could never join the Civil Service again. And escorted to the gate and off the premises.

There was no car to take me home – I was no longer one of theirs.

I stood at the bus stop and cried. I cried for me and for Scott and for Jersey and for everything... by the time the bus came I was practically incoherent.

The journey back to Harbury Green took about twenty minutes I think. I have no idea. I just slumped with my head against the window, staring out, not seeing anything, and wondering how my life could fall apart so spectacularly.

I was alone and lonely and scared – and missing Scott and Jersey more than I could even put into words.

And of course I couldn't ring Scott at Leighton Buzzard, or even write to him to tell him how it had gone, because Renza was there.

Renza would always be there.

I dragged myself off the bus in the High Street, shivering despite it being another scorching day, and kept my head down. I didn't want to face anyone. I was convinced the whole place – even if they didn't know about my work fiasco – would know that I'd once again been "living in sin" and would be delighted to see me back and looking a complete mess.

I wiped my eyes and my nose and stared in the nearest shop window to regain some sort of my composure. Now I had to go home and face Mum and Dad – disgraced and unemployed. Disgraced I knew they'd forgive, unemployed was another matter. We didn't have enough money for me to live at home and not have a job. I had to work. Everyone had to work. But, without a reference – there was obviously not going to be one from the Atomic – I knew I'd never get another decent job.

I'd ruined my entire life!

I stared into the shop window. It was the shoe shop. It sold boring old people's shoes. All year round their window display was of black and brown lace-ups.

"Assistant wanted. Full time. Apply within".

The notice was inches from my face. I sighed, and because I was wearing suitable job-applying clothes – I'd worn my navy polka dot coat dress with the white Peter Pan collar and cuffs for The Sacking – I walked in through the shoe shop's open door.

I got the job.

I was to start on Monday. The hours were 8.30 to 5.30. Wednesday was half-day closing and I'd get alternate Saturdays off. I have to wear a uniform – a dark blue skirt and light blue poplin blouse – they gave me a medium because it was all they had. I know it will swamp me. The salary wasn't great but it was certainly better than nothing.

I trudged home. Mum and Dad were both at work, and I ripped off the navy frock and put on my jeans and a T-shirt and huddled in the garden with the dogs and the cats, hating the blue sky and the sun because it reminded me of Jersey, and cried.

Then, because as I'd suspected there were dozens of new fan club applications from the girls who had been at Lords, I dragged out my Adler Tippa portable typewriter and wrote a long, long fan club letter about Narnia's Children in Jersey and what they'd be doing in the future, and about 'Livin' With You' and about anything else I could think of.

It ripped my already broken heart apart.

I read it through, then took it down to Barry to print off masses of copies. If he wondered why I looked like a zombie or why the original was splodged with tears he was kind enough not to mention it.

I spent the rest of the day folding the letters into envelopes and sending them out to fans – old and new – and, thanks to Stephan's stamp-supply, was able to post them all without having to face Mrs Nosey Norris at the post office.

And then, again, I went home and cried.

Renza's Diary
July 20th 1969

We spent a fabulous time with a friend of the band called John who lives near Heath and Reach and was in some sort of business, I forget what, and he invited us to his flat to watch the American moon landing that night. As midnight moved into the small hours of July 21st, we all crowded round his black and white television and had cider and Indian food, as we watched Neil Armstrong and Buzz Aldrin actually walk on the moon. Zak didn't think it was real and said it was all a big con, but how would we know? It was so exciting and historical. Scott and I loved it. We talked about space and Isaac Asimov and his books and lots of other things we both love.

I made sure that my uncle and auntie knew I was home so that if my parents asked they could cover for me. I didn't have time to visit them as my trip was so brief, but they didn't mind.

The whole visit passed so fast and soon I found myself holding on to Scott so tight he laughed, 'Hey, I need to breathe, and you're going to crush the life out of me,' as we said goodbye.

'I'll miss you so much.' I sobbed into his shoulder as he stroked my hair.

'I'll miss you, too, and I'll be thinking of you all the time and especially when you look at the moon, I'll be looking too.'
He held my face in his hands and kissed me so tenderly I almost fainted away. His eyes were brimming with tears and he looked so beautiful and so kissable I didn't want to leave. But John Barry would be at the station waiting for me and I had to tear myself away from him.

I cried, silently and privately, all the way from Victoria Railway station to the steps up to our flats in the strasse. Now all I could do was hold on to the memories. Until the next time.

Stella's Diary
July 21ˢᵗ 1969

Today I started work in the shoe shop. I already hated it and the uniform made me look like Little Orphan Annie. There were two older ladies and a girl from one of the outlying villages who was 16, and the manager, a grizzled old man who sat in a booth and watched us all like hawks.

The shoes were, as I knew, boring. We had to dust them when there were no customers. And climb tall ladders and lift the millions of boxes down and dust them too. And make sure they were all back in size, style, colour order. It was mind-numbing.

And when we did have a customer everyone else disappeared into the stock room and left me to it. I spent all day shoving hideous shoes on to ancient sweaty smelly feet, trying to ignore distorted, weeping corns and bunions.

It was clearly my penance.

And my first day was made even worse because I hadn't slept. Last night history was made when America landed their astronauts on the moon! Neil Armstrong and Buzz Aldrin *walked* on the moon! I stayed up all night, watching it with Mum and Dad and the cats and dogs, and could hardly believe what we were seeing. It was so exciting, so incredible – so almost impossible to take in – but also for me, so painful because I knew Scott and Renza would be watching it together.

I physically hurt. Everything hurt. I knew it would be like this.

Stella's Diary
July 31st 1969

I'm not proud of this diary entry – but I need to write these things down to tell the whole story.

Vix had been such a good friend since I got back. The best. She'd spent a lot of time with me, filling me in on all the local gossip and everything that had happened while I was away. She hadn't once said "I told you so". Not once. She had suggested we go out for a girls night out – like we used to – but I couldn't. I just couldn't.

She'd even said I ought to go for a drink with her and her Jeff – but I couldn't do that either. It wouldn't be fair to them. Because they'd be together and happy and I'd be the broken-hearted gooseberry and ruin their evening. I'd promised her I'd get glammed up one day and we'd go and hit the town again – but not yet. Not yet.

Instead I'd stayed in, every night after the hateful, hateful days in the shoe shop, and written to Scott.

I'd written him a ridiculous letter every single day. And, to my shame, sent them. I'd told him about what happened at work that day (usually nothing), how I hated my job, how I was now reading Dennis Wheatley's *They Used Dark Forces* where the characters travel through their enforced-dream-state to meet on the astral plain when they can't be together in real life, and that I'd tried this to be with him while we're asleep!

Seriously! Absolute tosh – but it was true – I'd done it, and of course it didn't work, but I was that desperate.

Desperate. Each letter has been more and more pathetically desperate.

I'd told him stuff about Vix and Jeff – even though he doesn't know them and wouldn't be remotely interested – and about my upcoming hospital appointment and about that old song that goes along the lines of "I go to sleep and imagine that you're here with me..." and so many more boring and insane things.

Anything to make it seem as if we were still together.

And, even worse, I'd phoned him at Leighton Buzzard a couple of times, but he'd been very distant and distracted so I'd just said goodbye and walked away from the phone box in tears.

I guessed Renza was there now so he really wouldn't want to talk to me. He probably wouldn't even open my letters. I sort of hoped he wouldn't. It was killing me, remembering how happy, how in love we were such a very, very short time before.

I know he'd said when Narnia's Children left Leighton Buzzard they'd go back to Jersey for a while, and the only update he did bother to tell me in one of the painful phone calls, was that after Jersey he'd probably share with Stephan in London until a permanent place for the band turned up.

He hadn't written to me at all and I knew how pathetic my letters sounded and that I was clearly now just irritating him by phoning him too – but I couldn't help it. I was being ridiculously feeble – I knew it – and should have had more pride and accepted that it was all over – but I couldn't.

I was clinging to the memories and the mad happiness amid the wreckage of our love affair. My heart was breaking and it hurt so much.

Stella's Diary
August 9th 1969

On Sundays, and my Saturdays off from the gruesome shoe shop, I'd been going out with Mum and Dad in the car, taking the dogs for walks over miles of countryside, or round the perimeters of stately homes – Mum loved a stately home! Most of the time I'd walked a bit then hurried back to the car and huddled up on the back seat alone and read. Dennis Wheatley of course. And cried.

I'd been home from Jersey for nearly four weeks and every day was still awful. I got through my days in a sort of cold daze, breaking down when I remembered how wonderful it been – and now there was only this emptiness for the rest of my life.

At least now, because I had no idea if Scott was in Jersey or Leighton Buzzard, I'd stopped writing the pathetic letters. I bet he was glad about that!

One of the weird things at the moment though, was how much I suddenly hated certain records. Oh, not any that reminded me of Narnia's Children, but new records on Radio One. I think it was because they were now part of this lonely, horrid life. My two major hates were 'Marrakesh Express' and 'Sugar, Sugar'. They were both in the chart and being played everywhere all the time and I loathed them with a vengeance and knew I always would.

But my life wasn't all bad because tonight, for the first time, I went out with the girls. With Vix, and Debbie and Sally – who had both elevated me to some sort of legendary superstar status because I'd broken the Official Secrets Act to run away with my rock star lover! – and a few of our other mutual friends and everyone was really kind to me and said I looked fab with a suntan and was lovely and skinny, and didn't mention Scott at all.

I wore the black trousers I'd bought with Eva – yep, cried my eyes out again – and the Julie Driscoll top – all dressed in black seemed very appropriate. We went in to Oxford, to our favourite Chinese restaurant in Summertown to start with where I ate practically nothing and refused to open my fortune cookie just in case, and then on to the Stage Club.

I'd always enjoyed going there – and at least I knew they'd only have a DJ and not a live group. I knew I couldn't have coped with a live group.

It was dark and lively and packed – and nothing at all like Lords, thank goodness – and because I'd been drinking cider – I doubt if anyone had heard of rye and dry and even if they had I'd never drink it again – and not eaten, I was a bit numb and floaty, even managed to enjoy myself in a miserable sort of way.

The DJ played The Stones' new record, 'Honky Tonk Women', and everyone rushed up to dance. I just stood there and swayed a bit. It was the most animated I'd been for weeks – even though Mick Jagger's voice reminded me of Zak.

Then the DJ, in his phoney transatlantic voice, said he was going to slow things down and to get ready for a smooch.

He played 'Nights in White Satin'.

It undid me. Completely. I barged through the swaying couples and managed to stagger into the Ladies and leaned against one of the sinks, clutching the taps for support. I could still hear it. Still hear those words...

"... oh, how I love you..."

I howled then. Really howled. A girl came out of one of the cubicles, looked at me in horror and ran out of the door.

Vix came in, searching for me, took one look at me and gathered me up in her arms.

'Don't...' I managed to splutter. 'I'll ruin your dress...'

'Bugger the dress,' Vix said, moving me gently away from the sink and splashing some cold water on my face. 'Come on, Stella... cry it out...'

The Ladies' door opened.

'Get out!' Vix howled. 'Now! Clear off! This lav is out of

449

order!'

The door closed again.

I sniffed back the tears that clogged not only my eyes but also my nose and my throat.

'Don't try to stop crying,' Vix said, manfully ignoring the mess I'd made of her brand new blue and white gingham Bardot frock. 'Let it all out. You'll feel better when you've...'

The door opened again. Vix got rid of whoever it was in the same way as before.

'It's all my fault,' I hiccupped. 'All my own fault. I knew this would happen. I bloody knew. And yet I kept kidding myself that it wouldn't end like this. I hate myself for being such a fool!'

'Oh, Stella,' Vix smoothed my hair away from my face. 'It's no one's fault. It happened. You fell in love. You've had the best time, probably a better time than most girls can even dream of. Yes, ok, it's probably over – but you've done it and had it and one day you'll look back and enjoy the memories.'

'I don't want memories!' I howled. 'I want Scott!'

'Ok... right now that's not what you want to hear – but trust me, it's true. Now, wash the worst of the gunge off your face – I don't think we're going to be able to rescue your eyelashes or the sequins... I've got some mascara though, so we might be able to do a bit of a repair job... come on, Stella. You can do this.'

Vix dived into one of the cubicles and came back with a mile of toilet roll and got me to blow my nose and wipe my eyes.

'That's better,' she looked at me. 'Trust Auntie Vix – ooh, no – I think I said that once before and look what happened. Anyway, come here... let's sort you out and turn you into a human being again.'

Between us we sort of managed to make my blotched and bloated face and washed-out eyes look reasonably acceptable.

'Thank you,' I sniffed. 'I don't deserve you.'

'Don't be daft,' Vix grinned, hugging me. 'It's what best friends are for. You'd do the same for me, wouldn't you?'

I nodded.

'Good — then let's go and face the music — oh, not *that* music — that one's finished.' She linked her arm through mine. 'Tell you what, I'll go and ask the DJ to play some Engelbert shall I? That way we'll all be in bloody tears.'

And I actually laughed.

Stella's Diary
September 7th 1969

I hadn't written anything in this diary for ages. There hadn't been much to say. However, since the night in the Stage Club I'd tried really hard to take Vix's advice and pull myself together. No one could change my life but me, I realised that, and despite the heartache, I made some tentative plans for the future – my future – my future without Scott.

I was still working in the shoe shop but I hated it more every day. That was the first thing I could change – find somewhere else to work, or find another way of life altogether. I'd started spending a lot of time in the library, making plans – some of them really mad, others, I thought, might, just might, make a difference and give me a purpose again. In the meantime, I'd sent out a lot more fan club stuff – again some of it totally plucked from the air because I was so out of touch with the band now. I'd also had the next hospital appointment and it wasn't the greatest news.

There will be further operations to remove all the rest of the old scar tissue and to deal with any fresh lesions inside me – and possibly a full hysterectomy because everything was such a mess, even though I'm so young. They told me all this in medical detail and sorrowful voices, but I didn't care. I really didn't care.

I tried putting on a brave face all the time and Mum and Dad and Vix were being so kind, but I should have listened to them all those months ago – I should have known this is how it would be without Scott. I'd played with fire and now I'd been well and truly burned.

However, there had been one bright spot – although I'd told no one about it – I'd had a very brief letter from Scott! Oh, nothing romantic or anything like that, (it started "Dear Stella" – not anything more affectionate or Twinkle any more) but telling me – in case I needed to know for the fan club stuff –

that Stephan had found Narnia's Children a flat in Pinner, and the address – and the phone number. And he'd ended it with "love, Scott". No kisses.

It was better than nothing. At least I knew where he was now – and if he hadn't wanted me to know, he wouldn't have told me, would he?

Renza's Diary
September 12th 1969

Scott decided to write at last. It's only the second letter I've received since I got back from my visit in July. Today's letter was from North Kensington where he's staying at Stephan's flat whilst a new place is found for the band. He thought they'd got one in Pinner, Harrow, but it wasn't confirmed at the time of writing. The others are all staying with friends in other parts of London for the time being.

Despite all his talk of me spending time with him in Jersey and my saving up and booking time off work, he's sorry he didn't make it happen, things got too hectic.

Reading this I started to panic, worrying that now our relationship had moved on in a grown-up way, he wasn't interested any longer; that's the real reason my trip to Jersey fell through I bet. My mind was a mess. I thought everything between us had been sorted and now I can't be sure of anything. He didn't want me after-all.

They've been gigging all over the country and things seem to be going well. They'd been in the studio again and recorded eight songs which had been sent to them by a guy who's a really well known song-writer. They'll be recording a song called 'Morning Papers' as their next single, and the B side is possibly going to be ' Putting it All Behind Me.'

A Radio One producer will be producing it and so that should help plug it on radio. They're not using the same record producer who produced 'Livin' with You.' Scott didn't say why, but mentioned that their managers had just moved to really plush offices in London now that Doc Holliday was such a star and making them loads of money. Stephan who is still their Personal Manager is going to earn vast amounts from Doc and his band. Doc as well. No wonder he has a posh flat.

There were the usual declarations of undying love and how much he missed me. He said as he was writing he was playing his favourite record at the moment, 'Gotta See Jane,' by R. Dean Taylor, and it made missing me so hard. He said he always substituted Renza for Jane when singing it, and thought that would make me happy. Oh yeah! He wanted me to know he was having a guilty conscience about treating me badly recently, not writing often, and being a bit quiet on the phone, and he wanted to make it up to me soon. I could feel my heart filling with happiness as I read it, but in the back of my head the little voice of doubt started chattering again. What to believe?

His mum, Eva, who I've yet to meet, sent her love and said I can visit whenever I like, and I could go for Christmas if I wanted. I don't know if I can get time off – but I can try.

The last few months have been so difficult. I've been job hunting in England, sending out endless applications for job vacancies I've found in good quality magazines like The Lady and English Newspapers, a bit half-heartedly because of Scott's ever-changing attitude; nothing from him for ages and then he'd write again of his love and how he can't stand being away from me any longer, so I've started looking for a job in earnest again.

To be honest I think I might get a job in England whether we're together or not. I'm so fed up here and I need to get on with life. I can't – won't – work at the base forever, but Dad says I can't leave home legally until I'm eighteen and he won't let me have my own passport until then. At the moment I use my parent's passport to travel. It looks as if I'll be stuck here until my birthday next year.

Heidi and I have been out shopping now and again, she is fanatically into clothes, and we've been out to have coffee and cake: English people go to the pub, Germans eat cake. She's called round a few times to see me – Mum seems to approve – and I've spent a little time with her at her home chatting about England mainly. She loves hearing me talk as it helps improve her English and she is helping me with my German. She's heavily into British history, even the war, which I find a bit embarrassing discussing with her, she being a German after-all. She knows all about Scott and thinks it is too romantic for words. Her fiancé is a bit boring she says, and I have to wonder why she is engaged to him. She met Klaus recently when I was in Dortmund with him, at a disco, she was there with Mr Excitement himself and we bumped into them. We shared a table and she kept giving Klaus the eye. He didn't seem too interested but I'm afraid I couldn't care less. I wouldn't be surprised if she'd given him her number.

Yep, that's the most exciting thing that's happened to me in ages, well, not if you include 'Hair,' which Isolde and I went to see in Essen when she was home from College.

Poor Isolde nearly passed away in shock when the cast of men decided to walk across our seats from the stage, naked as the day they were born. I had to laugh at her poor face. I'd been half expecting it having heard all about it in England last year. But no one prepared us for the live sex on stage. I've never been so interested in my own shoes in years. She sat and giggled, hanging on to my arm as I gazed steadfastly at my shoes, tears of laughter and embarrassment washing my black eyeliner down my cheeks. She kept nattering away in German as she tried not to look. I hadn't a clue what she was saying but laughter is laughter in any language, and both of us were doubled up. How we didn't get chucked out I've no idea. Everyone kept telling us to shhh!

I kept recalling the poster of dishy Oliver Tobias in Carnaby Street, advertising Hair, when I went with Gideon, and one thing was as plain as the er…nose on his face; the German actor was no Oliver Tobias!

I hope Mum and Dad don't discover what 'Hair's' all about. I told them it was a musical set in a hairdressers, when they got tickets for us to go. They think Isolde is studying hair dressing at college.

Stella Deacon has been in touch with Sophia and Jasper,

writing to them as Fan Club Secretary, and we've had a few exchanges of letter as well. The fan club address is in Harbury Green, Berkshire. It sounds familiar but I can't think why. I know I've never been there. Anyway, Stella seems very nice and efficient. The kids enjoy hearing about it all – it's exciting for them.

Sometimes I'm tempted to write to Stella and ask her if she knows whether Scott has other girls or not, but how stupid that would be. Besides, she might think I'm some stupid kid and laugh at me. What if she told Scott what I'd said – he'd go nuts if he found out I've been checking up on him.

So it's just as well I can go out with Klaus now and again, and Heidi when she's not with her fiancé. I'd go round the bend otherwise. I don't see much of Isolde as she's mostly away at College, which is a pity, she and I get on really well and she likes a good laugh. There's only so much reading and listening to music on my own I can stomach, so when I get a chance to go out with Heidi or Klaus, I'll go.

I shall rub it in when I next write to Scott, just to throw him off balance like he does me. Somehow I think I need to let him know I'm not sitting here withering away waiting to hear from him, even if that is exactly what I'm doing.

Stella's Diary

September 26th 1969 – my 21st birthday…

I'm not sure where to start with writing about today. My 21st birthday. It was all a bit higgledy-piggledy really. Ok – Mum and Dad had said ages ago that they wanted me to have a birthday dinner at home, because Mum wanted to cook something special. My grandparents were going to be there and I'd invited Vix and Jeff much earlier in the year.

I had also, back in the distant happy days, invited Scott.

And, make of this what you will, I phoned him in Pinner and told him the invitation still stood. I know... I know... Anyway, he'd been fairly non-committal – disinterested, even – no surprise there, but yesterday I'd had another brief letter from him:

'Dear Stella, if the invite to your 21st still stands I can catch a train and be in Harbury Green by 6 o'clock, I've checked. I must catch the last train back to London as we have a gig on Saturday. I can't afford a card or a present but I would like to be there if your parents will allow me to come. Please ring me. Love, Scott.'

It had completely thrown me, I must admit – I didn't know whether to laugh or cry and wondered what the hell he'd told Renza – and oh, yes, of course I wanted him to be there and to see him again, more than anything in the world – but would it be like ripping the scab off a wound that had just, only just, started to heal?

I'd told Mum. She just said: "if you want him to be here, then that's perfectly all right with us. I think it might be a bit awkward, but it's your big day. I don't want him to ruin it for you, but if you think it's the right thing to do, then of course he's more than welcome. Yes, phone him, and tell him we'd like to see him – after all, his parents gave you such wonderful hospitality, so it would be rude of us not to do the same. It's up to you, Stella."

I rang him. It was an odd conversation. A bit distant and slightly stilted but friendly enough. Certainly not loving or romantic, but I hadn't expected that. And he said he'd be there.

I didn't offer to meet him from the train or anything, even though I really, really wanted to. I knew I had to play it cool. Anyway, Harbury Green was a small place, even if he didn't remember where my house was – and why would he after all this time? – he'd be able to find his own way easily enough.

This morning, Mum and Dad had to go to work, and I had to be in the dreaded shoe shop by 8.30 – on my 21st birthday! – so they gave me their presents early: a brand new, latest model Singer sewing machine, a fab huge Lowry block print (Lowry was my favourite artist and one of the ones I'd spent two years studying and trying to emulate in my Art A level), and a silver bangle to add to the collection I always wore on my right arm.

I was in tears. I hadn't expected anything because I'd already had the suitcase. I didn't deserve any of it. I knew how hard they must have saved and gone without to give me such fab things. And all I'd done was lie and bring trouble to their door and be a complete misery!

I hugged them and cried and cried and said an incoherent thank you over and over again.

Then we all had to go to work – and it was just another day.

Until the evening.

Mum had been preparing and cooking for ages and the dogs and cats were getting in the way and the house smelled gorgeous. I hoped I smelled pretty good too – I'd used all the Sea Jade toiletries and made a special effort with my hair and make-up – and I'd worn a bright orange micro-mini dress – made last year but never worn – and the long white boots.

Vix – in her favourite pink thigh skimmer – and Jeff arrived at the same time as my grandparents (who'd clubbed together and bought me a tiny heart shaped gold wristwatch on a bracelet – so beautiful – I cried all over them too!), and Vix and Jeff gave me another lovely silver bangle for the collection.

I'd had lots of cards, too. I was being so spoiled!

My nans both went out into the kitchen to help with the dinner and Dad gave the men a beer. I took Vix into my downstairs bed-sit room and told her about Scott.

'And he's coming? You're bloody mad! Don't expect me to speak to him!'

'Please, Vix – I know it's not right, but... oh, hell... look, I don't suppose he'll even turn up – but if he does, be nice to him, for my sake.'

'Nice to him? I'll ring his bloody neck!'

I laughed. I knew she'd be ok. She'd give me hell afterwards, but like Mum and Dad, I knew she wouldn't do anything to upset my birthday and I loved her for it.

Scott arrived at 6.45. I opened the door to him and nearly fainted. Oh that sounds so pathetic again – but it was so incredible seeing him again after so long. He was wearing all black – which reminded me of Jersey – including the long coat, and his hair, still very long by normal standards, had been cut a bit. He was still the most beautiful boy in the world.

'Um... hello... come in...'

'Sorry I'm a bit late – the train... er – happy birthday.'

'Thank you.'

We stared at one another. Not knowing what to do or say. It was so weird after everything we'd shared. I still loved him so very much.

'You look lovely,' he smiled at me. 'And I'm so pleased your parents wanted me to be here.'

Not exactly true.

'They'll be pleased to see you again. Come in and have a drink.'

He walked into our still-scruffy, still-untidy, still-homely living room. The dogs bounced round him and he patted them all. I introduced him to my grandparents and Jeff. He smiled nervously at everyone, Dad gave him a beer and Vix gave him "a look".

Then Mum, hair awry, glasses falling off her nose, popped through from the kitchen and smiled warmly. 'Scott! How nice to see you again. Are your parents well? Good. Leave your coat on the chair there with the rest of them. You've got a drink? Dinner won't be long, dear... try and find a seat...'

'Thank you,' he smiled at Mum. 'It's very kind of you – and I love your home.'

Mum beamed and vanished back into the kitchen.

I loved my mum.

We had dinner all crowded round the table in the kitchen. Mum had pulled out all the stops and produced an amazing meal of duck in cherry sauce, with sauté potatoes and garden peas. And a chocolate cake and cream for pudding. And there was a bottle of Mateus Rose on the table, as well as beer and Babycham.

It was fab!

The conversation and laughter roared round the table – we were such a mixed bunch. I didn't speak to Scott at all, but Mum and Dad and Jeff did, and both my nans. Vix ignored him and chatted to my grandads. It was nowhere near as awkward as I'd imagined – but very, very surreal.

Scott was here. Here. Really here. It kept going through my head. It was all like some bizarre dream.

Then they all toasted me and wished me happy birthday and my nans gave me a cardboard Key of the Door, and Mum and Dad gave me the real thing, and everyone laughed. Scott caught my eye and gave me the slow, sexy smile. I grinned back at him. It was going to be ok.

As soon as we'd all said thank you and how gorgeous the meal had been and offered to help clear and wash up and Mum had chivvied us out of the way and was scraping the left-overs for the animals, I grabbed some more beers and dragged Scott, Vix and Jeff through to my bed-sit room.

Jeff and Vix immediately sank down on to the floor cushions and started going through my LPs, deciding to play The Lovin'

Spoonful.

I sat next to Scott on the studio couch. Not touching. Just side-by-side.

He looked at me. 'Are you ok? Your letters sounded so...'

I blushed. 'Sorry about the letters... yes, I'm fine, thanks. Hate the shoe shop, but otherwise I'm ok. You? And the new flat? And the rest of the band?'

He shrugged. 'All ok. Nothing much changes. Except Rich has left.'

I hoped Rich had decided to settle down with his nurse girlfriend and hoped he'd be happy.

I knew we couldn't tiptoe round any longer.

'And how's Renza?'

He sighed. 'She's fine, too. And back in Germany with her family. She hopes to be back in the UK soon, though.'

'Oh, good. That'll be nice for you both.'

God! This was ridiculous!

'Talk to me...' I leaned against him. 'Properly. Oh, don't take any notice of them,' I indicated Jeff and Vix, now entwined on the cushions, 'they're otherwise engaged. Scott, please talk to me.'

He leaned back and pulled me against him. It was lovely to be in his arms again. The Lovin' Spoonful were singing 'A Younger Girl'. It was so appropriate, we both laughed. And then he told me. It wasn't all I wanted to hear, some of it was pretty heart-breaking really, but it made a lot of sense.

He and Renza had moved their love affair on. He was, for the first time, in a committed grown-up relationship with her. He loved her. Was in love with her. And he wouldn't and couldn't cheat on her. I tried not to look surprised at this point, I mean, I'd assumed they'd been sleeping together from the start – but clearly not. I kind of read between the lines here – he didn't need to spell it out.

I actually admired him for this. He'd just broken what was left of my heart, but it did prove that he was a nice boy, with principles – even if he was also a sexy rock-god superstar. He loved Renza, totally, was going to marry her, not yet – but one day – and yes, she was still, and always would be, the love of his life.

And, it also meant that he had at no time been sleeping with us both – which oddly made me happy – oddly, because it obviously meant our relationship had now also changed. So, where did that leave me?

Still hanging on in there, apparently. He said it was a mess, and he was really confused and he didn't want to lose me, but...

'But things can't be as they once were, can they?' I said. 'And please, don't say we can still be friends because we can't. I can't.'

He took my face in his hands and turned me to look at him. 'I know. Oh, I'm so screwed up. I wish...'

'That you'd never met me?'

'Sometimes...' he smiled. 'No, not really. It's been fun – more than fun. Even though I've felt guilty and mean and unfair to Renza.'

'But it's ok now. We both know where we stand – you and me, I mean – not Renza. And Renza need never know about – about us.'

'I hope she never does.' He looked at his watch. 'Oh God – I'll miss the train! I'm going to have to go. I don't want to, but...'

'It's ok,' I untangled myself and stood up and hauled him to his feet. 'I know... thank you for coming. You've made my birthday really special.'

Scott moved slightly away. 'I'll just go and say goodbye and thank you to your parents and get my coat.'

As soon as he'd left the room, Vix looked up. 'Hopefully you've got the message now.'

'You were *listening*?'

'Course I was. It was better than *Coronation Street*.'

I shook my head and barged out of the room. Scott was in the tiny hallway.

'I've said my goodbyes and thank-yous. Your family are fab, Stella. You're very lucky. Oh, and I know I said I couldn't afford anything but I got you this...' He pulled a paper bag out of his coat pocket. 'Look at it when I've gone. Ring me – soon. I'd like you to see the new flat. And, thank you...'

He kissed me gently. Briefly. Setting me on fire. Again.

Then I opened the door and he was gone into the darkness.

I leaned back against the door and looked inside the bag. It was a book. I took it out: *The Lion, The Witch and the Wardrobe*.... Narnia – of course!

I smiled and read what he'd written inside:

'*Always remember 7th December 1968*'

As if I'd ever forget.

Renza's Diary
October 11th 1969

Dad handed me a letter this afternoon with a Jersey stamp on it. It wasn't from Scott, the hand-writing was far too neat, a bit like Mum's actually. I could hardly open it my hands were shaking so much. It's the invitation, I'm going to Jersey, I thought, as I opened the rose perfumed pages with trembling fingers.

'Is that from his mother?' Dad asked trying to see what was written.

'Think so,' I said as I unfolded the pages and looked at the address. Of course it was.

'What's she want? She's never written before, not even after all the promises of invitations from your hippy.'

'What's this about an invitation?' Mum came downstairs and tried to grab the letter but I was far too quick and raced into the bathroom, locking the door.

'Sorry, got to go.' I shouted through the door. I wanted to read it first for a change.

There were several pages; she introduced herself as Scott's mum – as if I wouldn't know, we'd spoken on the phone before I left England – and apologised for not writing sooner. She said that her life is hectic and with a small child to look after, time slipped away all too easily. I nearly laughed out loud, she should look after five flipping kids and then she'd know what hectic really was.

She said Scott had told her we're getting married one day, but not too soon she hoped, because she was far too young to become a grandmother and as light followed day, she said, that's what would happen next. Not on your bloody life, I muttered, more than a bit annoyed. I'm never having kids. The flipping nerve.

Her name's Eva, and I am to call her Eva – I'd never had to call her anything before – and she was sure we'd eventually be

465

great friends, she couldn't wait to see me – *oh yeah, right* – and I was welcome in Jersey any time I wanted. Her home would be my home – everyone was keen to meet the love of Scott's life – *well, not that keen otherwise I'd have been over by now*. She's heard so much about me, seen my photos, Scott was right, I was indeed a beauty – *I'm going to throw up* – and the band always talk about me with great affection, she felt she knew me already.

Eva – well, she said call her Eva, went on to tell me about Jersey and life over there and what we could do together when I eventually visit – *eventually didn't sound like an invitation was being offered any time soon* – and I flipped to the last page to see if there was a mention of a visit. There wasn't. I turned back to where she was telling me about how wonderful Jersey was.

Their lives were very relaxed and they – she and Scott's step-father, Dan – didn't stand on ceremony, she said, so guests would just muck in and, as I was no doubt a great cook, having so much experience according to Scott, I'd be a great asset when I visited them. Well, that's nice Scott, exchanging one skivvy job for another by the sound of it, should I ever visit, which I'm seriously thinking of declining should I ever, ever get an invitation. Cheeky bloody woman!

Then she dropped the bombshell. Stella Deacon, who she was sure I'd heard about, had been over for a few weeks in the summer – *I bloody knew it, my instincts were right. The two-timing rat! A few weeks, weeks!* – I felt sick and dizzy and had to take some deep breaths before I could bear to read on – and so it hadn't been convenient – *convenient!* – to ask me over at the same time. Stella, was there on fan-club business at Stephan's request, and staying at Eva's was cheaper than a hotel, she wanted to assure me, nothing more. *Nothing more!* Just saying that implied there was, *something more!* I'm going to recommend Scott has his eyes and ears tested; Stella's been living in his home for weeks and he's been totally unaware of it.

Pain gripped my heart and I felt a cold sweat run through my body. I put the letter on the vanity unit and ran my wrists under the cold tap.

'What *are* you doing in there, come out now?' Mum yelled and banged on the door.

'Use the one upstairs,' I yelled back. My voice sounded strangled, even to me, as tears streamed down my face.

'I want to see that letter,' she banged again. 'Now!'

'Go away, it's private, go away.' I sat on the loo seat and wiped my hands and tears with the hand towel.

'We told you to forget him, he's not going to be bothered with you while you're here and he's there. What did his mum say? It's from her isn't it? It's not his writing. Got her to tell you he's chucking you?'

Eva's letter prattled on about what a nice girl Stella is, such a good cook – *what's with this cooking lark? Anyone would think she's really in need of staff to do her chores for her, not visitors.* She wrote about Scott's half-sister, Holly, and their horses and Narnia's Children gigging all over the island, and how she hoped I'd enjoy the music scene over there, when I visit. *When, not if then!* The band are becoming famous and quite the celebrities on the island. *Big flipping deal.* Reading it was making me cross. Perhaps that's her intention, to put me off Scott by dropping hints about Stella – letting me down gently – giving Stella a clear field.

Mum's given up banging on the door and I've managed to sneak up to my room without being spotted, to finish Eva's letter in peace. There's no way I'm going to let anyone else read it, especially the marriage bit!

For some reason I needed to put Gary Puckett and the Union Gap on my record player, 'Young Girl,' which I love, seemed just right to listen to as I read on.

Oh great, wonderful, Stella has been to the flat in Pinner a few times. Flipping news to me! More fan-club stuff I suppose. Why is she telling me all this? Bloody wonderful. I can't cry any more, I feel too angry. I need to digest it all.

I don't think I'm going to mention any of this to Scott when I write or talk to him on the phone. I'll just wait and see if he mentions any of it. I'll reply to his mum, politely and I won't rise to her bait either. Why would Eva make a point of telling me about Stella? Trying to warn me off gently?

Meantime, I'm going to buy some new outfits for the series of parties and dinner dances at the Mess throughout next week, when the Silver Anniversary of the base in the village is being celebrated, with loads of army and MoD bigwigs and German guests from the Rathaus (Town Hall), the local Council, and whatever. More flipping oompah I suppose.

I've seen a couple of really gorgeous cocktail dresses in a boutique in Dusseldorf which Heidi thinks I should buy for the early evening events, and I've seen a fabulous long skirt in heavy black and gold brocade which will go well with some new lace blouses I bought last time we went shopping. They're classic styles so I'm not too worried about wearing them – very Audrey Hepburn. I'm all right for shoes.

When I reply to Eva I shall make a big deal of the celebrations and my new clothes and mention Klaus and how wonderful he is. Put that in your pipe and smoke it! Hopefully she'll tell Scott. I might even tell Scott what a wonderful time I've been having, going out with Klaus, dancing, and anything else I can think of to make him as angry and hurt as I feel now. Playing softly in the background on British Forces Radio, Marvin Gaye's singing, 'I Heard it Through the Grapevine.' Ain't that a fact!

Renza's Diary
October 14th 1969

Things have been hectic, what with shopping for the celebrations with Heidi and then with Mum, I haven't had chance to read Scott's latest letter properly until now, let alone reply to his mother's letter. We've been working later at the base too, and I've had to help Mum a lot – the German builders are working in the cellar doing something or other, so we've been up at 5am because they come just before 6.30am and its pandemonium getting the kids up, breakfasted and ready for school before they turn up.

Thankfully the kids are playing on the swings with some German kids and Mum and Dad have gone for a walk, so I can read his letter in peace.

He sent it from their new address in Pinner, Harrow, and started off apologising for not writing for ages. Nothing new about that. He also included two pound notes towards a phone call he wanted me to make. He said he found it too difficult to get through to Germany, spending ages trying, and so it would be easier if I rang him instead. Well, at last he was paying for the calls. So far he's cost me an arm and a leg each time I've called him. Not that we chat that often any more.

They've got an upstairs flat in a big old house and there are three school teachers in the bottom flat. There are three bedrooms and he shares the biggest one with Mo, and Zak and Joss have their own. I can't help wondering if the wonderful Stella shacks up with him as well. I'm becoming bitter and twisted since Eva's letter; my imagination has been working overtime.

There's no more on Rich – he left suddenly, Scott said. No one knew why or where he'd gone. The news upset me. Rich has always been my friend, my ally. I'll miss him very much. But there's still Mo so it's not that bad, if I ever get to see him again – the way things are...

469

They liked Pinner, the flat overlooks the main Pinner Road so it's very busy there, and 'happening.' They've had some great gigs since moving there, and even ended back in Wing, near Leighton Buzzard for some of them. One was at a huge equestrian centre, in a sort of an arena, with over five hundred people. . .

'Livin' with You,' will be released in America in January, so a lot of hopes are being pinned on having a hit. Narnia's Children appear not to have made any money yet from all their hard work. But what they could potentially earn, even if the record did only marginally well in America, seemed to excite him – to me it was all a dream for the future.

'When are you coming over? You mentioned March in your last letter, please make it sooner. I'm going mad without you.' He wrote. 'Of course I still want to marry you and I always will, but personally I think that to get married at the moment would be rather stupid, we don't have any money! If any of our records make it then that would change everything. I love you and want to see you more than anything and I hope and pray you will come to London to live so I can see you every day and every night.'

I was so shocked reading this. Upset, hurt and disappointed – and it doesn't matter how often I've read it, I still can't work it all out. I'm confused and feel so unwanted, yet he says he loves me and wants me to come over... But then there's Eva's letter. I just don't know what's going on, especially with declarations of undying love again and then putting off getting married, not that I want to do it any time soon, I'm not stupid.

'Don't think I've changed my mind about marrying you, because I haven't and I hope it can be soon. Agreed, people have got married for love without money, but it is pretty futile I think.'

I'm beginning to wonder if he has a split personality, like Mum. That'd be just my luck.

Totally numbed by what he'd written, it's taken me a while

to digest the bit about Stephan and Doc Holliday and The Cards. Doc has sold over 2 million records (of 'The Egyptian') in England and America and Scott's calculated what it's worth to Stephan. A fortune. I still can't take that amount of money in, even though I think he's mentioned it before. I know he wishes the band were earning like that. However hard they work, they never have any money. It's so unfair.

I'm so confused. I rang him as soon as I could get to the post room, and it was wonderful, he was warm and loving in the things he said to me and, when I asked about getting married, reassured me that he wants to, but not yet. But I never thought we were going to get married any time soon anyway.

I asked him about Stella Deacon. I couldn't help myself, it sort of shot out of my mouth before I could stop myself.

I said I've found out in a letter from his mum, which arrived out of the blue a few days ago, that Stella's been over to Jersey to stay with his family, and that she's often at the Pinner flat for weekends. I told him I was interested to know if his eyesight has improved and if he's managed to catch sight of the lesser spotted Stella lurking in Jersey and Pinner, since he's always maintained he never sees her. I said I'm amazed his mum managed to have her as a house guest right under his very nose, without him knowing.

He was shocked, I could tell. He kept silent. *Probably safer. Give yourself time to think up an excuse.* So I said I was surprised Eva wanted to write to me, and he found his voice and said he thought it's because she knows we're getting married, and wants to get to know me. I said I'd not written back yet, but I would. I pressed him about Stella, reminding him to make an appointment at the optician's, since he's obviously going blind! He went very quiet again. This really annoyed me. I hate nagging but I couldn't help myself.

He mumbled something which sounded like 'I've never seen her in Pinner.'

'Well', I said, 'she must be invisible or something, the flat surely wasn't that big!' The stay in Jersey was never satisfactorily explained. I could tell he really couldn't think what to say. I told him Eva said Stella was apparently there on fan-club business for Stephan, and it was cheaper for Stella to stay with her than pay for a hotel. He muttered an apology for not telling me about Jersey because he knew it might upset me, but there's nothing to worry about. He didn't pass any comment when I told him I didn't believe him. I didn't want to nag him, so in the end let it all pass. For now. I'll bide my time.

Stella Deacon. I keep trying to picture her and what she's like. Older than me apparently, obviously very sophisticated, beautiful no doubt, and a writer too. I've gleaned something about her from what she writes in the band newsletters. She's met so many famous people I just bet she's the height of fashion.

Living in London the band has to be surrounded by beautiful and sophisticated women, all fashionable and really cool. How I hate being stuck in this bloody horrid backward place.

I really don't know what to think about Stella and Scott. It keeps niggling in the back of my mind and I am trying to dismiss it, but there it is, popping up all the time; a little bit of the green-eyed monster is beginning to lurk there – it's not very nice having such thoughts. Stella appears to be more involved with the band and especially Scott, and what he's doing than he's willing to tell me. The sooner I got back to England the better.

Stella's Diary
October 17th 1969 – Pinner...

I'd sent out another batch of fan club letters – all about what Narnia's Children *might* be doing in the future weeks because I actually don't *know* and have only picked up some bits of gossip from Scott and the rest of the band – on my way to the station to catch the train to London and then on to Pinner. Yes – on a Friday – because I'd left the shoe shop! I'd got other things lined up and leaving that awful, awful shop was one of the best things I'd ever done.

I was starting to get myself sorted out at last.

I'd been to the flat in Pinner a few times since my birthday, just to see Scott and say hi really, but today's visit was because I needed to clear up something I couldn't do over the phone.

Narnia's Children had the upstairs half of a big house on the main Pinner road: it was scruffy and a bit grubby and rather dingy and cold. There were three bedrooms and Scott shared the double with Mo. Zak and Joss had single rooms and live-in girlfriends now.

It simply wasn't the same any more. It wasn't just because there were other girls there – I took no notice of them and they had never really spoken to me – it was just – oh, I don't know – weird. Such a strange atmosphere.

I honestly couldn't be bothered to get to know the girls. I had nothing at all in common with them They were very glamorous and with-it and very confident and looked like models or pop stars and were about as far from the Dolly Rockers as you could get.

Although I had been amazed to discover that Zak's now-live-in girlfriend – all fake tan and cropped bleached hair and way-out clothes – was Prue!

Yes, Prue! The neatly-dressed little Dolly Rocker from Lords who had stalked him so relentlessly! She'd changed out of all recognition – and never seemed very happy when I saw her.

Maybe the reality wasn't as fab as the dream had been? Was it ever?

Zak seemed to have changed too – no longer jokey and funny, he seemed short-tempered and angry most of the time, and Joss simply ignored me. Mo was still friendly, but it really was no longer the same.

Those lovely, innocent, carefree, magical happy days at Leighton Buzzard – and yes, Jersey – were just like a dream now. It was all harsh and unfriendly in that flat, and everyone seemed to be snarling at everyone else. Everything had changed. Including Scott, of course. Or at least, our relationship.

Previously, when I'd stayed in Pinner for the weekend, I'd slept alone on the lumpy sofa in the living room. Today I wouldn't be staying at all.

I'd timed my arrival for mid-afternoon when the band should be up and about. They were – well, Mo and Scott were, watching a black and white film on the tiny television set. I rarely saw the other two in daylight and assumed they were still in bed with their ladies.

Mo went to make tea – so well trained – and I took off my fun fur and plonked down on the sofa beside Scott.

'Hi,' he looked at me. 'Ok?'

'Yep. You?'

'Yeah.'

Oh, things had changed! The words to 'Livin' with You' had never rung so true! 'Those golden days we shared… are over now…'

'Have you eaten?' I knew it was a daft question.

Scott shook his head. 'Not today. I think we had something yesterday.'

Mo came back with the tea in rather grubby mugs. 'Food? Less food here than in Leighton Buzzard. And that kitchen is so small I couldn't cook for all of us in there anyway. Are you offering?'

I smiled at them. 'Well, there's that Chinese take-away just round the corner. I passed it on my way here and it smelled really good.'

'It's great,' Scott said. 'But we rarely go there – we never have that much money to spend on take-aways.'

'Some things never change. Look, while the others are out of the way – because I don't intend feeding them, shall I go round and buy something for us? Prawn curry and rice suit you?'

'God, yes.' Mo laughed. 'I do love you, Stella! I wish Scott could marry you *and* Renza!'

Scott winced.

'No chance,' I laughed, probably a little more heartily than needed. Goodness, this brave-face stuff was difficult. 'No one gets to be that lucky. Sort out clean plates and forks then and as soon as we've finished our tea, I'll drag Scott out with me to carry the food.'

It was cold outside and I shivered, and flinched at the noise of the non-stop traffic hurtling up and down the road. I honestly hated every single thing about this place.

Scott and I chatted as we walked to the take-away but we didn't hold hands or anything like that. It was over. And it was still breaking my heart.

We returned to the flat with two carrier bags filled to the brim with Chinese food. Mo dished it up and said happily that anything left over could keep for later when they came back from the gig.

'We're playing in a really cool London club, tonight,' Mo mumbled through his curry. 'We've got a new roadie now, Art. He's ok. He's gone to get the van. Are you coming with us, Stella?'

'No, not tonight.' Or any other night. 'I'm going home. I only came to feed you and to leave this...'

I indicated the bulging tote bag.

Both Mo and Scott barely looked up from their plates.

'It's the fan club stuff. All of it – except the things with my address on of course. Envelopes, stamps, newsletters, names and addresses, photos – everything.'

Scott frowned. 'Why? Did Stephan ask you to bring it?'

'No. But I'm not going to be your fan club secretary anymore.'

They both stared at me.

'I can't carry on with it. It wouldn't be right. I hardly know anything about what the band is doing now and I probably won't have time anyway. You'll find someone else to take it on. It's been great fun.'

And my only remaining point of contact with the band. The last tenuous link was being broken.

'You don't have to do this?' Scott looked quite upset. 'You've been ace at it. Who's going to do it now?'

I shrugged. 'Renza? Prue? Someone who is with you all the time and knows everything about you – like I used to. Honestly, I can't carry on making things up – you need someone to take it on and handle it properly. God knows, you work your socks off for peanuts – you need all the PR help you can get. Just not from me.'

They looked a bit upset but neither of them argued with me.

I pushed my plate away. 'And now I think I can hear stirrings from Zak and Joss – so before they or their women emerge, I'll leave you to finish your food and dash – I don't want to miss the Paddington train.'

I stood up, pulled my coat on and headed for the staircase.

'Stella!' Scott called after me. 'Hang on!'

'Got to run,' I called over my shoulder. 'Have a great gig tonight. I'll ring you. Bye...'

And I was out of the door and down the road before the tears blinded me. Again.

Renza's Diary
October 20th 1969

What a week. I am exhausted from babysitting in-between attending the various events put on to celebrate the Silver Jubilee of the base.

We've had a round of cocktail parties with special musical interludes put on by various military bands and orchestras, and I've eaten far too much and had too many Bloody Mary's and Snowballs.

I've been able to wear my new green silk cocktail dress with the georgette sleeves and my dark blue taffeta which is ballerina length and which makes me feel like Audrey Hepburn when I put it on.

There've been formal dances, with the men in black tie and the ladies in full length evening dress and I've worn my long black and gold skirt as well as a full length evening dress Heidi hired for me from a friend's boutique in Cologne. I danced with the Brigadier who thought I was a German working on the base, and now I know why he always speaks to me in German whenever he meets me in the lift or on the stairs at work. I thought he was testing my German and I've really struggled to understand him, let alone answer him most of the time, besides he has a broad Yorkshire accent, and so his German sounds nothing like I've ever heard before. He had a shock when I said I was English! Silly bugger.

I've danced with the local mayor, the drunken postmaster from the village up the hill, and been propositioned by the latest resident drunk in the Mess. I've been the youngest at all these events and so game for all the lecherous men wanting an excuse to grope me on the dance floor in full view of the top brass. Delightful. I can't wait to tell Scott.

I've made quite a bit from babysitting too. I wasn't able to go to every event – there have been dozens during the day too – so it's been quite lucrative.

Renza's Diary
November 7th 1969

I've been thinking seriously about Scott and me (again) and how things are going and especially about the elusive Stella. Something needs to be done, things cannot go on like this. Yes, I know I keep saying it but I'll end up in the loony bin. Besides, this place is killing me, it's like being buried alive and if I don't get back to civilisation soon I'll end up old and shrivelled, even though the Jubilee celebrations were a welcome diversion from the day to day drudge of it all here. I'm too young to be stuck with the oldies doing fogey stuff all the time. It's really not cool. Get a grip girl!

I wrote to Scott to tell him I'll try to make it for Christmas, that we needed to talk and sort ourselves out – again – because I'm confused and he can't keep telling me he loves me and there's no one else – not even Stella. Right! I need to plan my future, I can't stand it here much longer and, with or without him, I have to change my life. I've asked about time off and my uncle said I could 'go to them' for at least part of the time. I just need to see if I can get a lift back – I've got £25 saved so far which is enough for the fare and everything.

I can't wait to see Scott again and to spend more time with him and perhaps even... Well, we'll see! The thought sends me! Then I come crashing down thinking about bloody Stella. I have to get answers. Until then there'll be nothing like *that!*

The band have been playing in Devon, and also in a posh club in London where there is an open top pink Jaguar car in the middle of the dance floor and the DJ plays records from a turntable inside it. Lots of famous people go there, like Mick Jagger and Marianne Faithfull, and apparently Zak has got friendly with Mick and Marianne's au pair!!! Grief!

Scott's last letter was full of their adventures in the hippest city on the planet. And where was I? Stuck in the 1930's!

Dave Cash from Radio One has been playing 'Livin' with You' a lot, and so have many of other shows as well. Their fans seem to really like it. The band's happy.

Scott has just got the *Abbey Road* LP by The Beatles and loves it. 'Hey Jude' was on when he was writing to me. I haven't bought it. I'm not sure if I want to buy it really. I love The Beatles but what I've heard hasn't grabbed me or turned me on enough to buy it yet.

Stella Deacon wrote a Newsletter to the kids, last month, which said the band might be going on the cruises on The Northern Star and The Southern Cross again at the end of the year. If this happens, how Scott thinks I'd be able to see him I just don't know. Stella said they might be going to some really amazing places again and she will write more about it later when they know what's definitely happening.

I think I'll ask Scott about this when I ring him next week. He's sure to have heard about it by then – Stella, whom he hardly knows exists, seems to know more of his business that he does! I know it's petty but she is beginning to do my head in. I know it's her job and of course she sees the band, but he hasn't helped by being so cagey. I wish he could put my mind at rest. That's why we need to see each other.

It's a small world! Our new neighbours, who arrived last month, and have a small daughter who plays with Lucy, chatted to Mum and me by the front step this evening, and Herbert, who works with Dad, said that Jasper – why am I not surprised! – told him my boyfriend was in a band, and he asked me if I knew someone called Geoff Green who was in a band his brother knows called Blue Bicycle.

Wait until Scott hears about this! Narnia's Children played with them way back, he will be so surprised. The bloke is now managing Pavement, and he was once in another band called Big Smoke.

Herbert's wife is from somewhere exotic like Thailand and she really made us all laugh the other day. She said she didn't like her flat because it was haunted and she's had to move into the spare room because of the horrible rumbling noise all night long.

As she started to describe it, Mum and I tried to hide our giggles. My parent's room shared a wall with Herbert and his wife's room, and we knew she could hear Dad snoring. He sounds like a train rumbling at high speed and when he was in the army in Korea, he used to wake up surrounded by boots where the blokes had pelted him with them, trying to shut him up.

We feel sorry for Herbert's wife as her English isn't good and she appears a lot younger than her husband. A few weeks ago she ran to ask Mum for help when her little girl was ill. She'd been to see the German doctor in town and got a prescription for suppositories to bring her high temperature down. . After ages trying to get the child to take them, during which time she'd been violently sick, she'd come to ask Mum what to do. Imagine Mum's amazement when she realised that she had been trying to force the suppositories down the girl's throat instead of putting them up her rear end!

The waxy pellets were huge; no wonder the poor child was vomiting!

I know I shouldn't think such things, but they are a weird family. Lucy came in the other day and asked if she could water their flowers and I filled a watering can and went with her to the flower bed Herbert had been digging and planting all afternoon, to help her hold the can. Even she knew the flowers were plastic, she couldn't stop giggling. Herbert had planted endless rows of plastic flowers. I thought bugger it and let Lucy tip water all over them. I can't wait for his wife to pick them for indoors.

Stella's Diary
December 6th 1969

Oh the irony! A year ago to the day – if not exactly the date – a year ago tonight, I thought I was going to die and I'd gone to the dance at St B's with Vix – and my life had changed for ever.

So much had happened in that year – most of it mad, and crazy and wonderful and magical and exciting. I'd said I'd have adventures if I survived – and I had. Ok, some of it had been complete rubbish and heartbreakingly sad – as is well documented in this diary – but looking back, I wouldn't change a thing. Well, maybe one – but there's no point in thinking like that.

No, it's been the best year of my life and one I'll never forget.

And now, a year on, in the darkening afternoon of the same sort of bleak, icy cold December day, it had come full circle. I was walking up that teeming busy road in Pinner for the last time.

This was the day I'd been dreading for ages – today I knew I'd be saying goodbye to Scott for ever. I hadn't told him – yet – but I doubted if it would come as a huge surprise. I knew, deep down, he'd welcome it.

My musical memory box had two tunes going round and round in my head as I headed towards the house for the last time: Bobbie Gentry's 'I'll Never Fall in Love Again' – oh, never had a woman sung truer words! And Cilla Black's poignant 'If I Thought You'd Ever Change Your Mind' – my current theme song.

I'd phoned Scott a couple of days ago and he'd told me casually, among other things, that Renza was coming over to stay with him for Christmas and would probably be moving in with him permanently in the New Year if her dad would let her have her own passport. He sounded ridiculously happy about it and didn't seem to notice that I'd gone quiet at all.

Men!

Anyway, I'd made sure Narnia's Children were gig-free today – I didn't want any distractions. I wanted to make sure the parting was as calm and painless as possible. For me, at least. I seriously thought Scott would simply be relieved that it was over.

I reached the house and, letting myself in the main door, walked upstairs to their flat. It was all very quiet. Hopefully the rest of the band and their female companions were still in bed or out Christmas shopping or something.

'Stella? Is that you? I'm in here.'

Scott's voice echoed from the bedroom. I pulled a face. I hoped he hadn't assumed today's visit was to rekindle – well, you know... that was long over. It was all over.

Gingerly I pushed open the door. Scott, fully dressed, was sitting on the vast double bed in the middle of the room, sorting through a pile of papers.

Still the most beautiful boy in the world. *Oh, how I love you...*

'Hi,' he smiled at me. 'You look cold. Is it snowing yet?'

'Not yet. I don't think it's quite that cold.' I shrugged off my fun fur and perched on the edge of the bed. 'What are you doing? Filing your love letters in alphabetical order?'

He laughed. 'I wish – no, I'm just looking through some paperwork that Stephan left – contracts, gigs, possible tours... that sort of thing.'

'Money?'

'No.'

'Boring.' I smiled at him. He deserved better.

I looked round the room – the room that he'd be sharing with Renza in a very few days. I'd rarely ventured in there before, only to deliver cups of tea or say hello or goodbye, and thought now it reminded me of the dismal, lost-love words of Cream's 'White Room' with its white walls and black curtains through which you could just see rows of dreary rooftops, and of course, being close to the tube station.

Another song I'd probably hate for ever.

I took a deep breath. 'You know why I'm here – and yes, I could have written you a letter or phoned – but I think we've been through too much for that. And I wanted to see you. You do know that on this Saturday, a year ago, we met, don't you?'

Scott looked up and smiled the gorgeous lop-sided smile. 'Our anniversary? Yeah, The 7th – see I remembered – is that today?'

'Tomorrow...'

'Best gig we ever did.' He stopped smiling and looked at me. 'God – we've had a heck of a year together, haven't we?'

We had. I couldn't think about it now.

'True,' I ploughed on. 'Mostly I've loved every minute of it – but now it's over because it has to be – and honestly, I hope you and Renza have a lovely life together. But I'll never forget you – you made me happy.'

'You made me laugh,' Scott grinned. 'And I'll never forget you, either. But, what are you going to do without...?'

'Without you?' I stretched my legs out in front of me. 'What am I going to do with the rest of my Scott-less life? Oh, I'm well-organised – as well as the freelance writing, I've got a new job to start after Christmas – only a temporary one, but that's my choice – working as an auxiliary nurse at the Churchill's Blood Donor Centre – they helped me to live – I want to give something back.'

Scott frowned. 'It sounds a bit...'

'Different? Yep, it's certainly that. I'll be working on a mobile unit that covers five counties, travelling with a team, staying in hotels, away from home – I think it sounds absolutely perfect.'

'You'll be taking blood out of real people?' He looked shocked.

I laughed. 'Yes – but we do get training first. I'm going to be a fully-fledged vampire... Anyway, it's pretty difficult to get a normal job when you've broken the Official Secrets Act and you're a bit short on the reference front. Mind you, the shoe shop gave me a glowing one, so that helped. And then – after the vampiring – I'm going back to Jersey to work for the summer season.'

'What? Without me being there?'

'Obviously. God, you are so big-headed! I'm planning to get a flat in St Helier and find someone to share with, then look for a job – in fact, I've kept in touch with your mum and she's looking forward to seeing me again... no, listen – and then, next September, I'm going to college.'

Scott pushed the paperwork away and stared at me. 'You really have got it sorted, haven't you? What are you studying? Where's the college?'

'English Literature and here in London – and no, we can't meet or bump into each other. Ever.'

He pulled a face. 'Ok. It all sounds very cool and grown-up and interesting – but won't you miss the gigging and the music and all that?'

'I've got that covered, too. I'm sounding out that new label – Island Records – to see if they need any freelance PR work done for their artists... So, you see, we've really come full circle and now I'm going, and thank you for – well, for being you and for being brilliant and and for making me happy – and – er – goodbye...'

I grabbed my coat and almost ran to the door.

Scott stood up. 'Goodbye, Stella – but... '

Yes – Stella. I was Stella now. I'd always be Stella. I'd never be Twinkle again.

He followed me across the room. 'It doesn't have to end like this, does it? I don't want it to end like this.'

'Nor do I. But it has to.' I turned back to him and kissed his cheek. 'Be happy. You and Renza...'

And then I ran out of the room and down the stairs, crashing the front door behind me.

He didn't even try to stop me. As I'd known he wouldn't.

Once out in the busy, noisy street I exhaled. My breath spiralled out, smoky in the icy air. I'd done it!

I'd rehearsed those words over and over again and I'd actually managed to say them all without breaking down once. He'd never know how hard I was crying inside. But I'd said it, and it was over. And, as I'd expected, Scott had at no time tried to get me to change my mind.

Now, icy cold, dead inside, I walked zombie-like towards the tube station, not seeing, not feeling, simply walking away from Scott for ever.

I managed to hold it together until I caught the Harbury Green train from Paddington. Sitting opposite two plump, rosy-cheeked women clutching their Christmas shopping from Oxford Street, I leaned my head against the window, and watched the sleet slithering down the darkening glass like frozen tears.

The train gathered speed through the winter evening, rattling along the tracks, singing a rhythmic song inside my head: oh, how I love you... oh, how I love you... oh, how I love you....

And then I cried my heart out. Because I'd never see him again and I'd love him forever. *Oh, how I love you...*

So silly really – after all, I'd known from the start that there was only ever going to be one woman in Scott's life – and it was never going to be me.

Renza's Diary
Christmas Week 1969 – Pinner

Just like my previous trips, the ferry sailing was a nightmare. Everyone was seasick, including the crew, and the Ladies was running in vomit. We got caught in a force 9 gale and had to anchor miles outside Folkestone for ages before it was safe to come into port. My lift this trip, Monty de Gruchy, one of only three unmarried men on the base, suggested we sit outside on deck as high up as possible, so that we'd get some air and not feel the boat moving so much. It was all very déjà vu, but this time I didn't care. I just wanted to die.

By the time Art, the new roadie, collected me in the new van from outside Victoria Coach Station, I was about to pass out. My period had started a few days ago and as usual I was almost bent double in agony and keeping a watch out for handy toilets. Monty left me to go on to meet friends in Streatham, reminding me to meet him in the same place after New Year, for our return trip. I was glad to see him go; totally embarrassed by my numerous loo stops on the trip from Dover. I felt sure he knew what my problem was.

Art seems nice enough, he doesn't know anything about Rich and why he left so I didn't push the point. He's blond, good looking, tall, and he had a groovy pair of yellow cords on, with a bright green shirt and a cravat of both colours. He reminds me of one of the Lemon Pipers. I notice he bites his nails, just like Scott. Yuk. Not so groovy.

I love being back in London again; the buzz vibrating through the van windows; music, colour and trendy people exploding everywhere in front of me – or so it seems after living in the dark ages, in the back of beyond, for eternity – I drank it all up thirstily.

The Christmas lights were dazzling and for the first time I'm beginning to feel Christmassy. The radio's blaring a selection of Christmas songs and I silently sing along to 'Santa Claus Is

Coming to Town' and 'White Christmas', getting more and more excited at the thought of seeing Scott again.

Art said the band had only just got in when he'd left to pick me up. They'd gone straight to bed for a few hours. Scott told him to look for the gorgeous girl with long blonde hair, almost to her bottom, and the best legs in London so, he said, that is how he knew how to spot me. I couldn't help it – I beamed in spite of my pain.

The Pinner house was Victorian and a bit shabby. Art helped me upstairs to the sitting room, carrying my bag for me. He knocked on the door before poking his head inside. I waited, wondering what to expect, hoping Scott would rush out and sweep me into his arms, but of course he didn't.

Mo grunted something and Art closed the door and shrugged. 'Mo's entertaining in there, so let's go into the kitchen and I'll make a cuppa.'

I followed him into a galley style kitchen, piled high with dirty dishes and cups. There was a bag of shopping on the only surface not covered in crockery. Someone seemed to have forgotten to unpack it. Art searched some cupboards for clean cups and managed to find two blue and white coffee cups which he inspected before running under the hot tap. He found the teapot and ran warm water in it whilst he waited for the kettle on the gas stove to boil.

I watched him silently, my stomach was killing me and I needed to sort myself out again but was too shy to ask for the loo. I tried not to wriggle about, but the pain and urgency to get to the loo was beginning to overwhelm me.

'Where can I powder my nose?' I heard myself ask – seriously; 'powder my nose.' Good God, he'll think I'm a moron.

'Oh yeah, course, through there,' he said pointing to the door opposite the sitting room. 'Sugar and milk?' He waved the tea caddy at me.

'Please,' I muttered as I backed out of the kitchen trying to

487

hide the back of my mini dress which I knew would give my secret away. I grabbed my case and dragged it into the bathroom behind me.

'Think I'll freshen up,' I called out, hoping my sudden reappearance in a different outfit wouldn't seem so odd.

The bathroom was narrow, with green lino on the floor and pale blue painted walls showing damp patches near the window. The plastic curtains had been blue floral a long time ago but were faded and the plastic hardened with age. The large bath had rust marks on the bottom and there was scale around the taps and plug hole, but it seemed clean. The sink was in a similar state and there was a bar of Imperial Leather on the side next to a grimy nailbrush. Several sponge bags were lined up along the side of the bath and the towels hanging on the back of the door would never pass the OMO whiteness test.

I took my dress off and rummaged in my case for a change of undies and dress. I managed to have a good wash, cleaned my teeth and re-did my face, glad I'd brought my own towel with me. Bliss. I felt human again. I pulled the lavatory chain and the cistern sounded like the white rapids emptying.

Just as I was about to leave I noticed a glass shelf with cosmetics on it. I thought they belonged to the band at first; I knew they all dabbled at times, but then I looked again and I realised the make-up and perfume belonged to someone else. Definitely female. My imagination began to go into over-drive: Stella, perhaps?

I stood in the kitchen doorway sipping my tea while Art knocked on the bedroom at the end of the corridor. He said that Scott normally shared with Mo, but because I was here Mo was sleeping in the sitting room, but we couldn't go in there as his girlfriend was staying over. Scott should be getting up by now. He knocked again and shouted for Scott to wake up. He'd made some tea for him too. I heard a voice from another room shouting for tea as well. The Krakens were awaking, well it was mid-afternoon after all.

My nerves were on edge waiting for Scott to appear. I kept licking my dry lips, checking the back of my dress for any tell-tale signs of my problem, and I kept thinking about the make-up in the bathroom. Of course, it might be someone else's — I kept trying to convince myself.

Art came into the kitchen to pour more tea and he asked if I wanted toast as he was making some for the others. I hadn't eaten since the ferry docked at Dover and so said yes. I offered to help but just as Art was about to answer me, a girl with long dark hair wearing only the top half of a pair of men's pyjama's walked into the kitchen barefooted. She nodded at me as I stared at her semi-nakedness, not a little bit shocked. I tried not to gawp. The girl took a slice of toast between her teeth, grabbed two cups of tea and disappeared without a word to Art or me. He didn't seem to notice her state of undress. I finished my tea and stood wondering what I should do next. Art carried on making tea and toast and offered me a slice with Marmite which I gladly accepted and was just biting into it when the door at the end opened and another scantily clad female ventured into the kitchen.

She wore a red and orange striped bra top and pink hipsters which left little to the imagination, they were so tight. She nodded at me and moved her hand in a 'hi' movement. I waved back. Art handed her two cups of tea and a plate of toast which she put down to light the cigarette Art offered her. He offered one to me as well but I shook my head.

She took a long drag, blew smoke out of the side of her mouth, closing her eyes as she leaned against the sink. I felt really uncomfortable and tried hard to think of something to say but my mind was blank. She had short blonde hair and the deepest sun tan I'd ever seen. Her nails were really long and bright red like the nails on her bare feet.

Was she Stella?

I noticed she had a huge bruise on her chin and on her

shoulders which looked new and was wondering if I should comment when Zak yelled from one of the rooms and she almost jumped out of her skin.

'Gone to bloody India for the tea, Prue?'

'I'm coming! Just coming!' she dropped her cigarette in the sink, grabbed the cups and plate of toast and, just like a waitress, carried them back to the room at the end of the corridor.

'Bastard!' Art muttered under his breath turning away from me to pour another cup of tea.

I tried not to look shocked.

'Here, take this in there and wake your bloke up.' Art handed me the tea and a plate of toast and pointed to Scott's room, 'time he got up.'

I knocked on the door and waited. No answer. I glanced back at Art who was watching me over the rim of his cup. He nodded. 'Just go in.'

I did. It was dark and there was a double bed in the centre of the room, various bed clothes seemed to be hanging off the bed and I could just make out Scott's hair spread across the pillow. He was on his stomach, his bronzed back naked, the muscles defined and hard all the way down to his tiny hips... he looked like a God, illuminated by a chink of light coming through the not fully drawn curtains.

He took my breath away.

I put the cups down and stood over him, wondering if I should speak or not, but my voice wouldn't come anyway, even if I could think of something to say. I just gazed at him, drinking in his beauty and stillness, stretching my hand out slowly to trace the shape of his waist down to his hip.

He stirred and I sprang back in horror in case he woke and found me groping him.

After what seemed an age he moved his head and his arm reached behind him, towards me. 'Don't be shy, lie down with me,' he muttered into his pillow.

490

I froze. Did he mean me? Did he think I was Stella? How did he know someone was there? Oh cripes, he'd felt me groping...

I held my breath, my heart pounding in my ears; that Keith Moon solo again. He turned over and brushed the hair from his face, looked right at me, intense: a wanton smile on his gorgeous soft lips. My knees shook. He held his hand out to me and as I reached for it he pulled himself almost fully upright, grabbed me by the waist and pulled me on top of him, crushing all the breath out of me.

Before I could catch my breath again his lips found mine and I felt myself floating towards the ceiling, light as air, my mouth devoured by his and his arms tight around me. I had to pull away in case I fainted, I felt so light headed and dizzy suddenly.

He pulled my head back, towards his chest, and I could smell Imperial Leather, and that familiar scent he had, all of his own. I nuzzled into him brushing my cheek against his smooth skin, lost in the sheer pleasure of his body. As he stroked my hair it was as if we had never been apart.

'Sorry I couldn't meet you,' he moved his face in my hair, stroking my neck sending shock-waves through me. 'We got in so late and I need my beauty sleep you know.'

'It's OK, Art looked after me,' I mumbled, voice croaking, my throat tight and dry.

'Get in with me.' He rolled me on my back and gazed deeply at me. I couldn't look away.

'Don't be silly, it's afternoon still,' I heard myself squeak. Wriggling from under him and managing to sit beside him, I pulled my dress over my thighs.

Scott threw his head back laughing out loud and I could feel myself blushing.

'You crack me up babe, you seriously do.'

'I don't mean to.'

I know I sounded lame, what must he really think? I bet Stella jumped into bed whatever the time of day. Those girls in the kitchen obviously did.

'Don't look so stricken.' He kissed my nose, 'I can see you're embarrassed, that's why I love you so much.' He squeezed my arm. 'You're so innocent and that's so sexy, you really turn me on.'

'I can't help it.'

I looked at my lap, feeling really stupid. Innocent, for goodness sake! I don't want to be innocent! I want to be sexy and sophisticated and a woman of the world – not a stupid little kid.

'If you're not getting in then I best get up and get dressed. We can make up for lost time later.'

He grinned at me, threw the covers off and swung his legs out of bed, revealing his complete nakedness. I stared open mouthed at him, not knowing where to look, but he just smiled at me, hands on his hips daring me to look away.

Even though I had brothers, I'd never really seen a full grown man naked so close to me – well unless you count the cast of *Hair* in Germany! My brothers were too little to count really, and the one and only time I'd been to bed with Scott, in Leighton Buzzard, he'd stayed under the covers, in the dark.

My eyes were drawn to him like iron filings to a magnet. He remained motionless watching me watching him. His eyes boring into my face as mine bored into him. I tried to swallow but ended up choking and he leaned over me, patting my back as I coughed, laughing quietly.

'I can see we're going to have some fun later,' he said taking my shaking hands in his and holding them against his chest. 'If you manage to survive that long and don't choke to death.'

What an idiot I am, I thought. Stupid, stupid, silly girl! Fancy coming over all unnecessary in front of him like that!

I pulled away and stood up, moving as far away from him as I could manage. 'I'll go and wait outside while you dress.'

'Bit late for modesty. Stay,' he said as he pulled on his jeans and a tee shirt. 'How was the trip over? I heard on the radio there was a huge storm in the Channel.'

'Yeah, it was bad, even the crew got sea-sick.'

'You're OK though?' He brushed his hair and smiled at me.

'Yeah, just tired really.'

'You can have a nice hot bath later, with me, I'll rub your back and you'll soon perk up.' He laughed putting his arms round me and holding me tight. 'I'm here to look after you, don't worry about anything.' He kissed me long and hard. 'I've missed you so much, I'm so happy you made it over and you're here at last.'

'Me too,' I mumbled into his chest.

It felt really good to be held by him again and I just wanted to remain there for the whole visit. All thoughts of Stella were gone with the touch of his lips and the feel of him against me.

I went into the sitting room while Scott went into the kitchen to make tea. Mo and his girlfriend, Cassie, had tidied it up nicely, you couldn't tell it had become a bedroom now I was going to be sharing with Scott. Mo smiled as we chatted about books and writing and being writers, whilst Cassie watched me carefully, giving me the once over. She was very pretty and a bit older than I first thought. She smiled at me eventually when she realised that Mo and I were just mates, I think.

'Mo's told me all about you and how long you and Scott have been together.' She sat on Mo's lap. 'You two are a serious item.'

'I guess so,' I said trying not to beam at the confirmation of my status.

'They are and a lovely couple too.' Mo winked at me. 'It's called lurve.'

Scott handed cups of tea round and Mo sent him into their room for a tin of biscuits his parents had sent him for Christmas. Zak came into the room with his tea and sat on the floor in front of the TV.

He nodded at me and switched the set on. 'Not going to your uncle's then?'

Scott shook his head. 'No, she can stay the whole time. He's telling her parents she's been with him if they ever check.' He grinned and blew me a kiss, 'He's really cool.'

The girl with the bruising came in, wearing a bit more this time. She sat next to Zak and put her arms round him, but he shrugged her off rudely. I saw the hurt on her face and felt so sorry for her.

'Renza, meet Prue.' Scott smiled at her and she looked at me briefly and nodded. I smiled back. Everyone seemed on edge all of a sudden.

The TV came on loudly and *Top of the Pops* flickered to life with Frank Sinatra singing, 'My Way'. Everyone laughed when Zak said that this was Ol' Blue Eyes' final retirement gig. He often retired apparently.

We watched Jimmy Savile introduce Pan's People who danced to someone and something I couldn't see or hear as Zak and Prue sat in front of the set having what seemed like a whispered row, blocking my view. He kept shoving her away when she touched him.

Mo and Cassie scowled at Zak, and Scott shook his head at me, raising his eyebrows.

The room was quite shabby and the furniture old and worn but it was large and there was an enormous sofa and lots of arm chairs, as well as a big dining table with six chairs.

Joss came in with his girlfriend, the beautiful dark-haired girl who'd been the first one I'd seen in the kitchen. She looked just like Joan Baez. She nodded to me and Joss came over and kissed me on the cheek.

'Hi Renza, great to see you, we all missed you. Say hello to Mandy, you met her earlier when she had fewer clothes on, I gather.'

'Hello Mandy, nice to see you again,' I smiled broadly.
She gave me a friendly wink. 'Likewise.'

'Art's made some grub so if you girls want to sort out some trays, we can eat soon and then get sorted.' Stephan came into the room and gave me the thumbs up sign and, surprised to see him, I nodded hello.

Seeing the look on my face Scott knelt beside my chair, 'We're going to see some friends play tonight, in town. Stephan's treat. Do you want to come or stay here?'

'Stay on my own?' I know I sounded like a baby, but I didn't want to be on my own, we had so little time as it was.

'No, silly, we can go together with the others, or I can stay here with you, on our own. Up to you.'

'I'll go, you want to – I can tell.'

'Great, you'll love it. They're playing Hatchet's Playground where we gig quite a lot.'

'I remember, you told me that you gigged there with Harmony Grass a while back.'

'Yeah. That was cool and you'll love The Baubles,' Scott peered round Zak's shoulder at the TV. 'Hey, let's see who's on mate.'

'Joe South's just been on and later it's going to be Peter Sarstedt.' Zak moved so we could see the tiny screen.

'Grub's up!'

Art came in with plates of baked beans and Fray Bentos meat pies. I wondered if the band ever ate anything else. He handed plates round and we ate off trays on our laps, no one sat at the table. Tomato sauce passed round and piled-high plates of bread and butter. We ate in silence straining to hear *Top of the Pops* since Zak had turned the sound down so low it was almost inaudible. I did recognise The Edwin Hawkins Singers as they performed 'Oh Happy Day'. They were followed by Canned Heat so I guessed they were singing 'Going Up The Country.'

Fab bands and groovy songs. I loved them. I've really missed seeing music shows and TV in general. German TV was all very serious and there was lots on about the Second World War and concentration camps all the time. The music was all boring and military sounding, or James Last.

After eating, Art took the plates away and said he'd wash up later when we all got back and Scott and I went into his room to change. My stomach wasn't aching and I was beginning to think my 'you-know-what,' was stopping, it does that sometimes, soon after it starts, which was such a relief. I felt almost human putting on my pale blue mini- skirt which did up with a huge safety pin, like a kilt. I had my white polo neck skinny-rib jumper and long white lace up boots on too, and finished off with a big black floppy felt artist's hat, and a long paisley silk scarf. I hoped I'd look hip enough and not as if I'd been in the sticks for ages.

Scott put a pair of dark purple cords on, hipsters, and a short cut-off black ribbed jumper which had short sleeves and a buttoned neck, which he left undone right down to under his breast. His hair shone and had grown more than I thought it would, so it was on his shoulders. He looked sexy enough to eat. I actually felt my mouth water.

I put my make-up on; my usual big black eyes, mauve eye-shadow and lots of mascara, a tiny bit of rouge and pale glossy lipstick. My hair, almost to my bottom now, shone with the highlighted shampoo I used to keep my golden blonde bright and glossy.

Scott sighed as he looked at me, 'I'm gonna watch you tonight, all the guys are going to be after you. You look good enough to eat – I may eat you later if you play your cards right.'

He kissed my neck and cheeks and hands and then slowly pressed his lips against mine and I felt his tongue dart between my lips as he pressed himself suggestively against me. I almost passed out.

'Put her down and leave that 'til, later you two.' Joss stood in the doorway, laughing. 'We're ready to go and we're waiting for you.'

The gig was amazing. The club was amazing. It had a glass floor and was all chrome and glass inside and full of beautiful people. I heard all the latest records, learned all the new dances, saw all the latest fashions and enjoyed being with

Narnia's Children who seemed to be famous wherever we went.

Girls and blokes kept coming up to them for autographs and to have their photos taken with them. I had my bottom pinched so many times I was sure I'd be black and blue.

The Baubles were so tight and groovy. Sean the keyboard player was really nice to me and I could tell he really liked Scott. I didn't know their songs, like Narnia's Children they write most of them, but I could tell the band were going places. Girls screamed all through their performance and they asked Narnia's Children up on stage to sing harmonies with them on a couple of songs which they obviously knew and had sung with them before. It was so groovy. Even the blokes were shouting and waving at both bands by the end of the gig.

Prue, Mandy, and Cassie stood with me a lot of the time and we got chatting eventually and I found them to be really nice, not at all stand-offish or too sophisticated to talk to me. They seemed to think that Scott and I were officially engaged, and said he often talked about us getting married. I was so far gone, it was so far out – I was happy as Larry, hearing what they said.

I took a deep breath. 'How's Stella these days?' I asked as casually as I could.

Mandy put her arm around me and squeezed me. 'Didn't Scott tell you? She's not their fan-club secretary any more. She's gone on to pastures new and greener.'

'No, he didn't. When did that happen?' Trying to sound only slightly interested.

'Oh a few weeks back, she was never going to be around long, she was just sort of filling in until she got a better offer.'

Cassie and Prue headed to the ladies and Mandy shook her head sadly when I asked if Prue had been in an accident, all that bruising. She told me that Zak had had a row with her, and settled it in his usual manner – hence the bruises. I was so shocked I gaped like a loon. I just couldn't imagine it.

'Why does she put up with it?' I was astonished.

'You tell me. We've all tried to make her see sense and the guys have almost come to blows with Zak over it.'

'How awful, poor Prue, she seems so nice too.' I couldn't take it in.

'Cassie and Mo might split up too.' Mandy put her lips to my ear as she said this. Mo was standing a few feet away by this time, the band having come off stage for the last time.

'Oh, that's sad. They seem really happy to me.' I liked them both and they seemed well matched. Just shows what I know.

'Well, you know about their problem, I guess,' she whispered, watching both Mo and the Ladies' door. 'Well, that's the reason, we think.'

'Oh, err, I don't think I heard about that.' I said, knowing full well I hadn't a clue. Scott never gossiped or told me much about the others and their lives.

'Had to have an abortion, it was all really sad and I think it is going to split them up. Cassie thinks Mo is starting to back off and things are not the same as before.' Really? An abortion? Dear God! Mandy just blew my brains! I was gob-smacked. Gordon Bennett! Scott, was right – I was very, very innocent...
Before I could say a word Mo came over as the girls came back from the loo. He smiled at Cassie and put his arm round her. She leaned against his shoulder and I felt so sad. I wondered why they couldn't have kept the baby, but then I guess being in a band and on the road all the time with little or no money, without a secure future, wasn't exactly the best situation in which to have a kid. It was tragic.

Zak came over and Prue went to him and said something I couldn't hear and his face changed to a really nasty expression. Mandy nudged me hard in the ribs. She'd seen it too. She walked over to Prue and took her arm and led her away from Zak and over to where we were all standing, and attempted to involve her in conversation about a girl standing not too far from us who looked 'famous', but none of us could place her.

Prue didn't know who she was either. I certainly had no idea.

Stephan and Art came across and told us it was time to go. Scott found me and swept me up into his arms, much to the annoyance of a group of trendy girls who had been his shadow all evening.

He laughed. 'Come on wife, time to go home and play doctors and nurses.'

***

We lay side by side, in bed, holding hands in the dark. Cosy and happy and whispering about the future. We'd had a long talk earlier about Stella and my fears, and although he never admitted they'd had a fling, I've decided to drop it because she's resigned as fan-club secretary and wouldn't be seeing the band again and you can't build a future on suspicion and resentment. I believe whatever it was is over. Scott chatted about the band, and how we would need to wait a couple of years to get married to see how things worked out with the band and everything. But he was determined we should marry.

I told him I'd applied for some jobs in London and that there was a really good chance I might be interviewed in London sometime in March, when I was 18, so I'd been told by the Civil Service. I'd applied for a job in a government department which had hostel accommodation attached to it — Mum and Dad would only allow me to come back if I had somewhere to live as well. I thought it was a good way to get back and then take things from there. Scott seemed to think it was a great idea, too.

'We're going on the cruises again in the spring though, so I hope we get to see each other when you come over for the interview.' He turned and stroked my hair and face as he spoke.

'I won't have any control over the date and stuff. I'll have to stay at my uncle's though, because Mum has already mentioned it to him on the phone when she told him I might be over, if I'm successful in getting an interview board.'

'Let's not worry about it now, something'll turn up, I'm

sure. And you'll be here in London. With me. That's all that matters.'

Scott moved across on top of me and soon we were lost in kissing and caresses and all conversation came to a halt.

Later on we woke and chatted some more about the future and our life together and made plans and imagined how it would be. Lots of doubts and worries I'd had were put to rest and for some reason I really believed it all, that it would happen, that we would be together forever.

Scott hummed into my ear as he held me tightly. 'I wrote this song for you, "You Never Should Have Gone Away".'

'I remember,' I sighed happily.

'And the words of 'Only One Woman,' you remember them too?' He bit my ear gently.

'I've never forgotten, of course I do.' I pressed up close and breathed in his lovely smell.

'That's OK then. Never forget I love you and never forget those words. Whatever happens, we will be together always. We will always find a way no matter what goes down. For the rest of our lives.'

***

We snuggled up together and I whispered 'I'll always love you too, no matter what happens.'

'We have lots of time and things will work out just fine, believe me. I'll make sure they do.' Scott kissed me long and hard.

The only sounds, other than our own, until then in that darkened room, had been the cassette player, rewinding and replaying The Marbles' Song, 'Only One Woman' because every single word was true. Now and forever.

Soon, even they were silent.

The End

Dedications and Acknowledgements

From Christina Jones:

To: Allan - my brother and my friend - the boy who was there for me all my life, who shared the Only One Woman reality and the fiction, and who so wanted to read this book.
Love and miss you always, Tina.

From Jane Risdon:

I'd like to dedicate Only One Woman to my husband for his continued belief in me and never ending support since the day we met. He and his band changed my life forever.
Also to our son and his family: something for the memory box.
This is also dedicated to the many musicians and song-writers who have embroidered all our lives with such fabulous musical memories over the years, and still continue to do so. Without these creative people the world would be a much darker place. You rock.
Thanks to family and friends for their much appreciated support.
And my thanks to the many online friends who've helped us spread the word about Only One Woman, and especially those who have read and enthusiastically reviewed our e-pub and Kindle editions to date. You are amazing.
And thanks to everyone, especially all our editors, at Accent Press for their hard work on our behalf.
Thanks one and all. Jane xx

Christina Jones

Christina Jones, the only child of a schoolteacher and a circus clown, has been writing all her life. As well as writing romantic comedy novels, she also contributes short stories and articles to many national magazines and newspapers.

She has won several awards for her writing: *Going the Distance* was a WH Smith Fresh Talent Winner; *Nothing to Lose* was shortlisted and runner-up for the Thumping Good Read Award with film and television rights sold; *Heaven Sent* was shortlisted in The Melissa Nathan Comedy Romance Awards and won a Category Award; *Love Potions* won the Pure Passion Award; *The Way to a Woman's Heart* was short-listed for the Rom-Com of the Year; and *An Enormously English Monsoon Wedding* won The Reviewer's Choice Award.

Twitter: @bucolicfrolics
Facebook: /ChristinaJonesAuthor
/christina.jones.1671

Jane Risdon

Jane Risdon has been writing since 2011 having had a successful career in the International Music Industry, alongside her musician husband, which has taken her all over the world managing musicians, singers, song-writers, and record producers in a variety of musical genres. She has lived and worked in North America, Europe, Singapore and Taiwan, and has been involved with Music Production, Soundtracks for Television and the Movies.

Jane's writing has been published in thirteen anthologies - mostly crime/thrillers - and she has had numerous short stories and articles published in online magazines and newsletters. She recently completed the first novel in the series, Ms Birdsong Investigates, about a former MI5 Officer, and two others are underway. Jane also has another novel (work in progress) set in the music business in Hollywood and two further crime novels being written at the present time.

Twitter: @Jane_Risdon
Facebook: /JaneRisdon2
Wordpress: www.janerisdon.wordpress.com

Proudly published by Accent Press

www.accentpress.co.uk